# Her Foreign Affair

## Shea McMaster

**LYRICAL PRESS**
Kensington Publishing Corp.
www.kensingtonbooks.com

Lyrical Press books are published by
Kensington Publishing Corp. 119 West 40th Street New York, NY 10018

All Kensington titles, imprints, and distributed lines are available at special
quantity discounts for bulk purchases for sales promotion, premiums, fund-
raising, and educational or institutional use.

Special book excerpts or customized printings can also be created to fit
specific needs. For details, write or phone the office of the Kensington
Special Sales Manager:
Kensington Publishing Corp.
119 West 40th Street
New York, NY 10018
Attn. Special Sales Department. Phone: 1-800-221-2647.

First Electronic Edition: June 2015
eISBN-13: 978-1-61650-727-5
eISBN-10: 1-61650-727-6

First Print Edition: June 2015
ISBN-13: 978-1-61650-728-2
ISBN-10: 1-61650-728-4

Printed in the United States of America

*Twenty-two years ago, she ran out on the love of her life—and took a secret with her.*

When Randi Jean Ferguson fell for Courtland Robinson while studying abroad in London, she was ready for a life of tea and crumpets. But when she discovered Court was being forced into a shotgun wedding, there was no way she could stay—or tell him she was also pregnant with his child. Now widowed, Randi is just starting to consider finding Court—when he shows up at her door. With his son. Randi's not ready to reveal everything to Court, but if she doesn't will both their children end up scarred?

The best thing to come out of Court's unhappy marriage was his son. But he's spent the last twenty-two years thinking about Randi, his California girl, his first—and only—love. Now a widower, he takes a chance he's only fantasized about and seeks her out. At last he'll solve his heart's greatest mystery—but that won't be the only surprise in store for him.

# Books by Shea McMaster

Her Foreign Affair
Rachel Dahlrumple

*Writing as Morgan Q. O'Reilly*

Frozen
Chinook, Wine and Sink Her

*The Open Window Series*
Til Death Undo Us
Courage to Love
Weathering the Storm

**Published by Kensington Publishing Corporation**

*To my own hero who has never given up on me. Mr. O'Reilly, you keep me pampered and well spoiled. I think we can handle another thirty years at least. After all, our child wants us to meet his grandchildren. He's a sadist for sure. He gets that from your side of the family.*

# Acknowledgements

Her Foreign Affair was inspired in part by Jennifer Greene's, Blame It On Paris, published by Harlequin Books. Her story was about the daughter. I kept wondering about the mother. I can only hope my story is as entertaining as hers. I have yet to find a book of hers that doesn't make me laugh and fall in love all over again.

To my friend KM, thank you for the use of your house, both as a place to visit and as a setting in this story. I hope you get the spa installed someday. Any other redesign ideas you like, feel free to run with them. Sorry about the dead tree. I know a tree would never die in your yard, but it served a small purpose here.

To the real Randy, thanks for the use of your name, even if I did have to feminize it. We all know there's nothing feminine about you except your great love for the ladies in your life. I'm sure your wife and daughters consider themselves lucky to have you. I'm just amazed after all that stupid high school stuff we're still friends *mumble* years later.

I relied heavily on the Internet for details on tea, though I do like drinking tea in many flavors. Randi's preferences might mirror my own somewhat. Then again maybe not. Some secrets are meant to be kept. Google TEA and see what you come up with. Truly a fun way to spend a rainy afternoon while sipping the perfect brew. In my mind, I have a wonderful teaware collection. Sadly, my husband looks at my overstuffed shelves and suggests collecting teapots would require a massive thinning of the books. We're at an impasse at the moment. Maybe he'll get a big blue teapot for Father's Day…

As always to the critique partners who threatened to kick my rear if I didn't finish at least one WIP, preferably this one first. You all got me moving when I was stuck and your continued devotion kept me going to the end. You all are my inspiration and my guiding stars.

Last but not least, my UK connections: Jane from New Zealand, Maya Blake from London, and Liz from Minnesota (your life-long Beatles obsession is paying big dividends all over the place). You all made the language better, as I freely admit, I was not able to travel there and do the research myself. My experience with London is limited to three days the summer I was fourteen. Any mistakes not caught by them are all my own and no disrespect to the country of England is intended. After all, a few of my very own ancestors came from there.

As always, thank you, Carlee, for your unflagging devotion to the creation of these flights of fancy.

*"But it's no use going back to yesterday, because I was a different person then."*
*~Lewis Carroll, Alice's Adventures in Wonderland*

# Prologue

*London, England*
*Mid-late 1980s*

A soft spring breeze tugged a long curl from Randi Jean Dailey's carefully styled up-do. She paid the cabbie his quid, stepped from the car with the help of the hotel doorman, and gave him a smile. The cabbie let out a satisfactory wolf-whistle before zipping back into London traffic.

Jean's heart pounded with excitement. Instead of climbing on the plane to go home after her semester abroad, she'd primped and polished and put on her perfect little black dress accented with proper pearls and sexy stilettos. The ones Court had bought for her two weeks prior. The ones that made her short legs look a mile long, he said. The black shoes she'd worn to seduce him last night. The ones that had driven him so mad with lust he'd made love to her all night long.

With a long bittersweet kiss, they'd parted at noon. His promise to follow her to California as soon as he possibly could were the last words spoken between them.

She adjusted the lace shawl around her shoulders and headed into the hotel where the Lynford International Importers new hire reception was being held. As an only-just-hired summer intern, she'd received her job acceptance and invitation to the reception shortly after Court had left her studio flat. The afternoon had been spent madly running around making arrangements to stay in England another three months. To start.

But that wasn't all the good news she had for Court. Instead of only the summer, she'd be extending her stay indefinitely. Forever. The thought made her dizzy with delight.

Upon reaching the doors to the reception hall, Jean stopped and rested a hand over her abdomen. She had one more surprise for Court. One she prayed would thrill him to his bones. One that would give him the leverage to work around his father's manipulations. Like the song from a few years before, their future was so bright, they'd both have to wear shades. A silly grin crossed her face as she started through the wide open doors.

Soft string ensemble music drifted across the room. The event was exactly as Court had predicted. Proper Englishmen and their ladies talking quietly, mingling, as much to see as to be seen. For a week, he'd bemoaned the fact that instead of seeing her off at the airport, he had to attend this stuffy reception put on by his father's company. Not interested in the décor, she searched the sea of bodies in semi-formal wear, looking for one particular blond head. The men wore sharp suits of worsted wool with silk ties, the women cocktail gowns in various levels of fashion and expense. The student interns and freshly graduated new hires were easy to pick out, by not only their youth, but by the less expensive clothing and the nervous smiles on their faces. Because Court's family owned the company, she looked beyond the students and concentrated on the older attendees. The people Court had known since the day he'd been born.

One bright head stood out. Danielle Richards, the hiring contact. If not for Danielle's call hours before, Jean would have been boarding a plane just then. Jean headed for Danielle, who certainly knew Court and could help Jean find him. She merely had to work her way through to the other side of the large ballroom.

Descending the steps into the crowd, she plowed ahead, exchanging nervous smiles with the three or four people she recognized from classes.

Among the glittering bodies, various scents perfumed the air and queasiness assaulted Jean for a moment. Something that had never bothered her before the past week. She and Court figured she had a mild touch of flu, or possibly food poisoning like she'd had right after arriving in January. The call from the student clinic this afternoon had negated that theory.

A glint of Danielle's bright copper hair through the crowd assured Jean she was still on the right path. A few more steps and her gaze briefly met Danielle's. Someone stepped in and cut off the line of sight before Jean could take a second look at what appeared to be mild alarm on the other woman's face. Jean glanced behind her to see what might be happening that would cause the hiring director's reaction. No, nothing unusual there. Jean pressed forward once again.

Like the sun prying back a thick layer of dark clouds, she saw his golden blond hair through a parting of bodies. His back to her, he stood near Danielle, part of a circle of immaculately groomed men and women, a mix of older and younger.

Finally, she eased past a knot of distinguished men and stood directly behind Court. On a deep breath, she assessed the situation. The group he stood with contained two older couples, important looking men and their society wives, all perfectly dressed and bejeweled. A younger woman with a sleek blond bob stood at Court's left. Too close, but he came from people who knew people and had friends he'd been raised with. This could be one such. Across the small circle, Danielle was the only other person Jean recognized. A person who'd been friendly. Although the expression on Danielle's face wasn't exactly comforting.

Court began to speak, and Jean was able to hear him clearly, see clearly as his left arm came up to encircle the waist of the blond woman at his side, the action surprising her. If his shoulders looked a bit stiff, the movement a tad forced, she seemed to be the only one who noticed.

"Danielle, I'd like you to be among the first to know, Bea and I will be married next weekend. There isn't time for formal invitations,"—his chuckle was forced—"we're expecting, however, we'd love you to attend."

The timbre was Court's, but the tone and the words couldn't be his. Dizziness surged in Jean's head. She took a step back and clamped both hands over her now roiling stomach. The air had evaporated from the room and darkness framed the edges of her vision.

"Court…" Danielle said, doing her best to keep her face clear of emotion. Jean could see it, could hear the strain, as the other woman's electric blue gaze locked on her.

Jean swallowed against rising nausea and took another step back, bumping into someone's chilled glass of something. The shock of cold liquid dribbling down her back froze her in place.

In an almost dreamlike parody of slow motion, Court's arm dropped from the woman, and he slowly turned. Jean's gaze flew to his face as it came into view. His skin took on an ashen cast, as his eyes widened above his slackening jaw. For a long moment, it was all she could see.

"Courtland?" The sharply spoken word from the blond woman broke the spell. "What is it, darling?"

Jean's breath rushed back into her starved lungs, and her heart jolted into triple time, rushing adrenalin into her system. It was the spark she needed to turn on her heel and push through the crowd.

"Jean!"

She heard him call after her. Heard Danielle call after her, but didn't stop. Escape was the one thought in her head. Later she'd think about Court's announcement. But now there was room for only one instinct pounding through her veins. Run.

Snippets of his history came to her as she forced her way past people now expressing their shock at her rudeness. The girl he'd practically been engaged to since they'd been in nappies. The horrible break up days before Jean had tripped him in the library. The stories of his family and how he was expected to take over the business one day, like generations of Lynfords and Robinsons before.

Above all, the vision she couldn't reconcile with the words he'd just said, Court's face smiling down at her. His voice saying, "I love you. I'll come for you. We'll have a wonderful life."

As she broke through the edge of the crowd and rushed into the lobby, she thought she heard Court call out her name one more time, but from a distance. She didn't look back. Couldn't look back. Adrenalin pounding through her veins powered her forward. A doorman opened the heavy outer door.

"Miss?"

His enquiry went unacknowledged as she rushed by, headed for the cab parked at the curb.

"Taxi!" she called out.

Surprised, the doorman who'd recently helped her from a cab, leaped to open the door for her.

"Miss? Everything all right?"

She shook her head and climbed into the cab.

"Where to, miss?"

"Home." It was all she could think of. She could be at Heathrow in a few hours where she'd wait until a seat opened on a plane headed for New York. From New York she'd get a plane to San Francisco. There, she'd figure it all out.

"Where's home, miss?"

"Away from here." Tears blurring her vision, she met the cabbie's gaze in the rearview mirror. "Just drive." No one had followed her out the door. Especially not Court. His words echoing in her head tore her heart to shreds. The cabbie turned around and slowly eased into traffic.

Unable to stand it, she gave into temptation and looked back through the tears welling in her eyes and spilling down her cheeks. The sidewalk remained empty of anyone she recognized. Only the doorman looked after her.

The image of Court's face rose in her mind. Merry blue eyes, laughing at her driven need to experience everything Anglo, jokes about her attempts to learn the Brit accent, the little presents of Earl Grey tea, crumpets and flowers he brought her. The rose petals he'd scattered on her bed last night where they made love pretending to be in an English garden. The flower pressed between the pages of her favorite novel, a sweetly scented bookmark and reminder of his promise they'd be together.

From the dark and dreary February day when she'd accidentally tripped him in the library, her world had been filled with sunshine and laughter. He took her places, both physical and emotional, she'd never have discovered without him. Small shops, hidden parks, intimate pubs, classic tea houses, historical sites, and the places known only to locals. To heaven, where he wrapped her in soft clouds of love, like the weekend in the country where they hiked green fields and pretended to be Robin Hood and Maid Marian. A better friend, guide, and lover she couldn't have asked for.

"I need an address, miss. Or an intersection at the very least."

Of course the man needed a direction. Jean wiped tears from her cheeks and wrapped her arms around her middle. "Houghton Street," she said. She needed a direction, too, knew where she was headed in the next twenty-four hours, but had to take baby steps to get there. "Houghton Street and then Heathrow." One step at a time.

# Chapter 1

*Twenty-two years later*
*East Bay Area, Northern California*

Bent over the open oven, Randi figured only serendipity could have timed her daughter's arrival for Thanksgiving dinner quite so well.

Already up for six hours, most of that time spent in the kitchen, Randi was ready for her first glass of wine. A real glass, not a sip from the bottle she'd poured over the bird. So much for her resolve to become a new woman in her fabulous forties. A couple years in and she still harbored doubts about how fabulous the forties were. However, a person should always seek to improve herself, right? All well and good, nevertheless, this new woman clung to a few old habits she didn't want to give up, such as nipping from the bottle of wine intended for basting the turkey.

"Mom!" Birdie's voice rang through the house like a bell.

"In the kitchen," she called back. Steam from the oven frizzed her hair and bathed her face as she basted the bird. There went the efforts of an hour spent plucking eyebrows and applying her makeup just so. Well, instead of a fashion plate, the picture of a sophisticated California hostess, she'd be Wyatt's picture of the perfect woman—glowing from the heat of the kitchen and probably smelling of turkey as well. Too bad he wasn't here to celebrate. Death had a way of ruining family gatherings.

Instead, Randi expected her father and Birdie, both bringing visitors from out of town with no place else to go. Strays had always been Randi's specialty, especially for holiday dinners.

"Smells great, we're starving!" Birdie moved into Randi's peripheral vision. As bright as a sunny day with her long, honey blond hair, Birdie lit up any room, especially with her smile, cheerful disposition, and her clothing. Occasionally, Randi considered her child's bubbly nature positively nauseating. But not today. The semester had dragged on and contact with her daughter remained too infrequent. Stanford may have been a mere hour across the Bay, but it might as well have been across the country for all the time Birdie had to spare.

Randi shoved the heavy bird back into the lower of the stacked double ovens and straightened with a hand on the small of her back as she lifted the door shut. Yeah, cool sophisticate she so was not. Had she wanted to present such an image, she would have ordered the complete meal, cooked and ready to serve, delivered from the upscale grocery store down the hill. "Bird should be done on schedule this year. This time I bought a fresh one, not frozen."

"Your dinners are always perfect, and thirty minutes late doesn't count. Mom, come meet our guests."

*Ah yes.* The mysterious Drew, a grad student from overseas Birdie had met the previous week after tripping over his big feet in a coffee shop. Not only Drew, but his father, as well, visiting the states on business, timed for Drew's first big American holiday. The widowed father. A match to her widowed mother status.

Great. It was bad enough her father also asked to bring a guest, a single man of a certain age. In other words, old enough for Randi. But now her daughter had joined the game? Lately, it seemed as if an invisible milestone had passed, one declaring her mourning period complete, and, apparently, someone had declared open season on finding dates for her. Funny, her heart hadn't reached the same conclusion yet.

Well, let these possible future dates get a good look at the new woman. The one thinking about thinking of dating again.

Since Birdie generally preferred jeans, Randi raised an eyebrow at the dress her daughter wore. Navy flats were more in keeping with her personality, though Birdie showed off a pair of still nicely tanned legs. Randi was about to comment, but Birdie beat her to it.

"Wow." Birdie stopped and stared for moment. "Great look," she whispered, then took Randi's arm and dragged her into the foyer where two tall men stood. So the extra hour of shaving, shining, plucking, and painting had been worth it? Despite the steamy glow she certainly sported at the moment, and no time to powder it away.

Not wanting to acknowledge the matchmaking attempt of her daughter—the man was a foreigner for crying out loud and wouldn't be around long enough to get to know—she wiped her hands on her apron, then extended one to the younger of the two. Dark blond, he had deep blue eyes and a smile every bit as cheery as Birdie's. As Randi gripped his hand, hers warmed with dreaded perspiration. She made her shake firm and brief, dropping his hand almost immediately.

"Mom, this is Drew. Drew, my mother Rand—"

"Jean?"

"—ee Ferguson," Birdie stumbled to a stop.

Drew hadn't interrupted. No, it was the man behind him. The boy's father. The one Randi didn't want to look at. The resonance of his voice, the rich British accent that made the plain name she'd used for one semester sound exotic, it was an illusion, an echo from the past, a hallucination induced from too little sleep.

Reluctantly, Randi let her gaze slide past Drew's startled eyes and collide with those of the older man one step back, looking more stunned than startled. More amazed than surprised.

"Not Jean Dailey?" he asked, head tilted a fraction as his gaze bore into her.

There was only one thought in her mind as her heart thudded to a momentary stop, and her blood froze into crystals. *It can't be.*

This must be a delusion leftover from last night's dreams. The ones brought on by the romance novel she'd found in a box last week. The one sitting on her bedside table still exuding the soft scent of the rose pressed between the pages of the love scene. He'd been invading her thoughts too much lately. He couldn't really be here, in her foyer. This scene was purely a figment of a mind set to wandering by plain old loneliness.

Randi grasped Birdie's arm, holding her as much to stay standing as to keep Birdie from moving to the side of the younger man. There was no way God would play this cruel a joke on her after so many years. Yet, as she stared into those blue, blue eyes, the years peeled away.

"Jean is my mother's middle name," Birdie supplied helpfully, despite her apparent confusion, breaking the silence that had held for nearly a full minute. Words abandoned Randi, leaving her throat too tight, too dry for speech. "Her full name is Randi Jean Dailey Ferguson."

Hell, no point in trying to hide her true identity now, as if that had ever been a remote possibility. Not only did Birdie give it all away, she babbled to fill in the extremely awkward silence.

The gaze of the apparition who resembled, well, *him*, sharpened, and his lips quirked in satisfaction. The heat of his regard wouldn't allow Randi to deny the exceedingly male presence in her house. All the air evaporated from the foyer, and her heart kick started so hard it threatened to leap from her chest. Her mind might be screaming denials, but her body knew. And despite the first sluicing of ice through her veins, heat rushed in behind.

Those damn blue eyes stared into hers, and a spark of something ancient and irrepressible settled in her heart, causing it to beat triple time.

Yup. God was that cruel.

From her past, the one man she never once imagined she'd ever see again stood in her foyer. Impossible that he should have found her. Dad would have never given her away had anyone knocked on his door looking for her. Google searches on the various combinations of her name turned up little other than notices in school newsletters. All those years ago she'd married, changed her name, given birth, and moved from the parental home to start a new life as a new woman. The girl he'd known as Jean Dailey became Randi Ferguson. All the heartache of betrayal had been left far behind in Merry Old England more than twenty-two years ago. The only reminder? The nearly twenty-two-year-old beauty standing at her side. The child who towered over her, so like her father, if the truth be known.

All those years ago, God had held her feet to the fire to face her future, but this time she faced the past. And why did that past still have to be so damn handsome?

No, not a hallucination. He was real. So very, very real.

It was him, looking barely five years older than he had so long ago. His thick hair still gleamed gold under the soft glow from the skylight, though there were hints of silver at his temples, and his forehead seemed a tad higher. Great, gray looked good on him. He was still lean, his eyes remained as piercingly blue. Light blue that looked right into her soul. His face had filled out a little, developed a few lines at the eyes, and the cheekbones were no longer quite so prominent, the jaw a slightly smoothed granite instead of freshly chiseled stone, but essentially the same.

Yes, he still looked the same while she'd grown rounder and squatter. Thank heavens for the impulse that sent her to the salon a week ago. At least she wasn't gray. At the moment. And of course, makeup, underwires, and Lycra hid a multitude of other imperfections.

Whereas he… Well, he looked damn fine in his light blue tailored shirt, gold cufflinks, perfect navy slacks, and expensive leather shoes.

Just like his son.

She wanted to push them out of her house right then, send them both back to England, far, far away from Birdie.

Oh, no, no, no. This did not fit with Randi's plans. She needed to regain control of the situation. Time. She needed time. Yes, she'd planned to tell Birdie all about this part of her past, but after Christmas. Before the New Year. After getting some more information from an investigative resource. Not like this, not now. Lord, not now! When Birdie was already looking at her as if she'd lost her mind.

Control. Right. Shut the rest away and pretend there was nothing going on. Randi eased up on her daughter's arm when she murmured a protest.

*Oh God. Birdie's attracted to…* She couldn't complete the thought too horrible to think.

A first date she'd said, right? Did that mean they hadn't progressed beyond coffee? No hand holding? No kissing? God forbid… How would she break this up without Birdie knowing she'd brought home not only her brother—half brother—but father, for dinner? Her very gorgeous, missing from her entire life, father.

As she watched his face, drinking in every detail, his eyes warmed, then hardened. He didn't seem nearly as surprised as she felt. Had he been looking for her? Had he used his son to find her through her daughter?

Birdie pinched her arm, bringing Randi back to the moment with a small jolt. Oh Lord, she was standing there like an idiot, everyone looking at her with expressions of curiosity and puzzlement. Hoping to find her cool hostess voice and not a strangled, choked voice, she gulped.

"Hello, Court."

# Chapter 2

Many things filled Courtland Bailey Robinson's head as he stared at the woman clutching her daughter's arm as if she were sinking. Not the least of which was satisfaction. Finally, a conclusion to the investigation he'd begun ten years before. A bittersweet triumph because, apparently, she'd been keeping things from him, including her real name.

"Jean," he repeated, then shook his head and corrected himself. "Randi. Sorry, but I know you as Jean."

All the years of searching aside, he had to drink her in with his eyes. God, she was beautiful. She'd fulfilled the promise of her youth. And then some.

Where she'd once been pretty, bright, fresh, and young, twenty-two years later, she'd become the most wonderful of creatures, a mature woman. Confidence radiated from her as she lifted her chin ever so slightly, her jade eyes challenging him for having the nerve to enter her domain. Her petite body, once slender, now showed soft curves behind the faded green apron stained with the efforts of her labors to produce a feast. He took in the surface details, as too many emotions to name whirled through his mind. He'd been thinking of her so much lately, for a moment he wondered if he were dreaming.

"You know each other?" Birdie, the beautiful young woman who he'd thought vaguely reminded him of someone, looked from her mother to him and back again, her little brow wrinkled in confusion. "Mom? Are you okay?" Birdie protectively covered her mother's hand on her arm.

After her initial cool greeting, Jean's—Randi's—face had paled under her smooth makeup, making the colors all wrong on her face. A second later, the pasty shade heated into the rosy glow he'd loved, though usually produced for a completely different reason. Her body had flushed that way, in the same perfect shade of dewy pink while…

"Dad?"

His son's query caused her gaze to dart in the lad's direction and forced Court to blink himself back into the present, his lips curving in a smile greatly at odds with the emotions swirling deep inside. Hadn't she trusted him enough to gift him with her real name? Then again, what he'd done, been forced to do, probably had proved him untrustworthy in her eyes. Still, the mystery of where she'd ended up was solved, and the relief it brought nearly knocked him to his knees.

"I don't usually bring roses to strange women, but Birdie said they were your favorite, and I'm delighted to say you aren't a stranger after all. Well, except for the name thing. Why didn't you ever tell me your whole name?"

Randi's wide, shocked gaze darted back to him, bounced over to Drew, and zoomed to him again as if searching for signs of something. Most people gushed over the similarities between him and Drew, so she was clearly noticing for herself. It didn't take much to ignore the reaction as usual. He held out the bouquet of soft pink roses, so pale they were nearly white. As he recalled, they were exactly her favorites.

"Oh. Thank you. Funny you should find these..."

She ignored the question about her name and reached for the flowers. For an instant, her hand tightened around the tissue and plastic wrapped stems until the knuckles turned white. It seemed as if she were almost tempted to beat him about the head and shoulders with the bouquet of her favorite posies.

He'd once nicked a rose like these from her landlady's garden and Jea—correction, had to remember—Randi had pressed it between the pages of her economics book. "Yes, those exact roses. Destiny, I'd say." Did she still have the dried flower? What about some of the petals he'd shaken onto her as she lay on the bed their last night together? No, she probably didn't have any of those mementos. Most likely they'd hit the dustbin later the next evening.

The moment of pending violence passed and Court let the air escape from his lungs as she held the flowers to her nose. "More like the Fates screwing with me again, I'd say."

For a moment, a pain to rival the anguish he'd felt the last time he'd looked into those eyes stabbed at his heart. At the worst moment of his life, when he'd turned around at that bloody reception, knowing what she'd overheard. He'd never forgotten the look, and it punched him harder now, faced with what he'd given up by bowing under family pressure, and his own conscience, to marry Beatrice. Though judging by Birdie's age, the bitter thought hit him twice as hard in the gut, Randi hadn't been down for long. Birdie couldn't be a full year younger than Drew.

"Mom?"

Court could see Birdie's curiosity growing by leaps and bounds, and he looked her over once again. Of course, she somewhat resembled her mother. And yet, there was something besides her hair coloring that didn't quite come from her mother that twigged at the back of his brain. A quality from her father, perhaps? Someone he may have met in the course of business without ever realizing it?

One question answered, his Jeannie's location, but a few hundred new questions popped into his head. Too many to cope with and not only for him. He could see the turmoil in her as well.

"Yes, darling." Randi came out of her trance, long lashes sweeping her cheeks as she blinked a few times. "Yes, I met Court when I studied in England. Remember, I told you I did a semester abroad?"

"Why did he know you as Jean?"

Birdie asked the first question at the tip of Court's tongue, though logic told him exactly why she'd used her middle name, or to be more specific, avoided her first name.

"Come, you can put these in water. I was just getting to the rolls, which are ready to be shaped." Ignoring the question, Randi Jean—yes, the double name worked better, he decided, as it described how she'd been with him so long ago—thrust the flowers at her daughter, turned, and led the way into the kitchen.

Though she walked away as if she couldn't get away from him fast enough, she spoke over her shoulder. "Gentlemen, may I get you something? We could open a bottle of wine, or I could make tea. Or there's a fresh pot of coffee ready to brew."

While entirely proper, the cool, crisp tone to her voice wasn't one he recognized.

"Have any Earl Grey?" Court couldn't help asking. It had been her preferred, especially with toasted crumpets slathered in butter and jam. It had become their favorite, their tea. These days, he mainly stuck to a basic blend of black, a Lynford signature, but every so often, he drank a cup of the Earl and remembered, wondering if she ever did the same.

"Not a single leaf. I do have a variety of others. In bags, of course."

He didn't remember this brisk, efficient woman. Had she gone through a metamorphosis with the name change? What had the years done to her? And tea bags? Seriously? The woman knew better. Bags were like drinking reconstituted dried coffee crystals. Done only when nothing else could be found and desperation ruled. "Coffee will do." She'd probably planned coffee all along, and the threat of using a tea bag only ensured she got her way.

"Please, make yourself at home." She waved a graceful, ring free hand toward a room less formal than the one directly past the foyer.

Visible through an arch, bar stools stood across the counter from the sink. A good spot to perch and chat with the women in the kitchen. Birdie smiled from the sink where she started the water running before turning to lift down a vase from a cabinet.

Birdie.

Strange name. Not for the first time, he wondered about it. A nickname? Randi Jean certainly knew of the slang custom of calling girls birds. So why the name? Court looked closer and wondered if the porcelain skin and honey blond hair came from the girl's father. Randi Jean had been a strawberry blond when they'd met. Her hair was now a deeper auburn, expertly colored no doubt. Not that he begrudged her a little primping. No, she looked bloody fine for her age. What would she be now…forty-two? Of course, three years younger than he. But enhanced or not, Birdie didn't have her mother's coloring. How old was Birdie, anyway?

"You never said, Birdie, where you are at university." He made himself comfortable on the high oak chair. Drew, like the affable whelp he resembled, settled on the next chair over. The pose was studied to hide the sharp intellect soaking in every detail. Court ignored the question in his son's eyes for the time being. Randi had her walls up and reinforced, apparently in no mood to catch up on old times. Precisely where he wanted to go, but for now, he'd play the role of guest and stick to superficial conversation. Or rather, hide his penetrating questions in layers of small talk. Now that he'd found her, he had time to ease his way in again.

"I'm in the last semester of my bachelor's. I'm a semester behind my original schedule because my father died two years ago…" A sad smile graced her sunny face for a moment. "At the start of spring term. Mom wanted me to stay in school, but I took a semester off anyway."

Court cut his gaze to Randi Jean on the far side of the kitchen. Back to him, she stiffened at her daughter's recital. A widow. A reasonable explanation for the lack of a wedding ring. He'd certainly shed his as soon as he could after a suitable mourning period.

"And you're still a semester ahead of your high school friends," Randi added, while Birdie shrugged and cut stems under running water.

"So, your birthday is when?"

"You know better, Court." The laughter sounded forced, but Randi Jean turned to him then. "A gentleman never inquires as to the age of a lady, and a lady would never reveal such a detail." Hands wrapped in her apron, she looked around as if she were trying to figure out where she stood and what needed doing next. She looked everywhere but directly at him. Her gaze skipped right over him as if he were a portrait on the wall, and a not very interesting one at that.

Not happy to see him? Definitely flustered, and a touch uneasy when her attention landed on Drew. Even though Court had met with an investigator yesterday with the express hope of finding Jean, he was off-balance that it had been so easy despite previous years of dead-ended attempts. The different name, and not just married versus maiden, certainly accounted for past failures. How long might he have sought out every Jean Dailey in the U.S. and never found her? The investigator had only stumbled across a tiny article from a small weekly paper a month ago about a woman starting her own CPA business. And yet, his son had most cleverly and unknowingly stumbled on the daughter of the very woman Court wanted to find. Might have to raise the lad's allowance for that.

Birdie laughed. "You always said you were never a lady, Mom."

"Now's as good a time as any for you to start acting like one. So,"— Court watched her gaze bypass him to zero in on Drew—"I hear you're a grad student at Stanford? What program?"

Clever woman, she'd changed the subject. For now he'd let her. Her house, he'd play her way. Actually, based on this reception, he was surprised she hadn't pushed him right back out the door, but that would have required explanations she might not want to make. Later, he'd ask the question again.

"International law," Drew answered readily enough, though his bright eyes didn't seem to miss much. Court ignored the question Drew silently asked and focused on the women. Randi Jean punched a button on a coffee maker and reached for a bowl perched on top of the refrigerator disguised to look like part of the cabinetry.

"Coffee will be ready in a minute."

He gave her a genial smile when she glanced his way. "Smells wonderful to me." He didn't mind waiting while trying to figure out where she might not want to tread in casual conversation. *Fancy me showing up on your doorstep after all these years, eh Jean? By the way, I didn't get a chance to tell you how beautiful you looked that night. You know the one, the night you nearly gave me a heart attack by showing up out of nowhere and then running out on me. Shame on you for leaving me at the mercy of those people.* Probably not a good icebreaker. Just a guess.

Tension filled the house as Birdie arranged the roses in a low crystal vase, and Randi Jean used her fists to beat the dough she'd dumped from the large white ceramic bowl onto the floured surface of her granite counters. All while listening to Drew ramble on.

The soft, warm coloring of her kitchen made a perfect background to her beauty, from the adobe colored walls, moss green granite countertops, to the whiskey stained paneling on her cabinets and built in appliances. Without much effort, he could picture the two of them at the tiny café table before the bay windows of the small breakfast nook, looking out on the front lawn of the sprawling ranch-style house. Despite the tension radiating from her, and his urge to make off-color jokes about her name because he still couldn't adjust to the change in his mind, comfort settled around him as he inhaled the scents of cooking. Coffee, cinnamon, nutmeg, fresh yeast, and a host of other aromas reminded him breakfast had been light.

A visual inspection of the area did bring to his notice a theme. Everywhere, on top of the cabinets, in the cabinets, on top shelves behind glass doors, and set about in decorative arrangements, a mixture of tea pots and service sets. And she didn't have any loose leaf Earl Grey in the house? A glance over his shoulder showed more displayed on shelves of the massive entertainment center. Pots and tea cups of all sizes, shapes, colors, in every style from Wedgewood to whimsical crowded together in a colorful jumble only an avid collector could arrange. There was a clue here. Court grinned to himself and turned back toward the kitchen. For a heartbeat, his gaze caught hers. She gave every appearance of being unsettled. Angry, hurt, confused, and yet... Abruptly, she looked away. Had that been longing he'd seen? Longing such as had sent him across the Atlantic and the entire North American Continent to find her?

While Randi Jean continued to interrogate Drew, Court sat back and watched, as he'd loved watching her play domestic during their short time together. Drew could hold his own in conversation, hence the law degree. It allowed Court to let his mind wander back and let him sort his own feelings. Something he'd tried to do often over the last few years as thoughts of this woman returned to him more and more.

What a time that had been. He'd been in the final push of his post graduate degree, and Jean had been there at exactly the time when he'd needed her. Badly. He'd tripped over her, literally, in the library where she'd been seated cross-legged on the floor between the shelves of the history section. He'd been passing through, his arms piled high with books, on his way to a quiet table at the back.

As she'd crawled about, helping him gather books, he'd fallen in love with her backside. Those had been the days when girls wore tight leggings and long tunics with ankle boots. Or very short skirts. She had been dressed in black leggings that day, and at one point, her long sweater had lifted enough her pretty bottom had been in his face as they scrambled for scattered papers.

One inhale and he'd breathed in her scent like a dog sniffing out a female in heat. Hardly classy, but had she backed up instead of crawling forward, he'd have tasted her and probably taken her right there on the library floor, like the dirty dog he was. She'd been adorable as she helped him carry everything to his usual table in a secluded corner, and he'd let her pile her own books beside his. He should have told her to leave, but he'd let her stay, unable to put her on the other side of the wall he'd erected against all women. The one she'd quite easily crawled right over with her trim little bum.

"Birdie, why don't you get out the deviled eggs and the relish tray?" Randi Jean paused long enough to get coffee mugs and carry the pot over to the counter where he and Drew sat. "Bring the sugar and cream while you're at it." Brusque as a pub landlady, she poured and handed the mugs over the sink. "I'll have some hot *hors d'oeuvres* in a bit. My father and another guest will join us soon."

Only her father? That jolted him out of his musings. "Your mother…?" Court probed gently and met her gaze steadily when she looked him in the eye for a moment before turning away.

"Seven years ago. Cancer."

"I am sorry." She'd been close to her mother. Without her mother's input, her father never would have allowed her to go overseas alone. The semester away had been a test to see if she could get out in the world on her own, and her mother had endorsed it. Stories she'd told had painted the picture of an overly protective father who never missed a weekly phone call and had hated the fact she was on the far side of the world where he couldn't monitor her dates or activities.

What had her homecoming been like?

Randi shrugged, as if easily dismissing her mother's death, and moved to a cabinet over another counter to the right. In the blink of an eye, she had a dark brown bottle out. Ah, not so nonchalant as she tried to portray if she was seeking a touch of liquid courage.

"Irish cream in your coffee, anyone?" she offered while pouring a generous amount into her own mug.

"Don't mind if I do," Court answered. Hell, it was pushing nine at night in England, and he needed a tot. Besides, if she wanted to get drunk, then by God, he'd join her. However, judging by Birdie's glance and tiny frown as she settled the final flower in the vase, this wasn't standard behavior for her mother.

Just how upset was Randi Jean that he was here? She'd been devastated, much as he'd been, at their last, oh-so-very-brief meeting. The shock on her face, and the way she'd run from him, had made it all too evident. The letters he'd written returned unopened. The phone calls refused. Old frustration rose up inside him.

How upset was she? To hell with that, how upset was he? He had fought against getting his hopes up. Had run a thousand scenes through his head after getting a long awaited e-mail from the private investigator he'd hired years ago. As the man had explained yesterday, Californians could file for private marriage licenses, making his job that much more difficult. The fact she'd never told him her first name had further complicated the search. And yet, every other Jean Dailey lead had been eliminated. So what remained must be the truth, right?

And so it was. Although, he wasn't entirely prepared for this meeting, didn't know what to say. He'd had no time to assess the situation, plan his approach, decide the angle of his opening. Or even whether or not he actually wanted to see her. Much less deal with the whole new identity thing. Sure, he'd expected the married name, but the first name too? The investigator had provided all the information he could without placing himself on her radar by contacting her directly or her neighbors, all the information Court used to make these decisions, and yet, here he was. In the presence of the object of his two decade long obsession.

The fact that Drew had unknowingly met and befriended the woman's daughter was a coincidence too bizarre to ignore. Sure, Court had suggested Stanford when Drew had first started thinking internationally. Perhaps he'd hoped for this connection. Hadn't believed in the long shot.

It wasn't often a man got blindsided or stumbled into the thing he'd wanted, and feared, the most. So far, he was whole. No missing limbs or punctured eyes. Not one bruise purpling his stomach, jaw, or cheek. After all the times he'd imagined meeting up with her again, this seemed almost a letdown. Why had he ever dreamed of her rushing into his arms with breathless anticipation? The woman couldn't even bring herself to look at him much less seem to want to embrace, or kiss, him.

"Drew," Randi addressed his son. Without missing a beat, she leaned over the sink and poured the alcoholic cream into Court's coffee, turning it a creamy shade of mocha. "How handy are you? It's Birdie's job to set the table, and it goes faster with an extra pair of hands."

"I learn fast." Drew grinned. "As long as I can tote my coffee along."

Court watched Randi's tense smile soften ever so slightly for the boy. Couldn't she manage the same for him? "Don't spill on the tablecloth just yet. We try to save that for dessert."

"Yes, ma'am, I'll do my best." Drew grabbed one of the egg halves and popped it into his mouth. Court recognized the groan of appreciation rumbling from the lad's throat as he reached for another. Happily munching, Drew followed Birdie and the vase of flowers to the dining room beyond a half-height wall topped with more of the green granite, leaving Court alone with Jean. Or Randi.

Despite the different name, he knew her and wanted very much to be alone with her, but there was only so much aloneness they could accomplish just then. They were as alone as they could be with the kids on the other side of the open doorway. Certainly not alone enough he could back her up against the wall and kiss her silly. At least without instigating more questions than he wanted to answer at the moment. In fact, he wanted to get answers before giving them. Not that she seemed to notice with her gaze following the kids as she positioned herself where she had a clear view of the dining room.

Unable to resist the rumbling of his stomach any longer, Court picked up an egg half and bit into it. The fluffy yolks had been mixed with some sort of mustard and piped back into the white. "Mmm," he echoed Drew's appraisal and popped the rest into his mouth, already reaching for a second.

"I meant to make them for you once. Never got the chance," Randi muttered, and resumed beating her dough after shooting a dark glare in his direction.

Court swallowed. "There're a lot of things neither of us got the chance to do for the other," he retorted, lifted his coffee mug, and left his seat. He was on the wrong side of the kitchen, too far away. In a recreation of the old days, he stood leaning his lower back against the counter, crowding her slightly while she worked, blocking her view of the kids on purpose. Whatever bee was up her bonnet didn't need to cross over to them.

"You're in my way," she said without meeting his gaze and took a healthy swallow of her coffee, almost as if she were desperate to induce numbness. "The kitchen is large enough you don't have to stand so close." Leaning back to glance beyond him, she called out to Birdie, "Use the white linens on the left side of the buffet." She eyed the kids for a moment, then turned her attention back to her labors.

Ah, but she didn't push him aside. "You used to like me in your way, Jean. Randi." He was near enough to smell the soft scents of her cosmetics adding up to a sexy, powdery, flowery smell mixed with a deep and sexy perfume, including the warm yeast of the dough she handled and the creamy coffee she sipped. No woman had ever smelled as complex or interesting as her.

Beatrice had always smelled of Chanel No. 5. Not even original and less than flattering on her. Poison would have suited her better, and not the perfume going for damn near four hundred pounds per ounce.

Still not looking at him, Randi began to rip off sections of dough, using her hands like claws. A desperate fantasy of ripping him to shreds? "I used to like a lot of things about you. Doesn't mean I still do."

Direct hit. Ouch.

Lips pinched and hands moving with practiced ease despite a slight tremor, she rolled the lumps of dough into balls and arranged them in a baking pan. Up close like this, the fine lines at the corner of her eyes were a little more pronounced.

"Jean," he said. Couldn't quite go with the Randi name. "I wrote to you... tried to explain...as best I could," he said quietly. Back then, in the days before Internet and a personal computer in every home, he'd been limited, and her parents had refused to accept his calls, well, the odds had been against him. That and having a new job and a new, breeding bride to focus on. One had blossomed under his attention. The other had unsheathed spiky thorns.

She threw a hapless ball of dough into the pan with such force he winced for the poor thing. "My name is Randi. Try to remember it, would you? Besides, what was there to explain? After all, a pregnant fiancé certainly took precedence over an American fling who was supposed to already be on an airplane out of the country."

"You were never a fling. Though now I have to wonder at the feelings you once professed. If you'd loved me as you said, why didn't I know about this other name?" Conscious of the children in the other room, where Birdie directed Drew in the best way to shake out and center a tablecloth, he spoke quietly but harshly, every ounce of his own pain from so long ago lancing the wound that had never properly healed.

She stared up at him, eyes round, mouth slightly open at his accusation. Before she could speak, he waved a hand to cut off her protest before it began. "I already had a ticket in hand. I planned to be on a plane twelve hours behind you. I wanted to show up here, in California, and surprise you. When other plans took precedence, I wrote to the address you gave me, but the letters came back."

A flush crept up her neck as she directed her gaze back to the task before her. Ah, she'd known about the letters being returned.

"There was nothing to explain. I heard it all. She was already pregnant. You told Danielle Richards the date of your wedding for heaven's sake. Only a week away. Bet you were sweating it that last week getting me out of your hair."

Angry green eyes looked up at him, overflowing with accusation. Fury rolled off her in waves. Her breasts heaved, gently bouncing with each tortured breath as she hissed at him, trying to keep their conversation just between them.

As guilty as he felt, as furious and confused as he was, the animated woman beside him fascinated him. Beatrice had never looked beautiful when angry, but Randi Jean couldn't seem to help it. Which made him feel, well, to tell the truth, randy. Probably why she'd used her middle name whilst in England.

"I was nothing more than a secretary with benefits to you. I typed your thesis, proofed it, and typed it again. And all the while, I kept your bed warm. Yeah, you got your paper typed and then you got a little extra." She turned her attention back to the counter and smashed the poor lump of dough before her. "Still operate that way, Court? Does your secretary type up your reports only to be rewarded with a game of slap and tickle on your desk?"

"Dammit, Jean." He ignored her last comment, as it had no bearing on the situation. He'd have to deal with that later. The look she shot him was extremely disgruntled. "Okay, I got it, but it's hard to make the switch."

"You can say it, Court. Randi. It's my name, not my physical state."

"It doesn't fit with my memories."

"As Lewis Carroll so eloquently put it in *Alice in Wonderland*: 'But it's no use going back to yesterday, because I was a different person then.' And I am a very different person from the naïve girl I was in London. For instance, I no longer fall prey to beautiful, smooth talking men."

"I'm not a predator, but fine. Randi. I'll try," he promised, but didn't put much stock in it. "I'd split with her three months earlier. We'd slept together exactly once in an attempt to get back together. It didn't work." Court winced at the memory. "You say I was a smooth talking stranger, but I see something else. I don't know how I bungled the whole thing, but she hated it and threw me out. We called off the engagement, which had been understood our entire lives. That was a month before I met you. I didn't know about the pregnancy until that day. I swear." Keeping his voice low was difficult. Fortunately, Birdie was vocal with her table setting lessons, allowing them some modicum of privacy in the kitchen.

Randi, glancing toward the dining room again, snorted her disbelief. "I was there. I heard the announcement. I saw you put your arm around her." The green gaze came back, spearing him with hurt and accusation.

He'd never told her, but Jean had saved his life. After his experience with Beatrice, he'd been reluctant to seduce or be seduced by the innocent American. He'd had a few experimental partners, all before sleeping with Beatrice, none of whom had ever screamed in orgasmic bliss. Not like when he'd fingered Jean to her first orgasm. From there, well, of course they'd had to conduct further experiments.

He ran a hand through his hair. Hell, Jean had been the one to convince him he was a sexual master. Before her, he'd had serious doubts. Bloody hell, he had doubts even now. No one had ever stirred him to the level of excitement she had. His body remembered even though he tried to remind himself jet lag was still a bit of a problem. Much like his body, she didn't want to hear about it now, although for a different reason.

She still hadn't been forced to leave. There'd been other reasons to stay. Why hadn't she? "I heard later that your application for the summer internship had come through and you'd accepted. Why did you leave?"

Once more, she looked up at him, her green eyes wide. "Why did I leave? I left because it was clear you were over and done with me. I stood there, waiting for you to turn around and notice me, and then you put your arm around that...*her*, and told Ms. Richards about your upcoming wedding, rushed because you two were expecting. How could I stay?" Her voice broke. Tears rose in her eyes. Tears she blinked back before they fell. "The only reason I wanted to stay was to be with you."

Inwardly wincing, he thought carefully about his response, wanting her to understand, to realize he hadn't had a choice, or not much of one. How differently would things have worked out if he'd fought harder? A question he'd asked himself plenty of times over the years. "I didn't know you were there. I thought you were gone." Lame excuse, but definitely the truth. Had he known Jean was there, or anywhere still within the country, he bloody well would have walked away from Beatrice, his family, and job—everything—just to be with Jean.

"Mom, which silver do you want us to use?" Birdie asked from the next room.

"Your choice," Randi returned without missing a beat, her mom voice back in control. "Don't forget the candlesticks on the sideboard. I polished them yesterday."

"Already saw them," Birdie chirped right back.

"I know that," Randi returned to their conversation as if she hadn't taken a side trip. "But then, I didn't usually do things quite the way you wanted me to, did I?" Another ball of dough suffered a beating before she threw it into the pan. "I never was, and never would be, the well-behaved little English woman you so obviously were raised to marry."

Court closed his eyes, remembering Danielle's expression as she'd looked over his shoulder. Half expecting to see the south wall caving in, judging by the horror on the woman's face, he'd turned and found himself looking into Jean's stricken eyes and pale face, her skin as white as chalk against the elegant black cocktail dress she wore. With her hair up and a string of pearls around her neck, she'd never looked more beautiful, more shocked, or more wounded. He'd reached for her thinking she was about to faint, but she'd backed away, a hand resting over her stomach as if to hold back the bile she'd been dealing with the previous week. She'd thought it had been a touch of the flu, but he hadn't caught it…

Before he could process the thought, the front door opened, and a man's gruff voice called out. "Hey, baby!"

Randi flinched.

Birdie shrieked with happiness. "Grandpa!"

Court looked to the right in time to see a colorful flash of Birdie hurrying toward the front door. Drew set down the handful of utensils he'd been putting out and sauntered after her. A glance to the woman on his left showed her fists pressed on the counter, knuckles white, head bowed. As if girding herself to face the lions of the coliseum, she inhaled deeply and lifted her head, back straightening.

"My father and a guest," she said through tight lips. "Behave yourself and don't go into details. I never told him your name, though I'm sure the kids will tell him we knew each other back when. Don't elaborate. Please. I don't want to go into it today. We'll talk later."

It was about all he could hope for just then. "As m'lady requests."

The look she gave him would have sent him to the bottom of the sea if such things were possible.

# Chapter 3

Still trembling with far too many emotions to process, Randi rounded the corner to greet her father and guest in the foyer. The younger of the two men carried a case sized box of wine. For forty-nine—Jordan, never married, liked to run marathons for fun, all facts imparted by Dad—he wasn't too bad. A little taller than Court, he had the lean build of a runner. Brown hair, neatly styled in a short cut, had strands of gray throughout, rather than just at the temples. Brown eyes assessed her from head to toe, then smiled.

"A full case, Dad?" Randi inquired as she gave her father a brief hug and kissed his cheek.

"You said you wanted extra, and you know the price break for a case. There're even a few bottles of Mumm in there." At sixty-five, RJ Dailey retained his vitality along with a head of thinning gray hair he kept slicked back. Today, in keeping with the relaxed attitude of the holiday, he wore a navy polo shirt and khaki pants. Jordan wore pretty much the same, in direct contrast to Court and Drew with their pressed, button-down shirts and wool slacks.

"Thanks. Um, Jordan? Nice to meet you. Why don't you follow me into the kitchen with that?" Once more Randi led a man into her domain, only to find Court blocking the way. She leveled her coldest glare at him. "Excuse me, Mr. Robinson."

"Pardon me." He stepped back barely far enough to clear the wine cooler under the counter to the left of the fridge. Those blue eyes of his sparkled with amusement, ignoring her irritation.

"Jordan, here." She moved aside a platter to make room for the box, which he easily set down.

"There, now we can do a proper introduction," the newcomer said. "Jordan Doyle." He held out a hand, and Randi quickly dusted one off on her apron.

"Randi Ferguson. Pardon the flour. I'm nearly done with the rolls. Jordan, this is Court. His son, Drew, is helping my daughter set the table." She could hear Birdie introducing Drew to her grandfather in the hallway.

Jordan smiled down at her as his large, warm hand engulfed hers. He stood tall enough that she felt shorter and rounder than normal.

Okay, so at five-two, it didn't take much to make her feel like a midget. Wyatt had been six-one, Birdie topped out at five-six, Dad six feet even, and Court, well, he was also six feet even. Drew, she'd place about six-one. Good thing she'd put on heels. Two extra inches didn't add much, but every little bit helped. She'd worn three inch heels a few times with Court, for example, that disastrous night. She'd discovered then that running on stilettos wasn't a talent she had. Somewhere along the way in her run from the reception to her flat, she'd twisted her ankle, which had left her limping for a week.

"Where would you like the wine?" Court asked from behind her. So much like old times, for a heartbeat she fought the temptation to lean back into his arms. Her body agreed, her neck tingling in anticipation of his kiss, right there, in that spot, the ticklish one right behind her ear. All this while holding Jordan's hand. Which reminded her of another reason why she remained annoyed with Court, she turned into a brainless idiot around him.

"Oh." She snatched back her hand from Jordan's grasp. "Why don't you see if there's enough room in the wine cooler? Dad? There's coffee and Irish cream, or the straight stuff over there." She pointed at the counter where she'd left the coffee service. "Why don't you two have a seat and help yourself to the trays? I'll throw some wrapped brie and prosciutto in the oven."

"Why don't you introduce me first?" Dad said, his eyes locked on Court.

"Oh, sorry. Court, this is my dad, RJ. Dad, Court."

"Pleased to meet you, sir." Court reached across the kitchen island and shook his hand.

"Didn't catch your last name…?" Dad raised his eyebrow in that most annoying expression he used when Randi tried to cut corners on information. Nailed her every single time when it was least convenient.

"Robinson, sir. Courtland Bailey Robinson."

Randi caught the wry twist of Court's lips. If only he knew. Was he imagining what meeting Dad would have been like so long ago?

And Dad certainly twigged to Court's full name, his lifted brow directed straight at her along with a glare of recognition. "Quite the interesting name there, sounds like—"

"Sounds like time for the football game to me," Randi interrupted, directing her own narrow-eyed glare of warning at her father. He knew the look well enough to back off for now, but he wouldn't be satisfied for long. Court was in his sights, and Randi's dread increased tenfold. Would she make it through this day with her secrets still buried? Desperate to hold off the unveiling of secrets as long as possible, she started toward the family room, subtly, or not, ushering her father and Jordan from the kitchen. "Who's playing this year, and what's the bet?"

Nobody fell for it, but at least Dad took the hint. She wasn't entirely off the hook; no doubt he'd call her to the carpet later. The man had a mind like a bloodhound mixed with a pit bull, which meant he could sniff out a lie and then kept worrying at it until she caved. The look he gave her now confirmed she'd only gained a few hours before the interrogation began.

From the moment she'd mentioned going abroad for a semester, he'd hated the five months she'd spent in England. Once she'd returned, and until she'd married Wyatt, he'd raved endlessly how he'd known all along she'd come home knocked-up. It was one of the few times in her life she'd been browbeaten into doing exactly as he wanted. When he'd presented Wyatt Ferguson, a rising sales manager, as an acceptable husband, and one willing to take on her shame, she'd looked into Wyatt's kind hazel eyes and agreed. It had been plain from the first moment that Wyatt was far more forgiving than her dad, and he'd lived up to the promise of being easier to live with.

With a grumble, Dad answered. "LSU is playing the Gators. The bet is for travel expenses. If LSU wins, Jordan pays his own tab. If they lose, I pay his expense report without complaining."

Predictable, but she was getting in on this action. The Gators were favored to win. "Hmm, throw me in for a long weekend in Napa at the B&B of my choice and I'll take your bet."

"You'll hire a tree service to take out the damn spruce so I don't have to hear about it anymore?" Dad's eyes bored into her from the family room to clear across the kitchen. The stupid dead tree she'd been trying to get him to take down for over a year. The one blight on her carefully landscaped backyard.

Randi blew a hank of bangs out of her eyes. "Fine. If LSU wins, I'll deal with the tree myself."

Dad rolled his eyes, then nodded at her hands. "I'd shake on it, but you'd probably squish that blob of dough into my hand."

Randi looked down at the poor mangled globule. The rolls would turn out interesting this year. If it wasn't the turkey, it would be something else.

Were there backups in the extra freezer? Did she have enough potatoes to mash if she didn't have more rolls? "Pour some Irish Cream in your coffee and consider us shaken."

"How you make it in the business world with that attitude, I'll never know." Dad shook his head and turned away to pour the coffee for himself and Jordan. "Let's go find the game, guys, and leave the women to the prep."

"Grandpa!" Birdie yelled from the dining room. "I heard that, and you know that doesn't fly in this house."

"Yeah, yeah, I'll carve the bird. Just make sure the right one is on the platter when it's time."

Birdie moved into the hall and glared at her grandfather, hands on hips. A moment later, the two of them broke into laughter and went their separate ways.

"Carve the bird?" Court murmured in her ear. Damn, she'd almost forgotten he was there.

"Turkey, bird, Birdie…" She looked over her shoulder and found him within kissing distance. Certainly smelling distance. And he smelled good. Some expensive cologne she didn't recognize.

"Ah. Birdie. A most interesting name. How did you come up with that?"

With a casual shrug, she said, "Nickname. Because she's so damn chipper, like a little bird." Randi put the last of the rolls in the buttered pan, covered them with a damp towel, and set them on top of the fridge to rise. Hopefully, they'd do it properly.

"Ah, so, what, exactly, is her name?"

Oh, so not going there. Not if she could help it. That would give the surprise away completely, and she didn't have a clue on how to approach that bit of news. She felt nervous enough watching Birdie lightly flirting with Drew as she directed him toward the cabinet with the china dishes. Banter seemed to cover most of it. At least they weren't putting their hands all over each other. Touches were limited to the bumping of shoulders. Heaven forbid Drew attempt to put his arms around Birdie. Randi would have to do something then. Would a pitcher of cold water be too drastic? She'd be seen as certifiable for sure, but would it keep the kids apart? Might be worth it.

Trying not to give herself away, she firmly turned away from the situation in the dining room and changed the subject on Court. "I hear you're a widower. When?" She moved to the far side of the kitchen, putting her back to him while she washed her hands and wrung out a sponge.

"Beatrice died in a car accident about six years ago. Drew and I have been baching it since."

"I'm sorry." Truly, she was. Death of a spouse pretty much spelled difficult.

"As much as I hate to say it, lest I come across as cold-hearted"—she turned in time to see him shrug as he spoke—"it more or less worked out for the best."

In order to wipe down the counter, she had to sidle up to where he loaded bottles of wine into the racks of the cooler one at a time. "Keep a couple bottles of the champagne up front, please."

"Have an ice bucket? There may not be room for all of this."

"Cabinet on the left. Top shelf." Randi began wiping the flour from the countertop. A swift wipe with a dishtowel and the counter sparkled, ready for the next task. If only she could deal with the half sibling issue as cleanly.

"Next to or behind the extensive tea service collection?"

Not ready to discuss what appeared to be an obsession with tea time, Randi ignored his probing question and directed hers back to his previous comment on his marriage. "Why was it for the best?"

"Tell me Birdie's real name, and I'll answer your question." He set the wine bucket down at her elbow and leaned toward her, interfering with the movement of her right arm. "A personal question for a personal question."

So he wasn't ready to go there, either. Fair enough. "What decided Drew on international law? I thought business was the family, well, business." Some sort of import company, if she remembered. Products from Spain? Or Italy? Or both by now?

"An extension of the family business. We've expanded globally. I need people with more expertise in international laws. He's fluent in French, Italian, and Spanish, and studying Chinese. After he finishes the year here, he'll move into an immersion program."

"He's here for a year?" Randi moved away from the tempting heat of him. He still smelled of expensive leather and a touch of bay rum, that was the scent she'd found so elusive. And creamy coffee.

It was easier to keep things light while she moved about the kitchen with her tasks. The rest of the appetizers she'd made and put in the fridge earlier came out now. Thank God for double ovens. Once more Wyatt had been ahead of her when renovating the kitchen. Double ovens and a huge Sub-Zero refrigerator. The man had liked to entertain, and he'd loved his food. All the more reason for her to start thinking heart-healthy in terms of her own diet. More than once, she'd asked herself if she'd indulged

Wyatt's preferences, hoping he'd have a heart attack. No, she honestly believed she hadn't tried to sabotage his health. He'd been set in certain ways, and no amount of cajoling had moved him an inch.

Randi sighed. This endless conjecture had to end sometime. Wyatt was gone. That's all there was to it, and she had a serious situation on her hands. A potential disaster in need of delicate handling. What chance did she have of getting away with subtly breaking up Birdie and Drew and leaving it all there?

A glance into the dining room showed the two putting the final touches on the table setting. How was she supposed to think through this situation with Court standing far too close? He occupied too many of her thoughts, which were scattered at best and completely destroyed at worst. She couldn't seem to string two thoughts together today. The top priorities, she reminded herself, were to get dinner to the table on time, keep Court and Jordan at a distance, keep Dad occupied enough that he didn't start wearing at her with questions she didn't want to answer, and, oh, keep her daughter and Court's son as far away from each other as possible. No worries. Easy. Could do it all in her sleep. If she'd managed to get any.

Consumed by a need to put more distance between them, hoping her mind would return, she arranged the remaining deviled eggs and relish plate on a tray. She nabbed a stack of napkins and carried everything out to the family room where the game announcers were beginning their warm up. With no coffee table, she set the tray on the leather sofa between the men.

"Thanks, sweet pea. Now don't block the screen."

"Thanks, Dad. It's a sixty inch screen. If you can't see around me, then I guess we don't need to be eating dinner today."

"Now, darlin', don't get yourself in a lather. I didn't mean that at all. If anything, you could stand to add a few pounds," Dad said. The suck up.

"Anything I can do to help?" Jordan asked. Just to be polite, she was sure, since his eyes seemed to be glued to her cleavage, such as it was hidden behind her apron, or not, as she stood bent over giving him pretty much a full view.

With a sigh, she straightened. "Thanks, but I've got more help than I need right now. Holler if this runs out. There's more coming."

Jordan's eyes cut from her cleavage to the kitchen where Court rattled ice into the stainless steel bucket. With a smooth movement, Jordan levered himself off the plush leather sofa and rose to tower over her. "I could do with a coffee refill."

She reached for the mug, but Jordan lifted it out of her reach. There were times tall people were truly irritating. Like when they weren't being useful as human ladders.

"I can get it for you," she offered.

"No need for you to wait on me all day. I can get my own refills." The smile he gave her was soft and warm, but it didn't do a blessed thing to stir up the pitter patter in her heart. Damn Court.

"Suit yourself. I think there's enough for one more cup, and then I'll put on a fresh pot."

"How's your coffee?" Jordan followed her into the kitchen. "Don't you get first dibs on refills?"

Now, that made her laugh. Her cup was ice cold by now. "I'm fine. One more round of coffee, and then we'll break out some wine." She waved toward Court and the champagne. "We have the first bottle on ice."

"And a back-up in the freezer," Court said. "Don't worry, I'll remember to pull it out." The way his eyes twinkled brought back the memory of the first time she'd stuck a couple beers in her tiny freezer against his advice. They'd been too busy to remember they were there, and the next morning, she'd opened the fridge looking for orange juice, only to find frozen beer sprayed all over the inside.

With a glare in Court's direction, hoping the flush rushing to her cheeks could be attributed to the ovens, she picked up the coffee pot and put a hand to it. "It's cold. Let me make fresh, and then I'll bring your cup out," she told Jordan. Two men hovering in her kitchen strained her ability to deal with life at the moment. One had to leave, and Court had found a task to keep him busy.

"No worries, I'll sit here, halfway between the kitchen and the game." Jordan gave her a wide smile and settled down at the breakfast bar where Court had sat earlier. He could put his back to the wall and keep an eye on the game and the kitchen at the same time through the arched opening.

She wanted nothing more than to scream at them all to go watch the game. Instead, she bit her lip and concentrated on rinsing out the coffee pot and going through the motions of setting up a fresh one.

Damn if Court didn't sidle up to her again.

"Got hot pads handy? The *hors d'oeuvres* look nearly done."

"Hanging on the front of the oven door," she muttered.

Court's body brushed up against her side as he turned just far enough to look over his shoulder. "What do you know? So they are. Cheeky little buggers, hiding out in plain sight."

"Imagine that. American ingenuity triumphs again."

Court chuckled and discreetly ran a hand down her back, settling at the base a mere second, long enough for her body to remember, to long for, to melt under the memory of his touch from so long ago, and yet, it felt as if it had been only yesterday.

No touching. Had to stop him from touching.

"Mom?" Birdie clattered into the kitchen. Court's hand dropped away. "Want us to fill the water glasses now?"

"You have the crystal on the table already?" How had she missed that?

"Everything's set, Mom, except for the water, wine, food, and people."

Randi peeked through the doorway to the dining room. Birdie had even placed the flowers in the center of the table and serving utensils on the sideboard. Everything sparkled. "Good job. Looks beautiful. No, no need to worry about the water right now. Go watch the game with Grandpa and give him a live person to argue with instead of the announcers *who can't hear him*," she raised her voice for the last part of the sentence.

"I can hear you!" he shouted back. "Got more eggs?"

"No more eggs. You get vegetables." She nodded at Birdie to get the refills.

"You're no fun, Randi. How did I raise such a dull daughter?"

"Like father like daughter," she shot back.

"That's not the way I remember it." Court's quiet comment sent a shiver down her spine.

The man may have been standing back to back with her, sliding hot packets of brie wrapped with prosciutto and phyllo dough onto a serving plate, but she could sense every inch of him along every inch of her back. She glanced at the clock on the wall. Hell. Today was going to be the longest of her life.

# Chapter 4

Firmly forcing his mind back to where it'd been before Randi's dad had arrived, Court transferred the baked bundles wrapped to look like mini presents onto a plate. Drew traipsed into the kitchen on Birdie's heels. Court stopped him and handed over the plate. Happy as usual, Drew took it, followed Birdie, and plopped down on the sofa next to her. For a moment, Court wanted to leap between them. They looked wrong together somehow, or was it too right? Like peas in a pod, they had the same coloring and apparently similar temperaments. Both unnaturally cheerful. A trait attributed to him, once upon a time. Right up until that spring so long ago.

Damn, he'd lost the thought. He needed to go through it from the beginning. Court ran a hand through his hair as if the stimulation could dredge up the memories.

Jean—Randi had applied for the summer internship because she loved London. She'd told him she needed to stay as long as possible to soak up all the real Earl Grey and crumpets she could. He'd gained a new appreciation for the everyday items by hanging with her. Hanging. Just one Americanism he'd picked up from her. So many cultural exchanges they'd made. The very thought brought a smile to his face. International Relations had been his favorite subject that spring. Too bad it wasn't eligible for addition to his transcripts.

And yet, she'd given up the opportunity because of one snippet of conversation she'd overheard. Okay, one incredibly damning snippet. Because she thought he'd thrown her, and what they'd had together, away. Because she thought he'd been toying with her, as if he were a modern day Lothario, with women falling at his feet, giving him a choice of lovers each night. Something he'd never been accused of. He'd been faithful to Beatrice until her death, and afterward, his affairs had been discreet with carefully selected companions.

He turned to watch her wash her hands, back stiff, movements jerky. Only once during their time together had he seen body language like this. Definitely upset. That time, so long ago, had been after a phone call from home. She'd once admitted discussions with her father could be difficult, but they seemed to get along fine now. What had changed?

Too many years had passed, or had they? A few minutes alone, that's all he needed. Time was precious and their audience too large. He needed to talk with her and there seemed to be a lull in the action.

"Pardon me," he muttered near her ear. "Where might I find the loo?"

Without softening a bit, she snapped out, "Off the foyer. There are two doors, one leads to the mudroom, the other is the powder room."

"Could you show me?" Possibly he could sidetrack her, get her to tell him about the photos lining the wall. "I wouldn't want to take a wrong turn and, say, end up in your bedroom."

The look she shot him embodied pure exasperation. He loved that look on her face. It meant he'd begun to get under her skin despite all her attempts to remain aloof. Not that she'd ever been able to cultivate aloofness. The quintessential California Girl back then, she'd never have cut it in London society. Beatrice and her coven would have sliced her to shreds in seconds. Thankfully, he'd avoided exclusive relationships since Beatrice, however, he couldn't help but wonder if Randi could slide into his society now, or would she find resistance?

Randi took one last glance at the other four people, though he could have assured her they were engrossed in the football game. Drew had become downright enamored with the sport in the three months he'd been stateside. While she grabbed a towel, Court untied the apron strings at her back. The exasperated look shot his way again, but she pulled the thing off over her head and laid it down beside the towel after her hands were dry. Without the camouflage, he could properly see the contours of her breasts where the thin knit ivory fabric molded to her body. His mouth went dry from wanting to touch her, so he shoved his hands into his pockets to keep from following through.

"This way," she muttered, and they made a clean escape into the hall, bordered on one side by a half height wall spanning the width of the house. On the other side, the full wall displayed an abundance of framed portraits. Beyond the half wall was a formal sitting room on the left. On the right, the dining room with another half wall and what looked like the back side of a chimney. Beyond, a cozy reading nook with windows looking into the backyard complete with swimming pool, deck, and a swath of green lawn.

"The bathroom is right over there." She pointed to an alcove off the foyer. "The door on the right, in case you can't tell it apart from the mud room, which has the laundry machines and a door to the garage." Sarcasm touched her soft voice. The vaulted ceiling with skylights certainly would have carried sound back to the others had she not kept her voice low.

"How about a tour of the gallery first?" He kept going straight instead of making the turn to where she pointed. The first portrait stopped him. "This must be your husband." Court pointed to a posed, formal photo.

"Must be." She stood with folded arms, toes in sandals tapping with impatience.

"What was his name?" The man looked like Paul Bunyan with his shaggy brown hair and close trimmed beard despite the entirely civilized suit and tie. Certainly a robust fellow with a barrel chest. Probably the kind of man with hair all over.

"Wyatt Ferguson." She all but snapped at him. "The powder room?"

Ignoring her almost desperate redirection, he commented on the man. "A good Scots name if ever I heard one." Must be onto something here, something she didn't want him to see?

"He was a good man," she said sharply.

Defensive? Interesting. "And a good father? Birdie doesn't look anything like him."

"He was a very good dad to her. He loved her above all else."

Court turned his head to look at her face. What was that tone? "Loved her above you?"

"Yes—no, I didn't mean that." Flustered, she blushed and waved a hand impatiently. "He adored his girls. No one ever doubted it. What you want is this direction."

Once more, he ignored her attempt to draw him away and turned his attention to the photos leading away from her. "Is Birdie your only child?" All the photos showed only Birdie growing up.

"Yes. I...we couldn't...have others."

Ah, a sore spot, must be getting closer to something here. He stepped down the hall, Birdie aging in reverse as they moved toward the single closed door at the end of the hall. At that point, Randi grabbed his arm, her nails digging into his flesh beneath his shirt, and tried to pull him back toward the foyer.

"Come *on*, what you want is this way." She tugged harder.

But one framed photo caught his eye. There it was. The answer to the question he'd asked earlier.

"Courtney Robin Ferguson, born February fourth, Nineteen eighty..."
The words he read from the brass plaque on the elaborate frame strangled
in his throat. One year... not even one full year after they'd met. It didn't
take a brilliant mind to do the math, and the psychologists had assured
his parents he had a particularly brilliant mind when it came to numbers.

Voice pitched an octave higher, Randi sounded as if she were choking.
"Yes, well, the powder room is this way." Randi tugged all the harder on
his arm, practically leaning away from him. Had he moved, she would
have fallen on her face.

Too bad he was stronger. But neither could he have moved if he'd
tried. Rooted to the floor, he stared at the photo of the smiling infant, arms
wide as if reaching for him. God, except for the dress and pink bow in
her hair, she looked exactly like...Drew. And only four months younger.
Either Birdie had been born premature, or...

Still resisting Randi's efforts to drag him away, he tried to clear the
lump from his throat. "Nice name you chose for her." Ice ran through his
veins, stinging and burning at the same time as his stomach tightened,
churning the coffee in his gut. Good God.

"I didn't name her," Randi growled, yet he could hear a hint of panic
underneath. As well she should be panicked. This news she never should
have kept to herself. She tugged harder on his arm, her nails digging in.
"Now, if you don't mind, I have cooking to do. If you need directions,
now's your chance."

A sudden inrush of oxygen filled his head like helium.
"Fine. Loo. Where?"

"This way."

Unable to see clearly, he grabbed her hand, following where she led.
The jolt of heat that zapped up his arm jump-started his stuttering heart.

When they reached the bathroom off the foyer, Randi tried to disengage
and step back. Oh no, she wasn't getting away so easily. Heart hardened,
shock fizzled out, and anger began to burn. He crowded her inside and
shut the door. The click of the lock he set sounded loud in the small room.

"Court," she turned on him with a furious whisper, "what are you doing?"
Her eyes widened at the expression on his face; her blustering wilted a bit.

"We need to talk, and this is about as private as we're likely to get,
unless you want to take me to your bedroom?" The lifted brow silenced
her. "No? I didn't think so. Too bad."

Not in a charitable frame of mind and wanting the answers she owed
him, he backed her against a small section of wall between a pedestal
sink and a chest next to the toilet. He kept going until one knee slipped

between her legs, their chests pressed together, and his arms braced against the wall on either side of her head.

"Court," she whispered again. "Get off me." Small fists pushed against his chest, but he hardly felt them.

Only one thought occupied his head. Nothing else mattered right then, and he'd have the answer or stir up the scene she obviously didn't want.

"She's mine, isn't she?" In his fury, he wanted to wrap a hand around Jean's throat. Not normally inclined to violence or manhandling women, he wondered in that instant if he could resort to such measures to get the answer. Plenty of his competitors had left the negotiating table wondering the same.

"She isn't." Randi's fist punctuated her lie, but he hardly felt it, his mind too busy keeping his hands back from choking the truth out of her.

But this was Jean no matter what name she used these days. Sweet, loving Jean. Lying Jean. Instead of choking her, he pressed her against the wall, fitting his body to hers as if they'd never been parted, leaving not one whisper of space between them.

"Then why is she named after me?" Swirling emotions churned faster inside him. Anger at not being told. Anguish for missing a lifetime of a daughter he should have been given the chance to cherish. Fury at Beatrice for holding him by the bollocks for sixteen wasted years, when he could have been with Jean and his daughter. Rage barely kept in check, the urge to throttle Jean stronger than he'd ever felt before because of the truth, the daughter and other secrets, she'd kept from him.

Agony ripped through him, nearly strong enough to drop him to his knees. No, he wouldn't have given up the years with Drew, but damn. Why did life have to be screwed up? He should have known. Should have had the choice, no matter how difficult, the chance to decide. She'd lied by omission, and he wanted to damn her for her silence. For her avoidance of his attempts at contact. For going so far as to marry another man to hide the truth.

"Tell me how Courtney Robin isn't named after me? How could anyone else choose that combination? It isn't an accident, Jean. Stop lying to me." Furiously spoken, he kept his voice low, though how he had the presence of mind to do it, he didn't know. Too many years of low volume arguments with old Bea?

"Randi, dammit, my name is Randi." One little fist pounded ineffectively against his shoulder again, but still he held her. She didn't have room to work up the momentum to do damage, and despite the heavy emotions battering both of them, he wanted this, craved this closeness, needed to feel her against him. The need for her had been growing steadily the past several years—face it, the need for her had never entirely disappeared. He might have dreamed of finding his Jean again, but he'd never dreamed of discovering a daughter. A daughter sitting in the other room. A daughter he'd met without recognizing. A daughter whose mother didn't want her secret exposed.

"The lies stop here. Tell me the truth."

"Oh, like you really care. What'd you do, set Drew on my trail?" She threw the accusation at him. "Was their meeting an accident at all? What are you doing here, Court? Why now?"

His control hanging by an unraveling silken thread, he spoke more harshly than he could remember doing since Beatrice's death, pressing her for the truth. "Tell me, Randi Jean. I know she's mine. She has to be. Tell me the bloody truth!"

His gaze glued to her like the gilt on the frame of the picture beside her head, he watched, as the color faded then heated her face until, with an anguished moan, the fight went out of her, and she dropped her head back against the wall, eyes averted. "All right, dammit, you're right. She's yours." Randi's voice barely reached the level of a whisper. "I...I..." Her eyes closed as she turned her head farther away. He moved his forearm closer, nudging her back to face him. "I almost died before he named her. Wyatt later told me that in my fever I kept muttering the names Court and Robin. He took it to mean Courtney Robin, so he put that name on the birth certificate."

A tear tracked down her cheek, washing away the worst of his anger, filling the void with something far softer, though no less agonizing. What had it cost her? The confession to her husband, the confession to him now? Had she confessed the details to her parents? Was this the reason the man had loved Birdie more than Randi? Court pushed his upper body back from the wall to cup her face in his hands. He swiped his thumb gently over her skin and lifted the tear. "He knew? You told him my name? He knew the baby wasn't his, and he still married you?" Would Court have been so generous?

Nodding, she continued with her story. "Yes, he did know your name. No one else knows. When I came to, I was horrified, but the paperwork had been filed." Randi slumped against the wall with no place to go but to curl against him. "I mean, my parents and Wyatt knew I was pregnant with another man's child, your child, but I would have put his name on her birth certificate. It didn't matter to him, he claimed her completely and would have gone along with it. As long as I never contacted you, that was his only stipulation. However, because I was so ill, he decided on following the truth about her parentage, in case, later… Anyhow, she doesn't know Wyatt isn't her biological father. I haven't told her. I was planning to…" her voice faded out, her attention absorbed by his chest as he tightened his hold.

Heart racing as if he'd won LeMans, Court held her while he tried to sort it all out.

What kind of man would marry a woman knowing she carried another man's child?

An honorable man. A man lucky enough to have this woman as his wife.

Someone he wanted to hate. Instead, he respected the bloke.

Court dropped his forehead so it rested against hers and drew in desperately needed air scented with the aromas of soft perfume and good cooking. His Jean.

Courtney Robin.

Why had she never contacted him? Had her husband truly forbidden it? That made some sort of sense. Of course he wouldn't want to lose his daughter to a man who'd turned his back on the mother. It hurt like hell to think that, but if Court were honest and put himself in the other man's shoes, he might have done the same.

Blue eyes, golden hair, and a sunny smile. Now it was perfectly clear who she reminded him of. She reminded him of himself at the same age…and Drew.

The truth slammed into him like a bullet train, and his head snapped up. "Oh hell. Drew's her brother." That's why their closeness bothered him. That's why Randi's gaze had seemed extra watchful, her actions furtive and nervous.

"I know, I know." Randi moaned. "We can't let them date."

Drew had been showing signs of interest, and Birdie had been shooting certain looks back. Damn. The train heading down that rail had to be stopped. "We have to tell them."

"Not now, not today, not with Dad and his friend in the house."

Exactly who was this Jordan bloke? "Friend as in…friend?"

Randi's eyes flew open as she looked up at him, and her mouth formed into a horrified "O." "No, no, no, not that kind of friend." She laughed a little. "Dad's so homophobic he'd run screaming from the house. No, Jordan is a consultant, and my father's attempt to match-make."

"Like hell," Court muttered. He'd just found her again, and he'd be damned if he'd let another man try to move in. Where did that come from? When he'd first thought of the idea to find her, he'd had no notion of starting up a relationship again…or had he been fooling himself? What did it mean that she'd lied to him, lived a lie, hid this elemental truth from him? Had she ever meant to tell him?

"Randi, the truth, really, why did you never tell me?"

A sob shook her and she tilted her head back, lids blinking rapidly to hold back tears. "I wanted to, but, God, Court, honestly? I didn't want to make things worse. I didn't want to hurt Wyatt. I didn't want to confuse Birdie. There were my parents to consider. And ultimately, I didn't want to make you choose between babies. I admit I was hurt and wanted to hurt you back, but not that way. Not by making you choose between one child and another. I knew I could make it on my own. I didn't know about…her. And if you'd known, and had still chosen her and her baby…Drew…" She gulped in her breath and swallowed heavily. "I couldn't have… I never would have…"

Court gathered her close, cuddling her against his chest, wanting to pull her into him until they could no longer find the line separating them. So like his sweet Jean to put someone else first. How would he have chosen? There was no way to tell. The emotions were too close, too mixed up. He needed time to think about all this. Not the least of which was how Randi had suffered.

Holding her close, his body remembered. Her scent filled his head; her breath against his chest warmed him like nothing had since he'd last held her. The tightening of his groin assured him she still moved him. Without pulling away, he dipped his head, loving the feel of her silky hair against his lips, her soft cheek against his. As naturally as breathing, they sought to touch each other. Her hands slid up his back, the heat easily penetrating the barrier of the cotton shirt he wore. Ravenous for more, his mouth found hers. Years melted away as they connected, like puzzle pieces finding their mates to make a whole picture. Heat infused him as she opened to him, allowing him in to taste the elixir of life he'd been forced to live without. The fire inside her fed the fire inside him, and he forgot to go slow, to be gentle.

"Everything all right in there? Randi?"

They both jumped at the sound of her father's voice, the pounding of his fist on the other side of the door an echo of the pounding of Court's heart. The rosy flush painting Randi's cheeks, her shortened breath pleased him. She'd been as affected as he.

"Randi?"

Court reluctantly loosened his hold on her.

"Yes, Dad, everything's okay. W… I'll be out in a minute," she called while wiggling out of Court's arms. The loss of her body heat was a physical deprivation. Almost like losing a limb. He rubbed his chest where their hearts had briefly beat in concert. Her body plastered against the front of him had quickly resumed its place as an essential element of his existence. Dammit, she belonged there.

"You sure? There were some strange noises coming from in there. Kind of like you're talking to yourself like you do when you don't feel well. Need Ex-Lax or Pepto?"

Randi slapped her hand over Court's twitching mouth. "Dad!" she exclaimed in horror. "A moment of privacy, if you please. You can use Birdie's bathroom, or mine if you need to."

"The Brit is missing too. He in there with you? Don't be hiding him from me. I have some questions for him."

"Dad! Go away!"

Finding it impossible to hold back his grin, despite the threat in the old man's voice, Court kissed her palm and watched a deep flush rise up from her chest and rush to the roots of her hair. As if his lips had scalded her, she snatched her hand away and turned to the mirror. At the sight of her running mascara and tousled hair, she grimaced and reached for a tissue to begin repairing the damage. To Court, she looked absolutely adorable. As beautiful as when she'd been livid with anger. More so.

"I'll be out in a few minutes. Why don't you check the backyard and see if Court went out there?" In the mirror, she crossed her eyes, and he almost laughed out loud.

"I think I want to stay right here and make sure you're okay."

Damn, but the old man was bloody tenacious. And, apparently, still as rabidly overprotective as he'd been years ago.

"I'm fine," Randi snapped and deftly repaired her face, or at least erased the smudges. Quick fingers combed through the layered cut until the soft strands fell into place and brushed the tops of her shoulders. She looked sexy as hell, all warm and tumbled as if just rolling from bed.

His eyes met hers in the mirror and damned if he didn't want to take her right up against the door with her father on the other side. Let the old bastard listen to his daughter being pleasured.

Randi waved at him, mimed combing his hair, and handed a tissue over her shoulder. He took the hint and looked in the mirror. Before he could laugh, Randi was there, her hand over his mouth again, eyes twinkling at her own repressed giggles.

"Randi? You coming out anytime soon?"

"I'm waiting for you to leave." To add emphasis, she leaned to the side and spun the toilet paper on its holder. "Do you mind?"

"Okay, okay, but you're acting mighty strange today. I'll go open the champagne, but only heaven knows what you'll be like with a little alcohol in you. You're not going menopausal are you?"

"Already did that when I had my hysterectomy, Dad."

Surprised, Court frowned. The reason she didn't have more children? When had it happened? When she fell ill after Birdie's arrival?

"Oh. You did?"

Exasperation escaped and she growled. "Dad! Go. Away."

Randi reached past Court and flipped a switch for a fan overhead, then leaned to listen at the door while he finger combed his hair into place.

Court raised a brow but she shook her head. The old man remained in place. Randi reached over and flushed the commode, and he turned on the water in the sink.

Finally, the footsteps retreated, and they both let out their breaths.

"Give me a couple minutes," Randi said, straightening her clothes. "If I don't talk with him now, he'll keep pressing for the truth. I'm sure he's figured out you're 'the damn bastard who knocked his girl up and sent her home.'"

Yeah, her father would see it that way. He shoved his hands into the pockets of his trousers to keep from reaching for her again. He'd have it out with the old man. Today. However, it didn't stop him from giving her his best sad puppy dog look.

"Oh for heaven's sake," she blew out the words. "I'm still mad at you."

"And this conversation isn't over. Not by a long shot. I'm pretty pissed myself."

A moment later, she was out the door, leaving him alone and wishing everyone else in the house to Mars.

# Chapter 5

"Good heavens, can't a person take a potty break every once in a while? It's the first time I've been off my feet all day." She gave her father a good glare for emphasis.

"If you're feeling poorly, and judging by the sounds coming from the powder room, you might be ready for the hospital, you can go lie down for a bit."

Rolling her eyes, she threw up her hands. "So now you're spying on me by listening at bathroom doors?" Not that she wouldn't put it past him, the man was that nosy.

"I don't call it spying when motivated by concern for your wellbeing." Bushy white brows lowered in his customary scowl.

Randi snorted and began to pull champagne glasses from a cabinet. "Did you do a head count?"

"I did, but came up short by two."

"Well, count me in. I'm pretty sure Court will be interested as well." She set six fluted champagne glasses on the counter in front of her dad.

"So are you going to confess, yet?"

"Confess what?" Time to baste the turkey, she turned away and reached for the hot pads. Court had returned them to their hooks. Good man. Been playing bachelor father for the past six years? Did it translate to knowing his way around a kitchen? So far, he'd proved helpful. And distracting.

Before she could get the oven open, her father crowded her from the left. "About the man who contributed the other half of the genetic material to create your daughter. Don't try to tell me the name is a coincidence." White brows lowered in an angry V. A look nowhere as intimidating as it had once been. "After Wyatt filed the birth certificate I asked him about her name and he said you'd named her after the father. The name is too close to be an accident."

Hadn't Wyatt been the chatty one when it suited him? "Smart man to put two and two together. And you've waited all this time to bring it up?"

"You were too ill, and then after, well, it didn't seem so important anymore."

"Because you fell in love with her. Well fine, now you know my biggest secret. Keep it to yourself. I'll tell her later. In the meantime, don't let her and Drew get cozy, if you understand my meaning."

"No problem." Dad straightened and began ripping the foil from around the cork. "But we're still going to talk about why he never came looking for his child."

"I never told him."

Let him think about that. Bending to see to the bird, Randi silently apologized to her daughter for siccing Grandpa on her. It was for the best, honestly. The less she and Drew cuddled up together, the less revulsion they'd feel later.

Family meeting. Tonight. The moment prying old grandpa disappeared with his guest.

Almost as if he'd heard the reference to him in her thoughts, Jordan entered on cue. She had the feeling he checked out her backside currently on prominent display. The one wide enough to block her father's view of the humongous TV.

"Randi, those brie wraps were out of this world. High class football munchies." Jordan at least kept a respectable distance away.

"Thanks, glad you liked them." She squirted juices over the bird and thought about adding more wine. Nah, more than one bottle was overkill and a waste of good wine. A few more passes with the baster and she decided the time had come to leave the lid off. Tom Turkey needed a little browning and he had thirty minutes left in the oven. Provided she'd guessed right this time. She glared at the little pop-up timer, not sure it was at all trustworthy.

Sure the factory put out a million of these a day and tested them by the handful, but what if she got the one that would have failed the test? What if she had the one in two million that didn't have enough wax to hold the little pin down until the right moment? What then? These things happened. Like the time she'd gotten a can of Pepsi Light, way back in high school, the one in the six-pack that was only half full and had a slice of lemon in it. Well, at least they'd used real lemons, but still, what a rip off and an example of spotty quality control. Accidents slipped through all the time.

"What's wrong, love?" Court asked, and she cut her glare in his direction. How'd he move so quietly on the tile floor of the hall? Arrogant SOB, using that endearment with her. He hadn't been fond of it back then, why now?

Pushing aside her urge to throttle him for reminding her how well they fit together physically, she snapped, "Nothing. Just wondering if I should put a thermometer in it."

"Believe in redundant systems, do you?"

She didn't appreciate the mocking nature of his lifted brow. The laughter rested there, twinkling in his damn beautiful blue eyes.

"Never hurts to be sure." All the same, she shut the oven and hung up her hot pads. Yeah, Dad watched from beneath his bushy brows. The man was still too protective by half.

"What can we do to help?" Court asked.

"Get out of my way? All of you?" Her female dominated house suddenly had far too many too-tall men in it. Three of the four stood around her. Dad had barely finished pouring the champagne when she grabbed the first flute.

"Let's have a toast," dear old Dad announced. "Birdie, Drew, come in here."

"Okay, but they're setting up a punt pass return."

At least that's what it sounded like Birdie had said.

"We'll make it quick," Randi promised. "I want these men out of my kitchen, and they won't leave until we do a toast."

Behind her, Court wrapped a hand around her right butt cheek and gave a little squeeze. His specialty, sneaky squeezes in public places where she couldn't react the way she wanted to. One time, he'd managed to squeeze a breast in the middle of a crowded coffee shop, complete with nipple tweak. And she'd had to endure what had almost been a full breast exam right there. In front of God and everybody. Princess Di herself could have walked in and Randi wouldn't have cared. Ten minutes later, they'd been back in her flat, ripping off their clothes.

"Okay, everyone with us?" Dad gave her a meaningful look. Oops, drifted off again and Court's hand slipped lower yet, easing deep into territory where, dammit, he was wanted, but not this moment. But to swat his hand away would draw attention to his actions. It wasn't as if she had room to move away, or even the strength. She still shook from the interlude in the powder room, and his touch weakened her knees. Her world had begun to unravel, and she was desperate to keep things as normal as possible, hoping she could weather the storm and survive the day. Just a few more hours...

"Sure, I'm ready. Got a good one for us?" Randi challenged her father.

Everyone raised their glasses in a ragged circle. Why did they all have to squeeze into the tightest corner of the kitchen? Court had to be baking, right up against the ovens with her. Time to open a window or two.

"Here's to the feast before us, the friends and family who join us, and our thanks for all the little miracles which have yet to be explained," her father said, his hazel gaze locked firmly on hers.

Around Randi, answers of *hear-hear* and the tinkle of fine crystal touching were drowned out by the buzzing in her head. The rat. Was he hoping Birdie would suddenly figure it out? Silence fell for a few seconds while people sipped their wine. Well, in her case, guzzling replaced sipping. Pinching her nose to hold back a sneeze, she held out her glass to forestall any comments on the toast. "Please, sir, may I have some more?"

Dad set down his glass and took hers. "That will require a second bottle."

"Good, the one in the freezer should be cold by now." There. See? She'd remembered it.

Dad slanted her a curious look, but she wasn't about to move or change expression if she could help it. Court had one long finger playing in a most delicious manner. One finger slid beneath the hem of her sweater, an action possible because she had yet to put on her apron again. An oversight she'd correct the second she was free. The sneaky finger traveled up her spine a few inches, tracing lazy circles then moving south to slip under the waistband of her slacks. With great concentration she squelched a shudder of pleasure. This so wasn't fair. And she'd never found a way to get him back for it. Not once. The scoundrel.

She shifted her hips, whether to encourage or discourage him, she couldn't have said with any degree of conviction. Of course he took it as encouragement, the tip of his finger wriggling into the top of the cleft between her rear cheeks.

"Mom?"

"Hmm?" How Court managed to do this to her, in this crowd, was almost unforgiveable. Except it felt so good. Especially with the champagne percolating in her blood. She felt warm and sultry, the tension in her shoulders easing while another tension began to rise again.

"Mom, you look a little flushed. You feeling okay?"

Blinking, she looked at Birdie, and for the millionth time, it struck her how much her daughter looked like Court. "Yeah, honey, I'm fine. Let's get some windows open and cool the house down a little. Anyone else feeling warm?" It took effort, but she managed to escape the crowd, and Court's seductive, sneaky hand, and headed for the door to the backyard. She didn't have to look to know he grinned, knowing he'd gotten to her—again.

Heels clacking on the tile softened to heels tapping on hardwood flooring as she stepped down into the sunken living room. It was tempting to drop into her favorite overstuffed chair in the reading nook, but she kept going until she stood on the rear deck, breathing in the autumn scents of dried grass, dead leaves, and someone's wood fire.

How could anyone be burning a fire on a day like this? The sky arched overhead in clear blue, the exact shade of Court's eyes. And Birdie's. Hell, and Drew's. Three cut from the same cloth. Desperate for more distance, she moved onto the patio surrounding the pool and into the sun. Ah, the scent of charcoal. The Wilsons were barbecuing their turkey again. She eyed the cool blue water in the pool. A dip sounded wonderful right then. Would the people inside think she was loco for jumping in fully clothed? Her gaze moved to the spa to the left. Now there was an idea. Later tonight, under the cover of darkness, she'd come out and...

"You forgot your champagne."

Should have known Court would find a way to follow her. She turned to face him, only to see Jordan right on his heels.

"Great day to be outside," Jordan said. He held a full glass as well as a small plate of appetizers. "Thought you might want a few bites yourself."

Had to like a man who wanted to feed her. "Thanks." She picked up one of the brie wraps.

Dammit all. The simple snack brought back a memory of Court feasting off her body in bed. One night, they'd splurged on several containers of Chinese seafood. He'd laid towels on the bed and then arranged their dinner with artistic precision. Shrimp curled around her nipples, fried rice heaped over her belly button, won tons and other delights scattered up and down her body. He'd alternately eaten from her and dropped morsels into her mouth, using his fingers to feed her and chopsticks to tease her. Wyatt had always wondered why Chinese food, spicy shrimp in particular, had turned her on. When Wyatt wanted to get laid, he'd brought home take-out. After Wyatt had died, she'd cleaned out the junk drawer and found it nearly full of wooden restaurant chopsticks.

Lord, was she so easy to manipulate?

A glance at Court's face gave her the answer. In a word—yes.

"Nice spot you have here. I like the way it backs to open space," Jordan said. "Your father tells me you did most of the landscaping."

Switching from spicy shrimp eaten in bed to eyesores in the landscaping took tremendous effort, but over all, she thought she handled it fine. "Well, I selected most of the plants, but a good landscaper helped me put it all in place." It was impossible to ignore the spruce in the back corner that hadn't survived a particularly hot summer. Like a black hole, it seemed to draw the eye without fail. "Even the dead thing can be credited to me." She nodded toward it.

"Ah, the famous, or should I say infamous, spruce tree?" Court's eyes twinkled. "What's the problem with getting it out?"

"Um, it's prickly? It's big?" Not so big, it only stood fifteen feet tall in comparison to the sixty feet tall redwoods that marched along the fence between her and the neighbor up the hill, but more than she wanted to deal with herself. "It's in a hard to reach spot and will be messy to take down. I don't want to smush the other trees and bushes nearby. Not to mention the solar panels for the pool heating system are back there."

"Hmm." Jordan squinted into the sunlight, one hand in his pants pocket while he rocked in his loafers. He had squint lines at the edges of his eyes, and his skin had a sun-roughened quality to it. Not unattractive, but his eyes weren't quite as handsome as Court's. Slight folds of skin gave him a heavy lidded look some women might consider sexy. "Could be done with proper planning. Have a chainsaw?"

He then turned those eyes on her, and she didn't feel one ounce of sexual attraction. Possibly because Court stood close by, his body heat reaching out to her, his scent wrapping around her and making her dizzy.

"No, I don't. I'll probably end up calling my landscaper to deal with it. I hate to pay for what should be a straightforward removal. Besides, I don't think he'll split it into burnable sized pieces for me."

Jordan chuckled. "That's no problem. My granddad had me swinging an axe by the time I turned nine. Wouldn't take an afternoon to take care of it."

"Why Mr. Doyle, that sounds like an offer to solve my little ol' problem."

Jordan did a double take at the Scarlett imitation and Randi could feel Court stiffening beside her. Especially when Jordan's smile widened into a grin. She couldn't recall any law about not flirting with guests. Probably the wine going to her head, but damn, Court needed a reminder other men found her attractive. Maybe it was she who needed the reminder. Oh hell, she'd better get some food in her system soon to counteract all the alcohol she wanted to drink.

"Depends on how the installation goes over the next couple of days, but it might be doable this weekend. I don't fly home until Tuesday."

"And where is home?" Court asked.

"New York. I grew up in the mountains up-state, but now live in Manhattan."

"I've heard Manhattan is exciting," Randi eased into the conversation again. Just to remind the boys she hadn't left before they started beating their chests. To think, scant hours ago she'd been hoping they'd get along and ignore her. The picture proved so ridiculous she bit back a laugh. "I've never been there personally, but friends who've been say it's exhilarating."

Jordan laughed. "Exhilarating is one word. It does have its moments of flash."

"Do you go to plays? The ballet? Concerts? Opera?"

"I try to avoid opera, but the rest, yes."

"Which concerts?" Randi asked. Was he a rock 'n roller or a classical music type?

"I once attended the symphony and a Stones concert in the same week."

Court chose that moment to rejoin the discussion. "Eclectic."

Randi shoved her elbow into Court's ribs for his almost sarcasm. Delivered in his accent, it was hard to tell.

Warming to his subject, Jordan smiled at her, pointedly ignoring Court. "I learned to appreciate the ballet when I dated a ballerina several years ago."

Oh, bad move. Never mention a woman from the past when trying to connect. Court apparently agreed with her, because he snorted barely loud enough for her to hear. Apparently, Jordan caught something in Court's face because he swiveled his head and nodded toward the dead tree.

"If things go well and your father frees me up, we could probably take care of that on Sunday."

"Hmm." Randi sipped her champagne. "Not to worry about now. I have bigger things on my plate, starting with a twenty pound turkey." She twisted her wrist to look at her watch and realized she hadn't put it on today. It was then she noticed the uneaten pastry still in her hand. Court was ahead of her when she turned to ask him the time.

"Sorry, you'll have to adjust for local time. I'm still on London." Unabashed, he grinned at her and held out his wrist while she rolled her eyes and did the calculation in a heartbeat. Sadly, she still kept up with such things. How could a simple TAG Heuer watch on a strong wrist make her go all hot and shivery at once? *Focus.* Twelve forty. Time to get the rolls in the oven and toss the salad.

"Ever consider using the second time zone feature?" She ignored his grin and didn't wait for his answer. Instead, she put the flaky appetizer in his hand. "If you gentlemen will excuse me..." She let the sentence trail off and sauntered toward the house. Knowing they both watched her, she put a tiny extra twitch in her hips.

Lord, dinner was going to be interminable.

# Chapter 6

How they made it through dinner without blurting out the truth of Birdie's parentage, Court would never know.

With what he'd learned earlier, and suspecting Randi's father had figured it out as well, Court did his best to help keep topics neutral, aiding Randi in her maneuvers to steer the dinner conversation. Old RJ had sent many a glare toward their end of the table, the burning glowers divided between him and Randi almost equally. Drew had taken it all in with his attention to details, looking like a prosecutor with a perpetually self-incriminating criminal in front of him. Court was able to redirect some of Drew's questions—heaven knew *he* was used to the subtle probing—but it proved as difficult as it did amusing. Add in Randi's father and his veiled questions about Court's past and things got even stickier.

Especially since Court couldn't keep his eyes off Birdie when he wasn't staring at Jean. Randi.

His girls. The thought still floored him, wonder being the only feeling he could handle while keeping on his toes verbally. Although his heart had clenched extra hard each time he looked at his beautiful daughter.

At long last the meal ended, and now he felt as stuffed as the bird had been. To keep from falling asleep on the sofa, he volunteered for kitchen clean up and enlisted Drew to help as a way to keep him busy and away from Birdie. Helping in the kitchen also meant more time in closer physical proximity to Randi, although the plan for Drew to avoid Birdie didn't pan out as she worked alongside her mother.

Jordan had apparently picked up the message Court had been sending out all afternoon. Back off. Randi had unfinished business with Court and damned if he'd let the other man horn in. RJ and his associate relaxed in the family room, this time with a professional game to occupy them, the old man on simmer for now.

True to his word, RJ had carved the bird. Despite being a sarcastic son of a bitch, he had a sharp mind Court couldn't help but respect. Randi had redirected any conversation drifting into forbidden territory, such as Randi's trip to England and how she and Court had met. The woman should be a high level diplomat. She had the ease of a tennis player deflecting direct questions and turning around subtle probing from all sides. It set his mind at ease in one area—Randi could easily transition into his world. His mother would be no problem for her to handle, as expert as she'd proved over dinner. An accomplished hostess, she'd kept the food circulating, the wine flowing, and the conversation had never faltered into uncomfortable silence as she dodged Drew's cross examination. It was probably because of her social skills he could make the transition to calling her Randi. Jean had never displayed such confidence, but rather a sweet, naïve innocence. Randi could take on the chilliest of socialites. More importantly, he could see her presiding at social functions and holding her own against London society.

However skillfully she maneuvered, Birdie had apparently sensed the undertone and regarded her mother with curiosity. Court had even felt her eyes on him a time or two from beside him at the table, as far away from Drew as Randi could seat her. Considering they were only six for dinner, it wasn't far. Had old RJ had his way, he would have had both girls beside him with all the strange men down at the other end of the table. Wouldn't have solved the problem like a dinner party for twenty or thirty would have, though.

Sitting between Randi and his daughter—daughter!—had been an exquisite torture in and of itself. On the one hand, he took every opportunity to touch Randi, whether by passing dishes or nudging her foot under the table. Her version of playing footsie had surely left a few bruises on his shin. Oh how he loved getting under her skin, even if it proved a tad painful. At least she hadn't ignored him, and he looked forward to making her pay later.

On the other hand, drawing out Birdie had been a delight. Used to women with agendas, these open California women were simply enchanting and more than once he'd caught glimpses of the young Jean in Birdie. A tilt of the head, a light touch on the arm, a smile or phrase which brought back that all too short period of supreme happiness. How he made it through the meal without pulling her into his arms just to hold he'd never know. Heart aching for the lost years, he threw himself into being a charming guest.

As a result of the effort to keep conversation away from their past relationship, he and Randi had grilled Jordan about the cultural smorgasbord of New York. Randi had an open invitation to visit should an event catch her eye. Jordan volunteered himself as the man to get her in the door.

In the door of his apartment came closer to the truth. The one with the view of Central Park. View, mind you. Even Court knew the term didn't necessarily mean it was across the street from Central Park.

Funny how the invitation had clearly excluded anyone else. RJ found it amusing, and Court caught him smirking into his stuffing. Thought his candidate had a chance with Randi, did he?

Court kept his chuckle to himself. He could beat Jordan's puny boasts. A country estate with semi-famous parklands she wouldn't have to share with another soul if she didn't want to. They could picnic in the nude and skinny dip in the pond without anyone being wiser for it. Take that, New York. Oh, and a flat in London on the banks of the Thames. One-two punch to the Yank.

"The china and crystal can go in the dishwasher," Randi said behind him. "The catch is you can't put anything else in there. The silver as well, but there can't be one spot of stainless steel."

"I don't mind washing by hand." At the surprise on her face, he grinned, dropped his cufflinks in a pocket, and rolled up his sleeves. "Hand the lad a towel so he can dry. You get to put away."

"You can stack them on the table"—she pointed at the breakfast table—"and I'll put them away later."

"Right-o." Drew selected a towel from the drawer Birdie opened nearby. "I'm ready, old man."

"I'm not so old I can't still twat your arse, pup." Actually, probably not, but Drew kindly refrained from disputing the fact. However, he did hear a feminine gasp from behind.

"It means to swat, Birdie," Randi said calmly.

"What's that?" Court looked over his shoulder. "Which word should I not use over here?"

"Twat," Drew answered, his gaze darting to Birdie and back. "Has only one meaning here. I'll explain later if need be. Just get to washin'. I'm wanting a nap, myself."

"Pardon me, ladies. And you, whelp, no words referring to sleep, if you please." It was a wonder he remained vertical. The rich aroma of brewing coffee set his nose to twitching, and he would have kissed Randi when she set down a cup for him had she stepped close enough.

"This should keep you going long enough to do your chores."

He wanted to kiss the wrinkle-nosed smirk right off her face.

"I know what we need," Birdie declared. "Grandpa, you can watch the game without sound."

The old man turned a frown in her direction. "What?"

Court watched as the girl manipulated buttons on the complicated system of remote controls with the ease of a NASA engineer. Closed captioning came up and music replaced the soundtrack of the game.

"We need something to energize us," Birdie announced.

*Cheeky little brat.* Court grinned as music from the eighties blasted from a speaker system for which Randi had definitely splashed down more than a few quid. Not only the media center, but everything about the house indicated fine living. Understated, but quality in the details. Grudgingly, he had to acknowledge she'd been well-cared for. It meant something. Didn't ease his guilt or frustration much.

"Damned way to watch a game," RJ grumbled.

Court grinned wider when Birdie refused to let her grandfather dictate to her. "You got to watch the other game. Just because you lost, it isn't my fault. Now, unless you want to be part of the cleanup crew, you can chill for a bit."

"A man has to be getting old when he takes lip from a bit of fluff like you."

"My grandpa, old? Never!" Birdie leaned over and kissed the old bugger on the cheek, then skipped away from the half-hearted swat aimed her way.

"Glory Days" from The Boss pumped out of the speakers, and Birdie danced back to the kitchen, singing along and doing an air guitar parody.

Damn but the song brought back memories. Didn't seem all that long ago when he and Randi danced to the music of the day. Everything from punk to big hair bands. Bruce Springsteen was meat and potatoes, she'd said back then. Good, old, basic American rock. No collection was complete without The Boss.

"Those dishes won't wash themselves," Randi said and set a stack of scraped but greasy dishes at his elbow.

"They'll be clean faster than your washer could do them."

"No doubt. Just don't chip them, and make sure they're clean. Turkey grease is sneaky." She reached across the sink and handed him a bottle of washing liquid. "One large spoonful should do it."

"Yes, boss."

The glare she directed at him could have boiled the water for tea. The same glare said she wanted to smack him, but felt hemmed in by the people around them. Also, she remained mad at him and didn't want him to know he affected her in any way. But he'd edged under her skin and was getting to her. At least she didn't hold herself aloof. No, not his Randi. How much of her feelings had she shut out over the years? Flustered and flushed, she tried to hold the glare, but he couldn't hold back his grin.

"Go on, you know you want to," he taunted her.

Lips pressed into a tight line, she shoved against his shoulder with hers. This was too much fun to let it go at that. "Is that the best you can do?"

"You're impossible," she muttered at the countertop.

Keeping his voice low enough only she could hear him over the running water, he taunted her further. "You can't wait to get your hands on me, and you know it." He plunged his hands into a sink full of suds. Now he appeared helpless, or so she'd think. "Come on, admit it. You're not really so livid at me, are you?"

With a growl of exasperation, she smacked him across the shoulder.

Court laughed as he leaned toward her and whispered in her ear. "Thank you, mistress, may I have another?"

Lord but he loved how she tried to hide her blush by scurrying to the other side of the island behind him. He couldn't remember the last time he'd seen a woman her age blush. Come to think of it, he couldn't remember the last time he'd seen a young woman blush, either. Kids these days could probably teach him more than a thing or two about sex. And wasn't that just a sad thought?

But for some reason, the thought of sex didn't depress him this time. The last twenty-two years had been hell as far as sex went. Beatrice had *allowed* it on their wedding night and once each month thereafter, but in between? Not a chance. Even though on their wedding night she'd admitted it had been much better than the first time, she'd declared the whole business messy and degrading. For several years they'd found a modicum of stability and had lived peacefully enough together, each busy with their own concerns. Business for him, charities for her. But as Drew hit his teens, things began disintegrating. Not because Drew turned especially difficult, he wasn't any more so than the average teen boy, but from his puberty on, the marriage had been every dreadful gothic novel come to life.

Cold bed, colder wife, the tolerable had crumbled into the distasteful far too quickly. It became all too apparent why the men of England, both now and in years past, often kept mistresses and endured their wives due to the advantages of blending certain families. In the end, his marriage had been nothing more than a business proposition. She gave him a son, and didn't find it her fault if the spare didn't appear after their limited couplings. After a couple of years, he'd passed on the grudgingly offered invitations to her bed. Had it not been for Drew and the pressure from their parents... water under the bridge now, much like the soap bubbles washing away down the rinse side of the sink.

Once Bea'd died, he'd ventured back into the physical occasionally by dating widowed or divorced friends, which had fed the gossip rags a story or two over the past six years. Not enough to make front page, just enough to be annoying and far more exaggerated than reality.

A pang for what life with Randi would have been like all these years hit him deep in the gut, and somehow, he managed to keep that upper lip stiff to hide it. Scenes like this would have been common. Hell, he might have even learned to mow the lawn and change the oil in his car had he followed through with his plans all those years ago. He felt like slashing out at something or someone for the loss. Or weeping like a girl, and that would never do.

"You're deep in thought," Drew commented.

Startled, Court mentally shook off his anger. "Hmm?"

"Good memories?"

Court barked out a short laugh. "A regular jumble of them. This one goes in the plus column, eh?" Out of habit, he turned his thoughts to the positive. Still protecting Drew from his deepest thoughts. Thoughts the lad might, or might not, understand.

"I think so." Drew kept pace, staying with him as plate after plate landed in the wire drain rack.

"Come to think of it, can't remember the last time I enjoyed washing dishes," Court confessed.

"Attractive surroundings sure help the process."

From the corner of his eye, he saw Drew's gaze move around the kitchen as the women sorted the leftovers, his expression carefully casual. Last night at dinner, the lad had confessed they'd not yet gone beyond meeting for coffee in the morning and accidental touches. Excellent news in light of the discussion still to come. Randi had the right of it, nip the attraction in the bud, or better yet, redirect it.

On the plus side, the lad seemed to like Randi as well as he liked Birdie, so how would he feel about the relationship? Drew hadn't ever connected with the few lady friends Court had introduced him to. He'd always put it down to a lawyer's cynical view of the world in general, but it didn't seem to be the case here. Abandoning his thoughts, he tuned into the conversation taking place behind him, Randi's warm voice washing over him, soothing a long ignored turmoil in his soul, in a scene so numbingly domestic it shouldn't have thrilled him the way it did.

"Do you want to take some of everything back to school?" Randi asked Birdie.

"Yes! Food service will be minimal through the weekend, and these are the best leftovers, anyway. I'd rather eat your turkey than their...whatever."

"Drew, do you want leftovers?"

"That would be fabulous, Mrs. Ferguson."

"Oh, please, you're an adult, Randi works."

"Ta."

RJ called over the music from the family room, "Don't forget my leftovers!"

"Have I ever let you go home without a care package?" Randi called back.

"No, just wanted to make sure you didn't start this year."

What had changed between Randi and her father? Court remembered each phone call from home had left her tense and frustrated, but now they bantered as if they were old friends. The old man didn't seem any less manipulative than he'd been back then. What had life been like for her upon returning home? How fast had her marriage been arranged?

Court pulled up a mental picture of Ferguson. He must have been several years older than Randi. That could explain the ability to keep her in style. What about her situation? Did she work? Had he left her life insurance? Stocks, bonds, property? From what he recalled of her background in economics and the financial courses she'd been taking in London, she should have a good grasp on keeping her nest egg healthy.

"Jordan, leftovers for you?" Randi called out.

"As much as I'd love some, don't have a way to keep them in the hotel room."

"Well, I'll give you a piece of pumpkin pie. That will keep for a day or so."

"If that long," he answered with a chuckle. "Thank you."

Behind him, first Birdie, then Randi began singing with the songs. Foil crackled and ripped, drawers opened and closed, plastic bags were shook out, and lids snapped in place, all in tune to the music rolling back the years in his head. Platters and pots appeared for rinsing.

"If you put these through the dishwasher, it will be easier." Randi at his elbow felt cozy and right.

"Is that so?"

"Less scrubbing and clanking around for you. Besides, don't want to ruin your beautiful manicure with steel wool pads."

"You like my manicure?" He lifted a hand and looked at his neatly trimmed nails. "Have a nice little chit who does them at my barber's. Worth every penny." It was also accompanied by a nice view down some impressive cleavage. He tipped well, in appreciation for the display. Not to mention, his lady friends appreciated the consideration. Didn't want a sharp nail interrupting intimate moments. Of which there had been none in far too long. Which might partly explain his almost violent need for Randi.

"It's beautiful. And keep your dirty thoughts to yourself," she hissed in his ear.

That obvious, was he? "Keep blowing in my ear, and I'd be happy to demonstrate some of my favorite fantasies," he whispered back. Then again, Randi created the need for Randi. Her sweet scent wafted around him, and he gazed down into her glazed eyes. Wine? Or desire? Perhaps a touch of both, he decided when her nipple grazed his arm. Hard as a diamond, the little berry wanted to play. He pressed against the cabinet to discourage his own reaction and prayed his tight briefs would do their job and help hide the evidence.

Mind back on his task, he adopted a no-nonsense tone and ordered, "Get me the last of the dishes. Stack them up, don't keep me in suspense here. The soap is giving out."

"It is not." Randi eyed him through long, luxurious lashes. Those eyes. He'd been a sucker for them from the first. Rich jade green, round and luminous, framed by mink lashes. Heart shaped face, clear ivory skin with a dusting of freckles her light coating of makeup couldn't completely hide. A soft sheen of perspiration made her skin look dewy and soft. She used the back of her wrist to brush some hair off her forehead. "Finish up and we can go for a stroll or find the swing out back."

"As you command, it becomes my greatest desire."

"Smart Alec."

"Hand them over, tasty wench."

That earned him a snort as she set down the last of the dirty dishes in the sink.

"Dried up old hag, is more like it." She grimaced and wearily leaned against the counter.

"We'll see. You look pretty juicy to me."

"Hmm, yeah, we'll see. NOT." She spun away.

Now what was she on about? They'd had a fine time in the loo. All they needed now was some privacy, preferably behind the closed door of her bedroom. Heat they had in plenty, the chemistry mixed properly, all they needed was time and space for combustion to occur. Granted, timing was a bit off, but they had later tonight to look forward to. Thanks be to Birdie for insisting on overnighting.

Ah Birdie, how would she react to all this? Would she hate them? Hate him? How deeply would the revelation rock her serene and secure world?

Nerves suddenly hit him in a way he hadn't felt in years. This secret of Randi's had the potential to rip huge holes in some innocent lives. Drew would probably take it in stride as he did all things, but what about Birdie? She seemed happy enough and well grounded, but what would it do to her to find out her life started with a secret? Would he and Randi get a chance to talk before the situation came to a head? Drew definitely had his eye on Birdie, hoping to get closer.

If only they could suspend this moment and draw it out, put off the inevitable, for he had absolutely no doubt that before the night was over, Birdie would know her true heritage. If he had to tell her himself, he would. The secret ended tonight. A thought which excited and scared the hell out of him.

Last dish washed and handed over to Drew soaking up his third drying towel, Court let the water out and rinsed the soap away. Would Randi be impressed he knew how to wipe out a sink? Just one of the many skills she'd once accused him of not having. A skill he'd learned soon after Beatrice's departure from this earth. Might have to show off his culinary skills. Breakfast? Did she have the proper ingredients on hand?

A dry towel landed on his shoulder, and he glanced back to see Randi eyeing him while rubbing lotion into her hands.

He turned off the water and pulled down the towel. "We done, boss?"

"For now. Good enough. If you'll move aside, I'll start the dishwasher, and then we can all go sit down with coffee, or brandy."

"Or both?"

"Mmm. Good idea. Actually, I have another mixture you might like."

"Bring it on." He stepped aside and bowed, waving his towel with a flourish.

"Cocoa butter cream if you want some." She indicated a container on the island.

He enjoyed the view as she bent to retrieve the washing liquid from under the sink and tended to the dish machine. He loved watching her move about the house. Naked and moving about the house would be even better. Naked and moving on top of him—or under him, he wasn't picky—would be best yet. Since she'd commented on his manicure, he took the hint and rubbed the lotion into his hands. Didn't want rough dishpan hands causing the wrong kind of friction later. Then again, rubbing this lotion into strategic parts of her could create the proper heat.

The music changed and he grinned. Taking Randi's hand, he dragged her to the foyer where there was more room to dance.

"No," she protested, but weakly, as he grasped both of her hands in his.

"Oh, yes." He led her into the rhythm. "Remember the Romantics?"

Randi groaned, but kept dancing to the lyrics about talking in her sleep, a most enchanting habit of hers, once upon a time. Probably still did and if given a chance to test it out, he'd take it. The kids poked their heads into the hall in time to see him spin her into his arms, then spin her out again, their own version of the swing.

"Look at that, she can dance!" Birdie laughed from the edge of the foyer, Drew peering over her shoulder.

"Yeah, yeah, the old lady can dance." Randi's breathless voice thrilled him right down to the bone, and he pulled her close.

Had she never danced with Ferguson? For some reason that pleased him immensely. He couldn't stand the thought of her dancing with anyone but him. They'd made magic when dancing. Magic so special it only happened once in a lifetime. "Yeah, she's still got it." Court laughed with the kids.

Randi looked up at him, eyes large enough for him to sink into the sea of green. The memories were there, right at the surface.

With the use of a favorite move, he pulled her close. "Yeah, darling," he murmured for her ears only. "Whether you want me or not, you've still got me."

# Chapter 7

The song came to an end and Randi laughed, using it as an excuse to step away from Court, her heart pumping as much from the exercise as being close to her old love. Dad killed the music, to the groans of Birdie and Drew, but Randi was grateful. She didn't have the stamina for dancing anymore, and being in Court's arms came close to stealing all her power to resist him. By the look in his eye, he knew it and heavily counted on her fading resistance. A quick stop in the kitchen to cram the remaining containers into the refrigerator bought her a few minutes while the kids plopped themselves down in front of the TV.

Winded, Randi paused in the pass-through from the kitchen to the family room and assessed the positions of the occupants. Dad had his corner of the sofa nearest the fireplace with Birdie settling down beside him. Drew sat to her left, close, but not too close in response to a look from Dad. Jordan sat beyond the curve of the sectional. Sit beside him, or in her rocking chair in front of the fireplace on the far side of the room? What she really should do was wiggle in between the kids. Drew didn't have his arm around Birdie—yet—although it was only a matter of time based on the way they smiled at each other.

Court stood behind her, most likely waiting for her to decide where she was going to sit. The sound for the game moving out of half time was back on. Football had never looked so unappealing, but to scurry off to her corner in the reading nook would be rude. Not to mention, there was that situation with the kids.

"What's the proper Thanksgiving etiquette here?" Court's breath tickled the side of her neck.

"Kick the kids off the sofa and we take their spots."

His nearly silent laugh teased her ear. "So cruel."

"The other option is to stretch out on the floor, or sit on the floor and insinuate ourselves between them by leaning back against the couch."

"Sounds hard." His hand cupped her bottom. "We don't want to abuse this pretty posterior."

If only... Man she'd love to sit on his hand for awhile and let it do more delicious things to her. Quashing a groan before it escaped, she made an attempt to push him back with her shoulder. "I have floor pillows. A nap on the carpet is a time-honored tradition. You can take the rocking chair, and I'll sit in the open spot by Jordan."

"No." His answer left no room for argument. She hadn't thought he'd like that suggestion much, so it came as no surprise.

Sneaky Court moved his hand, stroking her back in a way no one else would see, unless they looked at her face. Of course he didn't want her sitting next to Jordan. Court's breath warmed her ear while his finger drew a line down her spine, right past her waist and down between her buttocks. Without a pause, he glided his most wicked finger straight into the space between her legs. Right at the very top of her thighs.

"Would they miss us if we, say, wandered off to your bedroom?" He echoed her earlier thought as if reading her mind. "We still have lots to talk about. We've barely touched the subject of the last twenty-two and a half years."

Randi cleared her throat. "Bad form. Rude to guests and all that," she muttered. "We'll talk once the extra two leave."

"Who's to be polite for? Jordan? No loss there." His finger curved upward, stroking her through the layers of her clothing, wearing at her resolve to walk away. It wouldn't take much more for her already weak defenses to completely crumble. She wanted nothing more than to turn around and pick up where they'd left off in the powder room. But with her father shooting glances her direction, she didn't dare. The very fragile secret was close to exploding into the open, and she needed to hang on to it, just a little longer. Which meant shutting Court down.

"Down boy. Once the game is over, we'll usher the other two out the door. Until then, I have to play nice. If you want to plead jet lag and go lie down in your room, you're allowed."

"Only if you come with me."

If only she could. "No can do."

"Then I'll kick Drew to the floor. He's a good pup."

Aghast, she glanced over her shoulder. "He is not a pup."

"Oh, yes, he is. He's like one of those retrievers you Yanks are so attached to. Golden Retrievers? He's exactly like one. Makes friends with everyone, smiles all the time, happy to be wherever he is at the moment as long as he has someone to talk to."

Randi held back her chuckle, but smiled. That pretty much described Birdie as well if one were to try to compare her to a dog. No, a little chickadee or a canary fit better with her. She'd been well nicknamed.

"Anyhow, toss him a pillow and he'll make happy on the floor."

The look she gave Court over her shoulder this time should have made him wither away, but no, the devil she remembered grinned back at her.

"Fine." She reached for the coffee pot. "Anyone need a refill?" she called out to the room in general. Groans of denial came back.

"What's the special brew you wanted to make me?" Court asked.

"Take your seat and I'll bring it to you. Pillows are behind the sofa."

Randi watched from the corner of her eye as Court disrupted the lazy folks nearly comatose on the couch. From her secret stash, hidden at the very back of the liquor cabinet, she pulled out a dark brown bottle of hazelnut liqueur. She'd once overheard a man refer to it as panty-melter. Talk about setting herself up for trouble with a capital T. Right, as if she could have more trouble on her hands than she already had?

On a wave of recklessness, in went the liqueur followed by a healthy dose of cream. The good stuff, real, heavy whipping cream. Two extra miles on the treadmill this week. Mentally, she crossed her heart, then revised her vow. Next week.

Now she needed a good plan. Step one, get Dad and Jordan sent on their merry ways.

Step two. Shit, what was the best step two? Get Court aside and talk strategy or sit the kids down and go for broke? Because before this night ended, it would all have to come out. A glance into the family room solidified her conviction. Drew settled himself on the floor, pillow at Birdie's feet and his head on the pillow, feet aimed toward the TV. They looked a little too comfortable. How had they grown to be this comfortable with each other in only a week? Were they instinctively reacting to their close relationship, as in blood relationship, but mistaking it for attraction?

Shit. Step two, jump in with both feet. No time for strategy or finesse. It would be so much easier if she didn't like Drew. But she did. He was a nice kid. Reminded her a lot of Court way back when.

Lord, what would this do to his image of his father? What would this do to Birdie's image of her? Wyatt? Court and Drew? So many variations, this could go awry in so many ways it wasn't close to funny. It all depended on how Birdie received and processed the news.

Which led to step three, which depended entirely upon the kids and their reactions. Surprise certainly. Horror? Disgust? Feelings of betrayal almost a guarantee. She could only pray for forgiveness and understanding.

How many chances over the last two years had there been to tell Birdie the story of her life? One day the kid would actually read her paperwork in detail. Not that Randi had ever handed either of the certificates to her and said, "Hey, here look at this. This is who you really are."

Hmm. A thought to consider. She knew right where to find the certified copies of Birdie's birth and adoption certificates. For years they'd lived in Randi's purse alongside Birdie's shot records. Once she went off to college, Randi had filed them with the marriage certificate and vehicle titles. Right beside Wyatt's death certificate. All things that should be in a safe deposit box at the bank.

"With the vehicle titles?" Wyatt had asked her with a raised brow when he'd asked about the marriage certificate.

"They're all certificates of ownership, right?"

"But do I own you or do you own me?"

"Yes."

Wyatt had at least laughed and never questioned her logic again. As long as he could find what he needed when he needed it, he never complained. Then again, his method of finding things had been to ask her to find it for him. Great system. For him.

Randi leaned her head against the cabinet and said a silent prayer for strength and courage.

So. Step one. Get the extras off the stage.

She lifted the two mugs and waited until the play finished before walking in front of the viewers. She stopped long enough to hand one mug to Court, then stepped right over Drew and glided smoothly into her rocking chair.

With an audible sigh, she slid off her shoes and flexed her feet. A deep red line cut into her feet where the straps across her toes had been. Should have worn the black velvet slippers she'd picked up last week. So much for vanity and trying to impress two blind dates.

Set up by her daughter and her father. The pair of them looked mighty cozy on the sofa. A photo right now would portray almost the perfect family. Kick Jordan out of the picture and you'd have a girl sitting like a princess, surrounded by her father, grandfather and brother. Not a bad picture come to think of it. Getting up to find her camera would ruin the entire tableau. Nothing more than illusion anyway. No such thing as a perfect family existed anywhere.

From the first gulp of her laced coffee, she felt its magic slide into her blood, warming secret spaces in her body now protesting they'd been ignored too long. It seemed more than two years since Wyatt's passing.

Love had grown between them, softly at first. Slow and steady, directly opposite the instant explosion she'd experienced with Court. Enough love that she truly missed Wyatt's comforting, solid, steady presence and his ability to shelter her from any storm. She'd been well loved and her mourning deep and sincere.

Yet, she was a woman not quite ready for the nursing home. She still had desires. Desires that had ignited by a momentary connection with Court's darkening eyes. A sluicing of liquid heat traveled straight to her core. Heaven help her, she wanted him. Now. Right here.

At the sound of a throat clearing, she switched her gaze to her father and found him staring at her. She glared back, pointedly nodded toward Jordan, who dozed with his chin on his chest, and then the front of the house where his car was parked at the curb. Dad merely smiled and shook his head. At the two-minute warning, she gulped down the rest of her coffee and used sign language to inform him she wanted to see him in the kitchen.

"All right," he grumbled and heaved to his feet. "The Raiders are losing anyway. Sad day when Dallas stomps them into the mud this way."

"What mud?" Randi gave him a narrow-eyed glare as she chased him into the kitchen. The warm carpet gave way to cool vinyl under her bare feet, reminding her she wanted to get off them for the night very soon.

"All right, you dragged me in here." Dad put his cup in the sink. The pose he took, leaning against the counter, arms crossed, clearly signified he didn't want to budge.

"It's time you gather up your leftovers, and your guest, and go home. I'm sure Jordan would appreciate a nice, quiet hotel room about now. Or the ability to go trolling for companionship for the night. Either way, you've worn out your welcome for today."

Scowling for effect, he stood firm, looking immoveable. "I want to be here when you tell her."

"No." Randi crossed her arms and stood firm. Even if she did get a crick in her neck looking up at him. As he'd often told her, a person's size didn't matter. It was her determination, and Dad had run into her brand of it more than once. "This is my problem and I don't want to tell my daughter her whole life is not what it seems in front of a stranger. Jordan has no part in this, and I won't do that to her or Drew."

"I want my chance to grill the smooth-talking son of a bitch who sent my daughter home pregnant. Besides, I'm her grandfather," he pointed out.

"But you're not related to the other two. I'll call you tomorrow, unless she decides to disown me tonight, then she may very well end up on your doorstep. If the situation warrants your presence, then you can come back. Otherwise, we have things to work out around here before you play your role of outraged father." At his stubborn look, she threw up her hands in frustration. "You're making this extra hard on me. It's already a difficult situation, and you butting in like this is distracting me and taking away the energy I need to deal with this in a reasonable manner."

Anxious to drive her point absolutely home, she poked her finger against his breastbone. "Do NOT do this to me. I'm trying to do the right thing by my daughter, and a little support from you would be appreciated right now. I need to focus on her first, not your sense of injured chivalry."

At last he nodded, rubbing his chest where she'd poked him, and asked quietly, "How are you going to do it?"

"I don't know yet. I wanted to talk to Court first, but I think I'm out of time." Valuable time he'd used up by being pigheaded.

They looked into the family room where Birdie tried to rest a bare foot on Drew's head. He kept pushing it off, but they could see the sly smile on his face. The boy was going to strike and give Birdie what she had coming. Hopefully, it would be limited to tickles. She hoped Jordan had a strong heart as momentarily he'd be awakened by a screech loud enough to scare the dead.

Randi backed away from her father and stepped into Birdie's line of sight. Drew's as well. She gave them both a mother glare, and they settled down. She ignored Court's pout. Troublemaker. For a moment, the anger returned, and she bent the heat of her scowl on him. That innocent look so did not work on her anymore.

His eyes twinkled at her and he smiled, the special private smile, no less.

Damn him.

So the look still worked on her.

She rolled her eyes and turned away. "Your leftovers are all ready to go, Dad." This agitator wouldn't walk all over her this time.

Ten minutes later, she stood on the entry patio and waved as Dad drove off with Jordan. A minor skirmish out of the way. One which had been tougher than it should have been. This was not the right time, physically or emotionally, to go down this path, but she had no choice morally. Any minute now those kids could sneak off and do something that would scar them for life.

Court stood behind her, and when she turned, their eyes met.

"What are the kids doing?" she asked him.

"I believe they're thinking of hot-tubbing. Not a bad idea, actually. I could give you a foot rub." The accompanying lifted brow added he could rub other things as well.

"Not until we speak to them." She joined him on the top step and looked up. "I don't want to do this, but I think we need to do it now. Don't you?"

Court lifted a hand and used one finger to twirl a strand of her hair. "I think you're right. This discussion is going to be painful."

"True. Divide and conquer or sit them down together?"

"I don't want to do it alone, but it might be easier."

"I'm not sure there's an easy way to do it at all."

"I wish we could work out things between us first. Present them with a unified front."

Randi shrugged, turning away from his gaze. She couldn't deal with both situations at the same time. She wanted to be selfish and deal with the hurt and anger she'd held all these years. The aching loneliness that had struck her from time to time and had grown even stronger with Wyatt's death. She and Court should have been together. Instead, they'd lived with people they didn't love well enough to be married to and raised children they loved completely.

Court's hands slipped into her hair, his big hands forming to the shape of her skull.

Worn down from fighting the attraction all day, following instinct, she leaned against him, forehead tilted to his chest, and soaked in the comfort he offered. The feel of his strong body, solid where she leaned into him, his scent, the pulse of his blood and breath; it all came back to her, filling her, completing her as she wrapped her arms around his waist.

"Ah, sweet," he murmured against the top of her head. "I've missed you, dreamed of you, mourned the loss of this, the simplest of comforts, just holding you."

"I'm so confused!" All those feelings and more welled up from deep inside, overwhelming her, making her heart pound and throat tighten. The need to lash out, to hit something, or in this case someone, swamped her, almost taking her to her knees. By nature, she didn't resort to violence, but the feelings were too deep, held back too long, and so strong she shook with the effort to contain them.

Hands fisted, she clung to him as much as she wanted to escape. "I hate you, I need you, I can't bear your touch, and yet, I feel as if I've been slowly dying without it. I never want to see you again, but I'll kill you if you leave me. You've got me all torn up inside, and I don't know what I want right now, or five minutes from now, much less tonight or tomorrow."

Restless from the churning emotions, she tried to push away, but he held her tight and tilted her head to stare into her eyes.

"*I didn't know.*" The whispered words were urgent, as if wrenched from his heart, the agony she felt mirrored in his eyes. "I swear to God, any god you want, any major or minor deity, faerie, or sprite you name. I swear on my father's grave. I. Didn't. Know."

The truth in his eyes didn't help the hurt in her heart. Possibly it facilitated her understanding a little, but it didn't erase the years of secrecy and guilt. So much guilt. Guilt for not loving Wyatt as well as he'd loved her. Guilt for not coming clean with Birdie much sooner. Guilt for hating Court, his wife, and their child. So much to regret.

The time had come to let it all go. Her time for running away was over as of right now. She had to face her feelings for Court and tell Birdie of her heritage.

Tears welled up in her eyes, turning Court watery and wavy.

"Ah, love, don't cry, please don't cry. Anything but tears. Yell at me, beat me with those tiny fists, curse me to the ends of the earth, just, please, no tears. I can't bear your tears."

A late-blooming pot of gardenias sheltered on the steps lent a sweetness to the air as Court kissed the wet streaks from her cheeks. The tenderness with which he touched her, held her, did her in and the trickle became a waterfall.

"Ah, hell," he muttered and touched his lips to hers.

The sizzle that had been on simmer all day, rekindled into a blazing conflagration. Her hands slid up his back to cling to his shoulders as he held her head and devoured her mouth, the sweetness balanced by the saltiness of her tears.

The day caught up with her then. Lack of sleep, hours on her feet in the kitchen, the emotions and shock of seeing Court again, the tension created by her father's pestering, and the worry of unraveling Birdie's life without all the facts in place... God, could there be more? It all coalesced there in Court's embrace, and she dug her fingers into his flesh in a last attempt to hang on as what little sanity she had left slipped away, falling willing victim to his touch. Their breaths mingled, tongues tangled, legs entwined, and hands groped until they both pressed their hips toward each other. Nothing felt better than his kiss, his touch, his strong hands holding her so intimately.

The world faded away, wrapping them in the sweet scent of flowers. The troubles, worries, and aches all compressed down into one need. The need to fuse with this man. There was only one way to get closer, and she wanted it. Wanted it more than she'd ever wanted anything in her life. She needed to connect with his strength, needed the affirmation he offered.

"Mom?"

Mom didn't belong here, just Randi, a woman, and Court, a man. Mom was a dream person who didn't live in this moment. Didn't exist or belong to this world of only two people.

A choked giggle preceded Birdie's next, half-scandalized exclamation. "Mom? Mr. Robinson?"

"Bloody hell, Dad. In front of the neighbors?"

Drew's voice broke through the fog, shattering the moment.

Like a hot potato, Randi released Court and stepped back, heart pounding and chest heaving in a far too clichéd manner. Court resisted a moment longer, then released his hold. Unable to look at him or the kids, she closed her eyes and took in deep breaths, hoping to clear her mind and get control of her thundering pulse.

A car door slammed from across the street, and her neighbor called out, "Hey Randi, there're young kids here. Save the biology lessons for later!" Tuck's laugh echoed between the homes in the failing light of day.

Face hot, she glanced his way and waved. Like Brad Tucker had room to talk. The man had four children! Each and every last one of them had varying shades of their mother's red hair. It had been something of a not-so-funny neighborhood joke that maybe he had five since Birdie looked more like him than Wyatt. Of course everyone knew it wasn't true, but they didn't know the other side of the coin.

Someone's car roared to life, and it took all she had to raise her chin and face the children.

Right. At twenty-one and twenty-two, the tall, beautiful people in front of her could no longer be called children. They were adults who deserved to know the truth about their lives. Birdie especially.

"Hey, Randi."

Tuck's voice coming from close behind made her jump what felt like a foot. He chuckled. "Sorry, didn't mean to scare you. Kelly made me bring this over."

She turned, hand over her racing heart, to find a covered dish in his hands, but his eyes moved rapidly from Court to Birdie to Drew and back around again.

"Holy…" Tuck stopped and cleared his throat as he put on his lawyer face. The one which said no one was messing with his client and said client better bring him up to date right quick.

"Tuck, this is Court and Drew Robinson. Birdie brought them home for Thanksgiving…" she started to explain but at the look in his eyes, she faltered.

Blue eyes—so much like Birdie's people who did and didn't know better often teased them about the resemblance—drilled into her, asking questions and wanting answers right now. As her lawyer, neighbor, and friend, the look also reassured her he was on her side, ready to jump in and defend her if needed. "Anything else you want to tell me?"

"Court, Drew, this is our neighbor and friend, Brad Tucker. Also my lawyer." There, that should explain Tuck's seemingly odd question.

However, it didn't throw Tuck off one bit. She could see his sharp eyes had already taken in the physical resemblance of Birdie to the two men behind her, and he quickly moved on to sizing up Court with slightly narrowed eyes.

"So the old jokes were half right?" he asked quietly.

More footsteps came up the walk. As if Kelly could resist being nosy. Randi's heart beat faster, and she knew the end of her little secret approached like a flash flood. *Go away.* She silently tried to communicate the thought to the Tuckers. Of course, both ignored her.

"Oh. My. God." Kelly stopped and stared from one blond to the next just as her husband had. "Tuck, she really wasn't—"

Tuck threw an arm around his wife's shoulder, his hand coming to rest over her mouth. "And this is my wife, Kelly, the big mouth." He gave her a quelling glare before releasing her mouth. "This is why she isn't the lawyer of the family," he explained to the astonished crowd.

Randi glanced over her shoulder. Birdie and Drew both looked stunned. A glance in the other direction showed mild amusement and resignation on Court's face.

Heart sinking, she turned back to her neighbors. "Thanks, Kelly, Tuck, I'll catch up with you later."

Kelly's mouth gaped open and closed a few times before words emerged. "Oh Randi! I'm so, so, sorry…" Green eyes round as saucers had the grace to look horrified.

"I know, Kelly." Randi patted her friend's arm when all she wanted was for the earth to open up and swallow someone. Her or Kelly, she didn't care. "We'll talk, I promise."

"If you need us…" Tuck still eyed Court warily, but he backed off, dragging Kelly with him, the dish in his hand forgotten.

"I know your number." She gave them a half smile. Birdie began to make spluttering noises behind her. "Or I'll light-signal."

Since Wyatt's death, Tuck had told her if she ever needed him and couldn't get to a phone, she could always flash an SOS using a light switch or flashlight. She'd also learned enough Morse code there were times she'd done it to say goodnight and convey the message all was well. Although she probably wouldn't need the signal tonight, she liked knowing they were there if needed. One couldn't plan neighbors like this, but sometimes, they were handed over on a silver platter. A result of good Karma? Possibly. Then again, with Kelly's well-intentioned, but big mouth, maybe not.

Well, if she had any good Karma, she needed it now. Taking a deep breath, she turned to find Birdie and Drew frozen, their mouths gaping open.

"We need to talk," Randi said simply. "Let's go inside."

"I'll say!" Birdie squeaked. "I want to know what Aunt Kelly meant!"

"Yeah, I want to know why no one ever told me I have a sister," Drew said on a shaky chuckle. "I came damn close to damaging us both for life."

"Sister!" Birdie's eyes widened even more. "Omigod, omigod." She turned stricken eyes to Randi, and pointed a shaking finger at Court. "You mean...?"

Randi nodded wearily, her heart breaking at the look on her daughter's face.

"If he's...then..." Birdie turned to Drew and took another step back into the house, running into the foyer table. "Then he's...my brother?" The high-pitched screech made Randi wince at the shot of pain piercing her head.

"Let's take this inside," she said more firmly and stepped into the house, practically bulldozing Drew out of her way, leaving the men to follow, or not, at their choosing. She grasped Birdie's arm and marched her into the family room, Birdie too stunned to protest or fight. Once there, Randi gently pushed her down onto the sofa and took the rocking chair for herself, drawing it up so they sat face to face.

"Birdie, baby." Randi gulped and stared into her daughter's beautiful blue eyes. How to say this? Spit it out? Come at it from an angle? Start at the beginning and work up to it? She picked up Birdie's icy hand.

Aw Hell. There was no easy way, and when push came to shove, she believed in being forthright. "Birdie, I have to tell you... You need to know..." No brilliant words came to her. Randi drew in a deep breath, exactly as she'd do before diving into the pool. Birdie perched on the edge of the sofa, her face intent, her attention focused and confused. There was no way out but to go forward.

"As the Tuckers guessed, Wyatt wasn't your biological father."

# Chapter 8

"And you're just telling me this now?"

Randi flinched as Birdie's hand dropped away, and she sat with her mouth open wide enough to catch flies.

Drew settled on the far end of the sectional sofa, and Court stopped beside the rocking chair, his hand coming to rest on Randi's shoulder. A show of support? Lord, she needed one.

"Court is your biological father, which makes Drew your half brother." In a rush, Randi confirmed the words Birdie had choked out a few moments ago, and Court's hand tightened on her shoulder. She caught a flinch and cough from Drew at the edge of her vision. Gaze locked on Birdie, Randi reached for Court's hand, and his fingers enmeshed hers in his comforting grip.

Birdie's mouth snapped shut and dropped open again, her face losing all color for a moment and then flushing a hot red before going white again. Randi let go of Court and reached for Birdie's hand, but her daughter recoiled.

Birdie glanced from Drew to Court and back around again. "I don't believe you! It can't be…"

Heart breaking for the pain and confusion on her daughter's face, Randi kept nodding, unable to think of a way to convince her daughter, hoping for a look of relief in Birdie's eyes. Relief as in she hadn't yet gotten to the cuddling stage with Drew, or—heaven forbid!—further.

"He's…he"—she pointed one finger over Randi's shoulder—"is my *father*?" The rising note in Birdie's voice made it come out as a squeak. "*My* father? And this is the best way you could think of to tell me?"

Oh God, could this go any worse? "I'm sorry, so sorry!" Randi moaned and reached for Birdie again. At this point, Drew was Court's worry, and she didn't spare him a glance. "I wanted to find a better way. I never intended to dump it on you like this."

Birdie's face contorted into a mask of horror, and Randi feared what might erupt. She didn't expect, "You mean my real name is Courtney Robin Robinson?"

A louder choke disguised as a cough from the other end of the couch made all eyes turn toward Drew. His blue eyes were frozen wider than usual and despite his tan, he looked a little pale. Possibly a little green. "Courtney?" He swallowed and forced a grin. "Who'd have thought?"

"You thought Birdie was my real name?" Birdie stared at him as if he'd grown a second head, or the one on his shoulders had rolled off.

Drew shrugged. "I've seen it used as a real name."

"When?" Birdie demanded

"A couple of times..."

"If you say, *Bye, Bye Birdie* and *Hope Floats,* I will shoot you."

The only person in the room who seemed remotely amused, Drew's crooked grin trembled at the corner, seeming to regain his composure faster than anyone else, and Randi wondered exactly how he'd processed the revelation. "Okay, I won't say the movies."

Birdie threw up her hands with a growl, and Randi wanted to echo her. Another man who dealt with trauma by making jokes? What was it with guys? She glanced over her shoulder at Court who merely shrugged as if to say this was normal.

"Got to admit you got yourself one hell of a name there, Bird. Guess that means you'll be hanging around longer than a year abroad fling, eh? Aw damn." His head fell back, and he stared up at the ceiling, hands lying limp on his lap. "Glad you all spoke up now, wish you'd done it sooner, considering what I was...bloody hell." He straightened and scrubbed his face with both hands. "I suppose if I have to have a sister, I'm glad it's you. It'll take a few moments to flip-flop my thinking. But overall, yer, I'm glad to have a sister." Drew's sweet face brightened with a wide, toothy grin, to counteract his still pasty pallor. "And if Kevin Westerfield thinks this'll give him a chance of getting into your knickers, well, I already told him it'd never happen, but now I can back it up with a fist to his nose." Drew raised a fist and pantomimed a right hook.

Birdie gasped, and by the way her eyes lit up for a moment, apparently, she didn't think it was so awful that this Kevin person wanted to get close to her.

"Bloody hell." Drew's smile dropped and he paled again. "A sister. When's your birthday, Bird?"

"February."

"That means..." Drew frowned, then flicked his gaze toward his father.

"Yes." Court gave his son a crooked smile. "She was conceived roughly four months after you. About a month before I married your mother."

"Now there's a story I have to hear." One corner of Drew's mouth curled up in a matching crooked grin.

"I suspect you'll get your wish. Very soon." Court closed his eyes as his grip tightened on Randi's shoulder.

Randi couldn't help but grimace and give a weak, very weak, laugh. Oh yeah, there was a story.

"This isn't funny!" Birdie shouted.

Stunned by the angry vehemence of Birdie's voice, Randi swiveled her head to see the normally sunny face dark and stormy. Birdie had never been one to shout when upset and, yet, here sat a girl Randi didn't recognize. Birdie's eyes flashed with roiling emotions, her face a mottled mixture of red and white. She obviously couldn't process the shock as fast as her brother. "This is my life you've just turned on its nose!"

"I didn't mean to!" Forcing herself to stay seated when she wanted to jump up and pace, Randi defended herself. Birdie was upset enough for the time being, and pacing would only increase everyone's agitation. She needed to bring this under control and fisted her hands in her lap. If her neck got any tighter it might snap in two, which might be a blessing, actually, possibly even less painful than what she felt now. "It all happened so long ago, and the situation couldn't have been more complicated..."

"The nineteen eighties were not the Middle Ages!" Birdie argued back. "You should have told me from the beginning. You shouldn't have married my fa—my dad—Wyatt to hide your mistake. You didn't have to create a false life, a false identity for me."

Randi dropped her head back, and it thunked against her rocking chair, adding to the headache building inside her skull. "I didn't want to," she whispered. "I wanted you to know Court, but other people made different decisions, limiting my choices. However, I did have choices, and the one to marry Wyatt seemed like the best way to smooth out a difficult situation."

Randi glanced to the left at the painting hanging over the fireplace. It didn't appear to be much more than a seascape to anyone who didn't know, but Birdie knew it well. Wyatt had bought it as a gift to the family in general to commemorate his and Randi's fifth wedding anniversary. The year they'd moved into this house. Birdie looked as well, and it seemed to calm her. They'd all found the painting of Monterey Bay, done by a no-name artist, soothing and peace inspiring. It seemed to work its magic now when they needed it most.

"I don't see how." Birdie grabbed a sofa pillow and hugged it to her stomach, huddling around it as if holding her favorite teddy bear. "You'd better explain it to me." At least now she spoke in closer to normal tones and no longer shouted.

"I'm curious as well," Drew drawled and stretched out his legs, hands folded across his stomach.

Randi looked up at Court, pleading for... Lord, she didn't know what. Rescue from a white knight would be nice about now. Apparently, he got the message because he nodded and gave her shoulder a brief squeeze.

"I'll start it," Court said. He struck a pose, legs spread, hands clasped behind his back.

"No!" Birdie objected. "I want to hear it from her. That is if you are who you say you are. You are my mom, aren't you?" A hint of a sneer almost covered the flash of fear in Birdie's eyes and tempered the hurt and anger tearing through Randi.

"Of course I'm your mother! I even have the scars to prove it." Reining in her own temper, Randi held up her hands. "Okay, okay. Quite simply, while in London for my semester abroad, I met Court. We fell..." She swallowed hard, thinking of all the times she'd questioned this very fact herself. Court's hand tightened on her shoulder and certainty returned. "We fell in love and love followed its natural course. The day I was scheduled to leave, several things happened." Bracing herself, she lowered her arms and clung to the solid arms of the rocking chair.

She closed her eyes and let the memories flow. "Court and I had already said our goodbyes. My flight left that night, and he had a new hire reception he had to attend. He'd just completed his graduate degree, and it was time for him to step into the family business."

Birdie snorted and Randi opened her eyes. "You know all about family companies and what parents expect. You've seen it your whole life, because even though I work from home, I work for my father. It was the same for Court, and he'd been raised his whole life to work for his father."

"Um, actually, not only my father but my prospective father-in-law as well," he said, and Randi looked up at him. "See, Beatrice and I were products of an outdated fashion. We'd technically been engaged since we were children. The estates are side by side and the businesses compatible. Our marriage brought about a merger of both concerns."

Surprise made Randi blink. It certainly explained a few things. "You never mentioned that."

"I didn't see any point. Beatrice and I were over and done with at the time you and I met." Face carefully blank, he shrugged. "She and I spent one night together, decided we didn't suit after all, and parted ways." His gaze moved to Drew and softened with a father's pride. "Of course, all it took was one night to create you."

"Why'd you split in the first place?" Drew asked, then his eyes widened. "Are you saying you married her because she got pregnant?"

"In part. Many other factors went into the decision process. It wasn't so cut and dried."

"Right. The companies." Drew nodded, not looking like he completely agreed with the practice, but understood the system.

"And your grandparents' estate, which is willed to you as the first male child on their side in three generations."

"I don't see how all that matters," Birdie said. "Didn't you know my mother was pregnant? And with your child?"

"No, I didn't. But if I had known—"

Randi held up a hand again. "I had a chance to tell him, but by then I knew about the other baby." She glanced at Drew and apologetically grimaced. He smiled in return. "Drew. Only he didn't have a name then. Not yet. Please, let me do this in order."

"Oh, please do get on with it. I'm just dying to hear the story." Birdie imperiously waved for her to keep going.

Randi ignored the heavy sarcasm. Birdie certainly had the right to feel what she felt. "All right, so Court had family obligations. I knew this. I'd applied for a summer internship at the same company, but as no call came through, we both assumed I didn't get it. So instead of going to the new hire reception myself, which had been scheduled since before I'd left home, my flight was booked for the same time, making it impossible for him to see me off at the airport. We had plans for after my graduation, once he had some work experience, but nothing set in stone. We said goodbye, and then as I started to pack, the phone rang and I got the news I had the internship. I'd barely hung up when the phone rang again, only it was student health services. The doctor told me I was pregnant, despite the birth control I was on."

Birdie snorted. "Right." A roll of the eyes conveyed her disbelief.

"Antibiotics, my dear. Remember this little fact well, they can negate the effectiveness of birth control pills."

The nod from Birdie came reluctantly. They'd discussed it before. Randi had made sure of that early on.

"So." Randi drew in a deep breath and let it go. "I canceled my flight home, and made all the arrangements I needed in order to stay. I dressed up and went to the new hire reception with every intention of telling Court the happy news. What plans I had." Sadness and humiliation swamped her as if it were happening all over again. The look on his face, the disdain on *her—Beatrice? What a name—*face, the horror on Danielle Richards' face…and the sheer loathing of the two older couples standing near them. It had felt as if she faced an arena of man-eating tigers, all of them out for her blood. Except Court. His face alone had showed something else. Surprise, regret, and shame.

"Well it didn't work out quite the way I'd envisioned. I got to the reception in time to overhear the conversation about his…fiancé's pregnancy and how, to celebrate the happy event, they'd moved up the wedding date." Though she turned to look at Birdie, she clasped her hands over her stomach, remembering what it had felt like to carry her daughter.

"I'd opened my mouth to drop my own bombshell, but then I couldn't speak. All those people looking at me. They all seemed so pleased with the news, and Court looked so…so…right…beside…*her*. Like they'd been made for each other. Cut from the same cloth, so to speak." Feeling guilty for not being able to say the woman's name, she glanced at Drew who gave her a tiny smile and nod of encouragement. "I couldn't do it. I couldn't tell him. I couldn't force such a decision on him. He'd have been torn between two babies… And apparently, she'd been there first. I was the outsider. The foreigner. No way would I have ever gained the support of his parents. I didn't belong in his world."

Court gripped her shoulder. "We could have made it work, Jeannie. We would have worked something out."

She was already shaking her head. "No. It wouldn't have been fair to either child, you, or any of us, no matter what you chose. I'd seen my friends with divorced parents and how the splits affected them. I decided none of us needed such a complication. Especially the children. It would be too confusing with me in California and you in England. Too much distance."

Court moved in front of her and bent, hands on the arms of the chair, putting his face close to hers. "I think I should have been allowed to have a part in that decision," Court said quietly, his gaze locked on hers with an expression so tender, yet serious, she couldn't look away.

"Perhaps," she conceded. "But I was too numb and too hurt to consider your feelings. I thought it would be easier all around to come home and raise my child alone. If I couldn't have you, I'd have a part of you. And if you didn't know, you wouldn't be torn in two. I figured I was strong enough to raise Birdie on my own." She glanced sideways at her daughter. "And I do have my beautiful daughter to remind me of a precious time of my life."

"Oh for crying out loud! This is my life you made careless decisions with." Birdie's eruption broke the spell between Randi and Court, both of them turning their heads to see her glare as hot and as hurt as Randi had ever seen.

Court crouched, staying close, one hand falling to Randi's knee in a show of comfort as her head threatened to explode.

"I did not make a careless decision!" She choked back her shout and forced the words through gritted teeth.

Birdie subsided deep into her corner of the sofa. "Keep going."

Court settled on the carpet, keeping a hand on Randi while another deep breath helped restore a small amount of calm to her thundering pulse. "I flew out the next morning and made it home with no further trauma other than morning sickness. I managed to pass it off as air sickness for a day or two, but your grandmother finally got me to talk. Since I knew I didn't want an abortion, sooner or later, I'd have to tell them. I wouldn't be able to hide it for long and returning to Stanford in the fall would be impossible."

Birdie knew her views on abortion—although right for some people, Randi had never once considered it as a personal choice—Birdie seemed to relax a little, but the scowl didn't leave her face. "I bet Grandpa swallowed that like broken glass."

A humorless laugh escaped Randi. "Oh yeah. He yelled, he threatened, and tried to bully." But she'd stood firm, her mother beside her, refusing to get the abortion he insisted on. There was no point in telling Birdie any of that now. From the moment he'd held her, Birdie had been the apple of her grandfather's eye. "But your grandmother took my side, and he agreed to back off if I got married."

"Did you know Da—Wyatt...before?" Birdie's voice choked.

Swallowing the lump in her throat, Randi shook her head. "No. Grandpa hired him after I went to London. Grandpa brought him home for dinner a couple weeks after I'd shared my news. He was the fifth candidate brought home. And by far the nicest all around."

"Is that how you chose my dad?" Birdie sneered. "You interviewed applicants for the job?"

"If you choose to look at it that way, but like any job, it takes the right person. I suppose you could say dating is an interview process, if you want to boil it down to its essence. I had a couple choices before me. Live at home and listen to my father berate me for being irresponsible. Not an option if I wanted to keep my sanity and raise my child in a positive atmosphere. Drop out of school, get a job, and try to make it on my own. Difficult, but doable, in another state. Even back then, California was too expensive for any kind of decent life alone with an infant and no degree. Or I could marry a nice and decent man who promised to love my child as his own and live a normal life." She directed a pointed look at her daughter who stared back, not giving an inch.

*Keep moving,* she told herself. "Wyatt seemed kind and calm, and he inspired a feeling of peace in me. I didn't make the decision lightly and neither did he. We spent a week together, talking about our dreams, goals, and expectations. We figured out where we meshed and where we'd need to compromise. Even with our age difference we were surprisingly compatible. And we went into our marriage better prepared to work together than I expect most couples do." Talking about Wyatt didn't come easy with Court touching her, sitting close enough she could feel his body heat.

"But did you love him?"

"I learned to, and he learned to love me." Apparently, Birdie caught on to her feelings of tenderness for the man they'd both been so close to, because for a second, they shared a tiny smile. "If you listened to him talk, he always said he fell in love at first sight. Not quite, but close. It wasn't easy with my father doing a sales job on both of us, which was why Wyatt took a week off work and courted me. It was the only way we could talk. Now that I think about it, Wyatt knew your grandfather well enough.... I guess you could say a feeling of protectiveness seemed to rise up out of him. He became the shield between the two of us and the outside world."

Birdie gave her a long, thoughtful, and pained look before she nodded. "Okay, I believe you, though things have changed. Does Grandpa know... about..." Birdie's gaze flicked toward Court.

"Yeah, he figured it out when Court gave his full name earlier. I begged him to keep it to himself. I didn't want to draw Jordan into our drama."

"Good move, that." Drew nodded sagely.

"You haven't seen him on a tear. Just getting him out of the house tonight, well, it took some fancy tap dancing." Randi sighed and dropped her head back against the chair. "Anyhow, to get on with this story, I was prepared to drop out of school. Instead, Wyatt talked me into transferring to St. Mary's, which isn't far from here, and easing up on my class schedule. He had a tiny house in Albany, so it was convenient to the office for him and school for me. I went half time fall semester, took spring semester off to have you, then started up again in the fall, and graduated the following spring. I went to work for your grandfather, and we grew into a family. That's everything in a nutshell."

"Only if you forget about lying to me about who I am," Birdie replied sullenly. "I can't believe you lied to me. For all your harping about honesty all my life—"

"I only lied by omission, Birdie. I've been working up to telling you everything. It was never my intention to keep it from you forever. Wyatt and I wanted to tell you by your twenty-first birthday." Randi bowed her head and looked at her hands lying uselessly in her lap. "Fact is, sitting on my desk are some forms I am—was—preparing to send to a research agency. To find out more about Court, so I could tell you after Christmas. And had you ever looked, it's all there on your birth certificate. You just never looked at it. Attached to it is your adoption certificate. From when Wyatt legally adopted you."

"What?" Birdie came off the sofa. "Where is it?" she demanded.

Feeling as old as if two minutes had gone into every one she'd lived, Randi relied heavily on the sturdy arms of her rocking chair to push herself vertical. Court, rising gracefully to his feet, slipped a hand under her elbow, the warmth of him lending strength to her quickly waning reserves.

Birdie was already down the hall and opening the door to the master suite and Randi's office space. "It's in your files, right? You once told me...." Her voice trailed off as she moved deeper into Randi's room toward the filing cabinet in the little office nook where she worked.

Drew still sat on the sofa, looking a little lost and a lot bemused.

"Come on, Drew. You might as well see this too," she said to him.

With a shrug, he unfolded his tall frame until he, too, towered over her. "You know anyone can put a name on a birth certificate." He sent what appeared to be a significant look in his father's direction. "Doesn't make it true."

"I know," she said. "I'd planned to put Wyatt's name on Birdie's, but..." She sighed. "We'll get to that in a bit. She'll have the same question."

"What about the legalities of adoptions without informing the biological father?" Drew asked.

Randi shrugged. "My father knows a lot of influential people. It was handled quietly, and it's a bit late to question the matter now." She looked down the hall to where Birdie had disappeared. "We'd better continue this down there."

# Chapter 9

They found Birdie kneeling before the filing cabinet, the bottom drawer half open, a short stack of papers in her hand. The copy of her birth certificate from the hospital sat on top. A copy of the one filed with the government from what Court could make out.

"Why?" she asked her mother without looking up. Court held his breath having only had the abbreviated version in the loo.

"Because I almost died." Randi sighed.

"Died? You were dying?" Birdie looked up, tears streaking down her cheeks. Each one dug in like a claw in Court's guts.

"Hmm." Randi kneeled beside her daughter, and holding Birdie close, tipped her auburn head toward Birdie's shining gold lengths tumbling from a loose clip. "Remember we told you I was sick after you were born, which is why you were bottle fed?"

"Yeah, but I thought you meant like the flu or something."

Randi nodded to a framed photo on her desk, and Court followed her gaze. The young girl he'd known, looking tired but happy and extremely beautiful, held a baby in her arms while another man held them both. A stab of intense jealous pain jabbed him in the gut, but he forced it to subside as he focused on Randi's words.

"About five minutes after that photo was taken, something came undone inside. Unstoppable bleeding led to an emergency hysterectomy, and somewhere in there an infection set in. The hospital wanted the paperwork filled out, and I was delirious."

This conversation had to hurt her as badly as it hurt him. Damn, he and Drew should have stayed in the other room. They had their own discussion to have, and Birdie deserved a private conversation with her mother. But Randi spoke again, and he couldn't move to save his life. He wanted the same answers.

"Wyatt wanted you to someday know the truth. He loved you as much as any father ever loved a daughter. You were his in all the ways that counted." Randi's voice dropped to a broken whisper.

His daughter. Something clenched hard around the area of his heart.

Their daughter. Still needed to adjust to the thought.

"Wyatt did what he thought was the right thing since I couldn't. He named you, then took you home, not knowing if I'd live or not. That's true love, Birdie. He could have claimed you on the birth certificate, and no one would have fought it. Ever. But he had faith I'd live, and someday, you'd need to know the truth. I stayed in the hospital an extra three weeks, and during that time you two bonded as strongly as if he'd helped create you. Had I died, he would have kept and raised you himself, with the help of my parents. He adopted you, so you legally carry his name." Randi took the papers from Birdie and flipped through them until she found the adoption certificate.

Ah, there it was. Mystery solved as to why the husband had loved the daughter so much, possibly more than the mother. Made sense now. Had to admit a grudging admiration for the man posed with Randi in a second framed photo on the desk. A photo taken many years later in which the viewer could sense the loving relationship between them. He couldn't bear to think about it now. There was more to Randi's story, he'd bet his company on it. Much more had happened. He watched her face closely, and by the way she looked away, the shuttering of her eyes, the tightening of her lips, he knew she held something back. Some key detail, given away further by a significant pause and the sadness in her voice when she resumed her story.

"That's also why you were close to Grandma and are still close to Grandpa. The three of them took turns watching over you at home, then rotated out to stay with me at the hospital. They brought you in at least once a day so you could sleep on me, which allowed you and me to bond as well, though not as strongly initially as you did with the others. You and I formed our own bond later. It was an extremely difficult time for them, and Wyatt debated long and hard about the right thing to do. He gave you his last name, but for the sake of history, he put Court's name on the birth certificate. In case you ever developed a medical condition and some day needed to track down your biological family."

Court tapped Drew on the shoulder and tilted his head toward the door. Both women had tears streaming down their cheeks, weeping as they sat on the floor and clung to each other. He reacted instinctively. They needed to share a moment of grief in which he and Drew had no part.

Once they cleared the room, Drew murmured behind him, "Scary thing, that."

"Hmm?" He looked at Drew over his shoulder as they walked back to the family room.

"Women crying."

"Oh, yeah. It's called the better part of valor to leave them to it. They don't much appreciate us rushing in with tissues and solutions while trying to shush them."

"Uh-huh. You're a lily livered pansy when it comes to emotional women."

"I've seen you do your fair share of running, mate."

"Possibly," Drew acknowledged. He stopped in the kitchen, dim from the fading light, to find a glass, then filled it at the sink. "I'm curious, did you ever love Mum?"

Neither of them reached for the light switch. Some discussions were better had in shadows. Especially when it came to topics with potentially damaging emotional content. Such as the question just asked. The question he'd never wanted to answer.

"I don't know." He shrugged when Drew's eyes narrowed their gaze on him. "I didn't love her the way I loved—love—the woman in the other room. I suppose what your mother and I felt came from years of knowing each other. I pulled her pigtails in nursery school. She threw rocks at me and circled the girls against the boys. We spent summers tramping through the woods searching for Pooh's beehive, looking for the honey." He hoped like hell Drew heard the mute appeal for understanding.

"I suppose you could say we felt comfortable with each other, enough to go through the motions, but we had no grand passion for each other. Life was predictable and routine with Bea. Nothing like the glorious turmoil my Jeannie—Randi—put me through the few short months we had."

Drew toyed with the glass in his hands, but didn't look up. "So you... chose her because of me."

"Yes and no. I chose her because it was the right thing to do as I saw it at the time. I convinced myself the adorable American had been an angel who'd come to me in a time of need. After the debacle with your mother, I felt very emasculated. My Jeannie-girl fixed it. She gave me back my pride and validated me as a man. In a very odd way, she made it easier for me to step up and accept my responsibility." Though he never had quite been able to forget the look on her face before she turned and ran from him.

Drew's eyes met Court's dead on, piercing despite the fading light. "And were you sorry for...being forced to marry her?"

"What are you saying?"

A rare flicker of doubt flashed through Drew's eyes, his next question coming slowly. "Did you ever regret…did you ever consider…abortion?"

"Hell no!" Court stared at his son. "You are the very best thing to come from that union, and not for one minute did I ever consider throwing you away. It wasn't your mess. I am, and have always been, very proud to be a father. Your father. Even if things had worked out differently, I never would have abandoned you."

Drew nodded, relief evident in his posture. "I believe you. You both tried, but I always knew there was something not quite right between you two. I didn't know parents shared a bedroom until I went to Eton and the other boys started talking. I didn't know parents talked, and laughed, and spent time together. But I always knew you loved me. Mum did as well, in her own way. Some days I had to work hard to see it. What, with all her mutterings about duty, you would have thought she was a martyr right up there with Gandhi." Drew shrugged. "Once she died, I saw the world from a different angle."

"About that…" Court started pacing again. "The accident…"

"I know. You'd just handed her divorce papers."

Court stopped and spun on his heel. "Yes. Wait. How did you know? I made certain you weren't around when I handed them to her."

"Should have looked at the drapes a little closer. You didn't see me. Neither of you did. I'd been sneaking looks at some of the, um…" Drew's face colored in a way rarely seen, "…art books and when the library door opened, I jumped behind the nearest drape. Terribly clichéd romance, I know, but the cliché fit then. I heard it all. First time I'd ever heard her lose it. So different from her normal, unemotional tone, I'd never seen her angry before."

Slowly shaking his head, Court continued. "I can tell you there were only a handful of times I'd ever heard any emotion in her voice, and I'd known her all my life. What finally gave me the leverage was I'd discovered she'd had a lover on the side. Had for years. As near as I can tell, it was a close call as to who had really impregnated her." Court held up a hand. "Let me assure you, you are indeed my son. On that I have *no* doubts. Especially after seeing you side by side with your sister."

Although a look of relief crossed his face, he didn't question his origin. "So you were going to use it against her in court?" Drew asked.

"Yes. I'd grown tired of living with a woman of ice. But what really tipped the scale was I'd discovered most of the money I gave her for charities all those years had actually supported her lover and their hideaway. But the divorce papers didn't set her off…"

"No, it was the custody issue," Drew interrupted. "Although the thought of divorce shocked me, in a way I was glad you told her you wanted full custody. At least you spent time with me and didn't make me go to tea parties. But it did send her around the bend, didn't it?"

"Yes." Court stared out the now dark window, his mood pensive. He didn't have to tell Drew she'd wanted the maintenance money, not so much the boy himself. "I didn't wish her dead, but in the end, well, I'm betting God knew best."

Court didn't know what to say afterward, and Drew seemed wrapped in his own thoughts. They'd been over the trauma so many times they didn't need to do it again. After the argument, Beatrice had stormed from the house only to wrap her car around a tree less than a mile down the road. Court still lived with guilt and occasionally dreamt of the emergency lights flashing in the dark, reflecting off the wet road which had contributed to the slide. He also knew, although Drew had suffered under his mother's intention to make him into a proper gentleman, he missed her on occasion. Court scrubbed a hand over his face, jet lag and the emotions of the day taking their toll as silence fell. After a moment, his attention shifted back to the women, and by the way Drew cocked his head, Court assumed he did as well.

Sounds of sobbing at the end of the hall had faded sometime during their talk, and both men listened, doing their best to look as if they weren't. Long minutes later, Randi and Birdie emerged, Randi slowly leading their return to the family room, Birdie refusing to look at anyone, a stubborn tension about her body. Randi's eyes were red and swollen, her face still reflecting deep distress. Maybe they hadn't worked things out yet.

Without speaking, glasses of water were filled and people drifted to their previous seats.

Birdie finally looked at him and Court waited. Without a doubt she had questions, and she had a right to interrogate him. He wanted her to accept him. Forgive him. At least make a start at a relationship, if not a father daughter one, then as friends. As much as they could be friends. Birdie was a grown woman, but a young one. A daughter, who would still needed to be mentored. She also had to accept the fact he would be a part of her mother's life from here on out. A part of her life, as well.

"All right." Birdie finally spoke. "I'm named for you. I want to hear your side in all of this."

"What do you want me to say? Essentially, your mother hit the basic facts. I didn't know she was pregnant. I tried to contact her to explain, but she shut me out. Refused phone calls, returned my letters unopened. By then, I was deep in my new job and new married life. It nearly destroyed me to lose her, but I also needed to man up to my life and did the best I could to make it work. At the moment, my heart is at once dancing with joy, yet torn with grief, and a touch of anger. Now I'm learning what I've missed out on these past two decades."

Birdie still looked wary, but somewhat more accepting. If he'd hoped in his deepest dreams she'd rush to him and cry out with joy at finding her true father, he was sadly mistaken. Clearly, they'd need time. Especially when it came to Drew, who Birdie refused to look at.

"I can't change the past," he said softly, hoping to reach her somehow. "But we can take charge of the future. You were raised by a good man. I'm happy for that. I can't take his place, nor do I want to. I want my own place in your life. We'll have to figure it out as we go. Same with you and Drew. Instead of potential lovers, you now each have a sibling to turn to when you need a friend. At least I hope you two can be friends."

Birdie, his daughter—the very thought still made him giddy—stared from one person to the next, her gaze altogether avoiding Drew. Still too embarrassing to think about? How close had those two grown in the last few hours? How close had they come to snogging?

"Well, that's fine for you all, but where does this leave me?" Clearly Birdie's period of silence was over. "I mean, I had a dad, and he was great, but now you're telling me he wasn't my father, I wasn't his daughter, and that my real father didn't know about me until today?" She leaped to her feet and finally addressed Drew, though she attacked him with accusations. "Is that why you chose Stanford? Had you heard something about my mom? Did you seek us out on purpose?"

Without letting the boy answer, she spun to Court, and he braced for the barrage he deserved. "And what about you? Drew told me his mom's been gone six years. Why haven't you tried to find us?"

"First of all"—Court held up both hands—"I didn't know about you. Second, I'd talked with her parents only enough to learn your mother had married. Within a month of leaving me." Bitterness twisted his heart, especially now he knew the whole story, or well, most of it. Still had the bit about Randi almost dying after the birth he wanted more details about. "In my book—my twisted, heartbroken, beaten down book—her marriage told me she hadn't really loved me. Especially when the three letters I sent her all came back unopened, marked addressee unknown. Remember, the male heart is a terribly fragile organ. I was afraid to go further. Never in my heart did I dare hope for a reunion half this wonderful."

Okay, so at the moment, it didn't feel particularly wonderful, but the fact he'd found Jean, his Jean, even though she used another name, made the day spectacular. Learning of Birdie sent it to the stratosphere. It was too big to contain inside his sorely abused heart. They'd work out the rest; he knew they would.

Nevertheless, by no means was Birdie done with him. "You can find out anything on the Internet these days, you could have kept searching."

"And do you know how many Jean Daileys there are in the world? In the US? There are over a hundred in this area alone, never mind what her married name might be," Court told her. "I know because I've had contact with a private investigator."

Oh, but his daughter was a beautiful woman. Even angry and bristling, she had a quality about her he'd seen in his mother and sister, only Birdie didn't have the training of a lifetime such as came with tradition. She was as wild and free as a palomino running across the plains in an old Western movie. A glorious creature. So like her mother in that regard.

"If I'd known about you," Court said quietly, "wild horses, hurricanes, and cruel women wouldn't have kept me away. I'd have demanded my right to know you."

Birdie eased back a little, confusion and uncertainty flitting across her face. But it didn't stop her long. The next, most obvious, target of her anger sat in the rocking chair, just as shaken as anyone in the room. Possibly second only to Birdie herself, though Court was high on the list.

"And you." She glared at her mother. "You married a man you didn't love. You had choices."

"I did. I made the best choice given the circumstances." Randi sat up in her chair, clearly wanting to go to her daughter, even more clearly afraid to. "As I said before, abortion never crossed my mind."

"Why not? You threw him away." Birdie waved a hand toward Court. "Why not throw me away as well?"

Randi paled as if she'd been slapped, then her lips firmed in a determined line and she stood, going toe to toe with Birdie. The fact she had to look up at her daughter didn't lessen the impact one bit. "You were the best thing out of the whole deal, and I'd do it all again if you were my only reward."

The entire room froze, and not one person twitched for at least one full minute.

"When Daddy died, did you think about looking *him* up?" Birdie stabbed an accusing finger directly at Court. "Didn't you say something about that earlier?"

Now there was a question Court wanted to hear the answer to. Had she thought of him, wondered about him?

"I love you, Birdie," Randi said quietly, breaking the silence. "I love you more than anything else on this earth, and so did your dad. You weren't neglected, and you never wanted for anything. And it wasn't because we felt guilty. My only guilt comes from the fact I didn't love Wyatt as much as he loved us. I tried. I really did, and ultimately, we were as happy as any married couple could reasonably expect. Happy enough that you never felt the lack of anything. And that counts for something. As for searching for Court... I was about to start the process, but you have to remember, your dad hasn't yet been gone two years. I'm still adjusting, still mourning. Wyatt and I had our own love story. I loved him in my own way, and I miss him very much. I always will."

Mentally shuddering at the travesty that had been his marriage, the years of emptiness filled only with Drew and the growth of the company, Court felt envious for a moment, then decided his marriage to Beatrice had been just punishment for letting Randi go. He'd paid, and now he was done paying. And the evening had taken a rather too intense turn.

Birdie still stared at her mother as if she were a stranger she never wanted to see again. Although Birdie didn't speak, she wasn't cold. No, she trembled and her skin held a flush of high color, blue eyes flashing like lasers. Not one bit of ice anywhere. If anything, she looked like a dormant volcano getting ready to blow off twenty years of pressure.

"Look," he said softly, and Birdie flinched ever so slightly. "This has all been rather..."

Randi turned to him. "Melodramatic? Ready for the Made-for-TV-Movie-of-the-Month?"

"I had in mind a poorly produced Shakespearean tragedy, but the results are the same." The corner of his mouth crept up.

Randi gave him a tired smile, and the stresses of the day seemed to sweep over her all at once. She'd shown signs of exhaustion on the doorstep, but she'd rallied. Any reserves she'd drawn on to make it through this confession were now used up. She turned to Birdie and touched her arm, rubbing lightly, trying to offer comfort to the young woman standing as still as carved marble. "Sweetheart, you and Drew were considering a soak in the spa. Why don't you two go ahead and then get a good long sleep. In the morning, we'll talk some more and figure things out. All right?"

Birdie shook herself, as if coming out of a dream. "Um... I don't really..."

"Come on, Bird." Drew stood and stretched. "We're still friends. Let's go boil and form evil plots of revenge against the parents. They deserve to be double teamed."

Startled, Birdie looked over her shoulder. "Uh—okay."

Randi dropped her hand and stepped back, when all she probably wanted to do was wrap her arms around her tall daughter. The daughter, without looking at her mother, or him, turned toward the bedrooms at the end of the hall off the family room.

"Let me get my car keys, and we'll get the bags," Birdie said.

"The old codger and I will get the bags," Drew said. "Get me your keys. I need to find those hideous swim togs you made me buy."

Birdie blushed but handed over the keys, and Court found himself following Drew out to the car.

"Good going, old lag," Drew drawled. "You really know how to bring down the house. A trick you picked up from some of your actress friends?"

"Funny." He grabbed his case from the boot. "I'm sorry I never knew about her."

Drew's hand landed on his shoulder. "Me too. Woulda been a little more fun having her around, then again, I can only imagine Mum's reaction."

Court barked out a short harsh laugh. "You think she didn't throw my love for 'that American' in my face as often as possible already? She was very careful to never say a word in front of you, but anytime she wished to share her misery, she used it like a knife. With those two birds in our lives…" He sighed. "The times with them would have been heaven, while the times with her, would have been unimaginable."

"Well, things happen for a reason, you always say. Suppose it will be clear eventually." Drew slung the strap of Birdie's bag over his shoulder and picked up his own case.

Court shut the boot lid. "You're right, and they do. I wish the lessons didn't always have to be so painful."

"Ah, but how much sweeter the victory, eh?" Drew gave him a wink.

"What do you think of all this?" Court leaned against the car. His son had his own way of interpreting events. How little Randi truly realized the accuracy of comparing the lad to a retriever. Drew took things in, mulled them around a little bit, adjusted his stride, and didn't waste time sweating over petty details, but he would keep going until he had every detail gathered up.

"Not sure yet. Bloody ironic, don't you think? I am a bit horrified that I came damn close to putting the moves on my own sister, though. Cut it a little fine on the timing, old man."

Court shuddered. "You caught us as we discussed the need to tell you two."

Drew grinned. "That's what you call discussing things?"

Court shot him a mock glare, but secretly, he loved the teasing. Drew had no issues with him pursuing Randi once more.

"However," Drew said. "Had I known I had a sister over here, I might have done a little more investigating before tripping her. Why didn't you tell me you were looking for an old flame?"

Court shrugged. "Didn't know I'd find her this trip or if ever. Didn't know what would happen if I did find her. Didn't want to make myself look any more foolish than possible. And since I never suspected the involvement of a child, I certainly never expected you to be trying to date your own sister."

They shared chagrined smiles.

Drew clapped his hand on Court's shoulder. "Going to start things up again with Randi?" He took two steps toward the house, then stopped and looked back. "Do I call her Randi or Mother?"

Stunned, Court paused mid-stride, and stared at his son. "Why would you want to call her Mother?"

"I miss having a mum, and if you're going to marry her... Think she'd mind being adopted? Just her ability to cook alone is worthy of the title." Without waiting for a reply, Drew strode into the house, leaving Court gobsmacked in the cooling evening.

From inside, Court heard Birdie ask Drew, "So, Kevin Westerfield is talking about me? Really?"

"He's a player and not touching my sister." Drew growled at Birdie who answered with a huff. If she had another comment, Court couldn't hear it as they moved deeper into the house. For a moment, it sounded exactly like Court and his sister Liza had nearly thirty years before.

He rubbed his face and turned his thoughts to his son. Drew missed a mum. All in all, he shouldn't be terribly surprised. Sure, Bea may not have been the most attentive mother in the world—or rather, attentive in the wrong way as far as Drew had sometimes complained—but a boy loved his mum no matter what. Apparently, he'd done his grieving. One more sign of his easy affection and relaxed nature. Where he got that from, Court could only speculate.

He drew in a lungful of fresh air. Cool, but not cold. The air felt soft and held the fragrance of autumn, wood smoke and the decay of fallen leaves. A few hardy flowers clung to their bushes in protected corners.

Overhead, the first twinkling stars had begun to appear as the last vestiges of dusk faded behind the hills to the west.

Laughter could be heard as car engines turned over and doors slammed. The flickering lights of TVs glowed from a few windows, shadows of people moved behind others. From where he stood he could see five homes gathered around the circle, each one looking into each other's windows and probably lives. Neighbors who watched out for each other. Neighbors who shared in the everyday dramas. Much like the one across the street watching him from the window. Court acknowledged him with a nod that was returned, letting him know Randi had someone watching over. As she should. Only now, it would be him taking main watch. The neighbor—Tuck, she'd called him?—moved to the backup position.

He could have lived here. He could have loved this life. How much better would life have been for him, for Drew, if they'd lived here with Randi and Birdie? Would it have been better for Drew, knowing he had a sister? How much more miserable would Beatrice have made his life if they'd shared custody but not a house? Would he have fought for shared custody or abandoned his son to Beatrice?

But there had been that other life. The one he'd chosen without knowing all the facts. The one he'd been bred by ten generations to live. If he envied the Americans anything, it was their clean slates. Most of them didn't know their true origins and didn't care. Centuries of ancestry didn't watch them from dusty oils hanging on gallery walls. Few of them had the burden of being landed gentry, carrying on the ancient traditions, acting as stewards for the next generation. Waiting their turn to be a portrait on the gallery walls.

His daughter had been raised here. She'd learned to walk, ride a bike, kick a ball, and swim. All in the arms of her mother and another man.

It should have been him.

"Court?"

Randi's soft voice reached into his heart and twisted it around her little finger. Instead of whining about the years he'd missed, he should be thankful for the years ahead, years to come, years spent with his girls. Not Wyatt's girls. Court's girls. Though Wyatt had done a fine job caring for them in his place. Couldn't hate a bloke for that.

"Court? Is there a reason we're heating the outside?"

Hiking the strap of his bag up over his shoulder, he spun around and found Randi standing on the threshold, hands over her bare arms, rubbing up and down to chase away the goose bumps he could see in the light from the fixture.

"Just taking in the neighborhood." He stepped toward her, hoping she'd hold her ground, but alas, she moved back, letting him into the house. The door shut with a satisfying thump and click as she turned the deadbolt lock.

Home.

Not his home, but home nonetheless. The building offered comfort, the decorating extended a welcome, but it was the small woman beckoning him to follow her that made him feel warm and content for the first time in more years than he wanted to count.

"Your room is this way."

If he'd thought she'd lead him to the master suite on the left, he was wrong. A shame, really, because he'd noticed the size of the bed in her room. Far too big for one tiny little woman. Instead, she led him toward the family room and then down the hall to the back of the house.

"Looks like Drew is taking the rollout in the workroom. You get the official guest room."

"Nice enough, but lonely looking." The room was adequate with a double sized bed, dresser, bedside table, and lamp spilling out a warm pool of light into the otherwise dim room. A large window looked out over the side yard shadowed beneath tall redwoods.

"If you don't like it, I can call a cab and have it take you to the hotel down the hill." The cold, un-Jean-like, acerbic tone was back. Easier to think of her as Randi when she used the less friendly attitude. He could fix that.

Court dropped his bag on the bed and caught her shoulders before she could escape. "That would be far more lonely."

Stiffening her shoulders, she pointed her little nose in the air. "I'm sure the concierge could set you up somehow. The local bar, possibly even a service dedicated to relieving the loneliness of business travelers."

"I don't want anyone else, thank you very much." He spun her in his arms, recapturing her shoulders. "Now that the cat's out of the bag, what about us?"

"What about us?"

The fathomless eyes gazed up at him, and he forgot the twenty-two year gulf between them. The second chance before them was a gift and not one he'd let be scuppered. She had to understand this very simple fact, right? They had Drew's blessing. How long before Birdie came around? How long before this woman came around?

"Now that we're reunited, how do we keep from being apart again?"

Randi slowly blinked at him like a sleepy owl. "Who says we're reunited? Reacquainted, certainly. Reunited? Not likely, mate."

"Oh, now she remembers her Brit-speak."

A hank of hair curled over her eye. Moving slowly, gently he combed it back.

"So soft," he murmured. "You always had the softest hair, the softest skin, the softest sighs."

"And a soft, weak center." The grimace said she remembered typing his four hundred page thesis. "Well, I'm not so weak anymore." Her eyes hardened, and she shrugged his hands from her shoulders, physically withdrawing even as he saw the emotional gap widening. "I'm tired, and I'm going to bed now. Sleep as late as you like. The day after Thanksgiving is usually a slug day for us."

Retreat. She needed it for a bit. A chance to think things over and come around. Perhaps she had the right idea. A night to clear the head, so to speak. A chance to allow things to look better in the morning. So he returned to lighthearted banter. "What? You don't join the masses before sunrise and storm the stores? The newspapers and ads on the telly today made it seem all the thing."

"Not a chance. Did it once, refuse to do it ever again. I tend to make the gifts I give for Christmas rather than buy them. Sometimes, we travel instead. Birdie and I took my father to Mexico last year."

"Christmas in Mexico? Away from the home fires?"

Head tilted and eyes narrowed, she gave the impression she felt the answer more than obvious. "What do we have to stay home for? Birdie's grown and Dad's alone. Anyhow, bathroom is across the hall. You get to share it with the kids. Towels are on the counter."

He gave it one last shot, one more chance for her to invite him in. "Where will you be if I need you?"

"On the other side of the house, behind a locked door. Goodnight."

For a moment, she looked as if she had something else to say, but she turned away, leaving him in the guest room. He wanted to chase after her, but weariness visibly hung on her shoulders. Sounds came from the kitchen, and then lights dimmed. For tonight, he'd let things rest. But tomorrow, well now, that was a whole new day.

# Chapter 10

Randi closed her bedroom door, but chose not to lock it. The inner hussy half of her wished Court would ignore her warnings and storm her walls, just as he already had twice today. Third time's the charm, right? In this case, the old saying might be very true.

Hand to her forehead—as if she could hold in her brains—she closed her eyes and sighed. The drama of the day had gotten to her. Nothing a long soak in hot water followed by several hours of sleep wouldn't cure.

Still in darkness, she wandered to the bay window in the sitting alcove where she had her desk and computer. Bare feet registered the change from soft deep pile carpet to cool hardwood in the little office area. Out in the spa, Birdie and Drew lounged on opposite sides. Jets stirred up a froth of bubbles, sending ribbons of steam upward, giving the illusion of boiling the occupants. Underwater lights provided an eerie glow. Birdie threw back her head and laughed at something Drew said. The grip around Randi's heart loosened a bit. Thank God for Drew and what appeared to be his well-balanced personality. Although, he *had* displayed a lawyer's ability to ask seemingly innocuous, yet probing, questions. *Definitely one to watch,* she thought with a smile.

At least those two seemed to have found common ground. Parents who'd screwed up their lives. Mothers who'd screwed up their lives. Good. An ally for Birdie could only be a good start. Drew apparently wouldn't let her feel embarrassed over the obvious interest they'd been showing, and he seemed recovered from his own interest in her. It hadn't gone far enough it couldn't be redirected into a deeper friendship and alliance. If they used common sense, they'd each put down their instant attraction as recognizing a sibling and move forward.

With a stop at her dresser to remove her jewelry and put it away, she moved into the bathroom, shedding clothing as she went. Each piece deposited in the right basket. Dry cleaning and delicates. Light and dark.

Bath or shower? The simple decisions seemed insurmountable, but since she didn't want to mess with wet hair, she dropped the plug and started the tub filling. Cream cleanser took off what little remained of her makeup, pins held her hair up and, with a groan, she slipped into the sunken, tile-lined tub. Close the glass door, flip a lever, and she'd have a shower, but not tonight.

Tonight.

Talk about a way to drain emotions to the nth degree. As much as she needed to think about it, she couldn't. Her brain had grown numb. Short circuited. Fried. Shut down. She listened to the sound of the water and lazily used her toe to shut off the taps when the level rose high enough.

She must have drifted off because the next thing she knew, her chin dipped into cold water and shivers wracked her frame. Too tired to risk falling asleep again, she drained the tub and vigorously toweled the water away in an attempt to bring warm blood to the surface. She hurried to her bed, burrowing deep into the flannel sheets with the down comforter drawn up around her ears, leaving only her nose sticking out. The digital numbers on the clock glowed green; eleven-thirty-eight. Two hours? No wonder she'd become one of the pickled, the frozen, the foolish.

Thirty minutes later, still shivering, she pulled on a thick terry robe, shoved her feet into shearling slippers, and shuffled into the kitchen where only a dim under-cabinet light illuminated the silent house.

Once the kettle sat on the stovetop to heat, she reached into the cabinet for her favorite mug and a tea suitable for the moment.

Ah, somehow her mug had been pushed to the back, and behind it, a single tin of Earl Grey. The last of what she bought by special order each year. She could taste it now and wondered…

"Ah, so you lied earlier."

Randi screamed and dropped the tea tin, the crash of it as loud as gunfire in the sleeping house. Grabbing the first thing in reach, she swung with mug in hand to beat the intruder.

"Whoa! I'm not prepared to die by tea mug."

Court stood in the dim light, hands raised, chest bare over long flannel bottoms draped around his hips. Hair rumpled and feet bare, her every dream of the last twenty-two years come to life. Only better, because of his perfect physical presence.

"Hand over the mug, slowly now, and no one gets hurt." With exaggerated care, he reached for the purple mug and removed it from her hand by uncurling the fingers clenched in a death grip around the handle.

Heart beating so hard she feared it might leap from her chest if she didn't fall over from a heart attack first, she slapped his arm with her free hand. "Don't. You. EVER. Sneak up on me like that again!"

"All right, but for future note, in what way should I sneak up on you?"

Shaking, as much from cold as fright, she glared at him. So like him to make a joke at a time like this. A pathetic joke. She had to remember moments like this to stay strong against falling for his easy charm.

For in truth, as easy as it would be, going back, picking up a relationship with Court would be exactly the wrong thing to do. Birdie's reaction earlier tonight had made it very clear. Suddenly, all her plans to move ahead with her life, even the part about just thinking about starting to date again, seemed selfish. How could she even pretend she could *think* about a relationship with any man right now? She had her daughter to consider, their relationship to repair, before she could even maybe sort of dream of starting a new one. Even with an old love. Especially with an old love. Okay, specifically Court, Birdie's biological father. Too much baggage, too many old hurts, too many miles down that road. Going back was a bad plan. The wrong plan.

All clear to her now, she shook her head at the research project she'd been about to start. No need for it now. Court could answer Birdie's questions as the research had been intended to give her a picture of her father. No problem. She had a good start on getting all the details she could ever want. No need to worry about chasing down mysterious family histories in the case of—God forbid—catastrophic illness.

Court set the cup on the counter, one hand still holding her. "You're quaking. Not just a little trembling, but nearly enough to register on those earthquake monitors, or what is it you Californian's call them? Richter scales?" The twinkle in his eye gave him away. He knew exactly what he was talking about.

"I'm...c-c-c-cold." She tried to pull her hand away, and not be charmed by his teasing, but Court stepped closer and tugged her up against him, trapping her icy hands between them, resting on his very warm chest. She had to give him credit for not flinching. "An-an-and you s-c-c-c-cared me."

Breath choppy, head light, and knees weak, she didn't fight, but let him snuggle her close. Oh, but he smelled good, warm, and just like...Court. She buried her nose against his lightly stubbled neck, and he pulled her tighter until she felt her body shift into alignment with his, strong arms banding about her securely, comfortingly. Just being held against all that heated male skin nearly made her cry for the cruelty of being alone so long. The months and years of being on her own stretched out in front of her, a future when she couldn't even possibly start a new relationship. It just hurt too much to think about right now.

His chest expanded on a deep breath, and she felt a rumble from deep inside vibrate against her heart, tempting her with the promise of a future full of hugs just like this. Hadn't he said they could be together forever? Hadn't he implied that was exactly what he wanted? Or had he said it outright? She couldn't remember, but since she couldn't even think about thinking about such things…

Before her mind could take off on a flight of the imagination and talk her rational side into getting swept up in the fantasy of dreaming about just such a future, he spoke, his voice soft and very close to her ear. "I didn't mean to scare you. I did make noise, but you were enthralled by the tin of Earl Grey you said you didn't have."

"I'm t-t-tired and c-c-cold," she said through still chattering teeth, refusing to answer his accusation. She had reasons, which she had no intention of sharing with him. Hadn't she just decided he wasn't to be an intimate part of her life? Therefore, he didn't need to know any more about her. Or her ritual of self torture involving Earl Grey tea.

His head dipped over hers. "I see that, I feel it, and your little heart is racing to beat the band. Why are you cold?"

"Fell asleep in the bath."

"Thinking a cup of hot tea would take the chill away?"

Almost as well as he could just by holding her like this, but that was another thing he didn't need to know. "Yes."

"A good start, but I know a better way."

His hands rubbed up and down her spine as if to stimulate her blood flow. It worked. Very well, in fact. Might not need the tea after all, actually. Damn. Wasn't she old enough to be immune to this sort of thing? Where was menopause when a woman needed it? A hot flash would come in handy right about now. Another life moment stolen from her by her illness so long ago.

It would be so easy to stay here, to accept his comfort, to start up right where they'd left off in London. The part in the morning. Then she remembered the reception and the utter devastation she'd felt at his betrayal. The pain ripped through her as strong as it had then. "Stop."

Unable to bear the old feelings, she tried to pull away, but he held her closer.

"Stop what? I just said I know a better way to warm you up, that's all. Or are you letting your brain get in the way? I've told you before not to over-think things."

Frustrated, and thankful for the darkness hiding the rush of heat to her face, she slapped his chest. "If you're thinking skin to skin, think again."

"I look at you, and I remember skin to skin, or at least I think I do. It's been so long I think I need a refresher." The quizzical look on his face was amusing, and seductive, and working at the long hidden feelings she'd meant to keep buried deep, but she wouldn't let him know it. Not if she could in any way help it.

"Funny."

He so didn't believe her, because she could hear the smile in his voice when his lips brushed the top of her head. "Which tea do you want? I'll make it up and bring it to you."

Suspicion crept in, and she made no attempt to hide it. "Bring it to me where?" She pushed away far enough to look up at him.

Face as innocent as an angel, he spoke slowly and patiently, as if she were a young child. "You go snuggle up in bed, and I'll bring your tea."

Randi stared at him for a long moment, then nodded, as all the battle drained out of her in an instant. Why fight? He'd be gone in a few days, possibly as soon as tomorrow, why not take a little comfort, a touch of someone thinking about her? She'd grown used to Wyatt taking care of her, and for just a few moments, she wanted to be pampered again. Just a little bit. Just one mug of tea, what harm could come from that?

Court turned her around and gently shoved her toward the kitchen door. "Flavor?"

She considered her options, then shrugged. "Surprise me."

A test, and he knew it. He'd once told her an Englishman knew how to send messages just by the tea he picked to serve. Sort of like the language of flowers. Of course she'd never ever heard any reference to such a ritual involving tea, however, Court insisted it existed. Even crossed his heart to prove his sincerity.

After a week together and watching her fascination with all things British, he'd started the game, bringing small samples of different teas and reading off their list of attributes to her. Darjeeling for celebration, English Breakfast for a bright start, oolong, black, Formosa, Ceylon, green, and any odd blend he could find. But Earl Grey had been their constant. They'd explored every variation of the tea until they found the blend she'd enjoyed most, and he'd learned to appreciate it anew with her, or so he'd said. Had he mentioned it earlier to test her? Then of course, he'd had to catch her with a tin of it in her hand. Damn the man.

In her bedroom, she started to climb into bed, still wrapped in her robe and slippers, then decided flannel pajamas and socks would be the better choice. The robe offered too little of a barrier between her and the man about to enter her bedroom.

From the kitchen came the soft whistle of her kettle, its boiling protest short-lived. Only a few minutes until Court would join her, she hurried into her deep closet, one of two that opened into the bathroom. Where had those PJs gone? These days, she mostly slept in an old T-shirt of Wyatt's, so it took digging through several drawers before she found them buried beneath some old sweaters. She'd just shed the robe when Court called from the bedroom.

"Randi? I see the bed, but it's empty."

"Just a minute."

"Where are you?"

"I'll be out in a minute." She pulled the top of the mannish pajamas over her head, muffling her words. She'd just bent over, trying to get a leg into the bottoms, when Court appeared at the doorway.

"I didn't hear... Oh, there you are."

Startled, she straightened, one leg in, one leg out.

"Oh, no need to bother with those on my account." Court's smile produced a surge of heat in her blood completely unrelated to tea. "In fact, I insist you leave them off. A shame to cover your mouth-watering little bum."

Embarrassed, she laughed. "Little. Right." Shivering still, she managed to step into the other leg and jerk the bottoms up. "I haven't had a little bum since I was, oh, little. I said I'd be right out." Keeping her face turned away, she dug in another drawer until she found a pair of thick slouchy socks.

"I couldn't hear what you said, so I came looking."

Well, he certainly was looking. She could damn near feel his gaze trying to see beneath the worn fabric, but the pajamas were too loose to reveal much. A pair she'd purchased for Wyatt, they hadn't worked for him, so she'd trimmed the arms and legs and hemmed them to fit her while keeping the baggy fit. Perfect for cold, lonely winter nights. Now she'd found them, she'd start wearing them again. Socks in hand, she brushed past Court and marched toward the bed.

"If you think those old pajamas decrease your sex appeal, think again." Court laughed as he followed her, snapping out the lights and plunging the suite into darkness but for the bedside lamp. "Damn, I think they might be sexier than a silk negligee."

"Why am I not surprised?" she muttered. Where the covers were already pulled back, she turned to sit on the edge of the bed. Two heavy mugs sat on the bedside table, steam curling into the air, their murky depths softened with cream.

"Two sugars, right?"

"Not anymore, but it'll do for now." She kept her attention directed at pulling the socks on. When the first one proved difficult, Court took the sock from her and knelt, his big hand heating her skin before he slid the sock up over her foot. Before she could protest, he slipped the second one on, his hand lingering only a moment on her calf.

"You're half frozen," he said.

"I told you so. I'm quite capable of figuring out the inadequacies of my body temperature." She tried to swing her feet up, but he stopped her.

"You're cold enough that this calls for desperate measures."

"What?"

Without answering, he plumped up the pillows, lifted her, then sat with his back supported by the headboard, and settled her between his bent knees, her back to his bare chest. "This would work faster without the flannel between us." A deft twitch of his wrist flung the covers over them. With a few tugs, he had her perfectly cocooned.

"But—"

He picked up one mug and carefully pressed it into her hands. "Here, wrap your fingers around that until it cools enough to drink. It's decaf."

Stunned by his take charge attitude, she did as he said, offering no resistance when he wrapped himself around her from behind. Strong arms and muscular legs embraced her. A solid presence when she needed it most, instinctively she leaned against him, seeking his body heat. Sure, Court had always had a confident manner about him, but their first time in bed he'd been careful, almost hesitant, thereafter always treating her as if she were the finest porcelain. While no less careful now, he'd lost the traces of tentativeness, touching her and holding her like a man who knew his way around a woman. A man who handled them regularly. All the more reason to leave the past in the past.

"Now, what were you doing in the bathtub?"

"Trying to relax enough to go to sleep." Like she'd be able to do that now with him around her like cling wrap.

His chuckle rumbled in his chest, the vibration a comfort at her back. "And yet, you fell asleep in the tub?"

"Yes."

"How long were you in there?"

"An hour or so," she said and shrugged. "Maybe closer to two." Lifting the mug, she inhaled and recognized the English breakfast blend. A sense of relief slipped into her. Court had taken the neutral angle at the moment, saving the big guns for later.

"Why didn't you just pour in more hot?"

She shrugged again. "Too tired. Too pruned."

Gentle fingers slipped under her hair and touched her neck. More shivers rippled through her, but this time not from cold. In fact, waves of warmth were beginning to sink into her, melting the outer icy layer.

"Drink your tea. If you want more, the second mug is for you as well, if not, I'll drink it."

"One should do me." She blew across the top of the steaming liquid and gingerly tested. "Perfect." She sighed.

He'd always known how to brew it perfectly. Then again, he'd taught her to drink it the British way. The only way, he'd once haughtily informed her, sending her into gales of giggles. Which she'd paid for in kisses and tickles that had turned into something more. Another shiver traveled down her spine, this one making her body clench and the warmth settled right between her legs. A sip of tea chased more heat downward, straight to her stomach.

"Hm, yes, perfect," he murmured a moment before his lips touched her neck.

"Stop," she protested, admittedly in a very weak manner considering the ripple of raised goose bumps on her skin. Gasping out such words hardly indicated a serious frame of mind.

"Stop, what?"

Damn him for ignoring her. "Please, stop…that." Oh Lord, his lips, right there…

Court kissed her, so softly she barely felt it, and yet, she felt nothing else, the small hairs on her neck stood up, reaching for him, stretching in erotic ecstasy. The little hussies. Didn't they know any better than to encourage him?

"This? You want me to stop this?" His breath touched her like fairy wings.

"Yes."

"Now I'm confused. Yes, this is the spot you like best? Or yes, this is what you want me to stop?"

His lips moved over her skin, skimming, tickling, sensuously torturing.

"Court, stop playing with me."

"But darling, what I do best, and want most, is to play with you. Drink your tea. Besides, this will warm you faster than anything else known to man."

"Court." He'd surely stolen her brains. Damn the man. A huge yawn snuck in and consumed her. The aftermath left her eyes watering, her body more relaxed. She gave up resisting and cuddled closer to Court.

"Drink up, my Juliet. No poison in this brew. Only tea to reheat you from the inside out."

Entranced by his voice, she tipped the cup at her lips and gulped down the contents. A little hotter than she liked for fast drinking, nonetheless he had a point. Heat, delicious melting heat, spread outward, racing along her veins and nerves.

"There you go, guzzling like an office worker on a five minute break." Court took the mug from her weakening fingers. "More?"

She shook her head and leaned it against one powerful bicep. This felt so very, very nice. She folded her hands against her chest and drew her knees up close. When Court lifted the other mug and drank, she could hear him gulping it down, the aroma of the tea, sweet and creamy, comforting in a long ago familiar way. With a final shudder, her body thawed out, relaxing completely, soaking in the heat faster and faster, making her feel heavy and limp.

"Sleepy, darling?"

"Yes." Her eyelids drooped and another yawn invaded, stealing control of her body for a minute.

Court shifted behind her, but it didn't matter, she had no energy to move. The light snapped off and darkness settled like another blanket. Only for a second did her logical brain scream out the dangers of this idea. The rest of her was too sleepy to listen.

"Warm now?"

"Umm-hmm."

His chuckle rumbled against her back. "Great powers of seduction I have if the first time in twenty-two years I get you into bed you fall asleep on me."

"But—"

His lips on her temple cut off her protest. "I know, darling. Long day on your feet, and your emotions trampled all over. Wonderful feast, by the way. Now rest." His hand smoothed her hair as they sank down to the mattress. "Sleep, love. We'll deal with seduction later," he whispered into her ear as her eyes closed.

"Sleep," she murmured. "Stay."

"I'm not going anywhere."

# Chapter 11

Awake, his body still on London time, Court snuggled his Jeannie in his arms, the covers pulled up around them, but mostly around her. He wasn't the cold one. In fact, a dousing of cold water would work rather well right now. Her sweet little bum wiggled into the bend where his hips fit behind her. If he grew any harder, her tushie was in danger. Worn and thin, her flannels didn't offer much of a barrier. One firm tug and they'd be crotchless, which suited his frame of mind just fine.

Lord, he needed to get the mind off making love with her. The day's events should have exhausted him as they had her, but his mind was alive, and his body awake in a way he barely remembered. The jolt had hit him the moment Birdie had pulled Randi from the kitchen and into the foyer.

The sight of her in such a way, flushed and startled, the shock to his system had been almost too much to recover from. But not quite. Too many years of polishing his sophisticated demeanor had made it possible to hand her the flowers, and even to flirt just a little. Ignoring the primitive impulse to grab her and take her against the wall had used all his will. Keeping himself from following through in the loo had tested the boundaries of his self control. And now, with her in his arms—he ruthlessly swallowed the growl of his primal beast along with the driving need to seize her, consume, and possess her.

So many thoughts to process. Now he'd found her, what next? Did he convince her to move to London or open an office in San Francisco? With Drew's interest in China, that might not be a bad idea. But more important, what had Randi been doing with her life, and would she give it up or modify it to be with him? The questions built so fast they threatened to fry out the few remaining working cells in his brain. For now, he just needed to be in her presence, breathe in the essence of her, just be with her. Holding, touching, watching her, listening to the music of her voice, reveling in the magic of her. The time to rediscover the beauty of her heart. Just to be. With her. And Birdie.

His daughter. A near-perfect, smaller replica of her brother. He needed time with her. Time to talk. Time to fill in the blanks of the past two decades.

Now that they'd found each other, they'd have time. He'd make sure of it, because he sure as hell wasn't letting go. Not for any reason.

Watching Randi sleep, as he had their final week in London, he relived every moment of their last night together. Dinner over lamb stew and wine. The shower of rose petals he'd dropped on her in bed. Their night lit by a single candle and the street lamps from outside her flat.

He'd made do with a bedsit, bathroom down the hall, in a crowded rooming house, but she'd had a tiny studio flat. The important thing, she'd once told him, being she had her own bathroom and micro kitchen. Yanks, he'd teased her, but secretly, he'd enjoyed the luxury of the bath after they'd discovered the delights of making love in a tub. Briefly he thought of the spa outside. Later, he'd find a way to make love to her there.

All his thoughts came back to the one theme. Making love to his Jean. Randi. Jean. Whatever name she used, one fact held true; she belonged with him.

Apparently, the reminders were still there for her as well. When he'd brought in the tea and set it on the table beside the bed, he'd seen the paperback and remembered. The one perfect rose she'd saved from the bouquet before he pulled the blooms apart to drop the petals on her. She'd tucked it between the pages, in the middle of the big love scene. Before finding her in the closet tonight, he'd lifted the book and carefully fanned the pages. There, right where she'd read to him, the dried bud, its faded fragrance a gentle perfume drawing out the sweetest memories. Eager to touch her, he'd called out and heard her muffled reply from somewhere deep inside the *en suite*.

She sighed in his arms, a tiny smile touching her lips. She shifted, pulling his arms closer about her as she turned her head. The Second Coming couldn't have stopped him from kissing her cheek. That was so sweet he kissed her jaw. One kiss led to another until she turned enough he could kiss her lips.

"Court." His name left her lips on a sigh so soft he almost didn't hear it.

"Jeannie." He nipped her lip, loving the way she parted for him, her breath a teasing whisper he breathed in. If it killed him, he'd hold back tonight. All her defenses were down, and she had every right to be angry with him. He also thought she might be talking in her sleep. Thank

God it was his name on her lips. It gave him hope that forgiveness was already taking place.

She and Birdie were wrong about one thing, though. He *had* come looking for them. Randi, actually. Birdie had been a bonus. This warranted a call to the private investigator. Didn't need the man's services any longer. Should he insist on DNA testing? Probably not a politically correct move, as volatile as Birdie's reaction had been to the discovery. Besides, in his heart he knew it wasn't necessary.

Randi made the last quarter turn, which brought her front flush with his.

Sweet mercy, the quake that shot through him when her thigh gently connected with his groin made him see stars. He grabbed her leg and moved it away, trapping it firmly between his knees. The little she-devil moaned, frustrated at his diversion. Right, she felt frustrated. He'd made a gentleman's vow to keep his hands to himself, but here she was, teasing, pushing, cuddling up to him as if they'd never been apart.

"Sleep, darling. You need sleep."

"Mmm," she mumbled something he didn't quite understand. Agreement or denial? Sounded like denial to him, but maybe it was her hand resting on his pecs that made it seem that way. She snuggled into him, nestling her nose against his throat. "Warm."

"Yes, darling, I'm glad you're warm. I'm toasty myself. Sleep, Jeannie."

She settled, seemingly drifting deeper, and he breathed a sigh of relief. Should she choose to turn her wicked lips loose on him, he'd be lost. A poor excuse for a gentleman trying to not take advantage of a lady. A lady he wanted for more than just one night.

What were those scores from the game last week? Manchester United versus Everton. Then again, forget football, being in the middle of a good rugby scrum would work about now.

Randi's hair drifted, teasing his forearm with the sleek silkiness of it. Satin smooth and smelling of sunshine, turkey, vanilla, and just the barest hint of roses, he wanted to feast on her.

Now that she'd warmed up, he should slip from the bed and get his phone. Yesterday may have been an American holiday, but the rest of the world had kept moving. There were surely messages and e-mails he needed to deal with. The quiet of the sleeping household would make this the ideal time to get some business done. But with her in his arms, he didn't want to let go for anything. No business deal was worth the pain of leaving her at this very moment. It could all wait.

Leaving. The very thought sent a chill through him. Sunday, just two short days away, he was due to climb on a plane and return to England.

Not an attractive prospect on his part. A rapid mental review of his upcoming schedule didn't allow hope for staying longer. The contract with Attenborough had already been set back a week and to put it off longer would hurt both sides. Could the meeting be held in New York? Would Randi like to take a trip? Could he bribe her with shopping?

The flexing of her little hand over his pecs made him think of bribing her another way. Her palm slid until her fingers framed one of his nipples and he suppressed a groan. In an effort to forestall further explorations, he pulled her close, redirecting her arm around his waist.

It was a hell of a thing to be in bed, embracing the woman who'd been in his dreams for half his life and not be able to make love to her. She trusted—trusted! the silly chit—that he would hold her and keep her safe. Safe from what, now there was the question of the century. Safe from himself? Was that the insult or the injury?

Finally, she drifted into a deep sleep, and half aroused, he relaxed enough to join her, pulled under by the dregs of jet lag.

\* \* \* \*

In her dream, warmth invaded everything. The soft blanket around her became a living, breathing entity, there solely for the purpose of keeping her warm. Slowly, she drifted out of the soft layers of sleep only to wonder at the arms around her. Court's scent soothed her, forestalling any panic she might have felt. This felt right in a way she barely remembered. One arm pillowed her head, the other rested across her waist, his hand inside her pajama bottoms, cupping one rounded cheek. Her vow to leave their past behind them seemed silly now. It had been so long, surely she deserved some comfort. A woman needed to touch and be touched. Oh how she longed to touch all that glorious, warm skin.

Moving slowly, she pressed her lips to his neck. One night, one chance to share the best part of what they'd had, just one more time. They could do this without dredging up all those messy emotions, couldn't they? One night, one weekend, catch up, share some loving for old times' sake, then say goodbye, this time knowing their paths would most likely cross again someday. They could be sometimes lovers. Maybe.

But now, just for now, she needed this. Needed him. Only he could fill the yawning emptiness consuming her.

Unless she was mistaken and the thing poking her in the stomach didn't indicate his need for her, well then, she'd been out of the game far too long.

\* \* \* \*

As far as erotic dreams went, this one beat anything he'd ever previously dreamed. In his arms, his own sweet Jeannie moved her body against his. At some point, she'd grown lush curves. Nothing outrageous, just a little more padding filled out her breasts and added sassy curves to her hips, making them easier to hold. But it was Jeannie, just as he'd dreamed of her so many times, in so many ways. No one had ever touched him the way she had, in person and in every dream since their short time together so long ago.

But this dream topped them all. This dream came so close to real he could almost swear...

Soft lips closed around the head of his cock and wet heat wrapped him in an ecstasy that popped his eyes open.

Good Lord. Every prayer answered, Court groaned his thanks to his maker as his hand gripped her by the hair. "Jeannie-mine, my love..."

The wonderful sensation stopped as she lifted her head just enough to speak. "Oh good, you're awake." Warm breath bathed him. Soft lips brushed his skin.

"You don't have to stop on my account."

"Don't worry," she said with a truly evil chuckle. "Though I'm a little out of practice." She spoke so that her lips moved over the very tip. "But after counseling teens once they started to attract boys, I have to ask, how bad have you been? Girlfriends? One night stands? Women of convenience?"

"No one serious. I swear. No girlfriends, no one important." One or two friends who preferred to keep things discreet and as emotionally detached as possible. Divorcees who didn't want to mess up their settlements. If she pressed, he'd confess to those, but no way would he admit to anything else. Those days were now the past and only she mattered. "I have condoms in my luggage if they'd make you feel, um, more comfortable?" Any more comfortable and he'd have a heart attack. Out of practice? Not from his view.

"Hmm." The vibration around his cock grew electrifying, her hair brushing his hip sweet torture.

"Sweetheart? Darling? Please, don't keep me dangling like some poor worm about to be drowned." He'd been reduced to begging in less than twenty-four hours.

"You aren't dangling."

Well, no, he wasn't quite, but she had him at her mercy. He'd lived at the mercy of Beatrice long enough that he recognized the situation quite well. Only in this case, he liked it. He liked this form of sweet dominance from this woman and the way she took him in hand. Or in mouth, or both as it were, and swirled her tongue around him, just like...

"Oh, darling, yes, you remember…"

Her mouth closed about him once more, so very wet her saliva dripped down the length of his cock in a new sweet torture. She chased it, licking, sucking, working her tongue along his length, her mouth sheathing him until…oh sweet…

"Jesus!" When had she learned that trick? Her tight little throat convulsed around him and his entire body clenched, straining to hold back the fire of his semen coming to a boil. Just as he was about to let go, she pulled off, leaving him waving in the cool breeze.

Desperate, he reached for her, but she moved out of reach, sitting back on her heels.

"Jeannie…" he warned, but the cheeky wench just laughed at him.

"Done being the gentleman, Court?"

That did it. She'd provoked him enough. In one fluid motion, he rose up, and with forward momentum pushed her backward until her head lay near the footboard. It took only a nanosecond to realize her pajamas had disappeared. Probably somewhere around the time his had. "Been busy, haven't you?" His body covering hers, he settled between her sweet, soft, and smooth thighs. "Good thing you have such a big bed."

"I guess so." She laughed up at him, but he held the upper hand. Oh yes, she'd pay for her teasing.

In the shadows made deeper by the canopy of gauzy silk panels draped from the massive carved wooden frame of her bed, he found her hands and wrestled them over her head where he held them with one hand. To silence her laughter, he took her mouth, kissing her like a parched man at the fountain of youth, plundering, conquering, his tongue accepting only her surrender. So much for her mirth. Satisfaction filled him as she responded, kissing back and writhing beneath him, soft skin rubbing against him, and more he wanted to explore. Whimpers rose from the back of her throat, but he'd be damned if he'd give in to her carnal demands just yet. He'd waited so very long, needing her more than he needed air, and didn't want to rush like the youth he'd been.

With his free hand, he touched her, eagerly relearning every surface of her body with his fingertips. He traced the shape of her jaw, the downy softness of her cheek, the long sleek column of her throat down to the delicate structure of her collarbone. Still ticklish, she bucked and moaned as he trailed his fingers over the sensitive skin of her underarm. Ah, that was fun, but he wanted her compliant, not battling, so he moved on to explore the outer curve of her breast. The softest skin he'd touched yet, he lingered, stroking, teasing the flesh, torturing the woman. Communicating how much she liked it with her kiss, she sucked on his tongue as she had his cock. In fact, if he didn't take care, that very randy part of him would slip right inside her before he had a say in the timing.

He eased the kiss, puffing like a long distance runner, but able to speak. "Do not move your hands," he ordered. "Move your hands and I'll stop."

"Damn you," she swore without any heat.

"Do you want me to stop now?" He toyed with her skin, delicately stroking the side of her breast, following the rounded base of it, his fingers moving slowly, up and over, down and around.

"No, dammit, don't stop."

"Such a dirty mouth you've grown."

"Court," she said with a growl and tried to lift her pelvis, whether to unseat him or get him better situated, he wasn't sure, but either way it felt fantastic, her soft, wet, heat erotically cradling him.

Lightheaded, he didn't fight the instinct to slide over her flesh just once. So perfect. She fit him just right. No one had ever matched as perfectly as she did.

"Hold onto the post if you need to, but if your arms come down, I'll stop. Understood?"

She groaned, but reached for the thick post as soon as he released her wrists.

"Do you understand? Say it, Randi." In time, possibly, he could get used to that name. Randy daily. It certainly seemed to fit, and he grinned in the dark at the thought of loving her daily. He could see to it she stayed randy, just for him.

"Yes. Yes, I understand. There. Happy?" She grumped at him, but he knew it was all bluff.

"Oh yes, very happy. Now enjoy the ride." He shifted so both hands held her breasts, circling, pushing them upward, her nipples like cherries on top of a decadent dessert against his lips.

She wasn't quite big enough he could hold her nipples side by side, but each breast was a bountiful handful, warm, and the skin so unbelievably soft, and pliable.

"You're perfect." He suckled one nipple, then used his teeth to lightly tug when she arched up, seeking more. "I just wish I could see you."

She stiffened as if ready to push him away. "No!"

"No?" Now she had his curiosity up. "What don't you want me to see? Hmm?" He suckled the other, equally responsive, nipple into his mouth, and she melted back onto the bed. "Got a racy tat?"

"You'd have to stop too long, and I don't want you to."

"I'll let it go for now, but I will turn on the light sooner or later."
He switched back to the first nipple and smiled at the deep shudder that
moved through her.

"Just don't stop... not now." The breathy plea fanned the
flame inside him.

Loving the suppleness of her breasts, he buried his face between them
and inhaled. A few hours of warmth, sleep and arousal had brought out
the delicate fragrance his body remembered. She was here, and his, this
night, and as much as he wanted to plunge into her and drive them both
insane, he wanted to savor. Remember. Rediscover. Draw it out as long
as humanly possible. With his goal in mind, he began licking a small
trail around her breast. Tiny touches of his tongue left damp dots on her
skin like the short white lines on the road. Dashes that spiraled up to the
delicious peak where he indulged in suckling until she writhed, arching
and pressing her breast up into his mouth. Then he pulled back and blew a
gentle breeze over the path, chilling the now cool spots. Writhing changed
to a sensuous shiver.

Panting, she twisted, presenting the other breast for the same. Ah yes,
the Libra in her. Everything must be balanced. Equal treatment for all
parts. He could do that. If anything, he drew out the teasing longer on the
second breast, smiling to himself at how she quivered and moaned.

"Dammit, Court. Dig in the drawer, grab a condom, then get up here
and take care of me."

In the process of inching his way down her body, he paused just above
her belly button. "You have wellys?"

"Wellys? Aren't those rubber boots?"

"Rubbers, wellys, johnnys, condoms, all the same. Why do
you have them?"

"Girlfriends. Gag gift. I tossed them in the drawer." She tried to sit up,
but he held her down. Not that he had to exert any force to do it, one hand
on her stomach sufficed.

"Are they any good?" How good could gag condoms be? Why did she
have them if pregnancy wasn't the concern?

"Kimono? Crown? Trojan? Take your pick. The point being, just pick
one and put it on... fast!"

"Easy, love, we have time—"

"Have you waited two years for an orgasm?" She all but growled at
him, her head lifted, the better to aim a glare at him in the dim light.

He chuckled at her desperation. Although it seemed a lifetime for him.
A lifetime since he'd had her.

"Then take your time the next time."

Ah, the next time. Of course there'd be one. And one after that, and another… He continued his journey down her body, enjoying her smooth skin where he nipped the curve of her waist, before finding the neatly trimmed bed of curls a most delightful contrast. "Just enjoy, love. I'll see you get your reward for patience."

The protest that started as a growl ended as a mewl when he teased the tender folds guarding her center. She wailed his name at the touch of his tongue delving between those soft, sweet folds already coated with heavenly honey. His Randi. This taste slammed straight into his heart and soul. This nectar he'd sipped before was a soothing balm that filled him with the desire to love her as long as possible.

With his thumbs, he stroked her skin and eased her open, exposing the delicate lining he could feel pulsing around his tongue. So hot, so wet, the special tang that was all hers worked like an elixir from the fountain of youth, taking him back to younger days when they'd burned like supernovas. All heat and hurry. Too hot to slow down and draw it out. Quantity over quality. Had she not learned the reverse with her husband? Had she continued to burn so bright she'd burned him out? Had the man never tied her up and drawn out the pleasure?

If this bed were made for anything, it was sex play. The thick posters were strong enough he could tie her spread eagled on the bed and teach her how to anticipate and savor. How to explode and come back, awake and eager for more. Until, of course, she grew too tired for more.

He drove his tongue deep inside and stroked her smooth walls, noting how firm she was and the strength with which she gripped him. That was just his tongue. Suddenly, her urgency seized him. He slid his hands under her hips and lifted her to his mouth. Was she close enough? Nuzzling her, he dragged his tongue up her sweet flesh until he found her clit. Sparing time for only one swirl of the tongue around her tiny button, he gently suckled. One, two…three… she stilled, her cry cut off as she paused, breathless for two heartbeats, then cried out as she came, shaking and bucking against his mouth. The soft wail was far too restrained for the girl he remembered, but he had no time to ponder it now. He needed to be in her.

While she shook and thrashed, nails digging into the wood of the post she still held, he pushed away just long enough to pull open the bedside drawer and wrap his fingers around a square packet. In record time, the empty wrapper was flung aside and the ultra-thin condom rolled on.

"Court," she gasped.

"I'm here, love. I'm here."

"Now, Court, now," she begged.

When a lady asked so prettily, who was he to deny her? Profound relief, peace, and soul searing heat collided under his skin. She still fit him like a glove, her quaking muscles taking him in, gripping him as the next orgasm took her. Oh Lord, he'd be lucky to last two thrusts. The memory was too strong, the reality too real, the sensation better than he recalled. She had him in a tight grip, soft and firm at the same time. Slick and hot, she filled his senses as he filled her body. Randi opened her eyes, and in the dark room, they glimmered as she reached for him, gasping his name.

"Now, Court, now," she whimpered and pulled him down into her embrace.

Now, it was. Ever her devoted worshiper, he let himself go and tasted heaven.

# Chapter 12

Soft, gray, pre-dawn light filled the room while Randi stretched beneath her silky sheets. Pure indulgence, the light-as-air, four hundred thread-count bedding had been purchased as a treat to remind herself what it felt like to be touched sensuously. Inhaling deeply, she drew in the scent of man and lovemaking.

Court. Her eyes flew open to find him watching her. How long had he been staring and why did her body instantly flood with need for him? After so many years, in less than twelve hours he'd made his way back into her bed, the very essence of him once more under her skin. Her naked skin, under the same covers as his naked skin. His leg touching hers.

"Good morning," he said softly and bent to place a gentle kiss on her lips. "You're so beautiful."

"So are you." She combed her fingers through her hair, noting his looked only slightly mussed.

The grin he gave her sent her pulse galloping. "Don't look at me like that, or we'll never get out of this bed." His tone teased, but his eyes promised.

She smiled. "And this would be a bad thing, how?"

"It would be highly detrimental to the economy of both our countries."

"Oh?"

The tip of his index finger stroked down the side of her face, sending tendrils of sensual fire along her nerve endings.

"If I don't take care of business, and the company flounders, it would put many people on the dole. And I'm not only talking about my employees. The ripple effect would be astounding as my suppliers rely on me to keep ordering their products. The drop in demand for their products would continue on down to craftsmen and growers all looking for markets. Why, if my company were to disappear tomorrow, it could cause panic in many markets around the globe."

Randi laughed at the look of mock horror upon his face. "So, you're saying that I, a lone, simple, plain woman, have the power to destroy the world economy just by keeping you here in my bed?"

"Surely you are the same Randi Jean Dailey—and I do love your full name—who attended the world famous London School of Economics? You, amazing, beautiful woman that you are, last I heard, were working on a degree which would put you right in the middle of financial analysis, so surely you understand the implications?" One long finger traced her eyebrow.

The smile dropped off her face. "I am. However, I didn't finish my degree in quite the way I planned."

"Ah, the baby. Birdie. Tell me what happened?" Concern in his eyes kept her from shrugging him off.

"As I mentioned earlier, it took an extra year, but I finished my degree. From then on I've worked part time for Dad, from home, like I do now."

"So you were able to be home for her?"

"Yes. All in all, it worked out well. We were able to buy this house about the time she turned five, and here I've been ever since."

"It seems like a fine place to raise children."

"It is." Enough small talk. Next he'd be asking about Wyatt, and she didn't want to go there. Not in this bed. "So, you're not entirely on vacation?"

"You Yanks may have had a holiday yesterday"—he tapped her chin—"but my world kept right on rolling. I'm already hours late checking in with my secretary. But before I do, I have a question for you."

"Shoot." She gathered the sheet up under her arms, though it was hardly worth the effort considering the tissue thin quality of the fabric. She needed the comforter to provide any level of concealment, although she didn't think Court would allow it. He already eyed the sheet as if he wanted to pull it away.

"I have a business meeting next week I simply cannot put off. However, I may be able to move the meeting to New York. If I were able to get the other party to agree, would you go with me? Christmas shopping in New York is said to be incredible."

Surprised, she blinked and stared up at him. "After one night together you want to extend it?" Never had she imagined anything beyond today, much less including travel.

"Indefinitely." He grinned down at her. "I want to hear all the details you flew right over a few minutes ago. I want to see your face light up in ecstasy over and over again. I want to watch you sleep and try to decipher all the little things you mutter. I want to hold you, wine and dine you in style, even to the point I'll accompany you while shopping. I want to spoil you and just breathe in the experience of being with you. Please?"

Flabbergasted, she threw an arm over her face. "Wow. Court, sheesh, I don't know. I haven't even thought about today, much less next week. We haven't talked about your plans for the weekend, and yet you want me to pack a bag and run off to New York with you?" So not in her plans. He wanted to resume the relationship she'd decided to keep in the over and done with column. Okay, okay, so she'd nudged it into the occasional fling column. Self honesty was highly over-rated.

"New York if Attenborough agrees to it. Otherwise, what's the state of your passport?"

Helpless to stop the nervous laughter, she tried to choke it back.

"What's so funny?" Court lifted her arm and peeked at her face.

"I'm overwhelmed, that's what."

He slipped an arm under her head and scooped her up against his chest, taking her with him as he lay back against the pillows. "There's no time to do this slowly and gently. I'm greedy for you, love. I have today and tomorrow here, and a flight out on Sunday. The only question is, do I stop in New York or keep going on to London? I'm pretty sure I can talk Attenborough into New York, he might even be there now as he has family in the area. I don't know at the moment, but I will soon. If I could, I'd put the meeting off another week and stay here. Or make him come to San Francisco."

In Court's arms, her cheek resting on his chest, it all seemed to make sense. New York? She hadn't ever stopped there. With the city dressed up for the holidays it was sure to be spectacular.

Too bad Birdie still had three weeks of school, it would be fun to take her along. But that wasn't the point, was it? The point was for Randi to spend time with Court. Shopping, dining, and loving. Did she dare? Certainly, the easy route, but was it too easy? Didn't make it wrong, did it? Who said right had to be hard? They had history and were already past the awkward do-we-or-don't-we stage, because they definitely had. Made love. Most of the night.

"So, is your passport current?"

Randi listened to the increasing beat of his heart. He meant it. "Passport is current."

"Shall I have my secretary make the arrangements?"

When had she last done something so impulsive? Probably London. With Court. Look where that had gotten her. Birdie. Okay, arguably the best thing she'd ever done in her life, but still. Heaven knew there'd been nothing impulsive about her marriage to Wyatt, other than speed, but he'd been carefully selected. Everything else in her life had been plotted, planned in detail, each angle considered and analyzed. Had she ever just jumped in the car and gone for a drive without at least outlining her path? Just how exciting had her life been since then?

The jarring ring of the telephone shattered the predawn peace.

"Damn," she muttered. "Only one person ever calls this early." She pushed up on her elbow and reached across Court to grab the handset. A push of the button stopped the ringing. She hoped neither Birdie nor Drew had been awakened by the phone.

With no effort to disguise her sleepy voice she answered, "Good morning, Dad."

Court's hand settled on her back, and she rested her cheek on his far shoulder as she lay draped across his body. The hair on his chest teased her nipples, and she rubbed against it. Such a nice bed he made.

"So? I'm in suspense here. Could hardly sleep last night."

"Nosy." There was little point scolding him further. Six AM was as late as he'd been willing to wait to call. She should have expected it. "It went as well as it could, I suppose. We told the kids, and they went out to the hot tub to plan evil ways to make us pay. I was asleep by the time they came in, so I don't know what they decided."

"And what about the smooth talking Brit? Did you talk to him at all after?"

Oh gee. How to explain that one when it wasn't any of his business? "We've spoken." There, close enough.

"What's going on there?"

"Dad, it's early. I didn't sleep well last night, and I have guests to tend to." Court's hand smoothing over her butt told her how he wanted to be tended to. "I don't know what's happening in the next few hours, but I suppose I should tell you now…." A long male finger slipped down between her legs, distracting her just as it was intended to. Well, okay, so she knew what was going to happen in the very near future, but Dad didn't need to know.

"Tell me what? Why are you groaning?"

"I'm still tired. Fell asleep in the tub last night, and my neck is telling me about it. Anyhow, I want to let you know I've just decided to take next week off." The large hand caressing her cupped and squeezed one cheek of her bottom.

"Take the week off? Why? You're taking two weeks at Christmas already. And today."

"Today is a company holiday, even if you don't choose to recognize it for yourself. Besides, I'm caught up, and we're in the slow season anyway. I'll keep the laptop with me for emergencies, but I want to get some Christmas shopping done."

"Where are you going?"

"I don't know yet for sure, but I'll have my cell, so you or Birdie can reach me. I just won't be home."

"Where are you going?" he asked again.

"I'll let you know when I find out. Love you." She hung up the phone and tossed the handset to the bedside table.

"So, I guess that's a yes to my question?" Court's fingers dipped deeper, easing between her folds of flesh, testing her moisture, spreading it around a little...

"Yes, yes, make the reservations. I'm yours for the next week." She twisted until she straddled his hips. Pressing up on her arms, she gazed down at him, into eyes heavily lidded with rising passion. "Although I'm still mad at you. I expect a nice hotel and show tickets for at least one night, maybe two."

"And a car with a driver at your disposal to cart around all your purchases," he promised, typically ignoring her declaration of ire. Granted, she wasn't sure she believed it herself anymore.

The foot massage he'd given her in the middle of the night had gone a long way toward restoring her good humor. Not to mention there'd been other massages in the night and long, slow, sweet kisses. His hands lightly gripped her hips, then slid down her legs from thigh to calf to the feet pressed against his legs. It seemed neither one could get enough of touching the other.

"Wow, first class all the way?"

"Always. You're a first class lady and deserve nothing less."

"I expect you to show me your best, Mr. Robinson. Take care of next week, then we'll talk about how to spend the next two days."

"My best? Darling, I've hardly begun, but I do believe you've already had a sample of some of my best moves." The thumbs rubbing her feet reminded her as her toes curled in appreciation.

"Oh, I'm sure you have more." She leaned down, extended her tongue, and touched it to the tip of his nose.

"Is that tongue a promise or a threat?"

"Which would you prefer?"

"Oh, a promise, by all means."

Randi pushed up until she knelt over him. Court's hands slid to her lower abdomen. Too late she remembered and felt his hands travel along her scar, his eyes taking in the detail revealed by the dim morning light.

"Is this what you didn't want me to see?" he asked quietly.

"Um, yeah, well, scars like this aren't sexy." The mood lost, she tried to move off Court, but he held her down by her thighs.

"What is it from? The hysterectomy you mentioned yesterday?"

"Yes."

"Why are you ashamed of the scarring?"

"It's ugly. I'm thinking about consulting with the cosmetic surgeon a friend of mine used this past summer. She'd lost a lot of weight, and he did an excellent job of tightening her up before she moved to Seattle."

Court shifted, then flipped her onto her back with himself between her legs. His glare confused her until he slowly kissed each inch of the scar that ran from below her belly button down to the edge of her pubic hair. "This isn't ugly. What's ugly is the fact you were ill after giving birth to our daughter. What happened?"

Court pressed his lips to her scar again, the gesture so tender she felt the hot prickle of tears at the back of her eyes.

"I started hemorrhaging, not long after the birth, which was vaginal and not a C-section. The doctor told Wyatt it was either do surgery or watch me bleed to death."

"They made the right choice. Battle scars are honorable marks. This is your battle scar." Kissing her, he continued to slowly travel the length of the incision mark.

"Doc said it was one of the fastest hysterectomies he's ever done."

"Was recovery tough?"

"Yes. I couldn't breast feed like I wanted to. By the time I came around—there was a bit of a problem with infection which caused the fever—my milk had dried up and she was used to the bottle. It took me all spring and most of the summer to recover. Wyatt had to hire a nurse to take care of both Birdie and me while he was at work, and then he took care of us when he got home."

"Sounds like you had a very rough time."

He didn't know the half of it, but she wasn't about to confess her depression. Or the prolonged bouts of crying alternated with bouts of staring into space praying for death. How Wyatt had managed to stick through those six months remained a mystery, but once she'd returned to school, Randi had slowly found herself coming back. Not as carefree a version of herself as she'd been, but one more mature. Able to take on the care of Birdie and resume her part of the household chores. Gratitude for Wyatt had turned into tender feeling and, eventually, love. He'd offered the plastic surgery at the time, but had also declared it would be for her peace of mind and not his. He didn't mind the scar one bit. Said it reminded him how precious she and Birdie were to him.

"We made it through, that's what counts," she said softly.

"Thank God for that." Court resumed kissing her abdomen. "I want to hear more, much more, but if I'm going to catch my secretary before she sneaks out early for the weekend, I need to call. Much as I hate to leave this very comfortable and most attractive spot."

Randi chuckled softly and wove her fingers into his beautiful thick hair. "I understand. I've sort of lost the feeling myself for the moment."

"I haven't lost the feeling." Court kissed her again. "But time is applying its own version of pressure. Once I get this little bit of business taken care of, I can then once more devote all my energy and attention to you and Birdie."

"Then go. I need to check my e-mail and send out my vacation notice as well. I'll start breakfast, and we can talk with the kids about the next couple days. Any idea what you want to do or see?"

"Wine country. I've tasted a few Napa Valley wines, and I want to learn more." He gave her stomach one last kiss, then crawled up her body, kissing a trail along the way, taking time to nuzzle and worship her breasts. "I'm so...very...glad...you lived." He ended at her lips and kissed what breath remained right out of her.

When at last he let her up for air, feeling the words in a way she never had before, she could only whisper, "Me too, Court. Me too."

# Chapter 13

"Where do you want all this wine?" Drew asked. The first of the three cases Randi had purchased that day preceded him into the kitchen. The more than a dozen cases Court had purchased were being shipped to New York where his office would then forward the entire lot on to England.

"Keep an extensive wine cellar, do you?" Randi had asked casually.

"A modest one."

"Compared to whom? The Ritz?"

Court had merely smiled.

"For now, just put them on the island." Randi cleared the way of paperwork just in time for Drew to slide the box onto the granite.

Court came next with the case he carried, barely dodging his son on his way back out for the last case while Birdie set down a bag of miscellaneous knickknacks and tasty morsels they'd also purchased.

"Right there." Randi pointed next to the other one.

"Where are you going to store this since the cooler is full?" He nodded to the under-counter appliance he'd filled with wine the day before.

"There's room in the one by the bar. The whites and sparkling wines can go in there. The reds can go in the racks." She waved toward the small bar on the other side of the half wall that defined the far edge of the dining area. Facing the cozy reading nook was a fireplace with a tiny bar area flanking it. "There's a little space in here as well." She pointed to a rack on the counter under the cabinet with the wine glasses.

"Your tea sets don't leave much room." The teasing smile Court gave her felt good. Every time she looked at him she felt good. Like he was dissolving the ice barrier around her heart that had entered her life upon leaving London. "How about a cuppa or two?'

"Excellent idea." Randi turned and perused the selection of tea sets around the kitchen. The ones in here she actually used. The others around the house were strictly for show. For the four of them, hmm, the extra large cobalt blue pot would work best. "Get that one down for me, please?"

"Ah, the spiffing one." It was easily within his grasp. "For when you want quantity as well as quality."

Randi rolled her eyes. "And the lime green sugar and creamer nearby."

"Colorful no less."

"They're cheery together." With the storm clouds hovering on Birdie's face as they had most of the day while she tried to find her place in her altered world, cheery was just the ticket. "Birdie, would you get out four mugs? Anyone want a turkey sandwich?"

Drew returned and nodded. "A bit of tea will hit the spot just right."

"Do I have time to check my e-mail?" Court asked. "I want to see if Martha got back to me."

Randi nodded. Martha, the secretary. A whiz with travel arrangements if Court's praise was to be believed. With a light pat on her butt that made Randi want to squirm, Court left the kitchen.

"What can I do to help?" Drew asked.

"Fill the kettle and warm the pot," Randi answered and pushed the huge teapot across the island to the side near the stove. "Darjeeling okay?"

"Fine by me."

"Birdie? Would you get it out?"

While the kettle came to a boil, she filled the infuser with loose leaf tea. Drew poured the boiling water over it, and Birdie set the timer for five minutes.

"A timer?" Drew raised a brow.

"I don't like it over-brewed," Randi replied firmly, and he let it go with a twitch of his lips.

By the time Randi had sandwiches assembled, a plate of cookies arranged, and most of a pumpkin pie cut, the kids had the perfectly brewed tea and dishes on the table. Court returned in time to hold out her seat for her.

"Ah, tea time. Nothing like it in the world."

"Well this is supper, not a fancy party tea. I can make more sandwiches if these won't hold you."

Drew winked from across the table while Birdie poured from the super pot. "If it doesn't hold us, I'll buy the pizza later." He eyed the six inch high stack of sandwiches as if he were considering not sharing. She'd forgotten just how much a young man could eat. Good thing Drew didn't live here full time. Of Birdie's friends from high school, the boys had been the hardest to satisfy. The food bill had plummeted the moment Birdie went off to college.

Court merely rolled his eyes and turned to Randi. "Martha came through. The arrangements are all made."

"Arrangements?" Birdie looked up as she set down the teapot. "What arrangements?"

The smile Court put on his face seemed to come to him easy enough, Randi decided. More practiced schmoozing? It seemed to work on Birdie, at least when she was focused on him. When it came to Randi, Birdie had developed an all-too-new cold shoulder. "I'm taking your mother to New York with me on Sunday. I'm just sad your school schedule is so demanding at the moment; I'd have liked to take you along as well and spend a week spoiling my girls with some Big Apple Christmas shopping."

Drew choked on his tea and had to reach for a napkin. "Wow, I never heard you offer to go shopping before." His wide grin showcased perfectly straight white teeth.

"I'd stay here and take everyone into San Francisco if I could, but Attenborough won't come this far west. He's agreed to New York, though. Otherwise, my next plan was to steal Randi off to London."

His hand on her leg was intimate and not missed by either of their kids. Drew's eyes sparkled, but Birdie's darkened and dulled.

Randi reached for the pot and hefted it to fill Court's cup. The extra, small grip on the front of the pot made it easier to lift and pour. The ritual of playing Mother allowed her to focus on anything but Birdie's displeasure, which added significantly to Randi's guilt. All day she'd tried to ignore the growing feeling inside.

The morning tastings and a stop for lunch had been pleasant and a lesson in how Court did business as he bought several cases at each stop. In fact, Randi nearly found herself turning green with envy over the unseen wine cellars in both his London flat and the country estate he bought the wines for. Almost. In fact, she'd been too busy watching Birdie getting to know Drew to think too much about Court's apparently endless funds.

Over lunch, Drew had told the story of how he'd waited to get Birdie's attention.

With a sheepish grin, he'd confessed. "I tripped her."

Randi had stared at first Drew, then Birdie. "How did it happen?"

"Well." Suddenly, a touch uncomfortable, which had been fascinating to see, Drew had played with his spoon while his ears turned red. "I'd noticed this little blonde from time to time over the semester. About a week ago, I was in the café and had the perfect opportunity to meet her.

So as she came toward my table, I stuck out my leg and she tripped over it. I didn't expect her to really fall on her face."

"You tripped me on purpose?" Birdie's brows had practically flown into her hair line.

"Well, yeah." Drew grinned. "I couldn't think of another way to get your attention so fast. I wasn't expecting you to saunter right on by me."

"I almost broke my arm, you idiot," Birdie said with a roll of her eyes. "And with my thesis due, where would I have been then?"

"I probably would have ended up typing it for you."

"Sounds a little too familiar to me," Court had muttered.

After lunch, Birdie had made a point of walking and talking with Court, and Randi had watched true affection grow on his part. What Birdie felt was still Birdie's secret, which, frankly, disconcerted Randi the most about this whole business.

Not that Court seemed to plan on denying his daughter. In fact, he seemed quite enamored with the change in his life and had focused on Birdie without ignoring Randi or Drew. Wyatt had never dreamed of denying Birdie, and she had reveled in his affection. In fact, due to the influence of her grandfather and Wyatt, Birdie related well to older men and seemed to respond to the father figure in Court. However, something remained under the surface, which Randi didn't recognize. A hint of suspicion? Wariness? An unnatural edge of aggressiveness that made Randi question Birdie's motive.

There'd never been any friction between mother and daughter over Wyatt's attention. Court was a new game, and the rules were changing faster than Randi liked. Birdie probably didn't recognize her feelings of rivalry, but to Randi, they became clearer with each passing hour. Even though it was hard to tell how much Birdie liked Court, she seemed to not like his attention to Randi at all and angled to be the focus of the limelight. Not that Randi intentionally gave her much competition. Birdie redirected a large portion of Court's intense focus away from Randi, allowing her a chance to process everything as it happened. He and Drew had slipped right into the fabric of their lives, and it felt eerily natural. So natural that Randi was trying to figure out if she felt threatened or not. Birdie's uncharacteristic reaction didn't help. The talk of a trip to New York didn't seem to soothe unsettled feelings at all.

"You know, Court," Randi said carefully, "maybe we should put off the trip until Birdie graduates. It's only a few weeks. We could all meet in New York after Christmas. Between semesters."

Court was already shaking his head. "The tickets are bought, including great seats for *Mama Mia* on Broadway. I don't want to back out now. We'll come up with something, perhaps talk you two into coming to England for a bit of winter in the country."

"Oh, now there's an idea," Drew agreed. "We have a good long break between semesters, Bird. It would be perfect if you could come for Christmas."

Randi so hated to be in her position. Although hope flared in Birdie's eyes. Maybe she liked him a little. "We'll need to talk to Grandpa. He's got something in mind, and I don't know if he's committed yet."

"We have the entire family coming to Lynford Hall." Court glanced from Drew to Randi and back again. "Including Bea's parents this year." His grimace to Drew was on the apologetic side. "It's the first time we've scheduled a gathering in years. They want to see Drew...."

"And you certainly don't want to flaunt your new family from the other side of the woodpile in front of them," Birdie interrupted. With a deep frown she drank down the rest of her tea, wiped her mouth, and stood from the table in the stunned silence filling the room.

Randi had never heard such bitterness from her daughter, and her mouth gaped in surprise. Before she could protest, Birdie spoke again. "It's for the best. Well, I don't know about you folks, but I've got a weekend of work ahead of me. Drew, if you want to come back with me, you'd best get your gear. Otherwise, I'm sure Mom wouldn't mind getting you back to campus."

"Birdie." Randi, Court, and Drew all said her name at once.

"Sit down, baby girl," Randi said.

"It isn't like that at all," Court added right on top of her words. It was enough to get Birdie to stand still. "I don't give a rip what they think. I'm more worried about what they might say to *you*. You have a grandmother, aunt, uncle, and cousins over there, all of whom are coming for Christmas. In addition, there will be Drew's other grandparents and half the neighborhood for Christmas dinner. I'd love to introduce you to all of them. I didn't think you'd be up for all that attention. Most of which will be curiosity, but there's a possibility of antagonism."

"With Mum's side around, there usually is," Drew said. "Not sure I'd want that show to be my introduction to the family."

"Well, it's moot anyway," Birdie said with a shrug. "I have to finish my thesis and figure out my finals schedule. So, Drew, you coming or staying?" Birdie pushed in her chair and gathered her dishes. Obviously, she expected Court would stay.

"May I take my sandwich to go?" he asked Randi.

"I'll wrap up sandwiches for both of you and get the leftovers." Randi stood to gather the food.

Court put a hand on her arm before addressing their daughter. "Birdie, what's this really all about?"

"I have to finish my degree. School takes priority over family drama. Which I've had my fill of, thank-you-very-much."

"Well, when you've had time to sort some of it out in your head, I hope you'll give me a call. I'm available to you at any hour. Pretty much as I'm sure your mother is."

Randi nodded, hoping Birdie would take the offer of a bridge.

"I'll think about it."

"I mean it, Birdie. Anytime, anywhere. You want to talk, I'm there, even if it's by phone from across the world. Should you ever make it to England, my homes are open to you, and the family and staff will know it." Court stood, his hand resting on Randi's shoulder a connection of solidarity. Two adults standing together in the attempt to connect with the children. Or rather, child, in this case. It was important Court stood beside, not in opposition to her. That meant something, but the real question was how did it affect Birdie? Did it calm her or enflame this unprecedented and lingering anger?

"Drew, I'll be ready in ten minutes."

"So will I, Bird."

Heavy heart dragging at her, Randi led Court into the kitchen.

"Do you think—" Court started to ask, but Randi shook her head to cut him off.

She couldn't talk right now. The little bit of tea she'd sipped churned in her stomach. What was going on inside Birdie's head? She was angry, but at who? At her and Wyatt because they'd never told Birdie of her true origins? At the necessary change of relationship with Drew? At Court for showing up out of the blue? Was Birdie mad at both her and Court for thinking about resuming their relationship? Certainly, that had been obvious by the way Court had stayed close beside Randi, touching her at every opportunity. Just small touches. A hand on the small of her back, brushing aside hair the breeze had whipped across her face, holding hands with their fingers laced together. All familiar touches Birdie had witnessed her entire life, but from another man. A man she'd believed with her whole heart had been her father, for whom she still grieved.

In the fuss of leaving, Drew found a moment to give Randi a hug and thanked her for the holiday. A simple, "I'll call," from Drew was enough to convey a message from son to father.

Randi forced Birdie into a hug and whispered, "I love you," to her daughter. Birdie clung for a moment with a hint of desperate emotion, then pushed away without a word.

Heart breaking at the inability to ease her daughter's distress, Randi stood in the driveway with Court as the kids pulled out and turned down the road. They watched until Birdie's vehicle, Wyatt's old sedan, disappeared around the corner.

"I take it that's unusual behavior for her."

Court's voice was quiet beside her, his arm behind her back comforting. A quick swipe of her hand across her cheek took care of the tear trickling down it.

"Yes. That's not my baby girl. That's a confused and angry young woman who has never lived in this house before. I don't know what to say to her. Sorry isn't enough. Explanations seem pathetic. I don't know how to atone for the grave disappointment I suddenly am to her."

Court drew her around and up against his chest. She snuggled into his embrace. "Hush, love. She just needs time. It was a big shock and not delivered in the best way. Not that I'm sure there was a better way. Is there a right way to impart such news? I'm still reeling from the shock. You alone carried all the pieces of the puzzle, and it was a shock to you. How can we expect her to easily accept so many changes in so little time? And without Ferguson here to add his point of view... Well, it will just take time for her to adjust."

"You're right. But I feel terribly guilty for leaving right now."

"Shush." Court tipped her head up and feathered a kiss across her lips. "As hard as it is for me to take it in, the simple fact is, our daughter is an adult. Can't hold her hand forever, Jeannie-mine. She'll need to deal with this in her own way and in her own time. We need time too. Time together. Time to soak it all in, time to know each other again. Time to slow down and find our way onto a more stable path. We're full adults now. In charge of our destiny."

Breathless, she looked up into those blue, blue eyes, glowing in the dusky evening falling about them. "You sound like you're talking forever."

"Perhaps." His eyes searched her face. "It's fast, I know, but the last thing I want is to lose touch with you again. Promise me that one thing for now. Promise me now we've found each other, whatever comes, we won't lose the connection. I don't care how we stay connected—phone, internet, mail, you in my bed, me in your bed—just as long as we do stay connected."

The intensity of his feelings was all there in his eyes for her to see. Some of it lived in her heart, tempered by her daughter's distress. The feelings this man stirred up in her hit with the speed and impact of a tornado, all the heat of a firestorm, completely overwhelming while promising to carry her away. After all that had happened, right now, she wanted to be carried away. A short time of living the fantasy couldn't be bad, could it?

"For tonight, anyway, I think we can try out the latter."

"Ah, me darlin', now you're talkin'." Court's accent thickened to Cockney, sending a finger of thrill through her. Not enough to banish her guilt over Birdie, but enough to ease it just a little. Enough to build on.

"I love it when you talk that way," she murmured.

Something of her sadness must have been in her eyes as Court gazed at her. "What say you we go in, chuck the tea, crack open a fine bottle of wine, then go for a hot tub? I dare you to do it in the altogether."

Tiny though it was, a smile lifted one corner of her mouth. "I'll race you there."

# Chapter 14

Randi hesitated only a moment before lifting her chin and heading toward the plane. Court heaved a sigh, flashed the gate attendant a smile along with his boarding pass, and followed. The woman still had a walk that drew male eyes like a magnet. Tottering on her modest heels, Randi sauntered down the ramp, her black gabardine trousers cinched at the waist framing her hips in an extremely flattering manner. Her ivory silk blouse, every bit as elegant as any on New York's Fifth Avenue, draped her curves perfectly.

In any case, he felt relieved she'd finally decided to come with him.

The last two nights had been exercises in patience and distraction as she swung from worrying about Birdie's reaction to making passionate love with him. He hoped that in New York they could settle in, relax on neutral ground, just the two of them, and talk. Randi had been avoiding discussions involving anything deep and emotional while he'd wanted to do nothing but talk about everything to do with the future.

Now wasn't that a switch-up? For the first time in his life, Court wanted to slip a ring on a woman's finger—the sooner the better to his way of thinking—one big enough to shout to the world his possession of her. Two to three carats at the very least. Possibly with a few colored stones to make it stand out more. Tiffany wasn't far from the hotel, he might even find time to slip away and find something suitable.

"Oh damn!" Randi's curse of dismay brought Court out of his daydream as she tried to right her rolling carry-on bag. "I knew I should have replaced this case."

Court leaned over, righted the luggage, retracted the pull handle, and lifted it. "I've got it." He liked playing hero for her, especially when it earned him a grateful smile and swift kiss.

"Seats?" the flight attendant asked, and Randi turned to follow her to their seats in the middle of the first class rows on the left side.

The sneaky little baggage slid into the aisle seat, then took advantage of him as he lifted their cases to the overhead bin. The warmth of her hand on his stomach while he was occupied with his hands in the air created a heat far beyond that of a simple touch. Looking down, he met her eyes, sparkling with wicked mischief as she smiled up at him before directing her gaze lower. Suddenly, the sated satisfaction after two nights and a full day of intense sex disappeared. Only three hours earlier, he'd spent himself deep inside her, and now he wanted her again.

"Move over," he told her gruffly, gave his case a final push, then slid into his seat just as she vacated it. Faced with her luscious behind, he grabbed her hips and pulled her onto his lap. "You can sit here a moment and hide the evidence."

Not only did she not squeal, she had the nerve to wiggle until her thighs framed the erection straining against his trousers trying to reach her.

"Ever done it on an airplane?" he murmured in her ear.

"No. Have you?"

"Not yet. Ask me again at the end of the flight."

Randi giggled, lifted herself off his lap, and settled into the window seat. "Need a blanket, darling?"

Court crossed his legs and growled at her. "I'll get you, me pretty."

"A drink?" The attractive brunette cabin attendant asked. "We'll serve breakfast after take-off."

"The lady will have coffee with cream and Frangelico." He smiled at Randi. It wouldn't take long to melt her panties, and then he'd have her for sure. Clever of her to introduce him to the concoction.

"You're wicked to tease me this way." Randi leaned closer to whisper in his ear when the attendant had left with their orders.

"I intend to tease you a hundred different ways before this week is over. Possibly even this day."

By the widening of her pupils and the hitch in her breathing, he could tell exactly how his promise affected her.

The more he thought about it, the more impatient he became. The flight took off, breakfast finally served, and Court made sure Randi had a second tiny bottle of liqueur for her coffee. The flush it put on her cheeks and the sparkle in her eyes was all he hoped for. At last the meal was cleared, and Randi released the latch on her seatbelt.

"Excuse me," she said softly.

"By all means." Ever the gentleman, he stood and pointed her toward the lavatory at the back of the First Class section. Other than a lifted brow, she didn't argue. Nor did she seem to notice as he followed her until she opened the door.

"Go ahead," he leaned toward her to whisper in her ear. "Make sure you wash up properly, though."

"Court," she protested.

"I'm waiting…"

Shaking her head, she closed the door, and he leaned against it, hands in his pockets. What this woman did to him defied even his fantastic memories. Not since their time in college had he been this primed. He felt young again, as if he'd slept all these years, only to wake as if not a day had passed. But it was better this time. So much better. He had staying power, he had moves, and recuperation like he'd forgotten about. It was all about quality. The quantity was a side benefit.

Behind him, he heard a flush followed by water in the sink. When the locking bolt slid open, he pushed away from the door and ever so casually slipped inside the tiny lavatory.

"You can't be serious." Randi's eyes widened as he locked the door and crowded her.

"Good planning to put the lid down. Now turn around, darling. We don't have long and don't forget to keep quiet."

"Oh for—" she squeaked as he spun her and reached around her for the fastening on her trousers.

"I can't wait, Jeannie. I need you." His hand slipped inside her clothes, under the elastic of her knickers, straight to the sweet heat he craved. "Ah, love, you feel so good and ready."

She melted against him. "Okay, okay. How do you want me?"

"Just bend over and hold on. Open up your blouse for me. I need to touch you."

The sheer naughtiness of it turned him on so much he'd be lucky to last long enough to get her off with him. But he was game to do his best. When her blouse hung open, he reached around and cupped her breasts, rubbing over the nipples pressing against the silk.

"Pop them out," he growled, lips to her ear.

"I don't want to take off my bra," she whimpered.

"Don't. Just pull the cups down enough for me to touch your nips."

"Oh Court." Not much of a protest as she followed orders.

"So sexy, darling. Very hot." He pinched her nipples, loving the feel of her extra soft flesh rolling between his fingers, bringing them to maximum arousal as he rubbed her own moisture over one. The scent would carry him all the way to New York.

"Fast," she gasped. "I want it hard and fast."

"And I love to give the lady what she wants." Teeth tugging on her earlobe, he pulled on her nipples as she pushed down her bottoms.

"Now, Court," she ordered and, bent over, braced herself with hands on the seat lid. "You got me hot, now make it all better."

Chuckling at his demanding kitten, he dealt with his own trousers, stroked her with the head of his cock until she moaned, then thrust deep inside.

For a handful of racing heartbeats he held still, savoring the skin to skin grip with which she held him, until she pushed back against him. Thankfully, she'd given up on the idea of condoms.

"Impatient, are we?" He chuckled and started moving, holding her hips still as he plunged and retreated, creating heat and friction as she flexed her inner muscles. The visual incredibly erotic as he caught glimpses of her breasts swaying from their movements, his cock disappearing between the cheeks of her heart shaped ass. It was down and dirty, dangerous sex, no frills style and perfect for the moment. The temperature in his balls increased when he felt her soft hand alternately rubbing her clit and squeezing his cock at the entrance to her quivering quim.

"Yes, yes," she urged him on. "I'm...almost..."

Bloody hell, she scorched him! The audacity of their actions, the danger of getting caught, the thrill of two hundred passengers and crew right outside the thin cardboard walls drove his excitement to the peak and tension began to uncoil at the base of his spine.

"Are you with me?"

"A little...more...fast...er...oh!"

Randi dropped her head to her arm, covering her mouth to muffle her sweet cries. Her bliss did him in. Her trembling grip pulled him straight into Nirvana.

# Chapter 15

"Here we are, my randy little lady." The desire proved too much to resist and he swept an arm under her knees, lifting her into his arms. The bellman held the door to the suite Court always booked when staying in New York. For the first time, he understood the fun behind the tradition, and Court carried Randi over the threshold completely ignoring her protest. Just being with her made him feel strong and manly, almost enough to drop her and beat his chest.

"Court, you'll hurt your back." She clung to his neck with a hint of exasperation, which made him grin even more.

"Never. You're light as a feather." He hefted her a little higher, just enough he could kiss her. "Besides, isn't every hero required to sweep his woman off her feet at least once a day?" What he really wanted to say—that he considered this practice for their honeymoon—he didn't think would be accepted quite yet. By the end of the week, possibly, but now was far too soon. He needed time to work on her. A thrill of lust hit him in a wave so strong he nearly dropped her on the sofa because the bedroom was five steps farther.

Not to mention, they had an avid audience. The bellman wheeled his cart into the bedroom. Court only noticed the man stopped when he said, "Beg pardon."

"What's that?" Randi swung her head around. "Oh for Pete's sake, let me down."

"If I must," Court murmured, but the employee backing out of the bedroom caught his attention as well. "Something wrong?"

The young man cleared his throat and did his best to arrange his expression into a blank mask. "Uh, it's possible the room has been… double booked?"

Randi, two steps ahead, pushed past the brass luggage cart, and Court caught up to her as she stopped just inside the bedroom door.

"Oh, for the love of…"

Court wrapped his arms around the now stiffening woman he wanted in his room while the naked one he didn't want, coincidentally already in the bed, screeched and pulled the sheet up to her chin.

"Court! I didn't expect you to have company," Catherine… somebody, said.

What was her last name? They'd had dinner a few times, her father was a contact, but damn him if he could remember her name, which wasn't the same as her father's.

"No one said anything about…*her*." Catherine sneered the last word as if Randi were a maid or an amoeba. Probably the same thing in Catherine's mind.

"And nobody mentioned you," Randi retorted, then turned in his arms. In an extraordinary show of cool, she touched his collar and played with the button while avoiding his eyes. "Darling, you never told me this hotel provides full service. I'm impressed, apparently, they think of everything, including bed warmers. Unfortunately, this one isn't up my alley."

"What?" He wasn't sure what he expected, but surely not…this? Court shook his head in disbelief.

"Really, next time, have the hotel provide a bed warmer of each sex, if you truly want to impress me." Randi's dry tone belied the trembling of her stiff body, the glint of fire in her eyes, and the faint blush climbing her cheeks. "Might want to mention my taste in toy boys runs toward Swedish muscle men. I'll leave the underfed professional women to you."

"Wait. I don't know what this is about." Well, he suspected, but this wasn't something he'd planned. Not him, but who? Larry or Martha or someone in the hotel? Who would have notified Catherine of his last minute plans? He stopped Randi from leaving the room with an arm across her waist while Catherine spluttered in indignation from under the sheets.

"Let me go," Randi said quietly. "I'll call for housekeeping to bring up fresh linens." She hesitated a moment before looking over her shoulder. "And some air freshener to counteract the gallon of Obsession that somehow got spilled in here."

"Let me deal with this. We'll get another room." He spoke rapidly over Catherine's shriek of outrage. Had it not been his life, this scene would be somewhat funny. "Just let me call the front desk."

Randi had a point about the odor. The perfume in the room overpowered everything else, making his eyes water.

"Court?" Catherine's cultured New England nasal accent came out as a whine. "What is this? You promised me we'd get together on your next trip. When I heard you'd be here…"

Exasperated, and desperate to keep Randi from running to the next plane home, he glared at the unwelcome woman as the welcome one escaped and pushed past him. "You need to get your things and get out of here. I don't know how you got in, but you need to leave."

"What are you talking about?" Catherine had determination, he'd give her points there, but stupidity was another topic. "I'm here, just as you wanted me to be. Let her leave if she wants to."

"Catherine, get dressed. You have five minutes before security gets here to escort you out."

The woman shrieked. "You wouldn't dare! I can ruin you in New York!"

"No, you can't," he told her. There had never been a time when he needed her sponsorship in New York's business or social circles. He had twenty years of traveling those arenas, which was how he'd met her in the first place. Her father and uncle had proved useful a few times, but not anything of serious consequence. "Five minutes." He glanced at his watch and turned to follow Randi who reached for the phone.

The bellman stood stiffly and stared blankly at the wall. "Take the cart back to the hall while we clear this up," Court ordered.

By the time he reached Randi she had the front desk on the phone.

"Please send up housekeeping…what? Oh, there's an infestation. We need a complete scrubbing and change of linens—"

Court snatched the receiver from her hand. "Who is this?" His attempt at a glare had no impact as she glared back at him. Great, he hadn't set this up, not directly or specifically, yet he was the one in trouble.

"Oliver, sir. Is the lady serious about an…infestation?" The man in the lobby whispered the last word. As if it had the power to cause a panic should anyone overhear.

"Oliver, excellent. Apparently, my apartment has been double booked. What else is available immediately?" An arm around Randi's waist kept her from following their luggage out to the hall, though she didn't seem to be fighting to get away from him so much as trying not to laugh out loud.

"The penthouse is available. I can give it to you at the same rate as your usual apartment. I'll send housekeeping to deal with the, um, situation?"

"Yes, the master bedroom in particular needs a good airing out. Send up a bellman with the key. Our luggage is still on the cart. Thank you."

That out of the way, Court wrapped both arms around Randi who looked up at him with a brow lifted in inquiry.

"I appreciate you not carrying on," he said and drew her closer. Unaccountably, he felt a bit embarrassed and tried to hide it by burying his face in her hair.

"Does this happen to you often?"

"No, no, God no." Whatever had happened in the past, he'd never confess to. He certainly hadn't sanctioned it this time. "Please, continue to remain calm while we sort it out."

"Why shouldn't I? The cow in the other room is making enough noise for three."

Court winced. She'd spoken loud enough for Catherine to hear as she came stomping from the bedroom, dignity sorely hit, and clothing barely pulled on. Certainly not what he remembered of the woman's usual impeccable, sophisticated look.

"Cow? Did she call me a cow?"

"I wish you hadn't done that, darling." It was getting harder not to smile. Though he tended to agree with the sentiment, Catherine actually looked more like a scrawny witch with her dark hair falling down around her shoulders, dress askew, and her menacing eyes flashing in anger and embarrassment.

"You're right. I apologize. You'd never spend time with a cow, would you?" Randi grinned impishly up at him, and Court did crack a smile.

When the situation called for it, apparently Randi could bring out the inner bitch every woman seemed to have, though he'd never expected it from her. Thankfully, she seemed to see the hint of humor in the situation. Another sign she could most likely handle any social situation to come up in London. Nobody was going to push her around. Court's satisfaction rose another notch, and he rested his forehead against hers. "I'm sorry, darling, I didn't expect this, and I have no idea how she made it in here. We'll be in our new room in a matter of minutes."

Catherine was trying to slip her shoes on and having little success due to the stockings dangling from her fingers. "And just who are you to be calling me names? You're nobody in Manhattan!"

"Thank God," Randi muttered.

"Catherine, this beautiful woman is the mother of my daughter." Hoping Randi wouldn't take advantage of the opportunity to break away, he slid his hands up her arms until he cradled her face and held it just so he could look deeply into her eyes. Eyes that flashed fire at him and thrilled him deeply.

"You don't have a daughter! You told me! I met Drew last year, and you told me he was your only child." Catherine hit the side of his arm with her overpriced designer high heeled shoes. "You lying, cheating, sack of—"

"I've never been more wrong, Catherine," he cut her off without taking his eyes from Randi. "So very wrong, and I've never been happier about it in my life. I have a daughter who is almost as beautiful as her mother."

"You haven't heard the last of me!"

"Whoa there, lassie!" A new voice entered the fray, and Court reluctantly tore his gaze from Randi, though he did take a moment to secure her at his side before turning to face the newcomer. Leave it to Attenborough to show up at the least convenient time.

"Larry." Catherine drew herself up and spoke as if serving tea for the queen. "You might want to avoid this room. I understand the exterminators are on their way up to deal with an unwanted infestation."

"I don't get your point, love." Lawrence Attenborough stood aside and let Catherine swish past him.

"Ask your friend. Then again, you may wish to reconsider doing business with such a despicable worm." Nose lifted to the ceiling, she left the apartment only to be replaced by the floor butler, a middle-aged man known to Court only as Rupert.

"Mr. Robinson? The front desk rang."

"Ah yes, Rupert, thank you. Please see that Ms...um..."

"Miller," Attenborough supplied helpfully, his face a little too gleeful as he checked out Randi from head to toe.

"Right, Ms. Miller. Please find her a spot to recover her dignity, and then I'd like to have a word with you."

"Yes, sir." The butler left as quietly as he'd arrived. Good man, Rupert. Unless he'd been the one who'd let Catherine into the apartment in the first place.

"Now, Court, before you explain all the screeching, do introduce me to this very lovely lady."

Attenborough, who considered himself a lady's man, had Randi's hand in his and was lifting it to his mouth to kiss.

"Randi, may I present Lawrence Attenborough, my business contact this week, and no, he's no relation to Lord Attenborough, although he thinks it would be fun. Larry, this is Randi Ferguson, the mother of my daughter, as I'm sure you heard through the door."

The man's eyes flashed and lips quirked at hearing Randi's name, but chose to comment on the second bit of information instead. "A daughter?

Extraordinary. Do tell. How old is this long lost daughter? Surely she can't be more than a toddler, judging by the age of her mother."

"Thank you," Randi said. "You lie and flatter almost better than he does."

"I don't lie." Court stopped just short of snapping the words out. He had more to say but someone knocked on the door at that moment.

"Larry, get the door would you?" Court turned to Randi. "Have your handbag, darling?"

"Yes. I'm ready to go anywhere it doesn't smell like the perfume counter at Walmart." Though she was quick with the sarcasm, she did hitch the bag strap over her shoulder.

"Let's go to our new room, and then we'll get everything sorted, shall we?"

"Sir?" The bellman, a different one, stepped through the door.

"You have our key?"

"Yes, and Fiske will meet us at the elevator. Allow me to double check..."

"Yes, yes. Very good." Court waved him in. "I don't think anything came off the cart, but better to make sure."

At the door, they found Larry casually leaning against the jamb, and the first bellman missing.

"You sure know how to make an entrance," Larry said. "Where to now?"

"We're switching up." Court nodded out the door. "If you don't mind...?"

"Oh, I surely don't mind. In fact, I'll go along for the ride. I'm curious about your idea of switching up."

Now this he had to nip in the bud, or they'd never get rid of Larry. The man was a veritable font of gossip, which came in handy when one needed information. Not so handy when one unintentionally provided information. Such as unwanted socialites hiding in one's bed. "No, really—"

"Sir?"

And wasn't that just par for the course? This had begun to reach farcical proportions. Employing extreme patience in his tone, he answered the bellman peeking out from the bedroom. "Yes?"

"There's an open suitcase here..."

Court winced at the flimsy scrap of scarlet fabric dangling from the man's fingers. "Not ours. Rupert will know what to do with it."

The man dropped his hand, trying to hide the lingerie behind his back. "Of course. If you'd like to move on toward the elevator, I'll be right behind you."

"Right-O."

"Come right this way." Larry tucked Randi's arm in his, effectively tugging her out of Court's loose embrace. "I'm just dying to hear all about you and Court. When did you meet and make a little girl?"

"Oh, well…" Randi glanced at Court and he shrugged. The whole world would know by breakfast. Someone would be enterprising enough to dig out the story and print it in some rag. They'd find more information, faster than the PI he'd paid off on Friday. Unless, of course, something else more titillating came along. It usually did.

"I haven't exactly told the world our story. If you recall, until last week I didn't know there were extra chapters," he told her.

Larry leaned closer to Randi. "Now I'm positively hooked. You can't keep me dangling."

"I'm not sure I should tell you. If it were only Court's reputation at stake, there'd be no problem, I'm sure."

Court merely smiled at the small dig. She'd earned it.

"But since I have my daughter's feelings to consider, I don't want to see it splashed across the newspapers. How popular is Court in London these days? I haven't made a point of keeping up with the tabloids."

"I'm not sure he's ever made the gossip rags. There's usually someone with more flash about when our boy goes out on the town."

Randi nodded. "Good."

Thankfully, the elevator arrived then, however, Rupert hurried to intercept them.

"Where are you going?" Larry asked. "I'll escort the lady up while you have your word with Rupert."

Torn, Court looked to Randi who gave him a small crooked smile with a one-shoulder shrug. With a sigh, he waved them on. "The penthouse. The butler will meet you."

"The penthouse," Larry drawled with both brows raised. "Remarkable switch-up. We'll meet you there."

Court wasn't one to gnash his teeth, but this once, he was unquestionably close to grinding his molars to dust. Randi's hand on Larry's arm while he waved as the elevator door closed was positively guaranteed to drive a man insane.

"Excuse me. Sir?"

Court turned to the hapless hotel employee. "Did you find a spot for Ms. Miller to freshen up?"

"Yes. Were you not expecting her?"

Resigned to closing this loop, he slid his hands into his pants pockets. "No. Any idea how she got into the apartment?"

"Sorry, no, but I can find out."

Holding up a hand, Court shook his head. "It's done now, but please make note for the future. I won't appreciate surprise visitors. They've often been welcome in the past, but no more. The only woman allowed to surprise me will be my wife the next time we're here." Rupert had served him well before, and Court suspected the man kept a file on each guest. No detail stood a chance of being overlooked, and this one meant more than anything.

"Very good, sir. And congratulations. In advance."

Court grinned. "She hasn't agreed yet, but it's just a matter of time."

"Shall I pass a discreet word to the penthouse butler, Fiske?"

"I'll tell him, but please make sure the rest know." Any more scenes like the last one and Randi would make a beeline for her California house and never allow him access again. She may have agreed to this week, but he didn't have a good feeling on anything beyond. He needed this week to show, and convince her, this was it. The big IT. He wanted more than a week with her. Much more. Forever sounded about right.

"Very good. I'll see that housekeeping takes care of the room."

"Thank you." Court pressed the elevator button again. "Have you any recommendations of truly unique jewelers?"

"I'll get you a list of addresses. Fiske should be able to arrange for them to bring selections to the hotel."

"Good man, Rupert." The elevator arrived. "I look forward to it."

# Chapter 16

Before she had time to fully appreciate the handsome man hugging her arm to his side, the elevator pinged softly and the door slid open. A distinguished older man dressed in a black suit met them. This experience already surpassed any expectations she'd had, and now shot straight into the surreal realm. "Sir. Madam."

"You must be Fiske," Larry said.

She was grateful to him for taking charge of the situation.

Thoroughly overwhelmed by the events so far, Randi was happy to let him do so. Had she been left on her own, she might very well have turned on her heel and headed for home. Not only did she feel unprepared to deal with Court's women, the hotel was by far the most sophisticated she'd ever stepped foot in as an actual guest. Sure, she'd been to events and balls at hotels, and stayed in some pretty nice regular rooms, but never the very top, the elite luxury suites. Every detail said wealth and power in an oh-so-British way. Somewhat subtle, and clearly modern, the hallway reflected the magnificence of the hotel. The apartment they'd left was better decorated than her house. Now they were met by another butler. Who got escorted to a suite by a butler?

"I'm merely accompanying the lady while Mr. Robinson ties up some loose ends."

"Very good. If you'll follow me?"

He led them down a hall and around a corner. Randi's heels sank into thick carpeting selected to muffle all sound. In fact, she was loath to speak, fearing the butler might shush her like a librarian would. At a paneled door, he waved a card over a keypad, which activated the doors of yet another elevator. With Larry's hand on her lower back, she stepped inside. Fiske followed, leaving the bellman with the luggage cart in the hall.

"I'll send the elevator back. Take the luggage to the second level," the butler told the younger man.

Second level? Weren't they already on, like, the fiftieth floor? Randi glanced at Larry who merely smiled back. Not bad, in a floppy hair, Hugh Grant-cute kind of way. Careless bachelor, playboy, never-want-to-grow-up type. Not her style at all. All right, so he wasn't Court.

"Tip-top service here. Court must like you. Then again, I'm still waiting to hear the story about this daughter. Tell me, she can't be much older than five, can she?"

"She can," Randi answered shortly.

"No." Larry held a hand to his chest as if in shock, his summer lake blue eyes wide with mock surprise. A man who obviously smiled often, laugh lines fanned out from his eyes, the curves beside his mouth a bit pronounced. He looked and acted as if he were an old school chum of Court's. Highly possible, she supposed. All those years ago she and Court had kept to themselves, rarely meeting with groups at the pub. Time had been far too precious, and they'd wanted to be alone. "Court's a very naughty chap and never breathed a word of it to his oldest friends. I'll have to severely reprimand him over this."

The elevator doors slid open again and Fiske stepped out, graciously waving them into a sleek, modern-looking suite decorated in smoky blue and soft shades of silver and crisp white. Soothing and minimalist at the same time, it smacked of big dollars. Once the elevator was empty, he pressed a button on the wall, and the elevator closed up again. "You can send the lift down for guests from here. The intercom will screen them for you."

Taking in the setup, Randi nodded and accepted the card Fiske handed her.

"Nice," Larry said. "This way I can't sneak up on you two."

"Larry, you're an interesting person, but I don't see you spending much time here." Best get the point clear right away.

"Ah, love, that's where you're mistaken. Court and I have meetings, and we might as well conduct them here. Will you sit in?"

"Lord, I hope not," she said fervently. "I'm on vacation."

"Madam?"

"Yes, Mr. Fiske?" She turned to the butler.

"Tea is on its way up. We have time for a tour of the suite."

"Of course." With the steel and glass stairs leading to the aforementioned second level, a tour was very much in order.

"On this level, there's a full kitchen for use by the culinary team should you wish to dine *en suite*, a wet bar, powder room, dining, day bed in the alcove." Fiske led the way, pointing out the million dollar view and showing no sign of his thoughts as Larry followed, taking in the amenities.

As they neared the top of the stairs, the elevator pinged and doors on the upper level slid open. Court emerged, followed by the bellman with their luggage.

"Ah, there you are, Robinson." Larry stepped back and gently guided Randi toward Court.

"Mr. Robinson, I was just giving a tour of the suite."

"Excellent, Fiske. Ms. Ferguson is the lady in charge this week."

"Very good, sir." The butler turned to her. "Which room would you prefer?"

"The one with the biggest bath tub."

"This way." He waved toward the farthest door. "Everett, the luggage in the master, if you please."

"I say, Robinson, there's room for me here," Larry said.

"Not bloody likely, Attenborough. If I see your face before nine in the morning, I may toss you off the balcony."

His friend laughed and lifted Randi's hand. "Fine, I'll leave you to your tea, but I'll be knocking on your door at nine sharp. By then I'm sure you two will have your story coordinated. I expect to be entertained." The brush of his lips across the back of her hand was nice, but not tingle worthy. "Randi, a pleasure to meet you."

With great relief, Randi tossed down her purse and kicked off her shoes as Larry and the bellman boarded the elevator and left.

"Tea will be ready in ten minutes." Fiske turned and left them alone in the master bedroom also decorated in the same shades as the other rooms.

"What did you tell him?" Court loosened his tie and shrugged out of his jacket.

"Not a thing." Randi turned away from the stunning view and smiled. "Quite an introduction to New York."

With a sheepish grin, Court ran a hand through his hair, barely disturbing the short, precision cut. "Certainly one of the more exciting days I've had. I apologize…"

Randi placed her fingers over his lips. "Shh. I understand you didn't set that up. I'm sure there's a story there, and I may want to hear it someday but not today. I'm a bit tired and hungry." Court's lips were warm, and he kissed her fingers, sending heated jolts into her bloodstream. "Joining the Mile High Club didn't satisfy you?"

"Not in the least," he murmured and sucked her index finger into his warm mouth before releasing it. "Swedish muscle men, darling? Ouch."

"Only for toying with when you're not available."

Court turned to kissing her palm and wrist with slow, teasing touches. "I'd better make sure I'm available or see that you're too tired to go looking for Sven."

"The butler is downstairs," she breathlessly reminded him.

"So? He's paid to be discreet. He's here for our convenience and will adjust to our schedule."

"He's ours for the entire week?" She wasn't sure what excited her more, the luxury around them or Court's sensual attentions. Silly. She knew. Court and his kisses.

"Comes with the suite. Along with a few other things, from what I learned on the way up. I'm sure he'll be happy to sort out the details with you. All I need is coffee service and lunch during the hours I'm negotiating with Larry. I expect to kick him out by tea time. We'll do dinner with him one night, but otherwise, I'll leave the evening entertainment up to you. Just tell Fiske what you want, and he'll get the tickets and make the arrangements. I've told him to get a car with a driver to follow you all over town, collecting your shopping bags."

Randi found herself snuggling into Court's arms as he held her close. The fantasy was every bit as wonderful as she'd dreamed. Better. Too good to be true and too fantastic to last. But for a week she could live the dream. "I could get spoiled by this." His heart thumped comfortably beneath her cheek.

"I want to spoil you."

"Mmm. Don't get too caught up in that thought," she warned him softly and stepped back. That's all she needed, Court painting pretty pictures in her mind. If anything, this trip had already told her she was ill-equipped to deal with his version of reality. It was one thing to say he wanted to pick up where they'd left off, but too many years had passed, too many changes had taken place. Like her name, that girl of the past, Jean, wasn't really her. Had she ever been?

"Why not?" Court followed her, his footsteps silent on the carpeting. In just a few steps, he had her backed up against the elegant four poster bed. A simple wood frame painted a warm gold, it created a splash of color in the room.

"It will be hard enough parting at the end of the week, let's not add extra layers of difficulty, shall we?" Cautioning him in advance seemed wise.

"Who says we have to say good-bye at the end of the week?"

"Come on, Court." Closing her eyes, she let him pull her against his chest. It was a great comfort when she knew the words she had to say would hurt so much. She'd been thinking them all weekend, but the encounter downstairs reminded her of how true they were. "I know I can't hold you. What you're used to is so far removed from my life, it's as if I'd be no more than the village seamstress in your world. That display a bit ago was just one reminder of many that I'm too simple to hold your interest for long."

He started to protest, but she pressed a finger to his lips. "You admire, and are used to, clever, sophisticated women, and they adore you right back. I've seen it every time we step out into public. It's not just the women, it's the whole package. Your everyday lifestyle is so beyond what I know. I'm a suburban mom who lives a very small, insulated life. This world you live in is a fantasy, galaxies away from my existence."

Unable to stop him any longer, she didn't fight when he kissed her fingertip, then dipped his head. "You're more than woman enough for me. I'm just putting on a big show to dazzle you. This isn't every day for me, either."

Court's breath at her neck triggered her sexual response. In the back of her mind, she cataloged the physical sensations overloading her nervous system. Weakened knees, moisture between her legs, breath she couldn't seem to catch, and blood that flowed like hot honey through her veins.

"Catherine is not so much a woman as a plastic doll. She looks good from a distance, but close up, she's nothing more than a socialite looking for a bank account to keep her in style."

Breathless or not, she had to counter his insistence. "That may be, but she's obviously the kind of woman you're used to."

"Nice to know what you think of me." It looked as if he had more to say, but a discreet bell tinkled from below and Court's frown smoothed. "Ah. Tea must be ready. Let's go sort things with Fiske; then we'll get serious about resting up for tomorrow. We'll also fix your misconception about what sort of woman turns me on and how I hope this week will go."

Court's hand on her waist guided her out the door. "What do you think of having Chinese sent up? Had spicy shrimp lately?" he asked.

He remembered. Anticipation shimmered in a heated cascade right down her body and settled in her core. "I guess we'd better order extra towels."

# Chapter 17

"Is there anything else you require tonight, sir?"

Court shook his head while walking the older man toward the elevator. "I doubt very much we'll need you tonight, so get some rest. Madam has an ambitious schedule this week."

"Nothing out of the ordinary, sir. When did you want me to arrange for a jeweler to stop by?" Fiske asked quietly, and Court glanced up to the balcony near the master bedroom where Randi was getting ready for dinner.

"How late will her spa appointment go tomorrow?"

"At least four. I can tell the staff to drag things out a bit if you like."

"She's signed up for the full treatment already?"

"Yes, the complete package starting at one. Waxing first, followed by massage and facial, and finishing up with a pedicure and manicure."

"And they'll do it all here in the suite?" Fiske confirmed it with a nod. "Should I take the business meeting downstairs tomorrow afternoon?"

"If you like, sir, but you'll never know the spa staff is here. They're very discreet, and all the services will take place upstairs behind closed doors."

"What happened to the good old days of a beauty salon in the basement?"

The old man finally cracked a smile. "Guests prefer it this way."

"Ah well, we must move with the times, eh? All right, let's not worry about it." He heard a door open upstairs. "Eight will be soon enough in the morning, unless you have a schedule you must adhere to. As for the jeweler, can we arrange for a meeting about three? Book a small conference room downstairs?"

"Seven thirty will be acceptable for me, sir. I'll see what I can arrange for the jeweler. Good night."

Court heaved a sigh when the elevator door closed behind the butler. The man had wanted to stay and serve up the Chinese food delivered only minutes ago. It had practically taken swearing on the crown jewels and a promise to leave everything in the kitchen for clean up in the morning before Fiske would leave.

"Court?" Randi's voice carried softly down from the upper hallway. "Are we alone?"

"At last, love." He pressed a button on the keypad near the elevator. Do Not Disturb. Fiske assured him no one would dream of interrupting them before he showed up the next morning at half past seven. Court was positive Randi hadn't requested breakfast so early, but apparently, the man needed time for preparation. As long as he did it quietly, Court had no objection.

Movement on the stairs drew his attention, and he turned to watch Randi slowly descend, wearing only a thin white dressing robe, carrying a stack of towels. The winter sun had long set, and the lights had been dimmed, a few candles lit for a romantic ambiance.

"The food smells good."

"And you look even better." He moved to the bottom of the staircase and reached for her as her bare feet touched the floor. "Are you sure you don't want to do this in the bedroom?" Hunger gnawed at him. Hunger for dinner as well as for her. Lucky him, he'd get to take care of both at the same time. He could hardly wait.

"I'd rather not smell soy and ginger on the sheets all night long."

"As my lady wishes. Won't take me but a moment to reset the table. Fiske did insist."

They shared a laugh.

"I don't suppose he'd approve of his setting being rearranged."

"Doesn't matter what he approves of," Court told her. "Come, I'd like to eat while...the food...is still hot."

"What about me?" She pouted prettily.

"I fully expect you to get hotter the longer dinner carries on." He already trembled on the edge of anticipation.

"Oh, sir." She blushed and tilted her face up for a kiss.

"Come. I'm starving." He took the towels from her and laced their fingers together.

"Shall I close the curtains?"

Court smiled at her. "Why? No one can see us without a very high powered telescope, and even then the lights are low. If they want to put so much work into spying, shouldn't they have some reward?"

"All right. Then why don't I lose the robe? Since no one can see in."

"Good plan, but wait, I want to watch." He pointed toward the entertainment wall. "Why don't you find us some music?"

"I'm guessing you're not talking about hits of the eighties, are you?"

While she opened the cabinet doors, he set the towels down on a chair and started pulling the plates and silverware off the sturdy dining table with a view over Central Park. Looking north, the park was a dim area with tiny spots of lights peeking through the thick tree branches bare of leaves. The rest of Manhattan shimmered with lights from buildings, street lamps, and the never ending movement of vehicles. "A little blues or slow jazz would work. Or light classical. What do you like for mood music?"

"Oh, a little of this, a little of that. Ravel always works."

He laughed. "Surely we've grown beyond something as trite as *Bolero*?"

She answered him by finding dark and smoky jazz, a slow sax, piano, and drum trio.

Once the table was clear of breakables, he turned and met her gaze, equally as dark and smoky as the music wafting from the hidden sound system. "Oh, darling. Now you've gone and done it." The last time his pants had fit this tight was when he'd had her backed up against the wall in her powder room.

"And what is it I've done?" Low and sultry, her voice touched him like a silk scarf being dragged down his body.

"Now. Slide the useless robe off, and do it now. Nice and slow." He sat on the sofa and leaned back, feigning a relaxation he didn't feel. Her gazed settled on the erection straining against his slacks, and she smiled as mysterious as the woman herself. A smile that surely dated back to the first time a woman realized her power over man. Eve, Cleopatra, and Mata Hari had very likely smiled in this same way. If a man had to fall to his knees to worship a woman, he couldn't think of any other way he'd want to submit.

"Like this?" Her hands slowly worked loose the knot of the belt holding the robe closed.

"Step this way, darling, and hand me the belt."

Hips swaying to the beat, she sauntered up to him, stopping when she stood between his splayed legs. The knot slid apart, and the two sides dangled from her hands. "This belt?"

One end fell across his hand, and he held it between two fingers. "You don't need it anymore." Slowly rolling the cloth around his hand, he pulled it loose from one loop and then the other, leaving Randi holding the robe closed over her body. "Now the robe. Dance for me while you ease it off your body."

"What kind of dance?"

"The kind of dance where you stay right where you are."

"Mmm." Eyes twinkling, she moaned and swayed, her legs touching his as she moved. He knew she expected him to watch her body, instead, he watched her eyes as they strayed down his body and back up again. He could see the questions as if they were printed on her forehead. What would he do with the belt? Tie her up of course. How long would he draw out the teasing? As long as he could stand. How much of a certain night did he remember? Every single delicious second. He would show her he remembered it. Had doubts of his intentions, did she? By the end of the week, her doubts would be few, if any remained at all.

Because the suspense would work on her mind every bit as much as his plans would work on her body, he let her wonder, giving her no inkling of what lay in store.

One side of the robe slid off her shoulder, revealing white skin and the upper swell of a generous breast. God, she'd never looked more beautiful. Fighting for air, he did his best to hide his reaction, not that she missed the twitching of his cock beneath his trousers. Another shifting of cloth and the other shoulder slid into view. In the background, the sax wailed mournfully while a drum added a sensual backbeat Randi swayed to as the robe slid down her back, her two small hands holding the front close to her breasts.

"That's it, baby. Feel it," he encouraged her. "Good heavens, you're so damn gorgeous."

Heat flared in her eyes as candlelight danced over her skin. The robe draped down to her hips in the back, yet didn't reveal more than the soft upper slopes of her breasts. Moving with the music, she turned, showing him the long line of her spine, the dimples between her hips. Unable to resist, he reached up and touched her with a single finger. Starting at her nape, he trailed it down the shallow valley of her spine, feeling each slight bump of vertebrae. A quiver rippled across her skin leaving small pleasure bumps behind. Goose flesh. At the base of her spine, his finger caught on the robe, and he tugged it down, his nail lightly skimming her skin. Following the valley between her buttocks, he dragged the robe down her arms, past hands that no longer held onto the cloth. The filmy material settled in a soft heap around her feet.

With her back to him, she took tiny steps over the robe until one leg rested against his crotch. Using just the one finger, he skimmed up her inner thigh, then traced the lower curve of her bottom outward and around her hip. The finger continued across her lower back to the other side, out and down around the other hip and under the curve of her other cheek.

"Absolutely fucking gorgeous," he whispered.

"Is this all you plan to do? Tease my rear and call it beautiful?"

"No. I'm going to take your ass tonight. But first, our spicy shrimp is getting cold, and I know how you like your dinner hot." Before she could escape, he leaned forward and gently bit her, leaving just a tiny mark.

"Oooooooh," she cooed. "I hope there's more where that came from."

Bloody hell. If he didn't get her to the table, he'd take her right here and the food could go hang. He stood and reached around her, his hands moving from her waist up over her ribs to her breasts. The belt from the robe was still wrapped around his left hand, and he used it to rub over her nipple. "There's plenty waiting for you tonight. Be a good girl and you'll get to enjoy every bit of it."

"I'm good." Sultry eyes gazed over her shoulder. "I'll be even better by the time the night is over."

"You'll be exhausted by the time the night is over." If he could last that long himself. But then again, he'd gladly die trying. Heat from her soft skin penetrated his shirt when she leaned against him. "Let me show you the first of many wonders in store. We'll start with dinner."

"I'm starved."

He led her to the table, a large circle of mahogany set on a sturdy polished steel base with six steel and wood chairs set about it. Beyond, a large window framed just one nighttime view of the city. "Up you go." Hands on her waist, he helped her onto the cleared surface.

"No towel under me?" She lay back and shivered at the cool touch of the polished wood.

"I'll lay them about to catch any drips, but no, you get to feel the table under you. Cool, hard, impenetrable."

He watched as she shivered, but her eyes never left his.

"Hands over your head. Can't have you trying to rearrange the dinner once I get it served up," he told her. Obediently, she lifted her hands and clasped them at the top of her head. He moved around the table and used the belt to gently tie her wrists together with one end and secured the other end to a chair. "Okay?"

"Yes," she whispered.

Arranging the food on her body was almost as much fun as eating it off her would be. The large shrimp they both loved circled each breast. Potstickers fanned out around her belly button filled with dipping sauce. "Don't wiggle too much, or you'll spill it all," he cautioned. He spread her legs wide and arranged long noodles down her thighs. "You look positively delicious, darling." Peapods and wontons lined her ribs.

"Smells good. When do I get a bite?"

"A bite?" He leaned over, and with his lips, plucked a shrimp from her breast. "I get to do the biting, love." With the shrimp, he brushed her nipple until she moaned. "No wiggling," he reminded her. A pair of chopsticks worked particularly well for tweaking her other nipple before he lifted another shrimp and held it to her lips. "Open up, darling, and show me how you'll take care of me later."

What the woman could do with a prawn... He nearly scraped the food from her body right then. Instead, he watched her chew it while he removed his shirt. Not once did her gaze leave him as he stripped, not quite as provocatively as she had. The music still flowed from the speakers, and Randi's eyelids drooped with lust as she hummed along. He didn't think she even noticed.

Once bare, he picked up the chopsticks again. For each bit of food he ate from her body, he dropped a bite into her mouth. His tongue lapped up the drips and shared them with her in deep kisses. When he reached the noodles on her legs, he used his mouth on her beautiful pussy, drenching the noodles in her juices, then sharing with her. With the last noodle, he teased her, using the chopsticks to lightly hold her clit while he licked and suckled on her flesh. Each tiny pinch brought a moan and more wetness from her until she panted and begged him to finish. The ability to hold back was beyond him. He climbed onto the table and kneeled between her thighs. Spreading her legs on top of his thighs, he admired her body while guiding himself into position.

Their eyes met, and he could nearly see the sparks fly between them.

"I love you, Randi," he said. "I'll never let you forget it."

Not giving her a chance to answer, he relished her gasp as he pulled her onto him, fusing their bodies. The gasp turned into a cry, and as she shuddered around him, his control fled. He pulled back once and immediately reversed, thrusting into her body. Nothing had ever felt this good. Shouting her name, he released deep inside her, his name a sweet cry from her arching throat.

# Chapter 18

A long night of lovemaking notwithstanding, Randi felt energized the next morning. And grateful she'd brought her most formal business clothes, which she imagined were still casual by New York standards.

"Where'd my California girl go?" Court fit his body against her back as she fastened a pearl stud in her earlobe. His lips on the opposite side of her neck brought back every sensuous memory of the night before. "I can still taste the ginger sauce on your skin."

"Mmm, that's my perfume, and I can't imagine it tastes so wonderful."

"You actually bought perfume that smells like Chinese food?"

Randi laughed softly, feeling softer and younger than she had in years. "It's from Hawaii, and I bought it in Chinatown."

"Better order more Chinese for lunch." Court's warm breath tickled her neck and weakened her knees.

"Don't you have plans to meet all day? And shouldn't Larry be here soon?"

"I think we can call it a day by noon. It'll do the man good to stew over-night."

"Mmm, what about my beauty treatments appointment? Ah, Court, you need to stop." She wiggled her hips in a vain attempt to shake him off. "At this rate, you'll be eating your eggs and bacon…"

"At the table, but with you as my plate. I'm suddenly ravenous." Court's hands traveled from her wool clad hips to her silk covered breasts.

She moaned, arching into his hands. The thought of him eating his food off her body… Lord, what a wonderful way to enjoy a meal. "Now I'll have to wear the jacket all day."

"No, you won't."

"Everyone will know where your hands have been."

"Perfect." Court tipped her head and ravaged the other side of her neck. "Delicious."

The gentle sound of a bell ringing and the ping of the elevator interrupted, and Court sighed heavily. "I suppose it's time."

Randi turned and raised her arms to drape over his shoulders. "Yes. I asked for breakfast by eight fifteen."

"A mite early, love."

With a sigh of soul deep contentment she accepted his light kiss on her powdered nose. "I like a leisurely meal."

"Tell me you weren't joking about the bacon and eggs."

"What?" Randi stepped back and straightened her clothes with the help of the mirror. Shaking her head, she reached for her jacket to pull over the ivory silk shell she wore.

"Leave it off for now." Court took the jacket from her hands. "Why on earth are you wearing black? You wear far too much black."

"It's classic and easy to accessorize. Please, my blouse is wrinkled. I'd like my jacket."

"It's hardly wrinkled at all. I doubt anyone else will notice. Besides, you don't belong in stuffy suits."

"It's a classic."

"You belong in green, love." Her jacket held by the collar, Court wrapped his other hand around her waist and guided her from the bedroom. "A flowing gown that clings to your body. Nothing fussy or stuffy for you."

"Cliché. Redheads in green is overdone. Besides, haven't you heard about this little time period called mourning? I believe it was made popular by one of your monarchs." She glanced up at him through her lashes as they took the stairs down. "Victoria? Name ring a bell?"

"So century before last. And if you were following the fashion, you'd be wearing pale lavender by now, but I think it's safe to say you can throw off the colors of mourning completely."

"I look horrible in lavender." At the bottom of the stairs she stopped and straightened his tie. Any excuse to touch him.

"All the more reason to toss away the widow's weeds." Careless of the suit jackets he carried, Court wrapped his arms around her. "I don't smell bacon, darling. What did you order for breakfast?"

"Yogurt, grapefruit, oatmeal, wheat toast, and orange juice."

"Hell's bells." Court groaned. "We had this discussion in California. That is not a proper breakfast. It won't hold me until lunch."

"You have your choice of coffee or tea, of course."

"I thought we agreed to a full English breakfast."

"You agreed. But then you put me in charge. I believe the only requirements were coffee and tea service during your meetings."

"Ahem."

Court looked up and over Randi's head at the feminine sound from the dining area. "Martha. You made it in time. Good." Court released Randi on one side and turned her. "This is Ms. Ferguson. Randi, this is my secretary, the ever indispensable Martha. Anything Fiske can't handle, turn it over to Martha."

The indispensable Martha was a revelation. In fact, the woman looked an awful lot like Randi herself had twenty years earlier. She smiled to cover the ice that suddenly dropped her stomach to her toes. "Martha, thank you for handling the last minute change of plans in moving the meeting stateside." Randi extended her hand. From the way Martha's gaze raked her from head to toe, she wondered just how indispensable Martha felt herself to be. The returned handshake was firm and brief.

"My pleasure, ma'am." The tight smile from the younger woman came nowhere close to reaching the icy green eyes. Green eyes enhanced by the forest green suit which perfectly showcased shoulder length golden red hair and shapely legs displayed to advantage by matching green leather pumps. Had Randi worn formal business wear at twenty-two, she would have been a dead ringer for this woman. Apparently, Martha also recognized the similarities and wasn't amused.

"My goodness, Court, it's almost like looking in a mirror from the past." At least Randi had the dubious pleasure of seeing Court do a double take, his head swiveling between one woman and the other.

"Blimey, you're right. I never noticed it before, but Martha could be your sister." Oblivious to the tension in the room, he took Randi's hand and tugged her toward the dining table. She could almost hear Martha's thoughts. No way did the younger woman buy the sister line. "Morning, Fiske. Tell me she doesn't have me on a starvation plan."

Fiske held a chair for Randi as he answered. "The heart healthy breakfast, sir. Complex carbohydrates, fruit, low fat dairy, and low cholesterol protein."

Court tossed their suit jackets over the back of the sofa before pulling out his own chair. "Low cholesterol?"

"Egg white omelet, sir."

Court groaned and hauled Randi close to his side. "Darling. Egg white omelet?"

"With onion, tomato, ham and cheese, and only half egg white. Now unhand me and fuel up."

"Martha, better come sit with us and keep my mind off this dire food by going over the schedule." Court pressed a kiss on Randi's lips and released her to shake out the white linen napkin. The chill around her intensified as she watched Court morph into mogul. It was an amazing transformation.

Not pleased with the sudden business tone that filled the air, Randi dug into her cup of yogurt, eating silently while Martha opened her leather planner and began flipping through documents as if they sat in a boardroom instead of at the breakfast table.

"The cards you requested arrived this morning," Martha said, and handed over two plastic credit cards. Court glanced at them, then set them down next to Randi's plate while his secretary next delivered a sheet of paper. She barely noted their existence as Martha plowed onward. "These are the notes you forwarded regarding the first part of today's meeting with Larry. He's particularly interested in items one through five and wants them to start arriving in his stores within the next three weeks. He's already late for the Christmas rush, but has an intense advertising campaign ready to go the moment the first shipments arrive."

"And the supplier in South Africa?" Court lifted his tea cup and drank while reading down the list.

"They have an ample supply of the Rooibos in a dozen blends. Shipment by the usual methods will be slow, but as the product is light in weight, we could guarantee delivery by air freight."

"Upping the cost significantly," Court said.

"Of course, however…"

"Yes, he waited until the last moment—again—and expects us to pull a miracle out of our hat. Good thing I anticipated him, and we have enough to get a minimal supply to him within a week if he agrees to the terms."

The business talk continued as Randi ate a few bites of each dish Fiske placed in front of her. Court ate without paying particular attention to the food, neither complimenting nor complaining, until he reached the grapefruit half, which he merely waved away.

If Martha wasn't handing him papers, Court ate with one hand and rested the other on Randi's thigh. She understood the significance of preparing for the day's meetings, but she objected to breakfast as the time to do it, and she was about to speak up when a stack of letters requiring Court's signature appeared from the leather folder.

Court spared Randi a rueful grin. "After all, I was out of the office for the entire week."

"Of course." She hid her grimace by sipping from her tea cup.

Martha briefly met her gaze with a look that voiced disapproval as if she'd shouted it from the roof top, but Court missed it entirely.

"What do you think of the tea?" he asked Randi.

"I've always enjoyed this blend. Of course, this particular Emperor's Puerh is distributed from the Bay Area. Not far from my house, as a matter of fact."

Court laughed and leaned over to kiss her cheek. "I knew all those teapots meant something more than a casual tea drinker."

With a slight shrug, she tried to dismiss his curiosity.

"Come now, tell me how deep your knowledge goes." He rested an arm on the back of her chair and reached for the teapot to refill her cup. "How did the collection get started?"

"It started when Mother gave us the large silver tea service for our wedding. From there it became a tradition." The collection had grown with each anniversary, some years a small whimsical tea pot had caught Wyatt's eye, others an elaborate set. Then a friend had noticed and bought her a tea-for-one set for a birthday. From there, the gifts had exploded to the point Randi had wistfully admired the diamonds and gold the husbands of her friends purchased each year. Randi got tea pots and tea sets.

"You should see this assortment, Martha." Court set down the pot and relaxed, leaving his arm loosely embracing Randi's shoulders. His body heat comforted her. "Close to a hundred sets if I'm not mistaken. Everything from Royal Doulton to some of the funkiest artist renditions you've ever seen. Cast iron, silver, bone china, ceramic, yixing, new, old, antique; I think I even noticed a Tony Carter in one cabinet and something hand carved in wood in another. I don't think I've seen such a collection outside a museum before."

"Amazing," the indispensable Martha murmured, clearly not impressed.

"I still can't get her to own up to her favorite tea after all this time."

"I don't have a favorite," Randi said.

"Used to be Earl Grey. What happened?"

Like she would really tell him the truth about that? "I decided to be eclectic and broaden my horizons."

"I'm curious to see how your palate has developed. I also want your opinion on a selection of Maté blends. In the meantime, these cards are for you. I know how much women like shopping, so I don't want you to feel restricted. One is for you and one is for Birdie. I hope she uses her legal name for things like credit cards because I used Courtney on the card."

"Court—" Outraged, Randi began to protest, but the cards were slipped into her hand as what served as a doorbell chimed, interrupting what surely would have been a scene by the time she finished. Later. She'd lodge her complaint in private and not in front of the audience around them

"There's Larry. Now, I want you back here for lunch. Larry will pester me to death if you aren't, and I don't want to be apart a moment longer than necessary. After that, Fiske assures me you'll get the entire pampering package." He paused enough to catch the growing irritation in her expression. Lowering his voice, he leaned close enough to whisper against her lips, "Humor me and buy something nice to wear for dinner out."

Well that was clear enough. He wanted something sexy enough to peel off her almost the moment she'd put it on. And green. Maybe. Maybe not.

Like a runaway locomotive, the business version of Court steamrollered right over her. She was barely given enough time to greet Larry—who very much noticed the wrinkled handprints over her breasts—shrug into her suit jacket, and shoulder her purse before she found herself on the elevator down to meet the driver who had her car standing ready. Tucked in her handbag were the new credit cards and the names of personal shoppers at Saks, Barneys, Bergdorf-Goodman, and Bloomingdale's. She also had Fiske's and Martha's cell numbers programmed into her phone. Just in case.

She didn't know whether to laugh or cry.

So she went shopping.

# Chapter 19

By noon Thursday, Randi was shopped, spa-ed and museumed out. Wandering the stores alone had quickly ceased to be fun, and there were only so many times she could be buffed, waxed, massaged, and polished. There were plenty more sights to see, but a little went a long way there. Especially alone with a driver standing by. As much as Court said he wanted to spend time with her, the indispensable Martha had kept him snowed under a mountain of paperwork between meetings with Larry. Monday night they'd had dinner out, and Court had presented her with a pair of exquisite emerald earrings. That was the last time they'd made long, leisurely love, deep into the night, with him exploring every newly waxed inch of her body. The mere memory was enough to make Randi shiver with heat.

Tuesday, she'd spent the morning pretending to shop, telling herself she loved it, then the afternoon visiting two museums, arriving back at the suite in time to catch a small scene which might have been innocent, or… No, Court wouldn't do that, would he? Larry was nowhere in sight, and the impeccably dressed Martha looked just mussed enough, her blouse wrinkled in just a way, the smile on her face satisfied and smug, lipstick slightly smeared. Court seemed a little distracted, a little tired, and the scent of Martha's perfume had been clinging to him as he greeted Randi with a hug. Then again, the woman's perfume had nearly permeated the suite and would most likely require a week's airing to clear out. Thankfully, the scent hadn't made it to the bedroom. Or had it?

Tired herself from a full day out, she gave Court the benefit of the doubt as he didn't seem to notice when Martha eventually excused herself. Larry claimed prior plans, so dinner was a quiet affair, eaten in the suite, and they'd both fallen asleep early. She'd managed to plead exhaustion to avoid making love, but that didn't stop Court from holding her all night long. At least the scent of his skin smelled nothing like another woman's perfume.

Wednesday started with relaxed morning loving and a shared shower. Court finished dressing first and went down to breakfast several minutes before Randi, who admittedly, was dragging her feet. Another day on her own stretched out ahead. Not even the glitter and anticipation of Christmas filling the air had made shopping for gifts feel like anything more than a chore. She'd do better ordering online. Soft soled flats on her feet, she didn't make a sound leaving the upstairs bedroom and overheard Court's exclamation of disgust.

"What is this bloody rubbish? Why is this even here?"

Martha's hated voice answered. "I thought you should know."

"When have I ever paid attention to the bleeding gossip rags?"

"This is what they're reading at home."

"Must be a slow week," he grumbled. Randi watched from the balcony as Court slapped down the folded paper beside his place setting. "Get rid of it. It has no bearing here."

Still silent, Randi swiftly made her way down the stairs and to the table before Court noticed and looked up. The napkin he placed over the paper wasn't subtle, nor did he hide his irritation well.

"Oh good, I haven't seen a paper in days." Randi leaned across him and snatched it from under the napkin.

"Randi, there's nothing in there worth reading. It's just one of those tabloids the masses love for their outrageousness."

"Oh, I disagree. I used to love reading the London tabloids. They're better entertainment than reality TV." Scanning the page, she held it away from him. There, at the very bottom, the last inch… with two photos squeezed in side by side…

*Spying eyes caught sight of New York socialite Catherine Miller en dishabille leaving the hotel apartment of one of our favorite Brit importers. Seems, despite the connections the Miller textile merchants can provide him, Lynford International Importers' most eligible bachelor, CEO Courtland Robinson, found new fields to plow in California. It took us a couple days to hit pay dirt, but the beauty on his arm is an heiress with wine connections, and the grapevine tells us last week he spent a quid or two bolstering his cellar with West Coast grape juice and his bedroom with a sun-kissed mature beauty, the recently widowed Randi Ferguson. Rumor has it these two have a past going back decades, and we can only wonder what they're doing in NYC and what he plans to do about*

*all the hearts he's broken in Manhattan, and more so, the many London*
*socialites who've been fluttering around the widower these past six years.*

"It's rubbish, of course." Court laughed, albeit a little forced.

"Of course it is," Randi said lightly. "After all, she had a point; I'm nobody on this side of the US, much less Europe. We strictly do business on the West Coast." She tossed the paper down and picked up her cup of yogurt. Looking up, she caught sight of what looked like a hard glint of malice in Martha's eyes. Had Martha been the one to provide the photos and details? What did she have to gain, if she had? Randi returned the direct gaze and did her best to look mildly amused. "So what happens now? Do I need to find a big hat and Jackie O sunglasses?"

Randi wanted to take Court aside to talk about it, but Larry arrived, up to date on the gossip rag and begging details. Fiske quietly assured her if one of the staff was responsible, he or she would be sacked immediately. Too bad Fiske couldn't sack Martha.

The incident introduced a sour note to her day, and Randi grumbled at herself for letting it bother her. The situation didn't improve when she returned for lunch and Martha hovered over Court, pushing the paperwork at him all through the meal, leaving Randi open to Larry's flirting. Court frowned, but he didn't put down his foot, either, letting work intrude on the midday meal despite Randi's protest.

They'd planned to eat out before the show, but a few photographers had been waiting when Randi emerged from the hotel for another lonely afternoon, this time at the Museum of Modern Art. Fortunately, a doorman intervened, and her driver whisked her off to the Museum of American Finance on Wall Street. A place she imagined few normal people would seek out. From there, she paid a visit to MarieBelle Cacao Bar and Tea Salon. The driver had suggested, and she'd declined, a visit to the Museum of Sex—it certainly was not a place she wanted to go alone. Perhaps Court would be interested tomorrow or the next day. She returned to the suite by way of the underground parking garage and zipped up a back elevator, straight into Fiske's capable care.

"Where are we dining tonight?" Randi asked.

Fiske served a light tea, featuring a Rooibos variation.

"What's wrong?" Though clearly worn by the heavy schedule, which Randi figured wasn't working out as well as he would have liked, Court nevertheless noticed when she pushed away the steaming cup of brew.

"A little too grassy for my likes. I might as well gather grass clippings from my yard instead of the savannah."

"Ditch the Rooibos, Fiske."

"Yes, sir."

"Dinner tonight?" Randi prompted him.

"I booked a table downstairs. Paparazzi aren't allowed in. Did they give you much trouble while you were out?"

Randi laughed. "They aren't interested in little old me. As you said, it must be a slow week for the celebrities. No, I discovered some off the beaten path locations."

When she told him how fascinating she'd found the finance museum, he laughed. "Only you, darling. Where else?"

"I had it on good authority the Museum of Sex would be an interesting stop, but I figured that one would be more fun with company." She didn't mean for her lip to wobble, but as miniscule as it was, Court saw it and pulled her onto his lap.

"I think we can swing it day after tomorrow," he murmured in her ear.

Arms wrapped around his shoulders, she rested her head against his with a small sigh. "I'd like that. A lot."

"I'm sorry I've been such a dud so far this week. We'll have a bit of fun tonight. You like ABBA, right?"

"You weren't a dud this morning." She trailed a painted fingernail across his lower lip.

"Get me going now, and we'll miss not only dinner but the show as well."

Tempting. Very tempting, but part of the fun of New York, as Jordan had expounded only last week, was the nightlife. The excitement and glitter of Broadway.

"Think you'll be up for it later tonight?"

"I could be dead as a stinking dodo and still have it up for you, darling. Just knowing you're in the hotel makes me half hard."

At dinner, Court drank a little too much, and mid-way through the first half of the show, his eyes closed. At least he didn't snore, but he did startle awake when Randi poked him in the shoulder at intermission.

"I'm sorry, Court, but I've got a terrible headache. Do you mind if we skip out on the second half?"

It took him a moment to gather himself. "Headache you say?"

"Yes. I think I had a little too much wine, and the mix of perfumes is killing me. But if you mind too terribly…"

"No, no. If you're not happy, we'll go."

They returned to the hotel, agreed on a bath in the enormous tub, but Court nodded off there, too.

"Come on, Mr. Excitement. I think our day is over."

Mumbled apologies on his lips, he'd fallen asleep right after gathering her into his arms. Randi stared out the tall windows toward the night sky. What was it she liked about driven, ambitious men? How many nights had Wyatt fallen asleep on her? Morning had always been his best time, and more often than not, she'd gone along with him, faking a quick orgasm so they could get out of bed sooner. Was it like that for most men? Wake up fresh in the morning? She always woke up with her schedule for the day running through her head. Never a sexy thought, although mornings with Court were still fresh and new, and outlining daily tasks didn't intrude until later.

Thursday morning they almost made love, but neither of them seemed to have the appetite for it. Court's apologies didn't bolster her mood one bit.

"I'll make it up to you, darling. I know this isn't what I promised you. You've been so very patient." His kisses were sweet and edged with a hint of something Randi didn't recognize. If pressed to identify it, she'd say guilt. The large bouquet of flowers at her place at the breakfast table pretty much nailed the lid on her depressed mood, and the memory of rumpled Martha crossed her mind only to be ruthlessly dismissed. Court felt guilty about falling asleep at the show. That was all. No need to make a big deal out of it.

"We should be completely finished by noon today," Court said as he kissed her goodbye at the elevator. "It's even possible I'll be free after today. I swear I'll make up for being a bore."

"Court, it's all right." She used her most soothing voice. "I understand about business, really, I do." Smoothing his shirt to avoid looking into his eyes, she patted his chest. This was one more facet of Court the businessman. The gap in their circumstances widened a few more inches. Not entirely different than the occasional instance with Wyatt, but on a far grander scale. With Court, this would be normal on any given day. Business first. He had too many people relying on him to let it take a back seat to his personal wishes.

"Well, I don't. You're an angel, Randi. See you at lunch."

At lunch he had more apologies.

"There's been a hang-up," Court said. "Larry and I have to run out to a meeting. I honestly don't know how long it will take. I'll call when I know what's happening." The kiss he gave her had been quick and poorly aimed at her forehead.

"Are you going out this afternoon?" Martha asked once they were alone.

"No, I think I'll stay in and do some catch up. I've neglected e-mail and my family."

"Very well. I have some paperwork and arrangements to make." The younger woman began gathering her folders and laptop.

"How long have you been with Court, Martha?" Randi hated asking the question, but the two worked so closely, and sometimes the expression on Martha's face looked a little too...no, Court wouldn't sleep with his secretary, would he?

Well, Randi herself had acted as his secretary all those years ago, and he'd been sleeping with her. Had he learned his lesson or learned he liked that sort of working relationship? She was tempted to blame the cold chill suddenly filling her on the iced tea at lunch.

"I've been with him about seven years. Long enough to know how miserable his marriage was. Poor man, absolutely lost when it finally ended." Pausing in her work, she sighed, a dreamy gaze in her eyes. "The entire situation was such a mess. He'd filed for divorce, and then she died. The speculation in the papers was bloody awful. I'm just glad I was there for him. We grew close over the whole situation." The change to a direct gaze aimed at Randi left no question of how Martha expected her to interpret that statement.

"I see." Randi wasn't sure she saw what Martha wanted to portray. Working together created its own version of close but didn't necessarily translate to the sexual realm, and so far, Court hadn't shown signs of anything beyond a working relationship. Still, the clichés about bosses and secretaries existed for a reason and occurred far too often to discount entirely. She was about to question the other woman further when Martha's cell phone rang.

Her phone always handy, Martha answered before the second ring. "Yes, Court?"

Well, that was on purpose.

"No, no, I'll take care of it. No problem. I'll let her know. Right. Got it." Martha clicked her phone shut and turned to Randi. "That was Court."

Randi nodded. "Obviously."

"This deal is falling apart. He asked me to reschedule your flight home. He won't be back until late tonight and then will have to fly out immediately. He's very sorry, and he'll call you when he can."

The news was delivered as if discussing what office supplies needed to be ordered, but Martha had a glint in her eyes Randi didn't trust. It had been obvious from the start she and Martha would never be buddies, but out and out enemies? Surely the woman was smarter than that.

"Don't let this distress you," Martha continued. "This happens all the time and is usually why he sticks to professional women who know when to make a discreet exit."

Now *that* she hadn't expected and blinked in surprise. "Professional women?"

"Yes, he has contacts with many escort services around the world. Women who are well paid to be interesting companions for rich businessmen."

Randi's heart stuttered to a near standstill. It felt as heavy as a lump of granite, but she did her best to hide her feelings from the cold bitch before her. The last had been a hit meant to weaken Randi's confidence. No way would she let Martha know how close it came to matching things Randi had wondered about. "I see. Well, I still need to make contact with my family. I'll take care of my own flight arrangements. I presume you can do whatever arranging you need to from your own room." At least for now, the suite was hers to command.

"Of course. Let me know if I may be of any assistance to you." Martha picked up her datebook and laptop. "You know how to reach me."

Randi nodded but didn't move until the elevator door closed on Martha.

"Ma'am?" Fiske's courteous inquiry surprised her enough she flinched. Where had he come from?

"Mr. Fiske." Turning slowly, she hoped she portrayed a solid façade of cool, collected calm.

"I couldn't help overhearing…" He cleared his throat uncomfortably. "If you'll pardon my butting in?"

The man had been nothing but kind to her and regarded her now with a look of fatherly concern. He also took a huge risk by offering a personal opinion. While Court had advised her to treat the man like furniture—but politely—she couldn't do it. He was a human being in a unique place to observe events and had years of practice doing such. "Please. If you have something to say, I'd love to hear it."

"I don't know Mr. Robinson well, but honestly, I'm not sure my image fits with what she just said."

Randi sighed and gave him a small smile. "I agree with you but, unfortunately, I've had some signs that lend just a tiny"—Randi indicated so by nearly pinching her thumb and forefinger together—"bit of credibility to her statements. I admit I don't trust her much, but she has been very efficient and mostly professional. Especially when she thinks Court is around." Hands on her hips, she frowned toward the elevator where Martha had just disappeared. "Would she risk a job she clearly loves by giving me information which could easily be checked out?"

"Before you make any rash decisions, perhaps you should give Mr. Robinson a call?"

Warmth from the man's concern filled her, and she smiled at him. "I was just coming to that very conclusion."

"Might I get you a pot of tea?"

"Yes. I'd love one."

"Earl Grey?" He gave her a fond smile.

So he had been watching while Court tried to test her tea knowledge and get her to confess to a favorite. The tea she'd learned to love with Court so long ago had become her favorite again. Each time she drank it with him, a new memory joined the best of the old ones.

Randi laughed. "Found me out did you? Yes, Earl Grey, please."

"I won't give you away." Fiske resumed his dignified butler manner and spun on his heel.

The first call to Court's phone rolled over to voicemail. Thinking he might temporarily be in a dead zone, she hung up. Two more tries had the same result.

Fiske set down the tea tray beside her at the table and poured out a cup. "No luck yet?"

Randi shook her head.

"Try one more time," he urged her.

Wondering how much Fiske had observed of the meetings this week, she did as he suggested. Cup lifted to her lips, she inhaled the distinct aroma of the tea as the phone began to ring. She smiled at the butler and took a tiny sip. Court answered his phone as the tea slid down her throat.

"Randi?" The connection was full of static, and for a moment she wondered if it had cut out.

"Court?" She carefully set the delicate bone china cup on its saucer.

"Can't talk...Marth...arrangements...all made. I... call...soon...as...can."

"Court, what arrangements?" Closing off one ear with a finger, she listened hard, her small phone pressed tightly against her ear, hoping for some word that didn't sound exasperated and impatient.

"Talk to Martha," he repeated sharply. "...has...all details...can't... helped..." Static burst in her ear a moment before his voice returned. "... go home...talk...soon—"

"Oh, okay." She bit her lip, not quite believing what she'd heard. "If you say so." A hint of doubt slipped through, but had he heard it?

"Stiff...lip—" The connection died, along with her hopes and dreams.

So. Martha had instructions to make all the arrangements, and Randi had her orders to go home. Just like that.

Reflexively, she set down her phone and reached for the tea cup, more to pass herself off as the mistress of cool than a need for tea. Didn't want Fiske to see her crumble to bits right here. However, after a brief sip, her stomach clenched, and the tea turned bitter in her mouth. With a shaking hand, she lowered the cup, which rattled into place on the saucer. So much for handling herself unemotionally.

"I don't think I want it after all, Mr. Fiske." Once more the essence of bergamot became poison, and it took all she had to not run to the bathroom and purge.

She would not do this, this falling apart thing. Once was enough for any lifetime, and she never needed to do it again. She was a big girl now and hadn't expected anything other than a pleasant affair with an old lover. Too easy, she'd once told herself, yet she'd gone and done it. And what did it prove? Only what she'd suspected from the beginning. Taking the easy path had certainly cost her—again. This time the heartache was on her for being seduced into dreaming of more. Well that was that. She'd had her fun, now it was time to go home and leave the past exactly where it belonged. In the past. She had a life, a perfectly good one, and the time had come for her to return to it.

"Ma'am, it was a bad connection..." It had also plainly been loud enough Fiske had overheard every word. "I'm sure there's a misunderstanding, so many words cut out...."

"No. It was clear enough. The Indispensable Martha has indeed been instructed to make arrangements, apparently for my departure. The words 'go home' were quite understandable."

Ice filled her veins, despite her self-talk, which was ridiculous, because this was exactly what she should have expected all along. Disposable women. Like the socialite downstairs. Well, her own exit would be more dignified. This all made sense in a very twisted way, even if the puzzle pieces didn't fit exactly at the moment. If she thought about it long enough, the pattern would sort itself into place. Eventually. Maybe.

Court was a powerful, driven man. His marriage had been hellish, it made sense he would turn to women he could spend some time with, then walk away from with no regrets. Hadn't scientists spent years proving the point that males, particularly the strongest ones, were naturally inclined to propagate the species, making them not naturally monogamous? Hadn't she personally seen many marriages fall apart because of a husband with wandering ways? Granted, she also knew just as many men who did remain monogamous and faithful. Her neighbors, the Tuckers, were just one such example. Her own marriage to Wyatt, though he'd been into his late thirties when they married. Presumably, he'd worked off his need to sow wild oats by then. Funny, she'd never asked about his previous love affairs.

But with Court, something didn't entirely add up. He'd come to California and hired a P.I. to find her. Had told Birdie she could contact him at any time. Why would he do any of those things if he were just looking for a loop to close? Those seemed like extreme actions merely for a short affair with a flame from long ago. He'd then arranged a week for time alone for just the two of them. Well, not exactly time alone, though he had been up front about the business involved. Yet, he'd just confirmed Martha had the arrangements, whatever they were, under control, which meant Randi's orders were to pack up and go home without a fuss. With the earrings and the credit cards as payoff?

Like hell.

Well, lesson learned. Men from the past brought too much baggage with them. Better to be done with it now. At least she'd taken the first crucial inertia-ending step into the dating game again. It should be easier to take the second step as soon as she got home. The next man to offer her a drink would get a smile and a thank you instead of a brush off. Correction, the next attractive man. She wasn't so desperate after all. She still had her standards and some pride. Even if she had just proved to everyone she could be bought off with a trip and some jewelry. Well, the jewelry she could still give back.

"Mr. Fiske, as soon as I get my flight rescheduled, I'll need a ride to the airport." She stood and straightened the jacket of her new burgundy suit, which she'd bought with her credit card, not Court's. His card had never left her purse. At least she'd retained that much of her pride. No more gifts from him, she decided.

Standing straight, eyes forward, the perfect picture of butler efficiency, Fiske answered crisply. "Yes, Ma'am."

Heart firmly wrapped in a bandage of resolutions, she turned toward the stairs.

By quarter to two, her packed bags stood near the suite door. In her purse, she carried the paperwork for a flight out at seven. The credit cards from Court she'd left in an envelope on the dresser with a note thanking him for the lovely time. Not a lie. She'd had fun. A bit lonely, but then again, the museums she'd visited were better experienced without someone impatiently hovering, wanting to rush on when she wanted to sit and absorb. Next to the note, a wrapped tin of an exotic tea she'd found. With his connections and knowledge, it was one he probably already knew about, but it was new to her. The tea had been horribly expensive, but she'd been assured it was precious and worth the exorbitant price. Since she'd already purchased it for him, she saw no point in not giving it to him. In exchange for her keeping the earrings, although the prices paid weren't comparable.

In her purse she had small gifts for Birdie and her father. Nothing significant, just mementoes of her trip. Jewelry and cigar scissors, though she really shouldn't encourage Dad's bad habit. She hoped Birdie would like the diamond earrings as a graduation gift, and they'd laugh over a few of the tourist items in her suitcase.

After leaving a chaste kiss on Fiske's cheek, she'd left the hotel without a look back. Now she merely had to drink in the atmosphere of the café not far from the hotel. A place she'd discovered had excellent mochas and acceptable WiFi service, it was a busy, chaotic atmosphere in direct contrast to the quiet elegance of the hotel. The car would pick her up in an hour, more or less. Fiske had promised to call her cell phone when it was ready. She didn't want to miss her plane due to rush hour traffic.

"Randi?"

Deep in an e-mail from a friend, she didn't register the male voice directed at her until the chair opposite her moved and Jordan sat down. She glanced at the clock and saw thirty minutes had passed. Not long now until she had to go.

"It is you," he said and flashed a wide smile. "I didn't expect to see you here."

"Oh, hi." She gave him what felt like a very weak smile in return. She hadn't expected Jordan to be the next man to turn up in her life. So be it. She let her smile grow and warm, earning a surprised blink from him and a relaxing of his seemingly forced grin. A date with him would just be the second step easing her back into the singles market. If he came out to California again, she'd find a way to go out with him. Possibly fix him dinner as he'd enjoyed her cooking at Thanksgiving. "No, I don't suppose you would expect to find me here when I belong on the other coast."

"What are you doing here? When did you decide to come, where are you staying, and how long are you staying?"

In an effort to enforce her resolve to be friendly, Randi began the shutdown sequence of her computer. Other than Kelly's groveling over the incident on the steps on Thanksgiving, there were no interesting e-mails anyway. Birdie hadn't answered, and Dad had declared business dead, as usual, between the holidays.

"I made a snap decision to come right after Thanksgiving. I've been staying over there," she said and vaguely waved toward the tall hotel. "I'm heading home in just a bit. I need to walk back there to catch my ride in about thirty minutes."

"That's the Brit hotel."

It was almost more than she could do to not pat his hand and reward his brilliant deduction with a smile. Instead, she merely nodded.

"You came with Robinson?" Jordan pinned her to the chair with his gaze. "Where is he?"

"In meetings. He really should have headed back to London." She shrugged. "I'm shopped out, so I'm heading home."

"No," Jordan protested. "You just got here. If you've only seen Fifth Avenue, then you haven't seen the best parts of New York. You must stay and let me play tour guide."

Tempting, but she really did long for home. New York was cold and expensive. Never mind she had no real interest in Jordan—well, that could change, if given a chance. A girl always needed friends, didn't she?— and she didn't want to run into Court. It would probably be a repeat of seeing him with his arm around some taller, younger, prettier woman who dressed better than she did.

And didn't that thought feel like a knife between her ribs. With supreme effort she blinked back the threatening tears.

For the first time, she truly understood Dorothy's desire to get herself and Toto home to Kansas, and had to remind herself she'd chosen to go home and really was fine with ending her affair with Court. "Thanks, but I want to be there for Birdie as she finishes up the semester. I shouldn't have left her at this time."

Jordan stared at her for a long moment, and she wondered how much Dad had told him. Who ever said men didn't gossip? "You really want to go?"

"Yes, I really want to go." No doubts there. Home was exactly where she wanted to be.

"He treated you so poorly?"

Randi forced her laugh. "No, not at all. I've had run of the city. I'm just pining for sunshine." She pulled the collar of her new leather coat up around her ears. The faux fur collar was soft and helped minimize the chill blasting into the café each time someone opened the door.

"You've been abandoned to your own devices by a man too callous to realize how lonely you are."

Who knew the man she'd considered self-absorbed could be so perceptive? So, she wouldn't go out with him after all. She just needed to date, not see an analyst. "Jordan, it's not your concern. There are times when business simply must come first. Timing was off, that's all." Randi shrugged and looked out the window as a sleek town car in the hotel's signature silver and blue pulled up in front of the hotel across the street. "And there's my ride." She slipped her laptop into its case as her phone began to ring. She grabbed it and made note of Fiske's number. Since she'd seen the car, she felt no compunction to answer and slipped it into her purse.

Jordan stood and took the computer bag from her. "Let me walk you out and try to convince you to change your mind."

The warm smile he gave her conveyed appreciation. Randi slung her purse strap over her shoulder and slipped her arm through his. "You can try."

\* \* \* \*

"Larry, if you do this to me next year, I'll never do business with you again." Court tapped on the window separating them from the cab driver. Still a full block and a half from the hotel, traffic stood still, and he was restless anyway. "We'll climb out here. How much?" He peeled off some bills, probably over-tipping by two hundred percent.

Brisk air slapped him in the face as Larry followed him onto the curb.

"Are you crazy? I swear it's cold enough to drop a foot of snow."

Court didn't care if Larry froze solid. All he wanted was Randi in his arms, and if it meant trekking through six feet of snow, it didn't matter. The next three days, and nights—especially the nights—were hers, and he'd tag along wherever she wanted to go. He'd promised her shopping, dining, and touring. The business demands of this week had been unusually cruel, and he'd felt like a cad sending her out the door each day with only cold plastic and a driver for company. So much for seducing her into his plan to never be apart. Falling asleep during the first half of the boisterous musical hadn't been especially swift, either. Or in the bath afterward. Instead of clocking him, she'd been sweet, making him feel all the more guilty for not living up to the promises he'd made. But enough of that. He'd work double time to make it up to her.

"Not a cloud in the sky, Larry. Anyhow, as I was saying, you get your Christmas orders in by the end of October next year. September would be better, but I know you too well for that. I won't do business this way again when it can be handled in a reasonable manner long before the holidays hit. Now, I promised Randi that I'd ordered you and Martha to go home and I mean it. I want you two out of our hair."

People carrying bags and packages jostled for space on the sidewalk. In the distance, under the hotel portico, a stray beam of sunlight hit the hair of a woman. Red hair. Sparkling golden auburn. Court stretched to see if it was Randi. More than half a block away, there were enough people in the way he couldn't be sure, but it looked like her new coat. The woman stood beside a much taller man and hotel staff loaded luggage into a car just like the one he and Randi had used all week, with the exception of the cabs today.

He hadn't wanted to tie up their car and driver, and had left them for Randi to use. Though he wasn't sure why, as she hadn't stumbled through the door with armloads of bags each day. He'd seen a few, but if she'd bought more than three outfits and a few pieces of lingerie, he'd be surprised. Frowning over the thought—he should check the cards to see what she'd spent, if she'd used his cards at all—he kept his eye on the woman. The man turned just enough for Court to recognize him as soon as the bellman's cart shuttled away.

Doyle? What the hell was he doing at the hotel? The woman next to him stood about shoulder high, like Randi. She turned to face the car, her profile clear for an instant as she bent to climb in. It was Randi, he was sure...and Doyle followed? What the hell?

He tried to speed up, but the crowds on the sidewalks closed in, hampering his progress, earning him more than a few curses.

"Court, what's going on? Slow down," Larry complained.

Ignoring his friend, Court reached for his phone as it started to vibrate with an incoming call.

"Randi?" he answered without looking at the ID.

"Sir? Is this Courtland Robinson?"

It sure didn't sound like Randi, and it took a moment to place the accented male voice as belonging to his butler. The one in England. "Martin? Is that you?" From clear across the ocean. "Look, I'm sorry to be rude, but I don't have time—"

"Thank God I've reached you, sir. I'm sorry to call like this, but your mother took a fall and broke her hip." The urgency in Martin's voice began to catch Court's attention. "She's asking for you and refuses to have surgery until she talks to you. Your sister can't get her to see reason. They say she needs a hip replacement, and only you can reassure her on this point."

Court stopped in the middle of the sidewalk. Still twenty yards away, a doorman closed the door, and the car pulled away from the curb into traffic. Even if he had a clear shot and could break into a run, he'd never catch her. "Martin, can this wait? I've got—"

"Court!" Martin shouted, shocking him into listening, really listening. "Didn't you hear anything I said? Your sixty eight-year-old mother fell down and broke her hip! She's in pain and needs surgery."

"Surgery?" The word broke through the last of his distraction, and Court shook his head to clear it. "New hip?"

"Yes," Martin said in obvious relief. "You were listening. I've contacted Martha, and she's getting you a plane home. I'll meet you at the airport as soon as you arrive."

"Right." Court closed his eyes and felt Larry's hand come to rest on his shoulder, offering silent support. "Home. Hip surgery. Tell her I'll be there as soon as I can. Which hospital? I'll get the number as soon as I make it back to the suite."

Court disconnected after Martin assured him Martha had all the information he needed. Maybe she could explain about Randi driving off with Doyle.

"Court?" Larry squeezed his shoulder. "What's up? Your mum?"

"Fell. Broken hip. Larry, wasn't that Randi climbing into the hotel car?" He surged forward into the crowd. "Where do you think Randi would go with Doyle?"

"Randi? Doyle? Who's Doyle, and what does it have to do with your mum? Or Randi for that matter?"

Court flung out his arm in frustration, meaning to point after the disappearing car. His cell phone flew from his hand and landed in the street. Cursing, he started to follow, but a yellow cab, horn blaring, sped past him forcing him back onto the sidewalk where a horrible crunching noise reached his ears.

"Dammit!"

Larry echoed the curses streaming from his mouth and held up a hand to stop further traffic from rolling over Court. He quickly picked up the pieces he could, and for the first time in many years, a sense of doom settled over him.

"I can't believe you did that," Larry said as he pulled Court back onto the sidewalk, completely ignoring the hand gestures aimed in their direction.

Court could only stare down at the mashed and broken pieces in his hands. "Randi."

"What's her number, mate? You can use my phone." Larry whipped it out. "Come on, tell me. We'll have her in a jiff, and you'll see that wasn't her."

From the ruined pieces of his phone, he tried to extract the SIM card, but it was cracked beyond repair. Of all the idiotic things to happen.

"Number, old man?"

"Don't know it off the top of my head. That's what phone memories are for." Court flung the remains into the nearest trash bin and resumed pushing through the crowd to the hotel. "Martha will know. Fiske has her number as well. Gotta get back to the room. She's probably there anyway."

# Chapter 20

He'd had to have Fiske call Martha's room and drag her up to the penthouse while he used the butler's phone to try and reach Randi. Unsuccessful—her phone rolled immediately to voicemail—he stared at his assistant as her lips pressed into a thin line and she glowered at him. In the bedroom, Fiske was taking care of the last of the packing, and Martha flipped through a stack of the necessary paperwork between frowns.

"Court, we have one hour to get to the airport for check in. We'll be ready to go in just a minute or two. My bags are already with the bellhops." Martha tapped a blunt nail on her leather folder. Just one of the details he'd noticed over the last few days. Her hands lacked the grace of motion Randi had in spades. Although she was fifteen years younger than Randi, she seemed older, her youthful skin covered up with heavy cosmetics. She lacked Randi's relaxed, West Coast, sun-kissed complexion. The curse of the English in winter, skin as pale as a whitefish belly. The long hours Martha worked to keep him organized were showing. At least she was well paid to put up with him, unlike Randi.

"Martha, am I or am I not the Lord and Master of the company?"

Since he'd never taken this position, this attitude, with her before, green eyes not nearly as pretty as Randi's blinked back at him.

"You are."

"Then I can damn well do as I please. I can get myself to the airport, so I want you to take the rest of the week off, and I'll see you back in the office on Monday. Go home and relax or, better yet, stay on through the weekend if you like and put it on your expense sheet. Spend the rest of the afternoon in the spa, get your hair and nails done by a real New York beautician, whatever you want to treat yourself. Put it on the company card. A bonus for all the hard work you do." He took her arm and guided her toward the elevator.

"But, Court, I…I…" The stricken look in her eyes was there for only a moment, then a curtain of almost steely determination covered it. "Don't you think you'll need me this weekend?"

"For what? I think I can handle the situation with my mother, and the office will have a new phone for me when I get back. So, what do you want just for you? Anything you want. A weekend in the Hamptons? Boston? Skiing in Vermont? A long weekend in Miami? Name it, it's yours." Especially if she could reach Randi so he could try to talk her into flying to London with him. "Where did you say Randi had gone?"

"I didn't. I merely told you she'd gone."

"Okay, so get her on the phone and tell her to get back here. Hope she isn't too deep into shopping." Surely she'd just been heading out to another department store and had bumped into Doyle by accident? He turned away and headed for the stairs. Damned if he needed a butler to pack his suitcase.

"She's gone, as in she's on her way to the airport if not already there."

Court stopped midstride and turned to look at his assistant. "What do you mean she's gone to the airport? Going where?"

"Home. She grew tired of waiting around." Martha shrugged and stepped close, resting a hand on his arm.

"Home? Didn't you tell her you were making reservations for The Russian Tearoom? Didn't you tell her we'd be wrapped up this afternoon and both you and Larry had orders to leave us alone?"

"I did, but it didn't make any difference." Martha spoke in a voice that sent chills down his spine. She'd never used such a soft seductive voice before, and he had a moment of panic. No, surely she didn't feel…

The hand moved to his chest as she dropped her leather folio. "What will it take for you to forget all the others? When will you realize I'm the one who's always there for you? We're meant to be together."

"What?" Court stepped back. "Impossible, Martha." He laughed uncomfortably.

"She's gone," Martha said and stepped closer. "Just like all the others walk away from you. Only I stick by you. I'm the only one who's always there for you, Court."

Something very close to sheer terror gripped his guts. "Martha, don't even joke about something like that." Randi had been patient with business this week. Had Martha not delivered the message properly? Randi wouldn't have walked away from such an evening. His heart clenched so hard, for a second, he wondered if he were having a heart attack. With a deep breath of air tainted by some awful perfume, he sidestepped Martha and took the stairs two at a time.

He reached the bedroom and found it empty. The bed as neat as it was each day after housekeeping came through. On the luggage rack, his suitcase sat open but fully packed. The room looked oddly barren. Fiske came from the bathroom with Court's shaving kit in hand. Court peered around him and into the tiled room and found it likewise empty, with an abandoned feel to it. A second glance showed Randi's toiletry case missing, the contents no longer strewn across the marble counter.

Maybe she'd moved her things to the guest room. He'd just turned to head that way when a white envelope propped up on the dresser caught his eye. On the surface, written in Randi's flowing script, he read his name. Hand shaking, his secretary and the butler looking on, Court reached for it, taking only a second to make note of the small wrapped package it'd been hiding, and ripped it open. A single sheet of writing paper unfolded in his hand, and the credit cards he'd given her fell to the floor.

*Court,*

*Thank you for the very lovely time in New York. I've never been so indulged. I'm sorry to leave early, but maybe in the end it's for the best. You have your continuing issues this week, and I need to see Birdie. She isn't answering her e-mails or signing onto Facebook, and I'm worried. This will also give you the ability to better focus on business without me hanging around, waiting for you to be free. I hate that I've been such a drag on your time and energy.*

*Thank you. From the bottom of my heart. Drop me an e-mail, and we'll see if we can arrange for Birdie to fly over and spend some time with you. I'm glad she knows the truth at last, and I'm thankful she has a chance to get to know the rest of her family.*

*In case you see this before I leave for the airport, I'll be at the café across the street. The car is picking me up at 3:45. If you don't show, don't worry. I really do understand that sometimes that's just the way things are.*

*Give my best to Larry. He really is a character.*

*I thought of you when I found the tea. I hope you enjoy it as I've enjoyed my time with you.*

*Love,*

*Randi*

*P.S. I don't know much about tipping butlers, but Fiske deserves a large one.*

He glanced at his watch. Four o'clock straight up. Too late. For the second time in his life, Randi had left him. Leaving behind an even larger, more painful hole in his heart this time that he immediately tried to close with rationalization. There had to be a misunderstanding; there usually was in cases like this. Wasn't there? At least he knew exactly where to find her this time.

"Court?" Martha's hand touched his arm again.

Upon glancing up, he noticed the butler and his suitcase were gone from the room.

"She's walked out on you. I've never left you hanging. I'm there every time you turn to me. I'm the only woman who really knows and understands you. I'm younger and have more energy to keep up with your demanding schedule. I know you don't like the food she's ordered for you this week. I've never ignored your wishes in anything. You're the center of my universe, and everything I do is for you."

He stared down at the woman he'd hired seven years ago. In that time, she'd been like an extension of himself, always there, always anticipating his needs in the office. Always sweeping up the left over debris, making sure he never forgot a birthday or anniversary, always there for the important events in Drew's life. He'd told himself at the time her impressive credentials and efficient style made her so valuable. Loyalty. Steadfast focus on the job. Taking it beyond to make sure his household staff knew his comings and goings, making sure they were ready for whatever his schedule demanded. All perfect features to have in an assistant, and he valued them…. No, what struck him now was not how she handled her job. She looked like Randi.

Like Randi would have looked as a young professional woman. Only harder. Overly polished and buffed. Not like Randi now. The softer Randi. A little rounded, a tiny bit wrinkled, but sweet and smiling, gentle and warm. Loving. Caring. Nurturing. The Randi he'd fallen in love with so long ago and had never stopped loving.

Martha was a shell. She had the appearance, but not the heart and soul of the original Randi. She was a computer who tracked and organized. Yes, she kept his schedule smooth, but that wasn't what he wanted in a lover. Fine for an employee, but not the woman he wanted to spend his life with.

Randi had run from him once before because of Beatrice. Had she seen something in Martha's behavior that made her think…no, God no. He'd never given Martha a moment's encouragement…had he?

Coming to his senses, he shook off her hand. "No. You need your own life. Go out and find it. Take two weeks. I'll have payroll deposit a bonus in your account. Travel, find a boyfriend, deep sea dive, or ski the Rockies, but do something not involving work or me." He took her by the shoulders and turned her toward the door. "I'm sorry if you think I've led you on, but there's only one woman I love, and I need to find her." Annoyingly, it would have to wait. Right now his mother needed him, dammit.

"Court! Don't do this," she pleaded, her face crumpling. "You need me. I need you. We're coffee and cream. We're springtime and rain."

"Perhaps, but I don't prefer those things. I prefer tea and milk, crumpets and jam. I prefer Randi. Roses pressed into sappy novels."

"She's old! I'm young! I'm prettier." Martha straightened her spine, then softened her face. "She's gone. I'm here."

Resisting the urge to roll his eyes, he merely said the only thing he could at the moment. "You're fired." He urged her into the open elevator and pushed the button. "Leave your laptop and cell phone at the front desk; they're company property. I'll have a generous severance posted to your account no later than tomorrow. Your corporate card will be canceled once the transfer is confirmed."

Right now, he was needed in London, and he didn't even have the means to reach Randi on her cell phone. Upon glancing around the room, his gaze found the laptop case still on the dresser. Yes, he could. He could send her an e-mail.

# Chapter 21

"Birdie?"

"Hi, Mom." Her daughter sounded distracted, not unusual when Randi called, instead of waiting for Birdie to call. "Are you calling from New York?"

"From the airport. Just wanted to let you know I'll be home later tonight. Thought you might like to come home for the weekend. Just the two of us, and I can help with proofing your thesis if you like."

A long pause followed. "Didn't work out?"

Randi swallowed the lump in her throat. She sat in the departure lounge and didn't feel like displaying tears for the entertainment of others. "Business sometimes gets in the way of fun. You've seen it before. I had a lovely time but, well, things came up." Over the connection, she heard the bleep of e-mail arriving, followed by the click of a mouse on Birdie's end.

"Huh."

Randi waited for Birdie to elaborate, then prompted, "Do you need to get that?"

"No, it can wait. I don't recognize the e-mail. I get junk all the time." Birdie's voice faded out for a moment, then came back.

"Not grandpa getting our e-mails mixed up again?" With the handles of *fergieb* and *fergier*, he often picked the first one that popped up, and all too often Randi's e-mails went to Birdie. Sometimes she sent them back. Sometimes she just forwarded them.

"Nah, I know his e-mail address. So what happened? You want me to pick you up from the airport?"

The unexpected proposal perked up her depressed ego. The friendly offer was a big improvement over the attitude of late, much more like the daughter she knew. "That would be wonderful. I was planning on a limo, but hey, I'd love to save a few bucks. I spent plenty on your Christmas present." Birdie certainly ought to be pleased with the diamond earrings

Randi actually planned to give her upon graduation. Nothing large or flashy, the earrings would be Birdie's first bit of real jewelry, aside from the pieces Wyatt had given her.

"Well, seein' as how you went to all that trouble of buying me a gift and all..."

Randi laughed. "You scamp. You don't get it until Christmas." Which should make it a bigger surprise when Birdie got the earrings for graduation.

Birdie laughed as well. "All right, you spoil sport. Just tell me you didn't get any Statue of Liberty tchotchkes."

"Nope, no tourist junk, I swear." She crossed her fingers. One or two in the stockings didn't count, right?

"So, do you want me to invite Drew for the weekend?"

The question was unexpected, though the thought had crossed her mind. Randi answered carefully. "Do you want to invite him?"

"I don't know."

The loud speaker crackled to attention, and the standard early boarding announcement blared out.

"That's me," she said as soon as relative silence returned. "I've got a first class ticket."

"Really spoiled you, did he? Okay, well." Birdie huffed. "I guess we can be just the two of us."

"Do you mind? I'm not sure where I stand with Court right now, and I'd hate to drag Drew into it."

"No problem. Call as soon as you hit the ground. I should be at the baggage claim drive through by the time you have your suitcase."

"Thanks. See you in a few hours." For the first time in days, she felt hopeful Birdie might be over her upset. With luck, now they could talk things out and return to a somewhat normal life. Good advice all around, and advice she should follow herself.

* * * *

Court frowned at his computer screen. Birdie? He checked the e-mail address Drew had sent him. Ah. That made sense, the addresses were different by one letter, the last one of course. Damn awkward balancing the laptop on his actual lap in the back of a taxi. He'd already sent an e-mail off to Martin to get him a new phone. This time, something with a tough case.

So Birdie felt friendly enough to provide him with Randi's proper information. It also gave him an opening. A chance to communicate with his daughter. There went that soft feeling in his heart again. He could go with this. With a click on the touchpad, he opened a new e-mail message and verified the address.

*Dear Birdie...*

# Chapter 22

"Excuse me, sir?"

Court adjusted his focus from staring out the window at the frost covered Sussex landscape to his butler's reflection in the glass. Draped in white from the surprise snow shower they'd had the day before, the South Downs sparkled under a weak winter sun. After three weeks of dealing with everyone's problems but his own, he felt numb, as if encased in the icy crystals hanging on the trees.

Three weeks of doctors, hospitals, and nursing homes for his mother who wouldn't behave for anyone but him, and only then because he threatened to walk away. Mum's recovery kept him from straying farther than an hour from hospital and home, which ruled out jumping on a plane to California. He'd also been tied down conducting interviews for Martha's replacement, something he didn't dare trust to personnel after they'd tried to send him another Martha. All alongside getting the house ready for bringing Mum home, rearranging the parlor, and updating the bathroom for an invalid. Followed by the Christmas preparations. Not to mention doing business without the help of a competent assistant.

Still, with all those balls in the air, away from town like this, there was too much time left to think about Randi and far too few stolen moments to do anything about it. Small chunks of time, just long enough to seduce him into calling Randi only to say hello before someone else knocked on his door. Quick e-mails dashed off from his new phone saying nothing more than, *I miss you*, before an urgent message of one sort or another made it through. On the whole, he'd probably sent four messages total that contained more than three words, and not by much. Messages which prompted only terse answers, none explaining her abrupt departure. Three weeks of near silence from the one person he wanted to talk to more than anyone else in the world were about to drive him mad.

The latest problem gnawing at him had to do with Randi, of course, and the significance of Doyle answering her phone night before last. The one time he had hours stretching ahead of him, alone in the house with no possible way he could be interrupted—short of a natural disaster—it had never occurred to him she might not be available to talk. So he'd stayed up to the wee hours, settled in with a whisky and a fully charged phone, intending to not let her off until they'd talked everything out. Taken aback by the vicious stab of jealousy, so painful it had nearly doubled him over, he'd taken the coward's way out and hung up the phone, and spent the rest of the night staring into the fire while downing the entire bottle.

All he wanted—now the hangover had gone—was to be alone to meditate on the problem before calling again.

Instead, the house positively seethed with holiday preparations. Extra staff hired for the holidays moved about the house, decorating for Christmas, the sound of their chatter drifting through the library door. Martin, his household manager—heaven forbid anyone call the man a butler these days—stood at the entrance.

"Sir?" Martin said again.

Without turning from the window, Court responded to the summons. "Yes?"

"There's a young lady to see you."

"I'm not interested in company, Martin. Get her card, or name, or whatever, find out what she wants, and tell her I'll call week after next." Or not. The last thing he needed so close to Christmas was one more person needing something from him. Unless Randi had knocked wanting admittance, which didn't seem likely considering her lack of response. She'd been casual on the phone, pleading pressing business to ring off almost as soon as she'd picked up. The long e-mail he was still trying to write hadn't made it to her yet, mainly because nothing he wrote sounded right.

"I don't think that will work for her, sir. She has a suitcase with her and says her name is—"

"Courtney Robin Ferguson." The clear American accent was recognizable, the sharp tone was not. Court turned from the window, and had he not been startled he might have laughed when she glared up at his nonplussed butler and snapped, "How can it take you so long to deliver a message?"

His daughter pushed past the gaping Martin and strode into the library.

Stupefied, Court found himself blinking, his heart slamming in his chest. "Birdie?" What was she doing here?

"Sorry to be rude, but I'm cold. Lord, your country is damp." She met him by the fireplace where a sturdy log burned, and dropped her shoulder bag beside one of the chairs. Ruddy patches on her pale face stood out like red flags as she held her hands to the blaze.

Court cupped her cold cheek, their gazes meeting and holding. So very beautiful, his daughter, defiant and lost-looking at the same time. "Do I get to hug you?"

Her shrug may have been careless, but her eyes took on a suddenly shy cast. He interpreted the look as a yes and pulled her into his arms, holding her chilled head to his shoulder, breathing in the scent of cold air mixed with airplane antiseptic on her hair.

"Does your mother know you're here? Nobody said anything about you coming."

Birdie pulled away and grimaced. "I'm not twelve, you know. I'm twenty-one and able to travel without my mommy."

A shake of the head only slightly cleared his mind. "Forgive me. I'm still adjusting to the idea of having a daughter, much less realizing she's a full grown, independent woman." Court dropped his hands and turned his head toward his man. "Tea please, and whatever snack Cook has handy."

"Yes, sir." Aloof demeanor somewhat restored, Martin backed through the door and quietly pulled it shut.

Feeling somewhat nonplussed himself, Court found refuge in the tradition of hospitality. "You look all done in."

He gestured toward a wing chair next to the fire. A glance at the mantel clock and a quick calculation to adjust for California time, and he guessed it was about two in the morning. Or was it three? No, about two. Randi was probably still awake in any event. According to Drew, there should have been a party to celebrate the completion of Birdie's degree. He'd stayed on an extra couple of days for the party, otherwise it would have been him coming through the door. If Birdie hadn't showed, Randi was likely going mad with worry. Why hadn't he heard from Drew who was there, surely providing moral support for Randi? Or would it be the opportunist Doyle, holding her hand? He'd have to have a chat with Drew and get the story. If Drew were at Randi's, he'd know the details. Why hadn't Randi said something? Unless the party hadn't yet happened and Birdie hadn't yet been missed, and wouldn't be for hours.

"What are you doing here? I figured you'd be sleeping off the effects of your final exams and getting ready for your surprise party. Or was that supposed to have been last night?"

What he took to be a guilty flush stained her cheeks before Birdie thrust her stubborn chin in the air with a mutinous set to her jaw. "I decided to skip the party."

"So it was to have been last night?"

Birdie leaned forward and held her hands to the flames. "Do you know how rotten it is trying to get here by cab from Heathrow? Nearly two hours, and that was after an hour in customs. Cab driver said the snow made it take twice as long. I'm sure it's all old hat to you," she grumbled.

"I usually opt to stay in the London flat most of the time and especially when traveling. I save coming out here for long weekends and special business events." And unavoidable family emergencies.

"Well, after flying all night, I'm beat."

Deep circles darkened the delicate skin beneath her eyes, and the outer rim of her lips looked pinched and white. Drew had come home with a similar look last spring at the end of his first degree. Too easy a guess that she probably hadn't had a decent night's sleep in the last week or more.

"Martin said you came with a suitcase. I assume that means you'd like to stay for bit?"

"I know it's rude to show up unannounced, but you did say you'd be here through Christmas. If you don't mind, I'd like to stay at least a week. I'm sure your open invitation didn't include showing up out of the blue, right in the middle of the holidays, but I'd appreciate it if you forgave me this once." The smile she gave him was small and a bit unsure. If nothing else, he could relieve that worry right away.

Court smiled. She may not have called him, but she had turned to him, just as he'd said she could. What other answer could he give? "While an announcement with at least a few hours notice allows time to get a room ready, you're welcome at any of my homes, any day, any time. And had you sent your arrival information, I would have either come to get you myself or had a car waiting."

As if relieved of a great burden, Birdie slumped back in her chair. "Thank you. And yes, my mother taught me better manners than I've shown so far. It's just…"

"We threw you for a loop?" If she felt anything like he did, her world hung upside down with a few pockets turned inside out.

Familiar blue eyes stared up at him, wide with astonishment. "You understand…"

"I understand a great many things, Birdie."

Of course, there were also a great many more he didn't. However, the e-mails he'd exchanged with Birdie over the last few weeks had let him get to know her a tiny bit.

Clearing her throat, she straightened and assumed a position of extremely proper, and stiff, posture. "Courtney. I wish to be called by my real name. No more false life or false names for me."

"Courtney." Funny, but she didn't seem like a Courtney, not that he had any idea how a girl—woman—named Courtney should act any different from one named Birdie. "It will take some getting used to. I've had a hard enough time getting used to your mother's real name. Nor am I used to the feminine form of my name. I'm not sure it fits your personality."

"It feels funny to me too, but it also feels more grown up. Birdie is such a silly, little girl name."

Keeping a straight face took more concentration than he would have expected. "And you are not a silly, little girl, are you?"

She shook her head, and Court was hard pressed to name the sad feeling deep inside. Something precious had been lost, or had it been stolen? To him, she seemed so very young, far younger than her nearly twenty-two years.

"So, I ask again, does your mother know where you are?"

Bird—Courtney—stared back at him, as if her tired brain worked through a set of gears. "No. Maybe. I don't know. Depends if she's called out the FBI or CIA to search for me yet. Drew was in cahoots with her over the party, so he doesn't even know I'm here."

First things first, to put Randi's mind at ease, he reached for the cordless handset and punched in the number he'd dialed a hundred times since returning from the states. Dread clawed at his gut as he pushed the buttons. *Don't let Doyle answer the phone. Not tonight. Not at this hour.* It rang just once before Randi's ragged voice came through the receiver, as clear as if she stood in the next room. He breathed a sigh of relief. Doyle hadn't answered this time, and his heart skipped a beat just for the joy of hearing her voice again. Even more so when Court didn't hear anything resembling a male voice in the background.

"Randi, it's Court. I thought you might like to speak with someone who's just showed up on my doorstep." Without waiting for a response, he handed the phone to his daughter.

"Hi, Mom."

He didn't have to hear Randi's voice to know what she said. The exact words weren't necessary, for Courtney's face conveyed the gist of the message. Guilt clearly filled his daughter from head to toe as she swallowed deeply, and her eyes filled with tears.

"Mom, I'm sorry, I didn't mean to put you through so much worry, but honestly, it's time to cut the apron strings." Though Birdie rushed on, Court could feel Randi's shock and heartbreak half way around the world. "I'm an adult now, and I wanted to spend time with my father. I know about the party, and I'm sorry I messed up your plans, but when I called the airport it was catch the next flight out or wait nearly a week. Everything was booked. As it was, I just barely made the flight. I had no time to call."

Sure she could have, there was always time, especially for someone carrying a cell phone, but for some reason, this woman-child had chosen to ignore the worry her mother surely suffered. Other than punishment, what reason did Courtney have for tormenting her mother?

"No, I'm going to stay here for part of my break. It's the only time in the foreseeable future I'll have to get acquainted, and he said I was welcome. Yes, I know you taught me better, but I don't recall you acting any better."

Contrition immediately filled the girl's face, but she kept her lips clamped shut. Ah, the folly of youthful pride.

Truly, were he and Randi any better? Could three weeks of agonizing loneliness have been avoided if they'd stopped long enough to really talk to each other? Randi had yet to explain why she'd climbed into the hotel car with Doyle. Even after he'd explained his mother's emergency, Randi hadn't fully relaxed. The IT department was still trying to break Martha's password on the laptop he'd made her leave behind. Court suspected he'd find a few answers about whatever miscommunication had occurred once he had access to her files.

"Mom, I'll be home in time to start my master's program spring semester. I promise. Yes, I'll let you know when I'm coming in." Slumped in defeat under the relentless worry of a mother, Courtney sighed. "I took a cab to the airport. Yes, I brought my computer. Mom, this call is probably costing a fortune. I'll e-mail, I swear." Courtney rubbed her face with a weary hand. "Yes, I love you too. I will. Bye."

Martin opened the door and wheeled in the tea trolley. The scent of warm pastries was followed by evergreen from the wreaths and boughs being hung about the hall of the old manor house. Court took the phone from his daughter and placed it on his desk while she gathered herself and Martin fussed with the late morning tea.

"Lunch will be served in an hour," the butler said.

"Thank you, Martin. Will you put Miss Courtney's things in the front guest room?"

"Sir?"

"She'll be with us at least a week, possibly two. Should give you about two hours to get the back guestroom ready for my sister."

"Yes, sir." Martin poured the hot tea into a delicate china cup. "Cream or sugar, miss?"

Courtney roused herself from staring at the fire to ask, "What flavor tea is it?"

"Earl Grey, miss."

"I'll take it straight up."

"Yes, miss." Martin handed over the cup and saucer as if presenting the Queen's jewels.

A smile more like the Birdie from Thanksgiving graced her lips as she looked up at the manservant. "Thank you," she said without a hint of the anger that had propelled her through the door.

For the second time in the space of a few minutes, Court felt like laughing in a way he hadn't since New York. Without ceremony, Martin figuratively fell at her feet right then. Had life been a cartoon, Court knew he'd have seen stars bug out from Martin's eyes as the goofy grin spread across his face.

"In case you haven't figured it out, Martin, this is my daughter. Courtney, my butler—excuse me—household manager, John Martin."

Watching a man a good ten years her senior kiss her hand with all the intimacy of a lover gave Court pause. He cleared his throat and scowled as Martin recalled himself and rushed off.

"A butler?" Courtney regarded him with raised brow.

"Household manager." Court shrugged and poured his own cup. "Okay, butler. Though he reminds me of the other title often enough."

"A regular country gent, aren't you, Da—uh, Father?"

"If you're more comfortable, you may call me Court," he told her. "It's how we were introduced."

"No, you were introduced as Mr. Robinson."

With a grunt, Court sat with his cup and saucer in hand, Earl Grey straight up as Courtney had said. Since spending time with Randi, he'd cut back on the sugar and even the cream in his coffee and tea. "Take your pick, Father, Court, Da, or some other nickname if you like. It can be just between the two of us. Something with meaning to you. Whatever you feel comfortable with."

"Wyatt was always Dad or Daddy."

"Then you should continue to refer to him as such. He was your dad, Birdie."

A raised brow reminded Court of her mother. "I suppose it goes two ways, eh?"

"Birdie suits you, but I'll try to remember if it means so much to you."

"It doesn't matter." Utterly exhausted, she melted against the back of her chair. "I'm not sure who I am, so what does a name matter in the scheme of things?"

"You know who you are. That hasn't changed. The only difference is the picture has expanded. But the core, the heart of who you are, hasn't changed."

"Nothing's the same." Birdie considered him through tired eyes, and Court wanted to pick her up and cuddle her on his lap, as he would have done from the day of her birth if given the chance.

"Yes, it is. You just added a new branch to the family tree is all. Sort of like grafting a new variety of apple on to an existing tree. Granny Smith on one side, Golden Delicious on the other. Or maybe it would be Granny Smith and crabapple. Still talking apples, just a little wider variety." Ah, finally, a smile out of her.

"You being the Golden Delicious, my mom's branch being the crabapple." Birdie set down her empty cup and saucer on the trolley and helped herself to a refill. "I shouldn't have dropped in like this. Sounds like you have...family coming for the holidays."

"We do. My mother, who happens to be your grandmother, is coming home from the hospital in a couple hours. You may go with me to pick her up if you like. Drew—"

"Hospital?" Mindful of the cup in her hand, she sat up. "Is it serious?"

"A fall down the stairs while I was in New York. She had a hip replacement, and they're finally kicking her out of rehabilitation today. They tell me she's recovered remarkably. Personally, I think they've had enough of her bossy ways." Just in time for him to suffer her mood through Christmas. Lovely.

"Does she...will she...?"

"She knows about you, but obviously she doesn't know you're here." He smiled gently. Maybe it would be best if Birdie didn't go along to pick her up. Old Mum wasn't so happy about a bastard American granddaughter. One more reason he intended to stay as far away from the converted parlor as possible for the next few weeks.

"Anyhow, as I was saying, Drew comes home tomorrow. Later today my sister, your Aunt Liza, and her husband, your Uncle Albert—no Prince

Albert jokes allowed—and their children will arrive. Bryon and Jamie are four or five years younger than you and Drew."

"Prince Albert jokes? Oh, you mean like Prince Albert in a can."

"Got it in one. Over-played to death."

"Yeah, Grandpa still tries them out from time to time. Yeah, okay."

"Anyhow, you'll get to meet the bushel full and then decide for yourself which branch belongs to the crabapple variety."

"Do they..." Birdie's eyes cut away from him and she pretended to study the painting over the mantel. A rather stiff oil portrait of his parents in their wedding finery.

"Yes, they all know about you. I'm sorry to say that without meeting you, they're mixed on their opinions. Liza wanted to fly off and meet you immediately, but your grandmother, well, she's not quite as thrilled."

"I heard my mother's side. Now I want to hear yours," Birdie demanded.

"All right, but I get to do this my way, so there will be a bit of repeat, just from a different angle. Allow me a small indulgence, if you would."

Birdie nodded and settled back in her chair, tea cup and saucer in hand. Court rolled his head and cleared his throat, then stood and assumed his speaking position.

"Once upon a time, there was a boy, who—due to the neighboring estate and the daughter of said estate—was raised knowing he didn't ever have to play the dating game. While in many ways he considered this something of a relief, he also found it a bit of a disappointment. Took some of the sport out of life, but that's neither here nor there at the moment."

Birdie sat still and appeared to listen closely.

"Well, the boy and the girl grew up, went off to separate colleges, but kept in touch by way of regular family gatherings for holidays, weekend events, etc." Court waved a hand. "One Valentine's, they met up for a rare date and drank a little too much ale, an early celebration of the end of the boy's degree program. They'd sort of broken up over the previous break, but meant this date as a means to get things back on track. See, the parents had never accepted the break-up as real, so the wedding plans were still underway."

Court peeked at his daughter to see if she was still awake—she was—and he continued plowing on with the tale.

"Well, the date didn't go so well. In fact, it went so bloody awfully wrong, the girl kicked the boy out of her room and told him to never come back."

Birdie's eyes widened a little, and he gave her a sheepish smile before letting a grimace take over.

"Let me tell you, the considerable damage done to the male's ego, well, such damage can be quite traumatic. After all, he'd had some, er, practice and had been complimented most highly on his, ahem, style."

An unusual flush of heat crept up his neck. Perhaps this was a little too personal, but oh so key to the actions that followed. He began to slowly pace before the fire.

"Anyhow, the boy slunk back off to university, determined to get through his thesis and exams and never touch another woman again. The risk of additional humiliation was just too great. Once he completed his business degree, he was determined to convert to Catholicism and enter a monastic priesthood."

That earned him a tiny smile, and Birdie seemed to ease a bit.

"So, with this goal in mind, the campus library became the boy's new home. Night and day, he camped out at one certain table in the deepest, darkest uninhabited corner of the library. The history section was so dull, even the librarians avoided it to the fullest extent they could. One day, as usual, the boy headed for his table, carrying a stack of books right up to his chin, so he couldn't see the floor. He'd trod this path countless times before and knew each step of the way so well he could navigate it blind. No one ever visited his corner of the library."

Certainly, he was overdoing the drama, but she'd asked for his side of the story, and he'd do it his way.

"Well, foolish boy that he was, his arrogance was his downfall. Literally. One moment he strode along between the shelves, traversing a particularly boring section, somewhere about the Dark Ages, the next he was sprawled on his face with books and papers scattered everywhere. Before he could say Christopher Robin, a sweet, feminine voice with an adorable accent began chirping at him." Court paused his pacing to smile as he slipped into a falsetto voice. "'Ohmigod, Ohmigod,' she exclaimed. 'Are you all right? Are you okay? Do I need to get the paramedics? Did you break anything? Should I call for help?'" Dropping the poor imitation, he continued, "The cheeky little darling crawled right up on him, took his face in her hands, and he swore he'd gone to heaven, because he'd never seen such beauty in a mere mortal."

Caught up in the past, Court stared at the library shelves and dropped deeper into the memory, wondering if Randi remembered as well as he did. The musty smell of old books, the sweet sexy scent of charming young woman, and those eyes. They hadn't seemed real to him, so deep and clear a green it seemed as if dappled sunlight had lit her eyes from within.

"Green, green eyes, soft ivory skin dusted with freckles, hair shining like spun gold tinged with red…"

Birdie cleared her throat, breaking the moment, and Court looked away. Restless, he rolled his head a few times, then resumed his slow pacing, hands clasped behind his back. "She helped me pick up the papers and the books and carry them to my corner. She absolutely captivated me, but of course, I had sworn off females, so I tried to be distant. The cool, aloof, remote Brit to her California sunshine and American brazenness."

He peeked at Birdie's face and found she still appeared captivated.

"We stopped at the pub after studying that evening. Studying." He snorted. "I'd spent the session studying the way her eyes twinkled and trying to figure out just what she smelled like. Roses, but not just any roses. There was something more at odds with the puffed up hair, the heavy makeup, and the pile of clanking bracelets on her wrists. Remember, this was the era of punk, new age, new wave, big hair bands, and Madonna was teaching the world to wear lingerie on the outside. But I have to tell you, Madonna never looked as good as"—Court glanced at Birdie—"your mum did—does."

Birdie rolled her eyes and made a sound of disgust.

Court stopped pacing to shake a finger at her. "Don't discount the fashion. Guys loved it. Anyway, I ended up half carrying her home to my flat. She couldn't, or wouldn't, give me clear enough directions to find hers."

With a wave of a hand, he resumed pacing. "The point being, in a very short while, the boy and girl fell madly in love. So much so, that before he knew it, the boy had thrown away his vows of celibacy. The girl made him whole and, well, there's never been a more beautiful moment since the beginning of time. Chorus upon chorus of angels sang, the earth moved, stars fell to Earth, and every firework in China filled the sky."

A quick glance at Birdie showed her looking somewhat spellbound. Or were her eyes glazed with jetlag?

"Anyhow, they didn't have much time together. She had a ticket to return home in late May. In fact, her flight departed at the very hour the boy had to be at a very important reception. Their last week together marred only by a small case of the flu on the part of the girl. There weren't enough crumpets or pots of Earl Grey to ease her tummy, but they spent as much time together as possible."

Together. There was a word. Yes, they'd been together, as in joined, almost as many hours as they'd spent sleeping off their exertions. Oh yeah, he'd happily relive that week. Had tried to in New York…with rather mixed results. He shook off the thought and continued with his story.

"Their last day, the boy kissed her goodbye, and slipped from her flat just as the sun was rising on a glorious morning in May. There'd never been a more perfect day. The sky was a cloudless blue, still cool and fresh with all the promise of spring—which in itself is very unlike London—the trees bursting out in flower, the birds sang their little hearts out, colorful posies lined every scrubbed and gleaming walkway. The only blight was the heavy heart he carried away with him. He was walking away from the one girl he knew he'd love forever. The woman who had given him back his dignity, rescued his abused manhood and made him strong."

"You really loved her back then?" Birdie asked quietly.

"I really did. Still do. So…" Court continued as if she hadn't interrupted, sparing only a wink. "The boy made a stop by a travel agency on the way back to his flat and bought a ticket for America, one for first thing the next morning. He'd only be twelve hours behind instead of the year they'd discussed. Wouldn't she be surprised? With great anticipation he headed back to his flat, thinking to pack up before dressing for the important reception. Big deal, couldn't be skipped, otherwise he'd have bought a ticket on her flight."

Court stopped pacing and stared at the floor for a moment. "The thing is… He got a surprise—or three—that day."

He looked at his daughter, knowing the story already dragged on, trying to sort out the necessary information. He drew in a deep breath, rubbed his face with both hands, released his breath on a gusty exhale, and started moving again. "When I returned to my room, Beatrice, my ex-fiancé, was waiting for me.

"I'd forgotten to get my flat key back from her, so she'd used it to let herself in. That is to say she let in herself, her parents, and my parents. Before I could say one word, she flat out announced she was pregnant. Therefore, the wedding plans were on again, only on a smaller scale. The church and minister were set aside for the following week, and we'd just make do the best we could. By the way, our parents were pleased to hear about the plans being on again. A fact I couldn't dispute as they were sitting there, all of them nodding like those bobble head things."

Court stopped pacing at the frost covered window and looked out at only his memories.

"Of course, I didn't agree right off," he continued. "After all, a child out of wedlock wasn't the travesty of a hundred years earlier."

Grimacing at the painful memory, Court turned again, avoiding Birdie's eyes. "I told them of Randi, and my plans to go and get her back. Even if it meant staying in California for a year while she finished her degree, I'd

chosen in favor of true love. Well, we both know how that fight ended."
He resumed his pacing. "Both families presented logical arguments, and
I was reminded of my obligation, not only to Beatrice, but to the business
merger already taking place.

"So, we dressed for the reception, and with a fuming Beatrice on my
arm, we arrived in style. I had a goal in mind to get royally plastered,
blind, stinking drunk so I wouldn't watch the clock and imagine each step
of Jean's journey away from London. At four thirty, she'd load her luggage
into a cab. By five thirty, she'd have been at Heathrow and checking
in. See, we'd planned her exit journey so I'd know where she was at
each painful moment. I was determined to torture myself to the fullest
extent possible. And it was torture. At seven, when her plane would have
been pulling away from the concourse, I stood before Danielle Richards
from personnel, telling her of my new future, hoping she wouldn't ask
about your mother. I'd been recently informed her name would never
be uttered again, and to have Danielle ask about her would have been a
horror beyond imagining."

He turned at a gasp from Birdie. "Yes, damn bloody over-dramatized,
Victorian novel material," Court snarled. "I was caught up, and every
time I tried to escape, my path was blocked either by Beatrice and her
father, or my father. It was almost a bloody shotgun wedding. But I'm
getting ahead of myself. I'd just issued an informal invitation to Danielle
for Saturday next when her eyes shifted to a spot over my shoulder and
her face went still, frozen in a look of horror so unlike her I had to turn to
see what caused it."

Stopping by her chair, Court touched Birdie's cheek with two fingers,
and she had no choice but to look him in the eye.

"I turned, and I saw…the most beautiful sight I'd ever seen until the day
you took us home. Jean, my little ray of sunshine, dressed in a sparkling
black cocktail gown that paled against the glow of her skin. Skin that
turned a shade of ash as we gaped at each other. What I remember most
were those green, green eyes, wide and watery. And one more thing that
makes sense now. One trembling hand over her abdomen. At the time, I
thought it was the return of the stomach ailment she'd been fighting all
week. But now, I realize, she'd come to tell me she carried a precious gift."

As he stared down at his daughter, he saw her swallow deeply, as
caught up in the story as he, anguish in her eyes mirroring the ache in his
heart. "I swear, had she told me about you then, I would have grabbed her
hand and run us both to the airport for the next flight anywhere."

"What about…Drew?"

"I would have come back for him later, but at the time, I couldn't think that rationally. I tried to go after her, but both my father and Bea's grabbed me and hustled me out the other door. I was packed and driven to the country where they kept me occupied, pounding my duty into my head right up until the wedding. By then I'd tried calling your mum and had my calls rejected. A month or so later I was able to get a letter or two posted, and believe me, Bea made quite sure I knew the letters were returned unopened." He let his hand drop and stepped back from the girl. "I only had so much control, and faced with rejection, well…" He spread his hands in a gesture of futility. "I made the best of my life as the Fates had decreed it would be."

Too weary to carry on at the moment, he lowered himself into the other wing chair and picked up his now cold tea. "I got Drew away from his mother as much as I could and let him be a real kid, instead of the miniature lord she wanted. I tolerated marriage to Bea for the sake of both families until I couldn't stand it anymore. And when she died, Drew was in his version of the difficult teen years and took as much attention as the business. I had neither the time nor the courage to go searching for my lost love until this year. The rest…well, you know. Except the reason why your mother won't talk to me now? Did she tell you?"

"No, she didn't. I'm sorry I don't know. She won't say anything about New York other than she had a great time but got tired of shopping and decided to come home early."

"Not that she bought much," Court muttered to himself. Nothing at all on the credit cards tucked away in his wallet. "Anyhow, now you're here and the two of us can get to know each other. You'll see how Drew grew up and gain a little understanding how life is around here. I don't expect you to be a go-between for the issue between your mother and me. We'll work it out ourselves. Somehow."

For a moment, Birdie smiled softly at him, looking more like her mother than he'd ever seen. "So that brings us to your side of the family and how they'll react to me showing up. After your story, I can imagine how *un*thrilled your mother might be."

"Don't worry about it. You can stay out of her way as much or as little as you like. Your grandmother is staying in the parlor we've converted to a convalescent room for her. I imagine she'll hold court from there until she's ready to go home. She has her own busy life in London. Even though we live only a few miles from each other in town, we only see each other out here for holidays. Christmas, Easter, and the like."

"We see my grandfather at least once a month, sometimes more if he's feeling lonely."

Court gulped down the tea in his cup and leaned toward the trolley to refill it. "I don't remember your mother being close to him."

"Mmm." Birdie gazed into the fire almost as if the dancing flames hypnotized her, cup and saucer held in her hand forgotten. "When Grandma got sick, it changed things. Dad spent more time running the business while Mom and Grandpa took turns taking care of Grandma. I was pretty young, so I wasn't part of those conversations, but they worked out a few things between them."

"I'm glad to hear it."

They sat in silence for long minutes, simply being and enjoying the crackle of the flames consuming the wood. A sigh softly broke the silence, and Court glanced over to see Birdie's eyes drooping. He reached over and took the cup and saucer from her hands. Birdie's eyes blinked open owlishly.

Just like Drew's used to do.

Instinct kicked in, and Court almost didn't stop before bending to pick her up to carry her to bed. "Come on, puddin', I'll show you to your room."

Court stood by her chair and offered her a hand up. As if it were the most natural thing in the world, she stood and moved into his arms for another hug, this one freely given. In that moment, his heart was irrevocably captured by his little girl. This was his daughter, by God, and nothing or no one would stand in the way of them getting to know each other. He belonged to her, and whether or not she ever called him Father or Daddy, she had a firm hold on a corner of his heart reserved just for her.

The simple affirmation brushed away the cloud of gloom that had been hanging over his head while managing his mother's crisis. This Christmas would be absolutely perfect. For once his family would be whole. As whole as it could be without Randi there to share it. But Randi or not, Birdie was his, a part of him, and she was there to stay.

# Chapter 23

"Randi, please, you must come for Christmas. If nothing else, you've got to come and get Birdie." Court clutched the cordless phone to his ear when he really wanted to bang his head against the mantel in his library. Someone needed to referee. His mother, the old bat, and Birdie, the young hellion, had instantly taken to each other like Death to his scythe.

They had a love-hate relationship born in hell as far as he could ascertain. Helen sniped at Birdie, correcting her speech, her manners, posture, and anything else she could find wrong. Birdie sniped back, defying every instruction to the older woman's face all while playing nurse without a heart. Even the peacemakers, Liza and Drew, had given up after less than twenty four hours and retreated to their corners. After only one day home, Drew had fled to spend time with friends in the village, and Liza took her children on errands to buy last minute gifts. Albert hid out in the library with Court while his mother and daughter sparred in the parlor, seemingly adoring every minute of the last three days of their icily conducted war and physical therapy.

Before decamping, Drew had taken a moment to pass on Randi's reaction to Birdie's escape. While the call upon her arrival had relieved Randi's worries, it had also seemingly sent her into a deep blue funk. RJ hadn't said anything to Drew specifically, but he'd shown a deep level of concern, and, before leaving for the airport, Drew had overheard a conversation regarding depression and an inquiry about medications. He seemed to think at some point Randi might have suffered a debilitating round of the condition and wondered if it'd returned.

"Court."

The weariness in Randi's voice came through the phone, but he had no room to worry about it. Couldn't worry about it, or he'd start wondering if Doyle was there and if he were the reason for her fatigue. Or he'd worry that she might be slipping into a deep, dark hole. No, he had to convince her to come to him, and if it required bribery and tough love, then so be it. Not to mention, he really wanted her here, and he wasn't above taking advantage of the situation with their daughter.

"You're the one who extended an open invitation to Birdie," Randi continued right over his paranoia and justifications. "I'm *persona non grata* at the moment. I don't know what I said to her, but the last week of school, she quit talking to me again, so you get to be the hero. If you've changed your mind about spending time with your daughter, then you need to tell her. Lay down the law. She has a choice—straighten up or pack up. You don't have to tolerate bad behavior."

"That's just the thing, darling girl, she isn't behaving any worse than her grandmother. Underneath it all, they seem to actually like each other, and Birdie's the only one who can get Mum to do her exercises, but heaven forbid they admit it out loud. It's downright terrifying." Truly, he found it somewhat endearing as he hadn't expected his mother to speak to Birdie, much less let her take over as caregiver. Mum might never get to the hearts and flowers stage with Birdie, but Birdie was earning the old woman's respect. Now, if the rest of them could live through it...

"I can't do a thing about it, Court. You're a parent, surely you have some idea how to resolve these situations."

"I haven't a clue, love. I need you, Randi." There, he'd admitted weakness. Blast it all, this was a woman's domain, and he was man enough to admit he needed her.

The heaviness of her sigh weighed down his heart. "Typical. The flood waters rise up to their ankles, and men start screaming they're drowning."

"Sure, scoff all you want, you've got peace and quiet for the holidays. I've got high court drama with the princess challenging the dowager. I need you, the queen, to intercede and put them both in their places. Please, Randi. You've got me begging here. I'll do anything. I'll buy first class tickets. I'll buy a Rolls and liveried driver to meet you at the airport. I'll buy you all the diamonds, furs, and silks we never got the chance to buy in New..." The words dried up as an unseen hand clenched around his throat.

So far, she'd carefully dodged this topic. Something still bugged her, some detail she held back. If only he could get her to spit it out. If only he could get her to explain Doyle's presence, leaving with her and later, answering her phone.

Silence, heavy with unspoken accusations, stretched out across the satellite link until she spoke. "Did it ever occur to you I went to New York to be with you, not because I wanted a sugar daddy, Court?" Randi said so softly he barely heard her. "I don't want your money. I didn't want your money or pricey gifts in New York. I certainly hope you don't deal with Birdie by throwing money at her."

Surprise, so strong he straightened up, hit him like a fist between the eyes. "Is that what you think—thought?" The completely foreign concept as it applied to Randi stunned him to speechlessness.

"Court..." Randi sighed. "No, you don't get it, and if you don't understand it, then I certainly can't explain it to you."

"No, no, no, no, no." He pounded a fist on the mantel. "You do not get to throw out lines like that. No way. I don't accept it. You don't know what I do or don't understand. You'll have to spell it out for me. I'm not a bloody mind reader, especially from ten thousand miles away."

"And you don't know what I do or don't want from you."

"Do you even know? I know what I want from you, and it isn't purely sex." Though, if he had to admit it, the sex was spectacular enough to almost be a good enough reason in and of itself.

"You could have fooled me. I don't want to be bought off with credit cards and fancy trips as if I were the flavor of the week! Just one more of your quote-unquote professional girlfriends. Or do you call them escorts? Surely they weren't merely dates."

Okay, he'd wanted her to spill it. It certainly wasn't what he'd expected, however, she didn't sound depressed anymore. Anger was good, right? Anger was better than cold indifference and apathy. For the first time in weeks he felt energized and smiled into the phone. Finally, a breakthrough. Now, what the bloody hell was she going on about?

"A professional girlfriend? Did I treat you like a call girl? Is that what you thought? Is that why you left?"

"It's only one reason why I left. I understood you had business, and that's okay. But we were wrong to try and mix a pleasure trip with your business trip. I wouldn't have minded waiting around for you if I'd thought I wasn't just another Catherine waiting in your bed for you to have time to notice me. I would have stayed if I'd been sure..."

How could she ever think he considered her a casual woman? He knew he'd screwed up the week, but to make her feel disposable when she was anything but? Completely bewildered, he shook his head. "Sure of what? My affections? My God, I didn't invite you just so I could have a bedmate for the week. I thought I'd been clear about my feelings for you. If you'd stayed just fifteen minutes longer, the business was done, and I had plans to make up for all the time I didn't mean to leave you on your own. Randi,

I wanted you there because I love being with you. I meant for us to never be separated again."

Not a word from Randi, but he'd almost swear on a stack of bibles she was crying. He'd already gotten the message about the credit cards being a mistake. The few purchases she had made hadn't been on his cards. Had she really thought he'd been trying to pay her for sex? He felt like the lowest dog in the alley, but he'd sparked an emotional response from her. That had to mean something, and it gave him the faintest glimmer of hope.

"Granted,"—he kept speaking, hoping he'd stumble on the right combination of words to break this numbing deadlock—"just as you were driving away I got word of my mother's accident, but I would have brought you home with me. I wouldn't have sent you back to California. I'd counted on New York as a stepping stone to London. I fully intended to ease you around the world, and back into my life, step by step."

He heard the muffled sound of her blowing her nose.

"Darling, won't you tell me what happened? What sent you running for home?"

Silence from her end frightened him into believing she'd set the phone down and didn't hear the last question. A louder sniffle came across the line. No, she was still there. He went for broke.

"Please, Randi. Please come for Christmas. We'll talk about everything and sort things out. If you don't come here, I'm going there. Or I'll send the dowager and the princess. Yeah, maybe that's the better option. It would give the rest of us the nice, peaceful country Christmas we're all counting on. You're used to earthquakes out there. This will be nothing to you."

Finally, she laughed, if only a little. "Oh, no, you don't. You keep them. You invited her; she's your daughter. You deal with her. If you must send anyone, send Drew. Him I can deal with. All I have to do is feed him and let him watch football. And the way he's claimed his sunning spot in the backyard, well, that keeps all the neighbor girls happy, which in turn keeps him well occupied."

He could see her point. Drew's California tan and sun streaked hair had proved popular at home. "If you want to see Drew, you'll have to come here. He's rediscovered a filly in the village. She's home for the holidays as well, and he's trying to talk her into transferring to Stanford." If Court had to use the lad as bait to get Randi to fly around the world, he had no shame.

"Oh Lord." Randi finally chuckled. "A harem in every port, that one. A case of the apple not falling far from the tree."

How had she picked up on his apple tree analogy? "Nope. Not buying your analysis. Not a case of like father like son, there, you know."

"No? You say so, but Martha had a different story to tell."

Ah damn, and the distant, cool voice returned.

"Well, Martha has moved on. I fired her for trying to shag the boss." And a few other things he'd find out about just as soon as they unlocked her bloody computer.

"What? But you told her to make arrangements to send me home. You even told me to go home. I couldn't understand much else about our last call that day, but those very words certainly came through loud and clear! Fiske even heard the words."

"What?" It was his turn to be confused. "I never said any such thing." Damn cell connection. Good thing he'd trashed that phone. From now on, he'd buy the latest in cellular technology on an annual basis. Every six months if he had to. "What I said, and you obviously didn't hear, was along the lines of I'd told Martha to make reservations for dinner at the Russian Tea Room, and I'd ordered both *her and Larry* to go home."

"But—no!" She gasped on the other side of the world. "I distinctly heard 'go home' but not much of the rest. Only that we'd talk later…"

Angry at the miscommunication and her interpretation of it, he almost didn't hear the hiccup that sounded like a sob. Was this it? The final straw? First neglecting her, then having a garbled conversation completely misconstrued?

The anger drained away in an instant. "Aw, Jeannie, darling, no, no, no." No wonder she'd run. Hell. Wound finally lanced, he felt as if his heart bled straight onto the hearth before him. It hurt, but he also knew they'd just turned the corner. This he could work with. "I never wanted you to go home, not without me firmly attached to your hip." And his ring on her finger. Bloody Hell! However, this he could fix. "No, darling, Martha is gone. I don't know why she didn't tell you, don't know what she told you—"

"She told me you wanted her to make my flight arrangements. She said you had to fly out later that night and wanted me gone. Like this was routine for her, getting rid of your woman of the week."

"Darling, nothing could be further from the truth! I wanted her and Larry gone so we could do all the things I'd promised. You'd been so patient with me. I was a cad; I wanted to make it up to you."

For long moments, the only sounds were Randi's soft sobs and the crackling of the fire at his feet. He hated the distance between them and cursed the miles. If she were here, they'd already be in bed, making things right. All these weeks wasted because of a colossal miscommunication. A few garbled words that changed his world.

"Darling, please," he pleaded. "Come for Christmas. Come today. I want you here. I never wanted to be apart for even one minute."

"I'd decided the past held too much old baggage. I'd figured we'd had just another, shorter fling, and returned to our corners of the world."

"We were never a fling, Jeannie, not even in the beginning. It was never a fling between us. *Never*." Anger that she couldn't seem to grasp that one crucial fact seethed in him once more, burying the anguish for a moment. His clenched fist landed on the hard marble of the mantel. "If you get nothing else straight in your head, get this straight right now. I didn't want to say it on the phone, but darling, I love you. I need you. I want you. Right here, beside me always."

After a sigh filled with exasperation, she softly said, "Oh Court..." Hiccups and what sounded like either laughter or tears—he'd bet tears—filled the connection for several heartbeats. Finally, she quieted enough to ask, "So Martha is really gone? You really were blind to her attempts at seduction? It's what she'd implied, that she'd been sleeping with you, and...and..."

"Pure fabrication and solely on her part." He, not so softly, uttered a salty curse. "Jeannie—Randi, I never once slept with her; I swear to you. I didn't even realize how much she looked like you until you pointed it out. *You're* the one I love. *You're* the one I want. *You're* the one I tried to find everywhere I looked and not one female on this earth ever came close to being you. And now I've found you, I'm searching for a new secretary and have a line on a sturdy old dragon. She has iron gray hair and wears support tights, but she won't put up with any shite from me, Larry, or anyone else. I figure if I keep her in girdles I should be set for another ten years until she retires."

On the other end of the line, he could hear her make the in-between noise.

"Darling, are you laughing or crying?" He threw himself into the chair at his desk and pulled up a website for the airlines. By God, he'd have her here as fast as modern transportation could arrange it. While she took her time answering, he punched the button for the speaker phone to free up both hands to type in destinations.

Randi sniffled. "A little of both. But you aren't off the hook."

"Oh no, that I worked out. I'm sure I have several years of groveling left to do. But is it enough to get you to come and save me from the other women in my life?"

The library door crashed open, and Birdie stormed into the room, her face dark as a thunder cloud.

"That woman!"

"What's that?" Randi's voice sharpened, but remained low enough Birdie didn't take notice.

"She called me...a...of all the stupid, old-fashioned, useless insults!" Birdie growled as she approached the desk where she stopped and leaned on the top, hands flattened on the surface.

"What did she say now?" Court asked, acutely aware of Randi listening on the phone. It didn't stop him from working the online airline reservations.

"I can deal with the complaints about my posture, my speech, even my dress. I don't mind being called lazy for the first time in my life, but really, how low can a person go?" Typically, Birdie rushed right on without waiting for an answer. "She called me a bastard!" she exclaimed. "Of all the..."

"She called you what?" Randi's voice exploded from the speaker, and Birdie jumped back from the desk.

"Mom? Sorry, I didn't realize you two were on the phone." Birdie glanced at Court, one little plucked eyebrow raised.

"I want to hear exactly what happened. Was this Court's mother?" Randi's demand had Court and Birdie exchanging questioning glances. He'd never heard such sharp tones from his sweet girl. From the way Birdie's mouth gaped, it wasn't common for her, either.

"Uh, well, she was sort of provoked, Mom. Her physical therapy isn't easy, and I pushed her a little hard. She decided to curse my ancestry. I just laughed at her to tell you the truth."

"Don't you dare defend such behavior! No one calls my daughter a bastard and gets away unscathed."

Birdie started to speak, but Court waved her to silence. Taking advantage of Randi's outrage was just the angle he'd exploit to get her here.

"See? I can't leave them alone for two minutes. This is what we're all living with here, Randi. We need you." He winked at Birdie who'd begun to catch on, her eyes twinkling in conspiracy. "Now, I can have a limo at your door in an hour and you on a plane in three. Six, tops." Within fifteen hours, if he were lucky, she'd have the opportunity to tell him she loved him too. That one he wanted to hear face to face.

"All right, Court. However—"

Yes! His fingers paused in the midst of entering her name for the next flight out of San Francisco.

"Since Birdie disappeared, we've scrapped our plans for Aspen, and I won't leave Dad alone for Christmas. So buy a ticket for him as well and I'll come. I expect you to have a room for him, even if it means you have to sleep in the barn."

# Chapter 24

Twenty-four hours after Court's phone call, Randi stepped from customs and chewed on her bottom lip, not sure if she'd see Court or a stranger holding up a sign with her name. He'd promised a car and driver, but since it was the afternoon of Christmas Eve, and the airport was jammed, she didn't know what to expect.

While shrugging into her coat, a quick scan over the sea of travelers didn't show her anyone familiar. Determined to wade through the masses, she moved forward, and her rolling carry-on tried to fall off its precarious perch on top of her larger suitcase. The cantankerous little bag had been up to its usual tricks, and Randi wanted to drop-kick it into the nearest trash can. Pretty much like she wanted to drop-kick that awful woman who was damned lucky to be Birdie's grandmother and didn't have the sense to know it.

"Know what I'm buying you for Christmas," her father said with a growl. Randi knew he wanted to kill the carry-on, too, since he'd tripped over it the most.

"Already taken care of."

Court's amused voice made Randi look up, as with one hand, he took control of her errant luggage. The other arm he wrapped around her shoulders and pulled her close for a quick kiss, one she wanted to make deeper, but Court cut off when passing travelers bumped into his back. The kiss had been just long enough for her to breathe in his scent, lean against his solid form, and provide her a moment of solace in the noisy arrival area. He seemed entirely too cheerful in contrast to her jumping nervous energy. As usual, his presence calmed her, if only a little.

"'Allo, Randi."

Most of her anxiety over Birdie melted as she stared into his blue eyes, and she mentally knocked herself upside the head for being so stupid and stubborn about calling him all these weeks. She'd heard him say he loved her, but had he said it just to get her on a plane? Had he set Birdie up to manipulate her into flying over? Doing her best to assume a demeanor of cool detachment, much like he did with such British expertise, she stood as tall as possible in her low-heeled boots. Which, admittedly, wasn't saying much. Especially when his proximity effectively turned her knees to jelly and ramped up her over excited nerves. Wearing a black leather coat over a soft dark blue cashmere sweater and faded jeans, he still exuded an aura of power that drew eyes, especially hers.

"'Allo, Court." The Brit accents flying through the air zoomed her back nearly twenty-three years when she'd tried to fit in by adopting the cadence and music of the people around her.

"Still workin' on your accent, are you?"

Paying no mind to the racing of her heart and all the damn people stealing the oxygen from the terminal, she returned his teasing smile with her chilliest voice. "I'll get it sooner or later."

He laughed, ignoring her attempt to freeze him out, and dropped a light kiss on her nose. "Hello, RJ. The car is waiting, and the traffic wardens are about to haul my driver away. You're late."

"Bad weather almost got us re-routed to Birmingham. Then someone in customs had a burr up his butt," Dad grumbled. "Let's get out of this mess. I've seen holiday crowds before, but this is ridiculous."

"This way." Court turned toward the doors, but released her shoulder only to casually grasp her hand and hold it, looking for all the world as if this were an everyday event. In truth, Randi was worn down, her nerves stretched enough it felt as if he'd tossed her a lifeline, and she clung to him as if he were saving her. He responded by squeezing her hand, conveying a wealth of comfort without words.

The past weeks had taken their toll on Randi, and she knew every bit of it showed on her face. Every minute of second-guessing Court's motives, worrying about Birdie's swinging emotions, and keeping her father off her back had etched itself on her as a new line, or a new strand of gray that defied her stylist's color job. With only an hour to pack, and fueled by anger and the disintegration of the last straw of her tolerance for his family's attitude, she still wore the jeans she'd put on more than thirty hours earlier. She'd barely managed a twinset suitable for First Class. Heaven only knew what had finally ended up in her suitcase. She had managed to stuff bits of jewelry into her carryon and the presents for Dad and Birdie in her larger case, but what clothes and toiletries had actually made it, well, it was anybody's guess.

She supposed a handful of under things and socks had found their way into the suitcase corners, and whatever had remained in her toiletry case after New York would have to do. She'd fill in the holes with a trip to the local chemist or do without. The fact she had no gifts for any other members of his family, well it was just too much to contemplate. Court had a newly knitted scarf, only because the airlines had allowed her wooden needles and a couple balls of chunky yarn she'd found stashed in the corner of her craft room. Not a very good scarf, because she was years out of practice, but it had kept her agitated hands busy. Drew's half-done scarf didn't look much better. In fact, she wasn't sure he'd like the chunky mauve-ish yarn anyway. She could give it to Court's sister. Or a maid. Or a homeless person.

Unable to see over the crowd, Randi put her trust in Court and followed. She heard a squeal of recognition, but it didn't register that the squeal had contained Court's name until he came to a stop, with a woman hanging about his neck.

"Pammy," he said and allowed himself to be hugged. "Sorry, ducks, got my hands full here already. Randi, don't know if you ever met Pammy."

"Oh." The woman loosened her grip around his neck enough to glance at Randi, who made a strong effort to smooth her expression into one of polite interest. "'Lo there."

Not Court's usual fashion model, Pammy looked like one of the middle aged country club set, only a little more comfortable, her coat a little more worn at the edges, her makeup not quite magazine perfect. She was put together just well enough Randi felt grubby in comparison. God, had she really been about to buy his lines of love? Still had women hanging all over him wherever they went. At the airport even! *Tigers don't change their stripes*, she reminded herself.

"Hello." Randi gave a short nod while trying to reclaim her hand from Court. He held it tighter, not letting go of either her or her luggage.

"Ease up there, Pam," Court said with a chuckle. "We've got a long drive ahead of us. Catch up with you and Dave later? Been meaning to touch base about New Year's. May not work out this year, but let's talk later, all right?"

"Randi, eh? The one..." A brow needing a touch-up plucking raised until she apparently caught a look from Court. "Ah, okay. Sure. We've come to pick up our Davey. 'E's come back from a semester in Spain. We'll make New Year's work out somehow." Pammy turned her smile on Court even as she aimed a kiss for his lips. "Nice to meet you," she said to Randi and nodded at RJ before diving back into the crowd.

Once more moving forward, Court spoke as he tugged Randi along, their fingers still laced despite her attempts to break free. "I can't remember if we ever met up at the pub with Pammy and Dave. They got married the year after graduation. Knew Dave from Eton and met Pammy at university."

Most of his comments were hard to hear because of the crowds, but he kept talking until they burst from the multitude, nearly landing on top of a black Land Rover sitting at the curb in the frosty gray of the stormy afternoon, its shiny paint mostly hidden under a layer of road grime. By then Randi had stopped fighting for her hand. Staying on track had become a matter of survival, and clinging to him her only way out of the crowds.

"It's been snowing, and the roads are a colossal mess," Court said, his words carried by a cloud of steam. Against the silver sky, white flakes drifted down, looking like large white feathers.

"We already gathered the weather is bad." Dad's comment was dry enough to suck the moisture from the air.

A younger man, somewhere around thirty, leaped from the driver's seat and met them at the back. "Welcome, miss, sir." He gave them wide grins and lobbed their luggage into the cargo area.

"This way." Court wrapped an arm around her shoulders and directed her to the rear seat. "RJ, you take the front passenger."

Court settled into the back seat beside her. Not quite ready to face him, she reached for the seatbelt. Annoyance and too much caffeine, *not* exhaustion, made her hands tremble. Only a smidgen of relief followed when Court quietly took the buckle situation out of her hands and made sure she was secure in the middle spot, snugged right up against his side instead of on the far side of the seat. After buckling his own seatbelt, he threw an arm around her shoulder and pulled her against him. Resistance was futile as he only pulled her closer the more she tried to lean away from him.

"Rest love. We have a two hour drive, or more, based on the roads. Getting out of London will be dicey enough. Who knows what the M25 is like by now."

Tempting as it was to lie against him, she resisted long enough to look up at him. "Court…?"

"I know, you're still angry. With me, with Mum, with Birdie. I get it. But don't worry, all's well, love. You look exhausted." His blue eyes darkened as she started to protest. "Shh." He leaned down and pressed a kiss on her lips, lingering, letting her feel the warming caress of his touch.

On a sigh, too tired to fight for the moment, she gave up and kissed him back, then rested her head on his shoulder. Her eyes fluttered shut when his big hand came up and cupped her head, holding her in the warm spot where shoulder met neck.

"Try and sleep, love. All's well."

"But I don't sleep while traveling," she muttered in protest, hoping he'd keep calling her love. She'd prayed all the way around the world that he really meant it. And she'd included prayers that he'd stand up to his mother and not leave it to her to put the old woman in her place. At the thought, her agitation spiked once more, but Court's warmth dulled the sensation. His arms tightened around her, as if he sensed her jumping nerves and chaotic reactions and his embrace could hold it all at bay.

"Then rest. We'll be home as soon as possible."

Home. Why did that one word tug at her so? "Merry Christmas?"

He gave her a gentle squeeze. "The merriest."

Nuzzling her face into the safe haven he made for her, she let the tension drain from her body and didn't fight as his closeness lulled her into a light doze.

* * * *

"She asleep?"

Court looked up into the review mirror and met Martin's gaze before softly answering Randi's father. "Close." Nothing had felt so good since the last time he'd held her. This woman was meant to be with him. Her body knew it; her heart knew it. Just the pigheaded part of her upper level brain function seemed to deny every other instinct nature spoke to.

"Humph," RJ grunted. "About time. I had the flight attendant pour decaf, hoping it'd calm her down. Don't know what you said to get her all riled up, but she didn't sit still all the way around the world. Damn stubborn little mule. Only person more stubborn was her mother."

Not wanting to disturb her, Court softly returned the grunt to indicate he'd heard.

"Where're we going? Not that it will mean a whole lot to me until I can look at a proper map," RJ grumbled.

"Near Chichester in West Sussex, sir," Martin answered. Without looking away from the road, he reached between the front seats and extracted the A-Z map book. "We'll be taking the southbound M25 until Junction 10, then onto the A3. That'll take us in the direction of Chichester and the South Downs."

"A man always likes to know where he's going. Randi had no idea."

"She's never been to the house." Court kept his voice low, but Randi still stirred against him.

"And why not?"

"It just never worked out. We were both tied up in studies."

RJ's snort was disbelieving. "Not good enough to take home? Well, I'll get the story out of you later." He waved off Court's protest before it cleared his throat. "She told me what your mother called Birdie. Anyhow, we'd best let her sleep. She hasn't slept more than thirty minutes at a stretch since Birdie decided to go AWOL. Before then, I'm not sure she slept a whole lot more. Haven't seen her fall into a depression this deep since right after Birdie's birth. Not even Wyatt's death threw her this much. Someday I want to hear what really happened in New York."

That pretty much confirmed Court's suspicions and raised a whole bunch of new questions. Postpartum depression? Was that part of the reason her husband had hired nursing care? Randi looked washed out and thin. Too thin. How much due to worrying about her daughter, and how much due to her feelings about him, and what sent her scampering back to California? Birdie had only been away from home four days. Randi couldn't have lost so much weight in so little time. How hard a time had Birdie given her between New York and the end of the semester?

On top of all that, Court had his own worry. If RJ wanted to know about New York, Court wanted to know what Doyle had been doing back in California, and answering Randi's phone. Was he the reason Randi hadn't repeated the love word back to him?

"I just want to know one thing," Court said as quietly as he could. Randi had her anxiety moments, and that was fine. He'd even encouraged this one to get her around the world, but he had his. "What's the story with Doyle?"

RJ turned in the seat to look at him directly. "Concerned about Jordan, are you?" The older man's grin rubbed Court the wrong way. He kept his face as blank as possible, which only amused RJ more. "Give it a rest. Randi has no interest in Jordan, and he's played the field too long to get serious about any one woman. I merely used him to try and shake Randi out of mourning."

"Then why did he answer her phone?"

"Last week?"

Court nodded half an inch.

"He came back to fix some bugs. She invited us for dinner, and when the phone rang, she was up to her elbows in soapy water. I would have gotten it, but he was closer."

A two ton block of stone lifted from Court's shoulders. Just a simple disconnect. A misunderstanding. Miscommunication. Now all he had to do was figure out every detail of the misinformation Martha had fed Randi. And let Randi find her footing with his mother. Then they'd be right as rain.

Relishing the feel of her body snuggled up against his, he pressed a kiss to the top of her head. There was something to be said for home field advantage. At last he had it, and he'd reap the full benefit. She wasn't getting away from him a third bloody time. Desperation called for desperate measures. First chance he got, he'd nick her passport and lock it away until they were safely married.

\* \* \* \*

Randi drifted, distantly aware of the well-muffled road noises outside the car. Inside the car, she might very well have been in a comfortable sitting room were it not for the movement. Expensive leather gave her surroundings a masculine fragrance. Classical music spilled softly from the speakers, occasionally interrupted by weather updates, and she heard her father talking quietly with the driver. Court remained alert, but not speaking, probably to keep from disturbing her. Well, except for that little exchange.

Worried about Jordan? Silly man. Jordan was too into being Jordan, but he did make an amusing dinner guest, and he had taken down her dead tree. Dinner seemed like the least she could do for the man. Would probably invite him for dinner any time he traveled to California. Were her fears about other women as unfounded as Court's about Jordan? Court certainly hadn't let go of her to embrace Pammy at the airport. Maybe they were just old friends as he'd explained.

Something to think about when she wasn't so tired. For now, she once more drifted into a trance-like state. She could hear, feel, and smell, but for the life of her she could not respond. Never mind she didn't want Court to know she was sort of awake. It was a good way to learn things. At the moment, she heard the driver answer questions about the Robinson family estate, Lynford Hall. In the family for centuries, the land had been slowly whittled down to about two hundred forty acres surrounding the manor. Woodlands had once been managed to provide hunting for the royal court. Lands now allotted to the county as protected parks. Some of the remaining acres were farmed by community groups interested in organic food. Much of the land remained in a state of natural beauty, perfect for walking and communing with nature. They even had a few ponds and streams perfect for a spot of fishing.

It sounded lovely. What would it look like under a layer of snow? She had visions of fires crackling in hearths. Cozy bedrooms dominated by four poster beds draped with heavy velvet curtains. Every historical romance she'd ever read contributed to the hazy images rolling gently behind her eyelids until she felt the car slow. Almost there? Not wanting the moment to end, she nuzzled closer to Court.

"Almost home," he murmured. "Time to be wakin' up, love."

She moaned a protest that changed to appreciation when he tipped her head up and settled his lips over hers.

"I know how to wake you, darling," he whispered against her lips so only she could hear. Dangerously close to cupping her breast, he rubbed against the leather of her coat, teasing the underside with his thumb.

Rather than answer him, she returned his light kisses with soft nibbles. One large hand gently held the side of her face.

The car turned in a way she leaned more into him, and he tightened his arms. "Now if only Martin can keep driving in circles this way..."

The chuckle rumbling from his chest, and the spiraling thrill deep inside, pulled a smile from her. Before she could answer, the car pulled to a smooth stop. "We're home, Randi."

The way he said home... She tried to swallow down the sudden lump in her throat. Instead, she opened sleepy eyes and looked out the window. To see it all, she had to lean across Court, and still her view was limited.

"I don't see Birdie," Dad said on the blast of chilled air that blew through the car when he and Martin opened their doors at the same time.

"She's here. Or was when I left hours ago. Probably still is, unless she and her grandmother have finally taken each other out," Court muttered, and Randi looked away from the incredible house enough to shoot him a nervous glance. "Joking, love. Those two are peas in a pod. I'm relying on you to make them mind their manners and remember they're ladies."

Irritated all over again, she stiffened and pulled away from him. "Right. Since I've never even met your mother—"

"You have my permission to give tit for tat."

"Great." Ignoring his crooked grin, she slid across the seat and didn't fight when he half lifted her down from the car into lightly falling snow. Taking a moment to let her head clear, she paused and really looked at the house that welcomed with lights glowing warmly from nearly every single one of the numerous windows lining the front.

Although not the biggest pile of stones she'd ever seen, the house was impressive to say the least. If she were to compare it to something she'd seen in a movie, she might have to think Pride and Prejudice. Not quite on the scale of Darcy's Pemberly, yet something more than Elizabeth's Longbourn. Probably something in between. More than a bit grand, yet homey and friendly with plenty of trees and shrubs, most of them, she imagined, green and elegant when not covered in snow and ice. A tiny shiver followed a draft of icy air down her neck, and she pulled her collar close. To the side of the house she could see what appeared to be a large old wisteria, which seemed to hold up the arbor originally designed to support the now massive vines.

"Brrrr."

"A mite colder than California, I dare say."

"Bracing," her father said.

"Clean and fresh," she added after drawing in a deep breath. "Like Tahoe in the winter." The now late afternoon light was failing, but the snow cover lightened the landscape, muffling everything like a thick blanket. For the first time in hours she felt refreshed. Possibly she could deal with Birdie now. She hadn't been sure on the plane. The behavior Court described sounded nothing at all like the daughter she'd raised. Not to mention the grandmother. If it really were her intention to denigrate the granddaughter, then maybe Birdie's behavior was justified, although not excusable.

"Come on." Court rested a hand at the small of her back. "Martin will get the luggage, and here comes Drew to help. You'll be able to see the house better when the sun comes out and melts all the snow."

With a whoop, looking very much like he could play the role of Bingley, Drew flew down the wide stone steps. In the next moment, Randi found herself wrapped up in Drew's arms as he swung her away from Court. "At last! I'm so glad to see you."

After placing a loud wet kiss on her cheek, he finally set her down.

"It's only been a few days." She laughed and playfully swatted his arm.

"It's been a lifetime!"

"Go get my bags, you goofball." Thank God for Drew, whom she genuinely liked.

Grinning toothily, he all but bounded off.

Drew was easy. She just had to worry about Birdie's reception, and her own insecurities. No big deal. Happened every day. Water off a duck's back. Could do it in her sleep. If she ever managed to get any.

"That one I wouldn't mind keeping," her dad said.

"He comes along as part of the package deal," Court shot back, his gaze on her.

Dad shrugged in all too casual a manner. "So make it happen."

Stunned, Randi stared at the two men. Both of whom grinned back at her in response to her narrowed eyes. "What?" Something had just occurred, and it felt as if they'd gone behind her back even though she'd been right there. Men and their grunting communications. Might as well get out their clubs and beat rocks for all she understood.

"Works for me," Drew added his two cents worth before heading into the house, arms loaded with luggage.

"We'll talk later. Right now, I'm sure you'd love to rest, get a long hot shower, and a chance to dress for dinner." Court took her hand again, all but dragging her speechless little self into the house—okay, a house to Court, a mansion to her—in front of them. "Birdie!" he called out.

"In the library, Court," said another man about Court's age, and pointed to a slightly opened door off the grand foyer. Randi thought this one looked handsome enough, but there was a married feeling about him. Nothing specific told her this, not anything she could put her finger on, but his smile seemed friendly. Although, faced with the grandeur of the house, the man hardly registered on her jet-lagged senses. "Attenborough is trying to weasel out of dinner. He's whining about the weather."

"Gather the family, will you?" Court tossed out the order as they swept through the hall.

Without breaking stride, they continued into a room with three walls lined floor to ceiling with wooden bookcases filled with leather-bound books. All books. Not one inch of shelf open for a tiny *objet d'art*. Birdie stood behind a desk, glaring down at a phone. Between a pair of tall windows, a fire burned cheerily, just as Randi had imagined. At least one thing fit her expectations.

"They're back if you want to hear about the current road conditions, but honestly, you don't live so far away, do you?" Birdie demanded.

"About twenty minutes in good weather. Could be an hour or more in these conditions." Randi recognized Larry's disembodied voice coming from the speaker phone. "What would make it worth my while, chook? Who just came back?"

Birdie took a moment to wave at them. "Court just came back with my—I mean, he just picked up Randi from the airport."

"He drove all the way to London to pick up Randi? Well now, that might make it worth the struggle through inclement weather. But what about you? Who are you? You've never said."

"I'm Court's temporary assistant. Until he finds a replacement for Darling Martha." The way Birdie drew out the other woman's name did not indicate any sort of compliment.

"You're American, obviously, so I have to wonder where he picked you up. What's your name, chook?"

"You'll have to come to dinner to find out. Now, what's it going to be?"

Randi clapped a hand to her mouth. Beside her, Court shook with silent laughter. Their daughter easily held her own against one of the bigger gossips around. Obviously, she'd been warned of Larry's wicked flirting and penchant for dirty laundry.

"Oh, all right, baggage, I'll toss on my holiday togs, but mind you, just to see the incomparable Randi again. I mean to steal her away from that overgrown oaf who lost her and his daughter for twenty-two years." Larry's tone turned suspicious. "If Randi's there, could it be the daughter is as well? You wouldn't know her by chance, would you?"

"Sorry, you'll have to show up to find out all the gritty details, you nosy man. See you for dinner." Birdie punched the button with a grin and looked up. "Told you I could make a good secretary for you. Or rather, Executive Assistant. Complete with capital letters, and matching salary, mind you."

Court laughed. "I'm beginning to believe you." At Randi's gasp, he glanced down and winked as he reached for her coat. "But get your master's degree first. You'll be more useful and might actually earn the title."

Bemused, Randi let him take her coat. Before she could do more than hug Birdie, who clung to her tightly, a cacophony of voices erupted in the foyer and spilled into the library.

"Courtland, who is this American?" An older woman led the charge, leaning heavily on a cane while glaring at RJ. All manner of blond people followed. In her tiredness, Randi didn't bother to count. Randi let go to let Birdie embrace her grandfather. A moment later, she turned on the older woman and started fussing.

"Where's your walker? You're not ready to solo with a cane just yet." Despite the peevish words, Birdie was tender and attentive as the older woman took her arm and let Birdie escort her to a chair.

"Mind your manners, missy. I'm not on my last legs. I'm more than strong enough, and you well know it."

"Strong enough to walk across your room, sure, but not strong enough to tramp from one end of the house to the other. Who was there watching you?"

"Albert was doing a fine job until you started in on me. Oh fine, yes, get me the footstool. No, I don't want the lap robe. I'm not cold, for heaven's sake. Now stop worrying over me and introduce your mother."

Apparently, Court had exaggerated the war between the two. Randi cast a narrow-eyed glare his direction and noted he seemed to avoid her glance.

Hands in the air, Court waved for silence. "All right, all right, everyone come in and settle down. Find a seat. Liza find someone to bring up a few pots of tea while Martin gets the bags upstairs."

Randi watched the pretty woman, obviously Court's sister, nod and step out of the library. Still chilled, Randi moved toward the fireplace and stood near the wing chair her father settled into. Across from him, Court's mother eyed them both. Tall and thin, she had the regal bearing Randi associated with aristocracy and, even sitting, managed to look down her nose at them. She also looked freshly coifed, her white hair combed and curled into a set do. Presumably already dressed for dinner, she wore a cranberry red wool suit tailored with impeccable style, a sprig of holly pinned to her lapel. Several graduated strands of pearls circled her neck and a pair of rings, heavy with diamonds, graced her hands. Randi couldn't for the life of her remember if she'd packed anything remotely appropriate for a formal dinner. Certainly nothing like this.

Strong and encouraging, Court's arm circled her shoulders.

His lips moved at her temple. "Tit for tat, love."

She leaned into him, accepting the affectionate touch. Tit for tat. Whatever that meant. To show she was seeing through his story of constant strife, she pinched his waist and had the pleasure of feeling him flinch before he covered her hand.

Court's sister, half dressed for the coming festive dinner, her hair neatly curled and pinned, makeup applied, but wearing worn jeans and a soft sweater, came back into the library. "Tea's on the way for our travelers," she said cheerfully, oddly reminiscent of Birdie prior to Thanksgiving. Definitely a trait from Court's side of the family. It had never been one of hers.

"Thank you, Liza," Court said. "All right then, pay attention. I'm only going to say the names once. If you can't remember, then ask the individual later. I'm going to start at the top."

Randi watched Court's mother sit up, straightening her shoulders.

"First of all, this is Randi Jean Dailey Ferguson. I should have married her before she added Ferguson to her name, but my loss became someone else's gain. Wyatt Ferguson is a man to whom I owe my eternal gratitude. He took excellent care of the woman I love and the daughter she almost died giving birth to. I can't say I'm not jealous of his time with them, or his importance in their lives, but I am grateful for the love and care he lavished on them."

Unexpected tears pricked at the back of Randi's eyes as she stared up at Court. He kept throwing out those words today—love and marriage. How much had Martha lied about, hoping to clear away the competition? His gaze covered the room, then turned to her. "There's something I want to ask you, but I need one more piece of the proposal before I can lay it all out for you, so don't go running off."

"Okay," she whispered.

Someone cleared a throat, and Court smiled. "I guess I'd better get on with this, or we won't have time to clean up for dinner."

With a little sniff, she nodded. Court was on a roll. Far be it from her to hold him back now. Later, she'd have words about getting her on a plane under false pretenses.

Throwing out his other arm, he reached for Birdie. "This is my daughter. All of you know her, but I want to publically acknowledge her. Courtney Robin Ferguson Robinson. Commonly known as Birdie, and while I'm trying to break the habit, she prefers to be called Courtney."

Randi flinched in surprise and looked around the front of Court to see Birdie flush and shrug. "Really?"

"It feels more grown up."

"All right. I'll try."

"Thanks."

Court hugged them both to his sides, and when Birdie's hand took hold of her hand behind his back, Randi felt a huge weight fall away. There was hope. Maybe Birdie could forgive her.

"Sitting in the chair here," Court continued, "is another man to whom I owe my gratitude. RJ Dailey, Randi's father. In his own way, he made sure his daughter was cared for. I think we can find a way to get along from here on out."

A glance at her dad showed a short nod.

"And now for the Robinson side of the family. Randi, RJ, my mother Helen." The woman nodded stiffly. Probably figured she should have been introduced first. Some society ritual of one kind or another. "My sister, Liza, and her husband, Albert Pembroke." The man from the hallway. "Their sons, Bryon and Jamie." Younger replicas of Drew, still teens and somewhat gangly looking, each raised a hand. Randi smiled and watched them shoot their attention elsewhere as if embarrassed. No matter, she'd get to know them later.

Later. She would have a later with this family. For certain, Court meant to propose marriage to her, and she'd accept a second later, if she actually let him get the words all the way out. How they'd blend their lives together became a mere detail, but if she'd learned one thing since New York, it was how miserable she was without him. Telling herself they'd simply had a fling hadn't been working. She'd even tried a date with a man she met in the grocery store, but it just hadn't worked. The poor man would never be Court.

Martin entered the library, pushing a large trolley loaded with a pair of teapots to rival her Big Blue and stacks of teacups. Cookies lined a triple tea server. "I just heard a car pull up. Who are we expecting this early?"

"It's probably Attenborough, for all his complaining about road conditions."

Birdie snorted. "The poser. He had to have called from his car."

Martin's startled gaze flew to Birdie's face. Randi watched as the man all but melted under the glow of Birdie's smile. Oh lord, the butler was in love with her daughter. Did Court know? She looked up and saw him grimace. Okay. So he knew and didn't necessarily approve. This was a first for Court as the father of a beautiful girl. Men found his daughter attractive. Men who looked at her the way Court looked at Randi. Pretending to cough, she tried to hide her giggle. It didn't work, judging by the pained look Court gave her.

"There it is. This is the main core of my family, and I'll publically acknowledge Courtney at dinner. Until then, I'd like to keep things quiet. Larry will press for details, as usual, but don't give him an inch. The Catchpoles are joining us, as are a few others in a bit. Mother, would you please make your way to the drawing room? Our newest arrivals deserve a little time to freshen up after their travels, and the other guests will arrive"—Court glanced at a clock on the edge of his desk—"in little under two hours."

"So tell me about yourself," Randi heard Helen ask crisply.

Randi looked her way, thinking they'd have their chat now but, instead, found Helen's attention fully directed at RJ. Just as well. Randi wanted a one-on-one conversation after she'd had a chance to rest.

Unperturbed, RJ took the cup of tea the older woman offered him.

"What d'ya want to know, little lady?" he drawled. Randi turned away to hide her smile. Tit for tat. Dad got it. If the older woman tried to patronize him, he'd play the dumb hick to the hilt. Go Dad.

# Chapter 25

Court wanted nothing more than to pull Randi out of the room and have her to himself. Something had shifted in her attitude. Something had softened. It gave him hope she might not turn him away. He didn't think he could take one more rejection from her. Too much depended on her acceptance, and he didn't want to rush her. Well, not much anyway. Impatient with the relatives now surging around her, he stepped back and turned to deal with Larry.

"Dad." Drew caught up with him just outside the library door. "I found the missing item."

Court glanced back into the library, but no one seemed to have heard the announcement. "Good. Where did you find it?"

Drew followed as Court headed for the front door.

"Under Grandmother's pillow."

"The sneaky old bat." Court shook his head and grasped the knob at the same time a knock sounded from the outside. "Hang on to it for now. I'll get it from you at dinner." Yanking the door open, he caught Larry's fist as it fell for a second knock. "Come on in. You've been labeled a poser, you git."

"What?" Garment bag slung over one shoulder, a wrapped package under his arm, and a look of bewilderment on his face, Larry looked as silly as Randi thought. "Who would call me that?"

"My temporary assistant." The thick oak door closed heavily, shutting out the chilled night. "Expect to dress here, do you?"

"Oh, I'm much too curious to pass up an overnight. Do I get my usual room, or do I have to double up with Drew? Or, heaven forbid, you?"

"You're just lucky you don't get the barn." Court chuckled, thinking of Randi's threat. "You double with Drew. I already have my roommate assignment."

"Randi's really here?" Larry handed the wrapped parcel to Drew, hung his bag on the coat tree, and shrugged out of his jacket.

"Martin will move your car later," Court told him. "I don't think the valets are here just yet."

"Such hospitality. I came to meet your assistant. And if the fair Randi is here, might I presume the mystery daughter is as well?"

"She is. You'll get to meet her at dinner. People are about to go up to dress as we speak. Myself included." Court waved at Drew behind his back. "Why don't you wait in the drawing room with a snifter of brandy for a bit before doing the same? I'll send Albert along in a few minutes. I need to get Randi settled and give her a bit to rest and refresh. The poor thing hasn't had a nod of sleep in days."

"I thought she'd just arrived?" Attenborough let himself be guided into the drawing room where a girl newly hired from their usual caterers in Littlehampton had just finished lighting the fire. A bit nervous with this, her first job, she'd been growing more comfortable with the family, but Larry was enough to throw her off her stride for a minute. She smiled shyly and flushed when Larry smiled back. "Thank you, sweetheart. I feel it warming my cockles already."

"Care for a pot of tea?" she asked, anxiously wiping her hands on the apron she wore over a black skirt and white blouse.

"I'll be fine with the port and brandy, my dear."

"Yes, sir."

Court gave her nod, and she escaped, quietly closing the door behind her.

"You'll be all right here?" he asked his friend. "It's just for a few minutes."

"Don't leave me too long, or I'll go searching for the maid. Or to find this mysterious daughter of yours. At least give us a clue as to her true age. What I don't understand is why all the intrigue."

Court laughed. "I like torturing you. You'll find out soon enough. Relax, put your feet up. Albert will be along shortly."

"Go on. I can amuse myself drinking your fine liquor."

On an exhale of relief, Court shut the door behind himself. Why didn't he escort Larry into the library? He was certainly close enough to be considered family. Randi had the right idea after all, teasing Larry really was too much fun.

Once more he entered the library and stopped. Randi, delicate and pale, exhausted and glorious, talked with Liza and Albert while Birdie perched on the arm of her grandfather's chair. As if old RJ needed her protection from the dowager who was currently trying to grill him between little frowns shot at Randi. Bryon and Jamie were too engrossed in their handheld games to take much notice of any of the adults.

"Martin."

His man straightened up and turned his way. "Sir?"

"Attenborough's car is out front, his bag in the hall."

"I'll see to it."

"Randi's luggage is in my room?"

"And Sally has it unpacked, but sir…"

Martin's hesitant manner drew Court's attention from Randi. "What is it?"

"Sally didn't find any suitable clothing for dinner. In fact, she said…" Martin tried to school his face into perfect blandness, but his flush ruined it.

"Spit it out, man."

"Ahem. Well, sir, it seems Ms. Ferguson packed a couple of wrapped packages and mostly lingerie. A pair of jeans and a sweater. Lightweight sandals. Nothing at all appropriate for dinner, much less an English winter."

Biting his lip only worked for a second. "I see." Only lingerie? The prospect nearly made him dizzy before reality set in. "I doubt Liza has anything that will fit Randi. I hate to ask, but are there any pieces of Beatrice's clothes stuck in a closet somewhere?"

"No sir. As you requested, every scrap was donated to charity. However, I did take the liberty of calling to the boutique in the village. Ms. Sanders is running a few outfits over. I was able to get Ms. Ferguson's sizes from what she did pack. I told the shop to send you the bill and tack on ten percent for the extra service."

Just like Martin to be cheeky. As long as Randi had clothes, Court didn't care about the cost. "Excellent. The moment they arrive, send them up to my dressing room."

"Yes sir. Once this holiday is over, we need to have a quiet word."

"I know I'm running you through the wringer. Can't be helped." Court clapped him on the shoulder. "We'll get through this, and then I owe you a long, exotic vacation."

"Mustique?" His man rapidly blinked his eyes in surprise. "All expenses paid?"

"Absolutely. Right after the New Year. How does that sound?"

"After the wedding? Can't possibly leave before then."

"Ahead of me as usual." Court squeezed Martin's shoulder, then released him. "How could we manage such an event without you?" Indeed, Martin would be mortally offended to not direct the entire affair. "However, we have the here and now. Once the clothes are sorted, check on

Attenborough would you? I'm sending Albert and Liza his direction. Five minutes, Martin, and send a maid up with the pot of tea, as we discussed."

"On my way." The butler's mood deflated slightly, and he sighed but headed for the door. Martin's sigh reminded Court of Eeyore, but Court also knew the man did it mostly for show and would come through. He couldn't stand anything less than perfection.

Convincing Randi to retire took little effort. Getting his sister and her husband to let her go was the greater issue. Finally, he led her up the stairs. "I promise there's a fresh pot of tea waiting. Guaranteed to refresh you long enough to make it through Christmas dinner."

"I certainly hope so. Sure there isn't time for a cat nap?"

"There's just enough for a bit of tea, a somewhat unhurried shower, and time to dress." He threw open the door and swept her up into his arms.

"Court!" she exclaimed, and linked her arms around his neck before gathering her wits enough to ask, "Dress?"

Once inside, he shut the door with his shoulder while she looked around.

"This is your room?" She stiffened.

"Yes. I hope you don't mind, but I had your things brought here. We're a bit full. Hard to imagine with as many bedrooms as we have."

"Oh." She frowned. "I'm not sure I approve. Rather presumptuous of you, don't you think?"

Sensing a rising temper, Court bent his head to kiss her. He didn't start bold and brash in a way she'd certainly reject, but soft. Tender. Slow. Taking her little by little, doing his best to clear her mind of anything but loving him.

The main problem with his plan was he fell victim to the kiss as much as she did. Wanting to take her right there, he forced himself to ease away and head across the room. Randi's head dropped back as she too fought for air.

"What was I thinking of before? There was something..." she gasped.

"Dressing." Thankfully, she melted against him again. "If you're worried about clothes, Martin was able to dig up one or two items which might work. I hope you'll forgive us, but the maid who unpacked your luggage said you didn't have much besides lingerie. While I certainly wouldn't mind if you ate dinner in a silky negligee, I'd hardly let you do it with my family. I'd rather save that for dinner alone. Just the two of us."

"Oh." She stared up at him, green eyes wide and void of guile, so dreamy he could almost see starlight in them. Even her small frown was adorable. "Clothes? You mean, I didn't pack one dress?"

She really was in a fog. How could a woman not know what she'd packed? "Apparently not. I haven't seen the contents of your suitcase yet. Or were you going for the Madonna look again?"

"Your employees are discussing my wardrobe?" Her jaw dropped open as if the very idea was horrendous.

"It's all right, darling. They're paid to be discreet. Servants who publicly air family secrets find themselves unemployed." Although they would talk amongst themselves. "Eventually, you'll get used to being taken care of, by both me and the staff. Just remember we have your comfort and best interests at heart. Lord knows they've saved me from more than a few *faux pas* that could have embarrassed the family greatly."

He set her down beside the fireplace. Tea waited on a table next to a reading chair, but he didn't let her sit just yet, because he had the urge to kiss her again. He told himself he did it to get her mind off insignificant details. Since that worked so well, and she didn't seem motivated to undress herself, he started doing it for her.

In just a few moments, he had her layered tops off, leaving only her bra. A festive confection of red lace and green satin. If the rest of her lingerie was along these lines, the servants would be talking for years to come. She didn't protest when he unsnapped her jeans and pushed them far too easily over her hips, though he did close his eyes in a silent prayer of thanks. The panties matched the bra. Jeans at half mast, he gently pushed her into the chair and knelt to tug off her low-heeled leather ankle boots. It only took a moment to pull off pants and socks, which he tossed aside. That finished, he drew up an ottoman and inserted his knees between hers. Something about the action woke her up, and he had to act fast to keep her off balance for just a little longer. A point to remember, jet lag aided in making her compliant.

"Come here, darling." Gently tugging on her legs, he pulled her close enough she all but straddled his lap. Only the strongest of will power kept him from slipping his fingers beneath the thin panel covering her. With one deep inhale, he drew in her scent overlaid with the warming aroma of her arousal.

"Court, what are you doing?" She braced her hands on his chest.

Willpower, he reminded himself.

"There's something I want to share with you while we have a moment of quiet. It has the side benefit of helping you wake up just a little bit."

"You won't let up until you get your way, will you?" Randi leaned forward so her head rested on his shoulder, turned so she could watch him pour. "Not that I could ever resist you for long." Her sigh and all that lovely skin of hers made it hard to concentrate on the job before him.

"Not a chance, so you might as well go along."

"Pretty pot. Yixing Sky Dragon."

"Very good. I knew you were an expert at tea ware. Now pay attention. This tea is very special. Ever hear of Tieguanyin?" He lifted the small pot and poured enough to fill one tiny cup half way.

"Arguably the most expensive tea in the world. Named for the Buddhist deity Guan Yin also known as the Iron Goddess of Mercy. The package I left for you in New York. Reportedly the same blend used by the Chinese White House."

"Can't sneak anything past you. So you know how special this tea is. Mostly because you bought it for me, but also for its rarity. This is the first time I've brewed this particular blend of it."

"I've only had a taste. Merely a sample in New York." Randi sat up, leaving only enough room between them for the cup he now held.

"Our own little tea ceremony." Catching her gaze, he drew in a deep breath. The moment was now. She had to know this was special. Real. Forever. "Randi Jean Dailey Ferguson, I welcome you to my home. What's mine is yours. Everything. My resources, my strength, me, all of which pale in comparison to the love for you in my heart."

That tender organ pounding so hard for a moment he feared it'd jump from his chest and land in her lap, he held the small cup to her lips. A hint of moisture made her eyes look like deep mossy pools. Or was the moisture in his? Eyes staring into eyes, green into blue, the catch in her breath, the fluttering beat at the base of her throat matched his, and her trembling as she placed her hands lightly over his and carefully sipped from the cup echoed in his soul.

"Courtland Bailey Robinson, I accept your hospitality, even forgive you for assuming I'd share your bed, and offer my desire to share all that is mine with you." She gave him a tiny, wavering smile. "Most of all, I offer to you me, my heart, all my love, and every single one of my remaining days and nights."

An indescribable warmth filled him, rendering words unnecessary, nay, impossible for several heartbeats. They stared into each other's eyes, their hands connected where they wrapped around the tiny tea cup between them.

It was perfect. As perfect as each time they made love.

After a long, deep inhale, he too sipped, never once breaking eye contact. Rough though it was, he found his voice. "All that I am, body, heart, and soul, I give to you."

Randi's breath hitched again, her mouth parted, then closed. He'd rendered her speechless, and he smiled, feeling extremely satisfied. Holding onto the minimal excuse of a ceremony, he offered her another taste of the cup. She sipped and guided the cup back to his lips. As he drained it, the tip of her tongue slipped out just enough to capture a lone drop on her lip.

To hell with the ceremony. He thrust the clay vessel toward the table with one hand and hoped it landed right, because his other hand pulled her the last few inches right up onto his lap. Like the brilliant woman she was, she read his mind, or had the exact same thought, because her hands cupped his face, and she wrapped her legs around his body as their mouths met already open and hungering.

She loved him.

The exotic tea tasted exquisite on her tongue, and he drank from her mouth, taking in her hunger, desire, need for him.

Yes! Thank you, God! His heart sang, joining the mighty chorus reverberating in his head. Randi, in his arms, her love surrounding him, filling him… The years rolled back, and all that had been dusty, gray, and cold in his world burst into exotic color, light, and soul enriching heat. Jean, his Jeannie, was back, this time to stay, because now she'd confessed; nothing would keep them apart ever again. She'd even promised. He had her, and he wasn't letting go. Not for anything.

Not even the damn carriage clock, which chimed the first quarter hour from the mantel, could pry them more than a few inches apart.

Regretfully, Court eased the kiss into tender nibbles. "As much as I want to make love to your beautiful body, we have guests arriving in approximately one hour. One more cup of tea, and then it's off to the showers for you. I'll even help."

"You'll help me how?" The kisses she placed near his mouth and along his jaw were sweet temptations he steeled himself to resist. It took a strong man to hold out against such a sweet assault.

He ignored the question while refilling the cup. "What do you think of this tea?"

"You want to talk about tea now?" The soft seduction of her breath in his ear, lips on his earlobe, just about destroyed his plans.

"It's that or we skip Christmas and go straight to making love for three days." He offered the cup to her.

"You'd forget about Christmas for me?" she whispered, as she took the cup, irreverently drained it in one gulp, and set it on the tray.

He placed his hands on her waist and pulled her closer yet, snuggling her right up against his straining cock. "Yes, I would. But don't spoil my fun. I have plans, darling."

"Well then, I'm all yours."

He bent his neck and placed a kiss on the swell of her breast. "I'm absolutely mad for you, Jeannie-mine. But"—he surged to his feet with her legs tightening around his waist, arms about his neck, her lovely bum in his hands—"we don't have time for slacking off. If it weren't Christmas with guests, we'd hole up here and eat off each other." Ah there was the sweet flush he loved.

Bless her little soul, she tightened her grip around his neck, and pulled his head down to hers. "Kiss me, Court. Kiss me thoroughly, then make love to me in the shower."

"Darling, I thought you'd never ask."

\* \* \* \*

Randi clung to him, arms wrapped around Court's neck. His hands cupped her bottom and lifted her higher. "Kiss me," she heard herself begging. Fortunately, he complied, and by the time she somewhat regained her senses, he had her pinned against a tile wall with steam billowing around them.

"Didn't we forget something?"

Court grinned, looking entirely pleased and a touch smug, the smile guaranteed to capture her completely. "I think we might want to lose the clothes."

She laughed. Still in her Christmas underwear, she was silly enough as it was, but he was fully dressed, still wearing his shoes. Together they pulled off the wet clothes and left them in a heap in the corner of the huge shower.

"How old is this house?" she asked.

"At least three centuries," he answered, reaching for a bottle on a built-in shelf.

"I didn't know they made bathrooms like this back then."

"They didn't. This was once a dressing room. The dressing room was once a bedroom. This is why I can never remember how many bedrooms we currently have." Shampoo flowed into his hand. "Get your hair wet. You get the full treatment tonight. Tomorrow you get to take care of me." He nibbled on her earlobe, then worked the foaming liquid into her hair, his fingers strong yet gentle as they massaged her scalp. A refreshing lemony fragrance mixed with the rising steam.

"Keep moaning like that, and I won't finish washing you before pouncing."

"Promises." She wrapped her hands around his waist, loving the feel of his skin, and pulled him closer. Soap slipped down between them, creating slick friction where they touched from chest to belly to thigh. She particularly loved the feeling of his erection between them and moved against it.

Court groaned. "The lady likes to play with fire." He maneuvered her beneath the spray again, his fingers working with the water to rinse the lather from her hair.

"I like your torch, does that count?" Holding onto his waist, she leaned back, opening herself up to him, her head tipped back into the water. The flow ran down her body, teasing every bit as much as Court touching her.

"My torch likes you, so I suppose it does."

"And every good torch needs a holder." She moved against him again and felt him twitch in response.

When he spoke, the words came out gruffly. "A sheath for the knight's sword?"

"A place for everything and everything in its place."

Court pulled her against him, his hands slipping down to cup her bottom, holding her tight. "How many more bad clichés can we come up with?"

"Before you decide to stick that thing in me? I don't know. What are you waiting—"

The thought was left unfinished as he lifted her, impaled her on his body, and pinned her against the wall again, this time with the obvious intent of loving her senseless.

How he managed to find the spark of energy inside her, she didn't think she'd ever know. He filled her, challenged her, drove her higher. At last, the empty cold spot deep inside crumbled. Being with Court felt better than it ever had. Clinging to him, she let him take her where he would, which was heaven for just the two of them. His mouth ravaged hers, his hands gripped her bottom, his fingers rubbed where they could reach. When one finger rubbed in a spot that had rarely been touched, she wiggled and moaned.

"Do you want me to stop?" he asked.

"No, please, no…"

"You sure?" he asked roughly.

"Yes!"

"Easy, love, easy. Give it a min."

"Just like that, Court, yes!"

Three weeks of frustration gathered inside her and built up into one tight little bundle. The key to releasing it lay solely with Court, and he knew it. She felt his muscles bunching and straining as he held and touched her, creating fire that burned soul deep.

"That's my girl. Ah, Jeannie, I've missed you."

His finger twisted and touched the right nerves. Like a flame burning along a line of gun powder, a message ran down the fuse of her nervous system to the right bundle of tension, which he also managed to touch as she ground herself against him until she couldn't breathe. The tile warmed behind her back, and his chest braced her front, flattening her breasts between them. His body rubbed hers, and she moved against him, muscles clenching, embracing him deep within. Tempted to close her eyes, she couldn't because she didn't want to miss the expression on Court's face as the world around her shattered in an explosion of light, glitter, and mist. She heard voices cry out and echo back from the hard surfaces of the room.

"Stay with me, love," Court panted. A moment later, he drove deeper and buried his face against her neck. His hands tightened, driving her higher until a bright light exploded once more behind her eyes.

Slowly, so slowly, she drifted back from her release, and Court slipped his finger from her, sending another spasm of pleasure along her sensitized system.

"Easy, love." He kissed her neck and let her legs lower, one at a time until she stood once more, although his body still pinned her against the wall.

"So…" Unable to think of a fitting word, she let the thought drift away.

"So, right, love." Court rested his lips against her temple. "It's always like that with you."

"Yes." Only Court had ever made her burn, and yet, instead of using her up, she felt reborn. "Only you."

They took more time to wash with long caresses, and lingering touches, urgency calmed for the moment. At last Court twisted the taps and turned off the water.

"Much as I hate to move onward…" He reached for a thick towel and wrapped it around her.

After drying her hair and applying a slightly heavier than usual layer of makeup, Randi let him wrap her in his robe and lead her from the bathroom. In his dressing room, they found a simple black silk sheath and a wool suit in olive, which even Court had to admit didn't flatter her so well. Although it was a hair loose because she hadn't been eating lately, they decided on the black silk. His grumbles about the endless black stopped when she put on the emerald earrings he'd given her in New York.

"Heaven help me, Randi, you grow more beautiful with each passing moment. But you're missing something."

Speechless, she could only gape as he settled a necklace of diamonds and emeralds around her neck. The jewels sparkled where they lay against the black silk.

"I meant to give you this in New York..." His shrug made it unnecessary to spell out the rest.

"Court, I'm sorry—"

"No, love, I'm sorry. I treated you dreadfully. Forgive me?"

Finished fastening the clasp, he rested his hands on her shoulders as they both looked into the mirror.

"I shouldn't have left like I did."

"Water under the bridge. What a picture we make, you think?"

Nodding, she took the time to really look at the two of them together in the full length mirror, Court attired in a fine suit of black, she matching in the silk dress, which fell to an inch below her knees. Black flats suited her travel-weary feet just fine, though the lack of heels made her look very short against his height. Blond and red hair gleamed in the dimmed lights of the dressing room.

"This is how you'll look in candlelight, love. Absolutely gorgeous."

"You too." She meant it, but said it with a teasing lilt. "Are you sure we have to go downstairs?"

"Aye. We've delayed as long as possible. Far longer than we should have. Lord of the manor must make an appearance."

"Are you truly a Lord?"

Court laughed. "No, just owner of the biggest house in the neighborhood." A gentle finger traced the contour of her cheek as the carriage clock chimed the hour with eight strikes of the hammer. "And speaking of, we're later than I thought. The good people will be anxious for their dinner."

# Chapter 26

"How many people are here for dinner?"

Court grinned at the whispered question. At the bottom of the stairs, the swell of voices sharing holiday greetings was boisterous to say the least.

"Seventy, eighty, possibly ninety. I don't remember. Martin will know." It was really fifty as that was all the dining hall would accommodate in comfort, but the look on her face was priceless.

"So many?"

"A few are extended family sprung from nursing homes for the evening. We also have local merchants, barristers, doctors and the like. Even the local vicar who will slip away for midnight mass. In fact, most of the people will clear out for church, or will be picked up by the senior bus, saving us from having to kick them out."

With her arm tucked securely around his, Court had never felt more proud to escort a woman anywhere. At their appearance just inside the drawing room door, a hush began to settle as people noticed and turned their direction.

"Merry Christmas!" he called out and same came back in reply only from many more voices. "Sorry to have kept you waiting. Shall we go in to dinner now?" Without waiting for a reply, he turned with Randi still on his arm and led the way to the dining room.

With the crowd following them, Randi only had a moment to gape at what Court had to privately admit was something of a rather grand dining room. Especially when compared with the modest arrangement in her home. Her face paled a bit, and her hand tightened on his arm. A previous ancestor had decorated the room in his own interpretation of something the Tudor court might have recognized, from leaded windows to carved wood paneling, but without the dais and trestle tables. Bea had wanted to redo it, but Court had put his foot down, personally liking the rich design, especially for grand events such as this night.

At the door he and Randi formed a tiny receiving line. With his in-laws near the front of the line, right behind Larry who'd pushed his way in front, it seemed the best chance to quietly introduce her to the guests.

"Drew, please help people find their seats. Birdie goes at my left," he said quietly as his mother passed with Randi's father firmly in tow. "Larry."

"Randi, my love, I'm so pleased to see you again. Court's been teasing me unmercifully. You simply must introduce me to your daughter." His friend bent over Randi's hand, ignoring Court completely. Par for the course.

"You'll meet her in a few moments, Larry," Court said. "Get on with you now. There are a few other daughters who would appreciate help being seated."

"Oh sure, leave me to assist the sturdy farmer's girls and your elderly aunts." With a wink, he ambled off happily enough, leaving Court and Randi to greet the people looking her over with polite curiosity. The whole—house, room, crowd—had stunned Randi, but she didn't let it show now. Something that increased his pride.

"Randi, may I present Mr. and Mrs. Catchpole, my in-laws. Harry, Anne, this is Ms. Randi Ferguson of the United States."

Polite words of greeting were murmured, and the people eager to enter swept the stiff couple into the dining room. Hopefully, they'd be seated at the far end of the table near his mother. At least they didn't seem to recognize her name. Not yet. Although they'd surely heard of his daughter by now, which probably accounted for the disapproving glares. They weren't stupid by any means, and were probably putting the pieces together quite well on their own.

Finally, Court escorted Randi to her seat on his right. As he assisted her, the other ladies were helped into their chairs, and serving staff moved forward to begin pouring wine. Court stood for a moment before taking his seat.

It was times like these he enjoyed his life. Randi on his right with Drew to her right, Birdie on his left, with Larry on her left, his sister and her family filling seats on either side. Down at his mother's end of the table—far, far away—his in-laws, Randi's father, the vicar, and various aunts and uncles. Friends he'd grown up with and local dignitaries filled the ranks in between.

He lifted a glass of wine. "To friends and family, may the best of God's blessings rest upon your heads this night and always."

Glasses were raised, and Court settled in to enjoy dinner.

"Now really, is Birdie your real name?" Larry leaned toward Court's daughter with the question.

"Relax, Larry," Court said. "All will be revealed before the night is over. For now, all you need know is she's acting as my temporary assistant through the holidays. Once I get back to the office I have a real old dragon stepping in to take over for Martha."

Birdie gasped. "But I thought I had the job."

"As I said earlier, finish your schooling, and then you can come in as Miss Wolverton's assistant. You did well this week, but you'd be surprised what you can learn from someone like her. A year under her wing, and you'll be ready to take over just as she'll be ready for retirement. If you still want the job then, we'll talk."

"Sounds reasonable to me," Randi added.

"Oh, I think she's ready for the job now," Larry said, his gaze swinging from Randi to Birdie and back. "I knew I was right. Looks like Court, but sounds like Randi. This is the mystery daughter!"

"Shh, Larry," Court spoke quietly. "Don't give it away just yet."

Accusation in his eye, Larry leaned forward and stage whispered across the wide table, "She's a bit older than five, Randi."

"I never said she was younger, Larry."

"But you never said she was full grown. Is she older or younger than Drew?"

"About the same age," Court evaded before the women could speak up. "I'll tell you the entire tale *later*."

The rest of the meal was spent evading subtle questioning and exchanging secret smiles with Randi. When he could, he found ways to touch her. At long last, salad was cleared away and the table made ready for the mince pies and pudding. When everyone had fresh glasses of champagne, he stood and conversation slowly died down. Anticipation filled the hall.

"I know the earlier toast was a bit brief, but I wanted to savor the moment. Now our hunger has been appeased"—groans came from around the well-fed table—"I'd like to share with you the reason for my satisfaction this evening."

He spoke slowly while the staff quietly poured and served cups of tea, taking care to place a cup and saucer just so in front of each guest.

"We'll toast with champagne, but with dessert, I'd like you to enjoy a rare and special tea. It's said to be the most costly tea in the world, but that isn't why I chose it tonight. No, it's special in that a few weeks ago my love gifted me with a tin of it. Then, earlier this evening, my love and I drank it for the first time as we shared very meaningful vows. Vows which we'll soon, with her approval, repeat in front of God and the universe. I present to you, Randi Jean Dailey Ferguson." He held out his hand to her. She grasped it and at his gentle tug, she stood and glided under his arm. "Here's the official question. You've had more than enough time to think it over. Marry me?"

He watched as Randi's eyes slid toward Birdie. A silent communication passed between mother and daughter. The answer was already in her eyes before she said the word. "Yes."

"Stick with me, we're not done shocking them yet." Relief made his voice rough and hardly above a whisper under the cover of the applause from their guests. Although Birdie's blessing wasn't required, having it made things much smoother.

Turning his attention back to his guests, he raised his champagne glass for silence. "She's agreed, which is the correct answer to a question I intended to ask many years ago." There went the uneasy alliance with the Catchpoles. Their faces, already stony, now resembled the gargoyles hanging from the roof of Notre Dame. Regrettable, but not a serious loss. Their share of the business would still go to Drew, their only grandchild. Fortunately for Drew, he had a good relationship with them. It would all be okay.

"For a very short period of time, circumstances were in turmoil, and the fallout wasn't quite as I'd planned, but wonderful things still happened. Drew came to us, while on the far side of the world another miracle happened." With Randi under his arm, they turned to face Birdie. "Just a few months after Drew was born, in California another birth took place under the care of another man to whom I'll be eternally grateful. Though it nearly cost Randi her life, Courtney Robin came into the world with a smile and a golden halo. My daughter, both in blood and in my heart."

Shocked silence settled around the room. A splutter of indignation from the far end broke the silence, and Court looked down the length of the table, Randi stiffening under his arm. He couldn't quite hear all that was said, Harry Catchpole speaking soft but furiously to Helen. His mother calmly stared down first Harry, then Anne, both of whom had been friends of a lifetime. Friends she'd sided with more times than Court could count when it came to his marriage to their daughter.

"That's my granddaughter, Harry. I'll thank you to remember that when you speak of her, if you must. Now drink to her health and mind your manners."

Mother raised her champagne and lifted her gaze to his. "Carry on, Courtland, the tea is growing cold."

Doing his best not to chuckle, Court tightened his arm around Randi, who'd momentarily gone limp against his side. Not for one moment did he assume all battles would be so anticlimactic, but at least the world had been put on notice that Birdie was not to be snubbed.

"So," he continued as if there'd been no interruption at all, "for the first time, tonight I have my entire family under one roof. Randi will soon be my wife by law as much as she is already the wife of my heart. Drew remains my heir, but he'll have to share with the sister he tripped with his big feet in California."

"I suppose," Drew groused playfully, then grinned at his sister's mild glare. "I don't mind."

"So there we are. Blessings granted to grateful sinners. Let us drink to a happy future!" Court raised his glass to Randi's lips. Once she'd sipped, he turned the glass to place his lips in the same spot, and he sipped to his own happiness.

"Somewhere around here…" He set down the wine glass, as his guests drank their sparkling wine, many calling out their congratulations. "I have an engagement gift for you. Now where did it go?" Smiling at her frown, he patted his pockets.

Pretending to be lost, he glanced around their end of the table. "Wait, I think I see it. Drew, hand me Randi's cup if you will."

Her gaze never left his face, but the wrinkle of confusion remained creased between her brows. To the company he said, "Now for the tea." He raised the cup and said, "To your good health. Cheers!"

Accompanied by more toasts in answer, he brought the cup between them. "Our guests are tasting the Tieguanyin, but I have something a little more special for you. Take a look."

"What could be more speci…"

The fading of her voice thrilled him right down to the bone, or more to say, right down to his very marrow, resulting in a warm tingling somewhere south of his stomach. The light caught the facets within her cup, creating tiny pinpoints of rainbow light on her face, though not quite enough to compete with the sparkle and glow of her.

Resting in hot water at the bottom of a bone china cup lay a unique creation. Made of finely crafted silver mesh, shaped like a tea bag, complete with a diamond studded chain and tag, more than two hundred tiny, perfect diamonds sparkled from inside the silver fabric.

"Court?" she gasped. "What is this?"

"This is very special tea. Or rather, it's the teabag that is special. I know we've played with various brews whenever we've been together, and I was saving this one—" For their last night in New York. He swallowed against the pain of the lost moment and reminded himself this was much better. Although how his mother had gotten hold of it to hide under her pillow, well, he'd have to figure it out later. For now, he didn't even look toward the far end of the table. Safe to say the relationship with the in-laws would be irrevocably strained from here on out. His mother he could deal with at leisure.

"It's sparkling."

He smiled. "Yes, darling, it is. Not as sparkling as you are, especially when you smile, but it is quite a dazzling display." Together they bent their heads over the cup and watched the flashes of light swirl inside the precious metal bag.

"Why is it sparkling like that? Pretty fancy looking. And why the chain?"

"Well, this tea bag is actually crafted for a good cause. The proceeds of the auction where it was featured went to a children's hospital in Manchester."

"Oi! Court, whatcha got there?" Larry called out.

Ignoring his friend, he lifted it from the water. "Actually, there are no tea leaves in it. Only diamonds." Gasps from around the table barely touched his ears. His attention was solely for Randi.

"Diamonds!" Her eyes widened. "And you're dipping it in hot water?" She grabbed the tagged chain and lifted it from the cup. "Court! I don't think this was meant for dunking into water." Scolding him, she reached for a linen napkin, folded the enmeshed jewels inside, and started patting it. "Are you insane?"

He laughed, set down the cup, and took the bundle from her to finish drying. "I spoke with a jeweler who thought it would be a fun trick to play on my lady."

"I think you're crazy." She dropped back into the chair and shook her head slowly. "That has to cost a fortune and you just…" He recognized the horrified expression as she closed her eyes. "Goofball." The admonishment lacked heat.

Chuckling, he pulled the bag from the napkin and knelt on one knee at her feet, dangling it between them. "Happy Christmas, from your goofball."

Randi just stared at him, shaking her head and smiling in bemusement.

"A unique tea bag for my very special cup of tea."

She reached for the trinket, and he laid it against her hand. "Are those diamonds real? Not crystals or something?"

So untrusting. Had to work on that. A few dozen kisses a day would wear her down in no time.

"Yes, real diamonds. A whole bunch of them. Each one represents the number of times a day I think of you. There's no other like it in the world." Holding it by the tag, he gave it a little spin, both of them watching, mesmerized while it threw out dazzling sparks of light. Enough to silence the dining room.

"Just like these diamonds, you dazzle me, Randi. I love being dazzled. Especially by you."

She leaned forward and cupped his face between her soft hands. "I once thought your fire would burn me up and turn me to ash. But I was wrong. You light me up and energize me."

"Our blend is the perfect formula for us."

"Good Lord, man. Kiss her, you git!" Larry called out. "Vicar, how long will it take you to rustle up a wedding?"

"The usual. We can have it in a few weeks, what with paperwork and all. Have to go the normal route, you know." The old man's voice was robust with libations, but no less clear.

"Think you can pull it together by then?" Larry asked.

"I think we can wade through the bureaucracy, so we can marry in the local church. What do you think, darling?"

"I don't care when, where, or how." She slid to the floor to kneel with him, their bodies touching from knee to thigh, hip to hip, luscious breasts to his chest. "All I care is that it happens."

He circled his hands around her waist, and then his arms. This was where she belonged. Where he belonged.

"So, you're not angry with me anymore?"

"No, I'm not mad. Doesn't mean that won't change tomorrow, but for tonight... I don't think I've ever been happier."

Behind the impish grin, her face glowed brighter than the jewels in the necklace and the teabag combined. For a long moment, he could almost swear they were back in her flat that spring morning so very long ago. He certainly felt the same as the youth he'd been. Only stronger. Smarter. Wiser. Set securely on the path that would never again be without her.

"Since special licenses are no longer available at the snap of a finger, we'll have to treat it like a pot of tea. When the time is right, the time is right."

"You and your tea." She rubbed her nose against his.

"Yes. Me and my tea. That would be you. My perfect cup."

And nothing in his life had ever tasted as sweet as the kiss they shared. Unless it was the kiss they shared later that night...

But that's part of another story.

# Meet the Author

The softer, sweeter side of Morgan O'Reilly, Shea McMaster lives for traditional romance.

Born in New Orleans, raised in California, Shea/Morgan got moved to Alaska in 1977, where she attended high school before running back to California to get her English degree from Mills College. Alas, once back home she met and fell in love with her own forever true hero, a born and raised Alaska man. Since then she's had a love-hate relationship with America's largest state.

With her one and only son half way through college, and mostly out of the house, Shea is fortunate to spend her days engaged in daydreaming and turning those dreams into romantic novels and novellas featuring damsels in distress rescued by their own brains and hunky heroes.

Discover more about Shea at the following locations:

Website: http://sheamcmaster.com
FaceBook http://www.facebook.com/pages/Shea-McMaster/240251469328338

www.ingramcontent.com/pod-product-compliance
Lightning Source LLC
Chambersburg PA
CBHW020758250626
47155CB00003B/1128